"You're worse than a whore! A whore gives herself in order to eat—you give yourself for lust!"

Was ever a mother so brutally denounced by her daughter?

Passion

It was a denunciation that drove Mark Landless from her—he, the one true love of her life. And it was true. She had given herself to many men, and when Mark deserted her, she turned to others—the swashbuckling highwayman, Jack Moonlight; the sensitive young Frenchman, Etienne; and always in the background stalked the compelling, enigmatic figure of Captain Guy D'Eath.

Ecstasy

Infinite! Exquisite! Everlasting!

Books by Janette Seymour

Purity's Ecstasy
Purity's Passion
Purity's Shame

Published by POCKET BOOKS

PURITY'S SHAME

Janette Seymour

A KANGAROO BOOK
PUBLISHED BY POCKET BOOKS NEW YORK

Another *Original* publication of POCKET BOOKS

POCKET BOOKS, a Simon & Schuster division of
GULF & WESTERN CORPORATION
1230 Avenue of the Americas, New York, N.Y. 10020

ISBN: 0-671-82124-5

First Pocket Books printing June, 1978

Trademarks registered in the United States and other countries.

Printed in the U.S.A.

Chapter One

"Take your clothes off, girl—every last rag."

She gave a sharp intake of breath at his careless audacity, and she a lass who, despite a slender burden of years, had been badly used by men since her breasts had budded—and before that.

" 'Ere!" she exclaimed. " 'Oo do you a-fink you're a talkin' to, mister? I ain't undressin' in front o' you!"

Wearily, he closed his eyes and sighed. Really, the prudishness of the lower classes was beyond all understanding.

"Will you be so good as to strip?" he said with heavy patience. "And, having done that, will you attire yourself in . . . this?" He tossed her a scrap of diaphanous silk. It fell across a chair back that stood by the bed in that candlelit room.

"Wiv you a-standin' there?" she cried indignantly.

He could scarcely forbear to smile. His short acquaintance with the girl had commenced, that evening, in a Wapping tavern where she, working as a serving wench had in his full sight, and the sight of many others, allowed a Billingsgate fish vendor to maul her young breasts with his reeking fingers—and all for the price of a penny.

"I will turn my back, if it is your wish," he replied mildly, "though I give you my assurance that I have no designs upon your person."

Her pert, pretty face took on an expression of worldly wisdom. She looked at him, bright-eyed, down her tip-tilted nose.

"Ah, you're one o' that sort, eh?"

"As you say, I am one of that sort," he affirmed wearily. "Now, will you please be so kind as to change into the garment I have given you? Time is passing. The gentlemen will soon be here, and my master wishes that you be ready, and properly instructed, well before midnight."

"In-instructed? Wa'ja mean—instructed?" she demanded. "What's all this abaht, anyhow? You brings me 'ere, to this swell 'ouse, promise me five guineas . . . "

"Of which you have already received two in advance," he interjected. "And, if you decide to change your mind, I beg you to do so immediately, returning the money, of course. Another girl can be obtained."

" 'Ere, not so fast, mister," she snapped. " 'Oo said anyfink abaht chagin' me mind? I'm 'ere, and 'ere I stay, to earn th'other three bright 'uns. It's just that . . . well . . . a gel wants to know what she's a-lettin' 'erself in for, don't she?"

"Get yourself changed," he said. "And while you are doing so, I will explain, as well as I am able, what will be required of you this night."

She paused in the act of unlacing her bodice.

"There'll be the handy-dandy, I s'pose?" she said with a street urchin's cunning.

"There will, inevitably, be the handy-dandy," replied the other. "You will not, of course, object to that on moral, or other, grounds?"

"For five bright 'uns, let 'em all come," she responded cheerfully. "The army, the navy, and the marines!"

Beneath the coarse woolen bodice, she wore a shift with a drawstring neck. Dispassionately, he watched her unfasten it and shrug it down to her waist, baring pointed breasts and an unbelievably slender waist. She wore nothing under her skirt; the mode of wearing drawers—a newfangled conceit that had started as a necessity in the ballet and was slowly being taken up by older women of the respectable classes—was not one to commend itself to alehouse strumpets. With something like wistful regret, he watched the suave curve of her shapely rump as she stooped to step out of the skirt and shift. It was quite astonishing, he thought, that such a coarse young animal, coarsely bred in a city slum, half-starved from birth without a doubt, and a penny-whore since she had the wit to use her body, could, by a small miracle of nature, have achieved such perfection of form. A flower growing upon a muck heap.

"You're a saucy one, an' no mistake," she said. "Turn your back, indeed! I seen the way you looked at me."

"Put on the garment," he said brusquely, picking it up from the chair back and throwing it into her hands.

"You wuz goin' to tell me abaht tonight," she reminded him.

"Tonight's affair," he said, "an affair in which you are to play a not inconsiderable role, could be likened to . . . a charade."

"Huh?"

"A little piece of play-acting," he explained.

"Play-actin', is it?" she cried, shrugging herself into the wisp of silk. "I know their sort, the gennlemen what goes in for the play-actin'. Lawks! I could tell you a thing or two abaht gennlemen o' that sort. There

3

wuz this mucky old devil as made me dress up as a nun. . . ."

"There will be nothing of that sort tonight," he said sharply. "Tonight's activity will be carried out with gravity and—not to overstate the case—with reverence. The gentlemen who will partake in this . . . ceremony . . . are new members of a most exclusive club whose membership is limited to the highest in the land. They will be here tonight to perform a ritual, and you will play a part—a purely symbolic part—in that ritual."

"What part?" she demanded.

He drew a breath before replying. "That of . . . a sacrificial virgin."

They came by night. They came in crested coaches, landaus, phaetons drawn by high-stepping nags, and some came on horseback. They were all received by liveried and bewigged footmen at the door of the country mansion and led, by way of an ancient cloister for the mansion had once been an abbey), to a dimly lit chapel. There they were offered fine wines and strong spirits. They numbered twelve when they were all assembled. Most of them knew each other, if only by sight. The upper echelons of high society all knew each other.

"Good gad, Charles. What are you doing here?"

"I might ask the same of you, you devil."

"What's all this about?"

"Damned if I know."

"I was informed on very good authority that it would be something very out of the ordinary."

"I was told that there would be . . . " The confidence was deposited in his companion's ear.

"So was I. Damned amusing, isn't it?"

"And London's been such a confounded bore this season."

4

"This will liven things up tremendously."

"Quite."

"When they had all imbibed a considerable amount of drink, there issued into the chapel a personage in the black habiliments of an upper servant, or a secretary. He bowed deferentially to the assembled company, to which the gentlemen responded with cold stares, not liking the newcomer's epicine looks and manner.

He appeared not to notice their hostility, and he addressed them smoothly. "My lords, gentlemen, on behalf of my master, I bid you welcome this night. Before the commencement of the proceedings, I must first ask you to sign the visitors' book, and then to vest yourselves in ceremonial robes befitting the rite in which you will shortly take part."

"Damn you, fellow, where is this master of yours?" demanded someone loudly, red-faced and belligerent with drink.

"My master will appear before you in due course, my lord marquess," said the servitor mildly. "He is at present himself robing for the ceremony."

"Who is he, your master, hey?"

"My lord is known to all of you," was the response. "And now, sirs, if you will be so good as to sign the book."

Into the chapel trooped a line of footmen bearing what appeared to be academic robes of black silk, with hoods of scarlet and gold, one for each of the twelve gentlemen present. Assisted by the lackeys, they put them on and instantly took on the corporate appearance of a group of monks.

A large book was displayed open upon a lectern, together with pen and ink, one by one, the robed dozen wrote their names and high-sounding titles within it.

"My lords, gentlemen, will you now take your

5

places for the ceremony?" said the servitor. "Each to his own pew, and every pew bears the name and coat of arms of its owner."

He bowed them to their places till the twelve were all seated. He then withdrew, together with the line of footmen. The oaken doors of the chapel closed with a hollow thud that echoed and re-echoed in the vaulting high above. Then all was silent, no sound but the stentorian breathing of he whom the servitor had addressed as "my lord marquess"; he, far gone in drink, was nodding his head in sleep.

It was quite dark in the chapel, with only a single candelabrum burning above the central aisle, and two tall candlesticks, like a pair of winking stars, upon the altar. And then the somber notes of a pipe organ broke through the silence, sketching out the tune of *dies irae,* the hymn of the dead.

"My God—look at that!" One of the robed figures, turning in his seat, hissed the words to the man sitting behind him.

Down the aisle padded two strongly built men, whose powerful physiques were displayed for judgment by reason of their being entirely nude. They were masked, like torturers or executioners, with black hoods that entirely covered their heads, with hideous slits for the eyes. And they bore up on high, at arm's length above their heads, the prone figure of a young woman, clad in a wisp of white silk, whom they carried the length of the aisle and laid upon the altar. This done, they then departed.

The girl lay very still—as she had been carefully instructed to do. Only the rise and fall of her lightly draped breasts distinguished her from a waxen figure or a corpse.

The organ music ceased. One of the congregation shifted in his seat. Another was heard to snigger

6

drunkenly; someone cursed him to silence. In the ensuing stillness it was as if a chill had fallen upon the ancient building, bringing a shudder and a prickling of the skin, a creeping of the scalp, a moistening of the palm.

A concerted intake of breath from the assembled twelve greeted the sudden appearance, from an alcove behind the altar, of a figure similarly attired to themselves—save that, in place of a human head, it was goat-faced, with beard and muzzle, eyes of a staring greenness, and a curved sweep of goatish horns.

"Gad! 'Tis Old Nick himself!" cried someone.

The apparition came to the front of the altar and gazed down at the near-nude girl lying upon it. She, who had been assiduously schooled in her role and forewarned of the fearsome appearance presented by her fellow actor, nevertheless gave a cry of horror and made some shift to cover her lightly draped bosom with her hands.

The goat-headed creature then turned to face the congregation, and, raising its arms, commenced to mouth a string of unintelligible gibberish that presently was revealed, to those of his listeners who were not entirely befuddled with drink, as the "Lord's Prayer" declaimed backward, as in the black mass. This profanation having been completed, the grim celebrant, taking up a large silver chalice, filled it to the brim from a crystal decanter and sipped deeply of the liquid. Then, passing slowly down the aisle, the creature handed the chalice to each and every one of his congregation, and, like him, they drank from it. They were now thirteen in number.

There were some who, speaking of it afterward, attested that it was the drinking of the potion within the chalice that wrought the profound change within their minds, turning them from a mere collection of idle voluptuaries in search of fresh sensations for their jaded appetites into a pack of wild beasts. Those who had suffered the lassitude of drink were suddenly revived by the potion within the chalice. With flashing eyes and watering mouths, they gazed upon the figure of the girl upon the altar. And they cried out as one when the goat-headed creature, flinging wide his sable robe, revealed himself to be entirely nude beneath it, and in the full pride of manhood.

The girl, too, saw what the celebrant was about, and she relaxed herself with a quiet smile. What had passed before had caused her some puzzlement and disquiet. The mumbo-jumbo, the eerie music, the hideous goat mask—all were beyond her comprehension. This was different, this was something she understood, something that came well within the bounds of her experience. The handy-dandy was about to begin. She composed herself to enjoy it as well as she was able to—for it's a poor whore who makes hard labor of her calling.

They left their pews and crowded around the altar, those noble and high-born gentlemen. They watched with staring eyes as goat-head ripped the silk shift from the supine girl, then kneaded her breasts and her thighs. They crowded ever closer as the creature climbed upon the low altar and overtopped his complaisant "victim." They gave loud huzzahs when the celebrant made his brutal intrusion into her.

It was not consummated swiftly, nor without all the variations of attack that a mind far gone in lechery could devise. She, who had been used by more men than she could recall, whose quite exquisite young body, by dint of brutal use, had become—like some finely fashioned instrument that has too often been played upon by careless hands—insensitive to the purer refinements of passion, found herself being

8

borne aloft in the grip of a dark ecstasy over which she had not the slightest control. The slavering aristocrats were witness to the intensity of her breathless ardor. They marked every anguished expression that flittered across her screaming face, under the frenzied impalement of her hideously masked partner in lust. And when at last she was brought to her fulfillment, when the panting, goat-masked creature withdrew and left her sobbing and satiated, there was more than one noble gentleman who, having already divested himself of his nether garments, was ready to be next upon the altar.

Thereafter, they took her by turns, one following the other, without rest. All took turns upon the profaned altar, with goat-face regarding them with glittering, triumphant eyes.

Scions of the proudest houses in Regency England, noble lords who commanded stately homes and rolling acres, whose ancestries sounded like drum rolls down the halls of history—all had their way with a soft-smelling, shapely little amateur doxy who worked as a serving wench in a cheap Wapping alehouse. And, thanks to the curious effects of the hellish brew that they had imbibed from the silver chalice, they learned in her slender arms a strange and frightening splendor.

When they had all had their way with her—and some more than once—the goat-masked celebrant ordered the twelve to return to their places for the closing act of the rite. They obeyed without question naked as they all were, their loins satiated and their minds still aflame with the rememberance of what they had known. They stood, each in his crested pew, and watched the masked celebrant and listened to him chanting his obscene mumbo-jumbo.

The girl relaxed and composed herself for sleep—always supposing that she could possibly doze off with

9

that ranting going on. She felt . . . quite drained of feeling. Never in her short life had she been so used. Not that it had been an unpleasing experience; the very intensity of their assaults, the questing, lunging fury of their excursions upon her body, had quite numbed the growing pain of their repeated intrusions. But, oh, how weary she was, and her nipples ached intolerably. If only she could sleep. If only the feller in the horrible mask would cease his ranting, and him standing there mother-naked and still in his pride.

Now he had a knife in his hand. She knew all about that; the odd feller—him with the womanish way of walking and talking—had carefully explained all about that, told her that she shouldn't be alarmed.

As well as she had been able to understand it, this was to be the end of the play-acting. It was all what the odd feller had called . . . symbolic. She, a virgin (how they'd all laugh down in Wapping, to hear her so described!), having been ceremoniously deflowered by the congregation, was now to be sacrificed—in a symbolic way, of course—so that her body could never again be enjoyed by any man not a member of the secret cult.

Now the masked man was standing over her, so close that she could smell the man-like smell of him and feel his loins brush against her bare shoulder, so that she experienced, by his sheer proximity, a re-kindling of her own passion.

He was holding the knife on high, two-handed, pointing down toward her bare breasts, which rose, twin-peaked, to his terrible gaze. She knew a wayward twinge of fear when she saw, quite clearly despite the gloom, that the blade was honed and polished to a fine point, with a razor-sharp cutting edge.

It was her last act of realization. The next instant, the downward-plunging knife had pierced her beneath the left breast, entering her heart and cutting away her life.

She died—that poor little strumpet from the London streets—with the sound of thirteen men baying like mad dogs to the full moon.

Chapter Two

It was ten o'clock. The night watchman had just passed along the western side of The Steyne, beneath Purity Landless's window, and she had heard him call out the hour, announce a stormy night, but that, nevertheless, all was well. From far off, she could distinctly hear the breakers crashing upon the beach, with the muted accompaniment—familiar and dear to all dwellers in Brighton—of a million pebbles being rattled like beans in a basket. It had been stormy all that day. She and the children had been witness to the wrecking of a fishing yawl, which had been driven ashore right in front of the West Battery and in full view of the delighted promenaders.

Purity readdressed herself to her reflection in the pier glass, head to foot, clad as she was in a silk shift and stockings. She took up the gown of cloth-of-gold and held it in front of her, cocking her head to one side, regarding the effect appraisingly.

It was curious how fashions changed so drastically, even in a few short years, so that the cloth-of-gold, which had been *dernier cri* at the time of Robert's birth (she had worn it at his christening party), could now—with the aid of a cashmere scarf for a headdress —do service as a fancy dress for the ball at the Royal Pavilion that night. Or would it? She put it aside and tried the effect of her alternative choice: a gown of wild white silk embroidered with seed pearls. It was of similar vintage to the other. And she had to concede that it looked exactly like a nightgown. Had one really walked around in such scandalous clothes?

At that moment there came a tap on the door of her dressing room.

"Mama, are you dressed? We've come to say good night." It was Chastity's voice.

"Just a moment," said Purity, draping a peignoir around her shapely shoulders. "You can come in."

They entered. Chastity came in first. She was in her nightgown and peignoir, ready for bed, and Purity was forcibly struck with the realization that the child was a child no longer, but—in body, at least—a fully mature woman. After her came Robert, looking so absurdly like a three-quarter size replica of his father that it was quite risible. With them, trailing after and carrying a pile of clothes, was the ladies' maid, Hannah.

"Hannah's come to see if there's anything further you require her to do for you, Mama," explained Chastity. "Otherwise, I want her to iron my riding habit for the morrow."

"You are riding out tomorrow?" asked Purity. "With whom, dear?"

"With Emily Grandison," said the girl. Then she added, with a faint wrinkling of her pert nose, "And Simon Avondale."

It was a name that had been bandied about quite a lot recently. Purity kept a very straight face when she commented, "I'm sure Simon will provide a very good escort for you both. He's a nice boy."

Chastity made a moue. "He's quite silly, really," she said. "Dreadfully immature for his age."

"He's got himself a commission in the Blues," said Robert indignantly. "So he can't be all *that* silly."

Chastity turned her head slowly and treated her brother to a dark-eyed, long-lashed, smoldering stare of disdain.

"I believe you were allowed to stay up late, *little boy,* on condition that you behaved," she said. "And that, surely, includes *not* quibbling with your elders."

Robert's small jaw squared defiantly. The chin was cleft, like his father's. Like his father's, also, were the eyes: deep and intensely blue. Purity melted at the sight and the recollection of countless times she had seen that expression upon Mark's face.

"Children, children," she murmured placatingly, putting her arm around her son's shoulders. They felt so light and vulnerable: small-boned, unformed. "Don't quarrel. It's been such a nice day. Say good night to me, Robbie. I need to discuss female matters with Chastity and Hannah."

"Good night, Mama." He reached up, put an arm around her neck, and pulled her face down to meet his. Though he was going through the normal "skinny" period of early adolescence, there was a lot of strength in his wiry limbs.

"Good night, my darling. Sleep well."

"Can Tomkins take me to see if there's anything left of the wreck tomorrow?" he asked.

"Of course."

"Good night, Chastity."

Brother and sister put their tongues out at each other, and both laughed.

"Good night, Robbie," said Chastity fondly enough.

They heard his running feet on the stairs outside. Then came the sudden silence that betokened that he was indulging in his habitual—and forbidden—ride down on the hand rail.

"Was there something else you require, milady?" asked Hannah.

"No, thank you," responded her mistress. "You have done splendidly with my hair, and I shall manage very nicely with putting on my gown—when I have decided which one to wear."

"But, milady, if you were to disturb your coiffure while putting it on . . . I must stay."

Purity's hair—the crowning glory of she who was acknowledged to be one of the great beauties of England—was of a particular silver-gold color that was the despair of women and a constant lure to the eyes of susceptible males. It owed nothing to artifice, and it was of a natural orderliness that permitted her, on rising, merely to run her slender fingers through it in order to look as if she had stepped straight out of the premises of a Mayfair coiffeur. On the present occasion, the maid Hannah had essayed a quite elaborate arrangement of her mistress's hair by piling it up into a chignon, with corkscrew curls at the ears—after the mode that was current when the cloth-of-gold gown was new.

"It will not be at all necessary to stay, Hannah," Purity replied, taking up the cloth-of-gold again and holding it before her. "But before you go and attend to Miss Chastity's ironing, I should greatly appreciate your opinion about which gown I should wear, and yours, also, Chastity, darling."

"That one looks nice, milady," said Hannah, who was not a woman given to demonstrativeness. An upbringing in a parish orphanage and a face of uncompromising plainness is not conducive to it.

Chastity clapped her hands. "Mama, it looks lovely!" she cried. "You *must* wear it tonight." And she thought how merely to look at her mother was a

16

delight—standing there in the scanty shift that hid no secrets of her marvelous figure, so girlish, like one's own. The beautiful Lady Landless. Chastity gave a sigh of pure pleasure. What a tremendous source of pride it was to be the daughter of such a person. Difficult, also. Difficult and demanding. But vastly rewarding.

"You have convinced me, both of you," declared Purity. "The cloth-of-gold it shall be. I shall probably regret it, for you may be sure that, with all those stoves they burn, the Pavilion will be as hot as any conservatory after a few hours of dancing. But I cannot rid myself of the notion that wearing the white silk would be like going to a ball—albeit a fancy dress ball—in sleeping attire."

"Then I will help you put it on now, milady," said the maid.

"No, no," said Purity. "It will be another half an hour before the carriage is due. I shall remain in my shift, and perhaps I will drink a glass of wine before I dress. If I have any trouble with the buttons at the back, I can always call upon Sir Mark's assistance."

The maid curtsied and left.

"You will be the belle of the ball, Mama," said Chastity fondly.

"I shall soon be outshone," said Purity, "when you commence your first season next year, my darling. No one will spare me a glance when you appear."

The girl embraced her, her dark hair against Purity's silver-gold tresses, their arms entwined.

"Do you really think I shall be beautiful when I am a woman, Mama?" she whispered.

"You are a beautiful woman already, my Chastity," Purity assured her, and in truth.

"Simon Avondale says I'm beautiful," declared the girl. "But I don't listen to that kind of stuff, not from him. Do you think Simon is handsome, Mama?"

"Very handsome, dear," murmured Purity, smiling at her own reflection in the looking glass, over Purity's shoulder.

"*He* thinks he's handsome," came the response. "Humph! Mama, I find men rather alarming. Is that strange, do you think?" She lifted her head and faced Purity squarely. Dark-eyed, peach-skinned, she was of a beauty that was in dramatic contrast to the older woman's. They were like the East and the West winds together.

Purity smoothed the girl's cheek tenderly with her fingertips.

"I don't find it at all strange, my darling," she said. "Indeed, it would be strange, at your age, if you found them otherwise. But all that will change, I promise you."

Chastity said with sudden passion, clasping Purity closely to her again, "Mama, I don't want things to change, but to remain just as they are. I want to stay here with you and never go away. Never."

Purity was wise enough not to comment upon the girl's remark. She contented herself instead with stroking the soft hair, black as a raven's wing, that rested upon her shoulder.

Presently, she said, "To bed with you now, my darling, if you are riding out on the morrow."

"Yes," said Chastity, kissing her. "Good night, Mama. And I hope you and Papa have a lovely time at the ball."

"The event is bound to have a certain grotesque interest," said Purity. "Whatever may be said about life at the Royal Pavilion, the king and Lady Conyngham certainly provide society with an endless stream of scandal. Good night, my love."

"I shall require a verbatim report on all you see and hear," said Chastity. "And I'll expect nothing to be expurgated by reason of my tender years." She paused at the door. She was dark as a dryad, soft-bodied, moist-lipped, tremulous. "Mama, do you not think that Simon will cut a mighty fine figure in his new regimentals?"

Purity smiled. "Undoubtedly, my darling," she said.

The door closed behind the girl. With a fond sigh, Purity crossed to the console table by the shuttered window and poured herself a glass of Sherry from a decanter. She took the long-stemmed glass in her hand and gazed down into the pale, straw-tinted depths, her mind far away. . . .

So much had happened to her. She had known much pain and heartbreak. She had known, also, and still knew, so much delight and happiness. Mother of two. Adoptive mother of sweet Chastity. And mother —delivered of her own body after being conceived in the fire of pure passion, and suckled at her own breasts—of young Robbie. He had been born in the same month of the same year as the young Princess Victoria, the niece of "Prinny."

How hard it was to think of him as anyone but "Prinny." But the old, mad king had died long since, and now the prince regent was King George IV of England. He dwelled for the most part in his fantastical Chinese-*cum*-Indian palace in Brighton, with the latest—and perhaps the last, for the old voluptuary was now so obese that he had to be carried everywhere, and he lived on a diet of cherry brandy laced with laudanum—of his many mistresses: the vulgar, bad-tempered, bad-mannered, cold-hearted and grasping Lady Conyngham. And Colonel Sir Mark and Lady Landless of Clumber Grange, in the county of Wiltshire, had been invited that night to a fancy dress ball at the Royal Pavilion.

The ormolu clock on her mantelpiece thinly chimed the quarter-hour. Time to dress. All she had to do was put on the cloth-of-gold gown and a pair of golden slippers, then wind the cashmere shawl around her head, like a turban. She wondered if Mark was ready yet. He was to wear—complementary to her own costume—a long silk coat, which he had come by in India in the early part of his military career, together with a turban cloth. They hoped, both, to complement the architecture and furnishings of the king's Oriental folly.

She supposed that Mark would look dashingly romantic: he with his sun-bronzed face unmarked by the years, his splendid physique unimpaired. God, how she loved him and wanted him always. She felt her breath quicken, her loins stir, her skin prickle with wayward pleasure, her nipples move. This simply would not do.

"You are your husband's whore, my dear," she told her reflection in the looking glass. And she laughed.

The gown presented more problems than she had anticipated. In the first place, the undershift was too high in the neck for the gown, and it showed above the edge of the bodice. Off must come the shift; no one in the Royal Pavilion—least of all, the voluptuary king—would give a damn if Purity Landless was naked underneath.

With the cloth-of-gold finally smoothed over her hips, she found that—as she had intimated to the maid—the back buttoning was too fiddling and small for her fingers to manipulate with her hands held behind her. She needed secure Mark's assistance. Another sip of the wine, and then she went in search of him in his dressing room.

Mark never heard the door open. She caught him unaware, standing there, all unconcernedly tying a sash around his waist. He stood tall and straight as a guardsman, lean-flanked, broad of shoulder, spare of waist. The tightly fitted silk frock coat with the heavy gold embroidery showed off his torso to perfection;

20

likewise, the skintight jodhpurs in the Indian style, which announced his muscled calves and thighs. Her heart turned over with love and desire for him.

"Ahem!" She gave a small cough and greeted his gaze with a mischievous smile.

"Purity, my darling, are you ready?"

"Almost. Will you button me up, please?"

She turned her back to him, presenting her bare shoulders, the deep cleft down to her waist. He doted upon her back, as she knew well from countless occasions of loving.

"We are both ready in good time," he said. "Which is good, because the carriage will not easily get through the press of people who will be crowding around the Pavilion, though heaven knows what brings them out at such an hour and on such a night as this."

"To see us, I suppose," she said lightly.

"You look very beautiful tonight," he said. His voice was husky. "Your hair smells like all the flowers of Araby."

"Thank you, sir," she said primly. "Please continue with your task."

He moved closer to her. His hands, abandoning their task, slid inside the material, rested gently at her waist, molding the roundness of her hips. He kissed the side of her neck, the softness behind her ear.

"Purity!"

"I can feel each and every one of your coat buttons against my back," she said. Her eyes were closed, lips parted, ecstatic. "Do you remember, at the king's coronation in Westminster Abbey, when I had the reverse imprints of your Peninsular War medal and Waterloo Campaign medal for all to see on my bare shoulders? I seem to remember you had buttoned me up on that occasion also."

"That I did," he said. "That I did."

"Mark, if you touch me again like that, I think I shall go mad with sheer delight."

His hands were questing the small of her back, in the deep cleft that ended above her dimpled rump. She moaned with pleasure when they glided over her flesh, encircled her, and cupped the fullness of her breasts. She turned to face him, arms flung around his neck, pulling down his face to meet hers, slaking her thirst of passion between his open lips. The cloth-of-gold gown, untended, fell around her hips.

"Now—please, my darling—*now!*"

"The carriage . . . "

"Damn and blast the carriage!"

"The ball . . . "

"There's time for loving—and still time to be at the ball!"

He swept her up in his arms, strode across the room, then kicked open the door of their bedchamber. The great four-poster bed sighed beneath their combined weight as he laid her there and kneeled beside her, peeling off the silk coat, and while her fevered hands were unbuttoning the waistband of his tight jodhpurs and dragging them over his hips.

The cloth-of-gold gown lay in a shimmering pool between the bed and the door. . . .

The rhythm of their passion began, as always, like the slow movement of a great symphony, or like the beating of breakers on a rock-covered shore. Abandoning herself entirely to his lead, she let herself be borne up on the pulsating heartbeats of their combined ecstasy as, breasts to breasts, loins to loins, lips to lips, they played out the ancient mystery of man and woman; out into the darkness, above the storm-tossed sea; up on high, through the clouds and into the sunlight of eternal day.

She drifted languorously from out of the shallows of

22

slumber, her eyelids flickering open. Mark was in her arms, lying beside her and still sleeping; one hand was resting upon her flank, and his face was buried between her breasts. They had drifted together from satiety to dreamless slumber of the kind only enjoyed by lovers.

She stretched herself, gently, so as not to rouse him. He would awaken in his good time. And then he would take her again—as he always did, this stallion of a man whom she loved to such utter distraction. She relaxed and felt the delicious prickling of a new anticipation suffuse her body.

Soon he would awaken.

Soon they would . . .

"Oh, my God! Mark—*Mark!*"

He awoke with a start, his eyes flaring.

"Purity! Great heavens, what's the matter with you?"

"Mark, what time is it?"

"Zounds!" he exclaimed. Leaping from the bed, he snatched up his costume, pulled his gold hunter watch from a fob pocket, and snapped open the lid.

"It's past midnight!"

"We've missed the reception!"

Already struggling into the tight jodhpurs, he said, "I don't suppose the king will have missed us. We can slip in quietly and join the throng. Get into your gown, Purity."

"My hair's all messed up!" she wailed plaintively.

"Your hair looks wonderful," was his unhelpful response. "All you have to do is run a brush over it."

Somehow, they got dressed again—but there were distractions. She slapped his hand crossly when, while helping her on with the cloth-of-gold gown, he was so enchanted by the proud curve of her right breast that he was constrained to offer it a gentle caress. Purity, immediately remorseful for her hasty reaction, pla-

23

cated him with kisses, proffering herself again to his touch. All of this was time-consuming. . . .

But, presently, they were ready; Colonel Sir Mark and Lady Landless—she with an ermine cape over her costume, against the boisterous winter night, he with his military cape over all. Thus attired, they descended to their waiting carriage.

The coachman had fallen asleep in his box, or he might have thought to knock upon the door and prompt the butler to summon the master and mistress. Without wasting time on repining, Mark ordered the fellow to drive them straight to the Royal Pavilion, whose necklace of lights could clearly be seen at the far side of the wintry trees that bordered the open stretch of urban parkland known to Brighthelmstonians as The Steyne.

They drove through the gusty night, clasped together in the darkness of the carriage, hands held, her slender fingers enclosed within his palms, till they came at last to the sweeping curve of driveway leading to the front entrance of the Pavilion, where a line of guardsmen with spluttering flambeaux and a young officer with a highly polished helmet and a harassed expression eyed their arrival with much misgiving. Of crowds of eager onlookers from the public, there was no sign.

The young officer watched them alight and only slightly unbent when Mark presented him with their invitation card.

"May I assume we have missed the reception, Lieutenant?" asked Mark.

The other rolled his eyes. "Sir, you have missed that long since," he said. "Indeed, you are the last guests to arrive, sir, by a full hour. This way, if you please."

He turned around and led the way into the Pavilion. Purity and Mark exchanged a private grimace and followed his scarlet-clad back. He took them down a corridor that was decorated with an Oriental wall-paper of peonies and tall shoots of bamboo, in which brightly colored birds preened themselves against a sky of the deepest pink. Their feet trod upon Chinese silk carpets, and carved lanterns cast a pink gloom over all. They were walking toward the sound of a string ensemble playing a lively gavotte.

"They are dancing in the music room," said their guide.

He opened double doors and admitted them. The famous music room, thought by many to excuse the brittle vulgarity of the royal pleasure house, presented a brilliant sight under the glare of the great central chandelier that hung from the interior of the vast, gilded dome, its countless candles reflecting pinpoints of dazzling color from the jeweled and pomaded throng of ladies and gentlemen who advanced and re-tired, bowed and curtsied, and postured and simpered in time to the well-tuned strings.

"If we join in at the end," murmured Mark in her ear, "We might well enter unnoticed. Your hand, ma'am."

"Enchanted, sir," murmured Purity, extending her fingertips.

They waited for the next movement of the dance. She gathered up her skirt, took a deep breath, and they became as one with the rest.

At the next turn, when they were close again, Mark whispered, "The king is over there—to the left of the orchestra, lying on the yellow sofa. Don't look now."

A short gallop and another turn brought Purity to a position where she was facing the orchestra, and she took a sidelong glance toward an overstuffed sofa upon which reclined George IV of England. It was a sight that almost caused her to miss her step and collide with the lady nearest to her.

Some years had passed—three or more—since she

had set eyes on the royal voluptuary, and the king had greatly deteriorated in that time. He lay there, his pendulous belly swagged within a loose shirt of faintly Oriental cut, a mandarin's peacock-feathered hat set askew upon his dyed and becurled locks, a bemused expression in his pouched, pale blue eyes as he regarded the passing dancers. In his plump, beringed hand he held a large glass, from which he took copious drafts of a dark-colored liquor. Perched at the other end of the sofa, with the king's surprisingly small feet almost in her lap, was a grotesquely overdressed lady with a tall plume of osprey rising straight up from a bird's nest of frizzed hair, and with a pair of sharp, malevolent eyes that searched every passing face. This was the legendary—not to say notorious—Elizabeth Marchioness Conyngham, last of a long line of royal mistresses, all of whom had been older than their exhalted paramour, for, though the king possessed a swift eye—and a ready and roving hand—for the young and shapely, he greatly preferred something of more substantial build and mature vintage for his more permanent attachments. And his attachment to the unprepossessing Lady Conyngham was of quite longstanding. Their conduct at his coronation—a ceremony from which he had excluded his own estranged wife, Queen Caroline, who had knocked upon the doors of Westminster Abbey for admittance, and knocked in vain—had scandalized all society. Purity and Mark, who were present on that occasion, had seen the two of them. The newly crowned king was in his robes of velvet and ermine, and so drunk he could barely stand without assistance, sighing and making eyes at her. He had taken a diamond brooch from his breast, looked at her meaningly, and kissed it. She in turn took off her glove and kissed a ring she had on.

On their next turn together, Mark said, "If you have a sensation like that of a knife being plunged into your back, it is Lady Conyngham looking daggers at you."

"If she realizes that I am wearing nothing under this gown, we shall receive no more royal summonses," murmured Purity.

The music ceased with a flourish of violincello bravura. The two lines of dancers bowed and curtsied to each other. Mark took Purity's elbow and guided her toward the long buffet table that ran down the far end of the huge chamber.

"Lady Landless, ma'am. My dear Landless. How very nice to see you both." A tall figure detached itself from a group by the table and sauntered toward them.

"Your Grace, what a pleasure," said Purity, extending her hand.

The Duke of Wellington bowed over her fingertips, then looked up at her from under his arched brows, along the proud hook of his famous nose.

"Always a pleasure when old friends meet, ma'am," he said. "You're lookin' mighty well, I must say."

"Thank you, sir," said Purity. "And so, indeed, are you."

The victor of Waterloo had scarcely changed since she had first met him in Spain during the war against Napoleon. Like Mark, who was his near-contemporary, Wellington was as straight-backed as a ramrod and clear of eye. Only a slight grizzling at his well-thatched temples betrayed the passing years. His teeth were as white and perfect as those of a youth. Purity was amused to see that, with his characteristic contempt for frills and furbelows, the duke had scorned to put on fancy dress and was wearing a plain, tailed evening coat.

As the orchestra struck up again, Wellington cocked an eye at Mark. "You have a thirsty look about you, my dear fellow," he observed wryly. "Get yourself a glass of two of your sovereign's very tolerable champagne while I tread a measure with your lady wife." And, switching his gaze to Purity, he said, "By your leave, ma'am, shall we dance?"

"It will be a pleasure, sir."

It has to be recorded that Wellington's sweeping talents as soldier, statesman, and man of action did not extend to proficiency in the art of terpsichore. Not that he was greatly put out; but he contented himself by following the same steps as the man next to him. Fortunately, he had chanced upon a minuet, which is a dance of such slow tempo as to permit one to make sidelong glances, to prompt oneself from others; furthermore, the movements are very large and deliberate, and the lady, by making such broad gestures as ostentatiously gathering up her skirts, can signal to her partner that she is about to curtsy and that he must be prepared to bow. Purity led the victor of Waterloo very neatly through the first few movements.

"Have you spoken with the king?" he asked when they joined hands in a stately walk.

"We were late for the reception," said Purity. "I hope he, or Lady C., didn't notice."

"He will send for you," said Wellington. "He couldn't resist the most beautiful woman present tonight, Lady C. or no Lady C."

"He is looking quite dreadful," said Purity.

"You see him almost at his best," said Wellington flatly. "Tonight, for once, he is free of the gout. Moveover, he's taken his physicians' advice at last and given up the tight lacing, so that, though the shape of his belly is not greatly improved, at least he can breathe. Indeed, I declare that if he gave up the laudanum and cherry brandy, he might live another ten years . . . that, plus the bloodletting."

"The bloodletting?" repeated Purity, puzzled.

"Have you not heard? The caricaturists have finally

28

driven him to despair by lampooning his fatness. The poor fellow can't bring himself to stop eating and drinking, so he resorts to incessant bloodletting in the vain hope of reducing his weight, and in doing so he is undermining the remarkably fine constitution that has kept him alive through all his years of gluttony and excess."

"How awful!" exclaimed Purity. "Can his physicians not stop him?"

"They tried," said Wellington, "but it has become a vice with him. It is done secretly. Different surgeons are brought in, unknown to each other, to knife him. Our sovereign, ma'am, is almost literally bleeding himself to death. Ah, that would seem to be the end of the dance, and I must say I enjoyed it mightily. You dance well, ma'am. Indeed, you danced for the both of us. Come, I will show you something."

Extending his arm to her, Wellington led Purity across the chamber, bowing left and right to those who acknowledged him—and they were many. A door led out into a pleasant small apartment with a domed ceiling that was painted to represent sky, and whose walls were hung with pictures.

"Regard the gentleman with the horse, ma'am," said Wellington, indicating one of the paintings.

It represented a youthful officer in the uniform of the previous century, with powdered hair drawn back in a bow, a black scarf banding his neck, and a rose-pink sash knotted around his slender middle. One hand and arm was resting with casual elegance upon the saddle blanket of an Arab charger. Purity gazed up at the painted face with its steady, blue-eyed gaze, firm mouth, and resolute chin. And then she noticed the Star of the exclusive Order of the Garter pinned upon the left breast of the scarlet uniform coat.

"It can't be!" she exclaimed. "Surely not . . . "

"That is a true representation of our George when he was Prince of Wales," said Wellington.

"A flattering representation, surely."

"Gainsborough was too good an artist, ma'am, to have had to resort to flattery," said the duke. "That is he, as I first remember him. There was promise there, don't you think, ma'am? That's the face of a king if you ever saw one, eh?"

"What . . . what went wrong?" whispered Purity, aware that her eyes were unaccountably prickling and that there was a tightness in her throat.

Wellington spread his hands and hunched his shoulders. "You may well ask, ma'am," he said. "I can tell a little, but not much. The mother was as cold and sour a woman as ever bore a child. The father . . . well, there are many who aver that the last George cost England the American colonies. I tell you that by treating his grown son throughout his lifetime as if he had been a wayward child, he may well have cost England a king to be proud of and presented her with a drunken lecher."

"It was lack of love that destroyed him, then?" asked Purity.

"'Tis one way of expressing it, ma'am," said the duke. "What he lacked from the mother, he searched for in the arms of women older than himself. Poor devil."

"Sir, I think you have great affection for the king," said Purity.

Wellington shrugged. "I would put it no higher than pity, ma'am," he said. "A man must, in my view, carve out the shape of his own life and not repine over the hand of cards that fate has dealt him. Lack of love alone cannot excuse the—and you'll forgive my expression— pathetic sack of guts we see out there." He cocked a cold eye up at the portrait. "But

30

you'll agree, ma'am, 'tis a great pity that all that brave promise ended in ruination."

Together, her hand on his arm, they returned to the brilliant gathering in the music room, where Purity searched for a sign of Mark's tall figure. As she was doing so, she met a pair of regarding pale eyes fixed upon her from the other side of the room. Her fingers involuntarily tightened upon Wellington's sleeve. He looked down at her, then frowned to see her expression.

"What is it, ma'am?" he asked. "What ails you, pray?"

"That . . . that man over there," murmured Purity, "the big man dressed as a cavalier. Why is he staring at me so, and who is he?"

"As to why," replied Wellington, "your looking glass gives you the answer every time you seek your reflection. As to whom, the name of the fellow is D'Eath. Captain D'Eath, he calls himself, though captain of what I have no idea."

"He continues to stare," whispered Purity.

"That he does," said the duke. "I have a passing acquaintance with him, though I thoroughly dislike the fellow. Unless I mistake my man, he will presently ask me to introduce him to you. What, ma'am, shall be my answer?"

"Refuse!" replied Purity without hesitation.

"A sound decision, ma'am," said Wellington. "The man's a bad lot. I'll say no more. Ah, here comes my friend Landless, replete, I shouldn't wonder, with excellent champagne. I hand her back into your safe keeping, my dear fellow. Guard her well. Lady Landless is a pearl beyond price. Your servant, ma'am. Before I invite you to dance again, I swear that I will have me some lessons." The duke gave a self-deprecating smile, bowed, and walked away.

"Purity, my darling, you look rather pale," said

Mark. "Would you like to find a quiet room and lie down? I will inquire about the ladies' retiring room and . . . "

"No, Mark!" She was shocked by her own vehemence. "I want you to dance with me, now—right now."

"As you say, my darling," responded Mark mildly.

They joined the lines that were forming for a cotillion. Purity retained hold of his hand, clasping it tightly. Nor did she permit her eyes to leave his face. Nothing mattered but that she must not look to the side of the room where stood the large figure in the trappings of a cavalier, with a black doublet slashed with silver, a high lace collar from which rose a massive head, and eyes of the palest blue, eyes that had seemed both to strip her naked and peer within her mind. She shuddered.

The next movement of the dance brought her around to face that side of the room where peril lay. She could not but resist a glance. . . .

His broad back was toward her, and he was engaged in conversation with none other than . . . the duke. Even as she looked, Wellington was giving the man his wry, tight-lipped smile and shaking his head. Before she could avert her glance, the cavalier's head came around—and the pale gaze met hers.

He had just asked Wellington to introduce them— and had been refused!

Confirmation of the duke's prediction was in no way appeased, in her mind, by his carrying out of the promise to keep the stranger away from her. Purity knew, with a certainty that comes with instinct and brooks of no argument, however soothingly devised, that the stranger would find another means to make her acquaintance.

Why, then, she asked herself, did she not plead with

32

a headache, faintness—anything—and ask Mark to take her home?

They joined hands at the end of a movement.

"You really don't look well, my darling," said Mark. "Shall we slip out without anyone noticing and go back to bed?"

"No!"

A solitary violin sketched out the lilting tune that was the burden of the next movement. Purity picked up her skirts and followed the lively beat, around and around, till the vast, candlelit room became a blur of faces and colors, light shimmering on jewelry, winking in and out of many shadows.

He was watching her—that she knew.

Panting, breathless, they ended the cotillion.

"You look much better after your exertions, my love," said Mark. "The last movement has brought the rosiness back to your cheeks. It really is insufferably hot in here, is it not? Why does the king need so many stoves, do you suppose? Stay here and I'll go fetch you a glass of chilled champagne."

"Don't leave me, Mark!" she cried.

"I'm only going as far as the buffet table, my love," he said fondly, patting her cheek. "If I'm not back in half an hour, you may send for the Bow Street Runners to search me out, but 'tis not a contingency that's likely to occur."

Her mind screamed at him, *Don't leave me, Mark! Don't leave me,* or I shall be destroyed!

He was gone, lost in the press of people milling around the buffet table where bewigged footmen were plying wines and viands amidst a swirl of stark-white napery and gleaming silver and glassware. She closed her eyes.

She did not have long to wait. . . .

"Lady Landless, ma'am, may I have the inestimable honor to present . . . ?"

She opened her eyes and met the gaze of a foolish, pink countenance topped by a fool's cap and bells. For reasons best known to himself, he had seen fit to paint the end of his uncomely nose a bright red. After a moment's hesitation, she recognized him as a fellow member of Mark's London club, one who sometimes rode out with the Clumber foxhounds, and a member of Parliament and a baronet with a name something like Chivers, or perhaps Chalmers.

"Captain Guy D'Eath, ma'am. Pressed me insufferably to introduce him to you. Pray, where is Sir Mark? I must have words with him."

She was locked to the steady regard of those pale blue eyes that stripped her and saw into her mind.

"Over by the buffet table," she heard someone say, and surely it must have been she, herself.

"I'll go seek him out," said the fool in fool's cap and bells. "Your servant, ma'am, Captain D'Eath." He was gone.

"Why are you frightened of me?" asked D'Eath.

At close quarters, he did not loom so massively. Though broader than Mark, he was shorter than him by half a head. The impression of bulk was entirely engendered by the aura of maleness that surrounded him like a strange magnetism, coloring his every look and gesture: the way, from time to time, that his tongue emerged to moisten his very full lips; the manner in which, every so often, his forefinger would come up and slowly stroke the corner of his eye without disturbing the unwavering, ice-blue gaze he directed upon her, upon her face, her hair, her nervous hands, and her lightly-veiled breasts.

There was something else, and she had blurted it out, in answer to his sudden, shocking, and disarming question. It made him laugh. When he laughed, he threw back his head and drew the sound from the depths of his broad chest, and the thick muscles of his neck tautened.

"You are frightened of me because I am evil? How, my dear Lady Landless, can you possibly know that I am evil on such short acquaintance?"

She had gained a little in courage, and with it came some of her habitual assurance with men—all sorts of men. But she was still wary.

"When I was very young," she said evenly, "I had the misfortune to be caught up in the turmoil and horror of the French Revolution. At an age when most young girls live through agonies because they have a pimple on the chin, I saw men, women, and children being hanged. I saw drunken brutes despoil screaming girls while their own drunken womenfolk held the arms and legs of their victims. My own guardian they slaughtered like an ox. His sweet wife they drowned for their own amusement. One does not forget these things, *monsieur.*" *Unthinkingly, she slipped back into* the language of her childhood, and when it seemed that he was going to interrupt her, she held up her hand for his silence, then resumed. "Do not think I have lived the sheltered life of the English lady all my days, sir. I have seen things—evil things—that most of the people in this room would scarcely believe could happen. I have seen the slave market in Algiers, where people are bought and sold like animals, where women and girls are degraded publicly and flogged if they so much as protest. I know evil, Captain D'Eath. I know its shape, its color, its form. I even detect its scent, which is sometimes beguiling, as the scent of many poisonous flowers is beguiling."

"And you detect that evil in me?" The pale eyes were crinkled at the corners, as if with a secret amusement.

"You have put me to the question," replied Purity. "It was not of my choosing to be asked so bluntly why

I feared you. You must have your answer. Yes—it is because I think that you are evil."

Again, his fingertip slowly stroked the corner of his eye, smoothing away the crinkles of amusement.

"Nevertheless, you are attracted to me," he murmured, "as I am attracted to you." And, slowly and very deliberately, he lowered his ice-blue gaze to the daring scoop of her bodice, to where, beneath the flimsy cloth-of-gold, the deep cleft between her twin orbs ended in pink darkness. Purity instinctively lifted her hands and covered her bosom from his gaze.

"Not attracted," she said. "I am finding myself drawn to your attention by a strange compulsion, a compulsion which is beyond my control. There is in all of us a morbid fascination with evil. How else to explain the manifestations of evil in even the purest of hearts and minds? The entire population of ancient Rome, so we are told, flocked to attend the so-called 'games,' in which innocent human beings were torn apart by wild animals to make sport for the populace. I am not to be persuaded that *everyone* in Rome was a monster of evil on that account."

He licked his moist lips, bathed her with his eyes, and again she felt nude before his searching gaze.

"You argue well, Lady Landless," he murmured. "But, perhaps, are you not protesting too much?"

She felt her assurance waver. "Why so, sir?" she said.

"This . . . what you call morbid fascination . . . does it extend, in my case, to the . . . *physical?*"

"The . . . physical?" she repeated, and her glance wavered.

His hand reached out and touched her bare arm, high up, above her elbow, at the softness just below her shapely shoulder. She felt her skin prickle all over and her nipples stir and harden.

"Do your protests not mask a desire—what you

would call a compulsion—that has nothing to do with the heart and the mind, that concerns itself only with the flesh? In short, do you not desire me? Do you not wish to be possessed by me—physically?"

She shook her arm free of his touch. "Sir, your conduct is insufferable!" she cried. She was turning on her heels when his next words halted her.

"Have you returned recently to Château Feyelle, Lady Landless?"

She turned, her eyes staring widely.

"What do you know of Château Feyelle!" she cried.

"I know that you were brought up there," he said evenly. "I know that when you spoke of the horrors you experienced during the Terror, you lived through those horrors at the Château Feyelle." He smiled meaningly. "I assure you, Lady Landless, formerly Purity Jarsy, I know a very great deal about you."

He is trying to trick me, she thought, pretending to have an intimate knowledge of my past life that he really doesn't possess, somehow to trap me. . . .

"That, sir, is a trifle of information that you could have picked up anywhere," she responded coldly. "And now, if you will excuse me, I will go and find my hu——"

"What of the folk still living at Château Feyelle?" he said. "What of Hubert Playel and his wife, not to mention Yvette Lamont, whose man was killed at Waterloo along with Jacques Playel, son of Hubert?"

Suddenly, startlingly, she could not have stirred from his side for all the world.

"How do you know these people?" she said in awe. "Who . . . who *are* you?"

"I am—or would wish to be—your intimate friend," he said. "As to how I know your friends who live and work at the estate you set up in the ruins of the old De Feyelle château and grounds, I know them

37

because I have been there—recently—and have spoken to them about you."

"You have been to Normandy, to Château Feyelle?" she asked. "Surely, that is a very curious coincidence."

"It is no coincidence," he replied blandly. "I went to inquire about . . . you."

"About . . . *me?*" She stared at him in mingled astonishment and alarm, not lacking the admixture of a certain horror. "In heaven's name, why?"

Purity was destined not to hear D'Eath's answer to her question, at least not on that occasion, for at that instant, a simpering courtier sidled up to her and in mellifluous tones intimated to her that His Majesty requested and required the presence of Lady Landless. Would her Ladyship be so kind as to step this way, please?

Purity followed the creature, who reeked of perfume, like a Bond Street strumpet. Her mind was so wholly taken up with a disturbing train of thought that had been started by D'Eath's disturbing declaration that she was face-to-face with the reclining sovereign, and he had put a question to her, before she shook off her *malaise* and dragged herself back to the there and then.

"His Majesty has asked you how things are at Clumber Grange!" The shrill and scolding voice of Lady Conyngham was of considerable aid in clearing Purity's thoughts.

"Oh! Your Majesty, I do so apologize," she faltered. "I thank you. We have had a good year at Clumber. The harvest has been very fine. In the pheasant season, my husband and his friends shot three hundred brace and more." Can this—how did the duke put it? —pathetic sack of guts really be remotely interested in the goings-on at our country estate? she wondered to herself.

38

"I am mighty pleased to hear it, ma'am," said the king, his blue and rheumy eyes washing over her figure, lingering lovingly upon the generous round of her hips and the cleft of her bosom. Perhaps, she thought, he was wishing that he was the boy officer of the portrait. At that age, she would now be of his age of aspiration: a bit older than he. Mature. Experienced in love. A surrogate mother, with breasts to suckle. . . .

"You are putting on some weight, Lady Landless," said the royal mistress with a thin edge of malice to her voice. "All that child-bearing, I shouldn't wonder."

Purity forebore to mention that she had had only one child—and that he was a grown boy. But she observed, with a wayward twinge of unkindness, that Lady Conyngham had a dowager's hump at the back of her neck that stood out like the paunch of a pouter pigeon.

"Still charming the gentlemen out of their minds, ma'am, I see," said the monarch with a lecherous chuckle that set his numerous chins trembling. "I observed you twisting Captain D'Eath around your little finger just now."

Purity smiled wanly. "A pardonable exaggeration on your part, sir," she said. "In fact, I had only just been introduced to the captain, and I cannot flatter myself that my charms are so considerable as to bear upon a gentleman of so short an acquaintance."

"Ah, but Captain D'Eath is no ordinary gentleman, ma'am," responded the king.

"Indeed, sir," said Purity, keenly interested despite herself. "And why, pray, is that?"

"Why, he is a ladies' man of some repute, ma'am," was the reply.

"A damned fornicator, with bastards in every county of England," interposed Lady Conyngham, adding irrelevantly, "and also in Ireland, as I am told."

This sally reduced the king to a paroxysm of uncontrollable mirth, in the course of which his heavy face became suffused with a ruddy purple color and his thick chest was racked with a bronchial cough of great textural complexity. It took the ministrations of a pair of courtiers, one of them with a large glass charged with the monarch's favorite tipple, and the other gently massaging the royal back and shoulders to restore him.

"Ah, m'dear Elizabeth, you'll be the death of me," wheezed the king, fondly clasping his mistress's hand. "Do you not think, Lady Landless, that the marchioness has a devilishly humorous turn of phrase, eh?"

"Very risible, sir," replied Purity. So D'Eath was reputed to be a libertine? On the face of it, it was hardly surprising. And what else?

"He is also a murderous devil," said Lady Conyngham, as if in answer to Purity's unspoken question, "a duelist of note who has killed more than one man." Her small and malicious eyes narrowed greedily. "He is also reputed to be among the richest men in England."

"That is so, that is so," said the king. "Of his dueling, I cannot speak, but I can attest that D'Eath is, indeed, one of the wealthiest of my subjects." For an instant, he dropped his eyes in sudden confusion, and Purity remembered that, king or no king, he was forever at odds with Parliament on the subject of his debts and extravagances. Was it likely that D'Eath, like so many other rich men, had accommodated his sovereign with loans or gifts?

"Well, sir, I don't care much for the fellow, and that's the truth of it," declared Lady Conyngham. "And I cannot for the life of me imagine why you summon him so often to Brighton."

"Why, ma'am, because the fellow amuses me," said the king. And, again, his gaze wavered. Purity felt a conviction that her guess had been correct: the king was taking, or had taken, money from D'Eath. What was more, his mistress knew nothing of it.

The reply put Lady Conyngham out of countenance, for she stared rudely at Purity for a moment and said, "Well, sir, I do not think we need to take up any more of Lady Landless's time. I am sure she is anxious to return to dance with her many conquests."

"Ahem! Quite, quite," said the king. "Very pleased, as ever, to see you again, Lady Landless."

"Your Majesty." Purity dropped a curtsy, well aware that the king was leaning forward quite unashamedly to stare down her front. Let him stare—and be damned to that appalling old trollop at his side!

As Purity walked away in search of Mark, Lady Conyngham's coarse voice came clearly to her ears, loudly, delivered with no pretense of constraint: "I declare, the creature wasn't wearing a *stitch* under that absurd gown! And to think of a married woman of *her* age flaunting her breasts in that manner!"

Purity did not catch the king's mumbled reply.

"Mark, will you take me home, please?"

She found him talking to one of Wellington's aides shortly after meeting D'Eath's eyes. D'Eath had been dancing with a pretty brunette. He had looked sharply in Purity's direction, almost as if he had sensed that her gaze was upon him. He had smiled—a possessive smile that spoke volumes for his conviction that she had fallen under the spell of his overpowering maleness. Purity had felt her cheeks flame, to her shame and consternation, and she had fled to seek out Mark.

"Take you home? Of course, my darling," said Mark.

He put his arms around her protectively. And in this manner they walked together around the edge of the dance floor, past the wheeling and posturing lines of men and women. Purity had the wayward hope that Guy D'Eath was a witness to their departure and to the tenderly possessive way in which her husband was escorting her. Indeed, she wished it so dearly that it was only with difficulty that she restrained herself from glancing along the line of male dancers to see if his countenance had changed expression from smugness to chagrin.

Presently, cloaked and ready, they emerged into the blustery night. Their coachman detached himself from a group of his friends who were huddled together for warmth under one of the arched colonnades that fronted the exotic building and came running.

"Home!" ordered Mark.

It was warm inside the carriage, for a small charcoal burner heated its snug interior. There, also, were thick rugs of soft Merino wool that Mark solicitously draped across Purity's knees and shoulders. Then he put his arms around her. She responded to his embrace with a kiss of passion that shocked her with its unbidden intensity—and greatly delighted him. In the warm darkness, hastily—for she had a compulsion to make her sudden desires known to Mark, and there was so little time before they would cross The Steyne and be pulling up outside the house—she struggled with the cloth-of-gold gown beneath her ermine cape.

When she was done, she took his hand and guided it beneath the rug, beneath the cape, and experienced a thrill of fierce delight, as Mark gave a sudden intake of breath, to feel his hand close over the peaked crest of her right, bare breast.

"God! Purity, my love!"

His hands wound around her, finding her to be nude to the waist. Mouth to mouth they stoked the fires of their mutual passion, and she was moaning with delicious ecstasy as he did wonderful things with her breasts, the small of her back, and the soft curve of her dimpled belly. In an eternity of time that could not have lasted more than five minutes, the two lovers mounted the crest of a passion that only total abandonment of mind and body could possibly slake.

"Home it is, sir and milady." The coachman's voice interrupted them. They had not noticed the carriage stopping.

Purity pulled her cape tightly around her bare shoulders and held it together at the neck. Mark preceded her out of the vehicle, then helped her down.

" 'Night, sir and milady."

"Good night, Tomkinson."

Blessedly, the servants had been told not to wait up for them. Mark had his key, and he threw open the front door while Purity was still climbing the steps. They shut the door shut behind them quietly, so as not to disturb a soul in the sleeping house.

It was near darkness in the hallway at the foot of the staircase. One candle had been left on a console table to light their way to bed. By the candlelight, their lips met again. Mark's hands slid the cape from her shoulders. It fell to the floor.

"Not here, my darling—upstairs, in our bed."

They raced together, hand in hand, up the stairs, scorning to take the candle. Each one-handed, they stripped off what they could of their clothing on the way. Purity divested herself entirely of the cloth-of-gold gown and left it lying where it fell. She kicked off her golden slippers, then ran, barefoot and nude, to fling wide the door of their bedchamber. Mark was still struggling with his boots as she crossed to the window and threw open the shutters. The full moon, peeking through a sea of storm clouds, brilliantly illuminated their darkness and gave him a breath-robbing vision of her naked loveliness as she threw herself upon the bed to await him.

That night they transcended any experience of loving that either had known before.

It began with play—of the kind that they had devised together since the early days of their coupling together. She must be a coquette, and he was a simple country fellow who had never known a woman before. His instruction in the parts of a woman's body being both protracted and comprehensive, there was little lacking in his education by the time it came for him to put his knowledge to good use. This diversion was followed by a game of master and pupil, in which Purity played the role of a stupid and truculent schoolboy who not only could not repeat his Latin verbs, but who thumbed his nose at his kindly teacher, who was then constrained, in the interests of higher learning, to chastise the erring youth. The victim was laid across his master's knee and soundly slapped upon the bare rump. And it was only then that the astounded—and suddenly delighted—pedagogue discovered that he had been deceived: the lad's nubile sister, craving the attentions of the schoolmaster, had taken her brother's place. . . .

As in all good theater, when the actor's hearts are in it, the miracle of a strange alchemy turned make-believe into reality. And Purity and her Mark drifted, almost without noticing, from play to ecstasy beyond all imagining, to return only in the early hours before dawn, when, replete and contented, they smiled at each other in the moonlight.

"I am hungry."

"Me, too. I never touched a bite at the Pavilion. And it looked so good."

"What was there to eat there? Tell me, Mark. Describe it to me."

"Well . . . there was lobster in the shell, cold."

"Lobster—I adore it. Please do continue."

"There was an enormous dish—it must have been the size of a hearth rug—with cold roast game of every kind, all jointed, with little frills of paper around

44

each piece: grouse, pheasant, hare, woodcock, snipe, widgeon, wild duck, *et cetera*. And there was a piquant sauce served alongside."

"Mark Landless, you are putting me to the torture. I beg you *not* to stop!"

"For those of the dessert persuasion—and, as you know, my darling, I am more inclined to the savory—there was charlotte Russe . . . "

"Charlotte Russe! Mmmm—divine!"

"Iced *gâteaux* galore, orange and lemon sherbet, a *vol-au-vent* of pears, meringues, raspberry cream, custards, blancmanges, fruited jellies, apple pies. Need I go on?"

Purity leaped from the bed, her breasts jouncing. She snatched up her peignoir.

"Come, husband of mine," she said. "We are going to make a foray into the kitchen. If the servants have not eaten us out of house and home, there should be cold meats and desserts aplenty in the leftovers line."

"And a bottle of claret from the cellar!" interpolated Mark.

"Keep your claret. Open me a bottle of champagne. Tonight I feel like champagne. Tonight, I feel . . . *free!*"

"Free—free of what, pray?" asked Mark.

"Free of . . . "

"Yes?"

She turned away, grateful that the moon had been obscured by a cloud and that he could not see the expression that must have come upon her face. To her mind came the vision of a pair of demanding eyes that were colored ice-blue—that, and the memory of the instant when, D'Eath having taken hold of her arm, she had felt a dark desire—it had to be said; it now had to be admitted to herself—suffuse her whole being.

She had slaked that desire upon the well-known,

45

well-loved body of Mark Landless, her husband and lover. . . .

Or had she?

She was free . . .

Or . . . was she?

"It was only a turn of phrase," he said carelessly. "I mean, I feel free of cares, responsibilities. The children are both in bed and asleep, and we have made love beautifully. And now we are going to enjoy a superb predawn supper of cold cuts. Give me your hand."

The wind had intensified. When they opened their door, they could hear it moaning in the hall chimney below. On the way down to the kitchen quarters in the basement, they encountered a draft, which increased as they reached the hall, where Mark took up the candle that still burned there.

"Do you suppose someone left a window open?" he said.

"Surely not on a night like this," said Purity.

The door down into the kitchen quarters at the rear of the house was ajar. It was from there that the draft was coming. Three steps down, and they came to the door of the room that was occupied by the ladies' maid Hannah. It was propped open, and there was no doubt that it was from this room that the great and constant rush of wind was emerging. Mark peered within, shielding the candle from the blast.

"Are you awake, Hannah?" he called. "She doesn't seem to be about, Purity."

"Perhaps, like us, she is partaking of a predawn supper in the kitchen," replied Purity with a lightness of tone that most certainly did not match a curious sense of unease that, quite unaccountably, had closed in upon her. "Best to close the window and shutters, which, I see, are both wide open."

"What can have possessed the girl to do that on such a night?" said Mark, entering the narrow bed-

46

chamber and crossing to the window, through which Purity could see the silhouetted line of dark roofs in the street beyond the back garden.

Mark laid the candle on a table close to the window and addressed himself to reaching up for the raised sash, which was open to its fullest limit.

"My God!" he exclaimed.

"Mark, what *is* it?"

"Purity, come here!"

Her heart, taking up a sudden, pounding beat, she ran across to where he stood looking out of the window and down into the night. His hand reached out and took hold of hers, as if to steady her against what she was going to see.

The moon had disappeared behind a patch of clouds. It was pitch-black in the garden and in the flagged area below the window, which lay at the rear of the kitchen quarters. Some moments passed before Purity made out the shape of something propped up against the wall of the house, rising up from the area and ending at the windowsill, inches from where they stood. She reached out and touched—the top rung of a ladder.

"Mark!" she cried. "What does it mean? Why should Hannah use this to get out of the house in the night?"

"Or . . . did someone use it to get *in?*" he said harshly.

Their eyes met in the candlelight.

"Mark—*the children!*"

Purity was first to the door, leading him most of the way up the stairs, but he drew ahead of her when they came to the boy's bedchamber and flung the door wide open. A candle burned at the bedside; by its warm glow, they could see the tousled head upon the pillow, the peach-like down on the curve of a smooth cheek.

"Thank God!" cried Purity, her voice breaking upon the words. "Thank God that he's safe."

"Up to Chastity's room," said Mark.

The urgency had gone out of their pell-mell rush, the first and dreadful fright having been proved groundless. Purity even tapped upon Chastity's door, then shrugged when she received no reply.

"She sleeps like the dead, poor darling," she murmured fondly, then opened the door.

There was no light within, but Mark still carried the candle. The room was large, and the four-poster bed was at the end farthest from the door. Moreover, the bed curtains were partly drawn in such a manner as to render it impossible for them to immediately see if it bore an occupant.

As they crossed the room, their nostrils were assailed by an alien odor: sweetish, aromatic.

"Chastity, my darling . . . "

"She's not here!" Purity screamed, and she was instantly taken in Mark's grasp to steady her.

The bed was in complete disarray; the sheets and blankets were pulled roughly aside, as when the occupant makes a hasty abandonment—or is roughly taken from the bed. A scrap of torn lace and silk lay, half fallen to the floor, over the edge of the bed. Mark reached out and picked it up.

"What's this? Do you know, Purity?" he whispered.

"It's . . . it's part of her nightgown," she answered, "part of the bodice."

There was something else: a small bottle, uncorked and empty. Mark picked it up and held it briefly to his nostrils. It was the source of the odor that pervaded the room.

"She . . . has been taken, hasn't she, Mark?"

He nodded.

"She has been taken," he said.

Chapter Three

Morning brought blue skies and a sharp frost that made early promenaders put on thick scarves and walk swiftly with their heads bowed against the piercing wind. Out at sea, a full-rigged ship bowed on a westerly course down-Channel, half reefed down.

To the Landlesses' handsome terrace house in The Steyne came three men from the Brighton magistrate's office. One of them was the night watchman—the selfsame one who had called out the hours of the previous night. All three were simple, uneducated fellows. They stood awkwardly in the elegant drawing room, twisting their battered tall hats between work-roughened fingers and glancing shyly toward Mark Landless as he paced up and down before them, and occasionally stealing a look at the beautiful woman in the armchair, with the miraculous silver-gold hair and the tragic, lovely face.

"The girl was hale and well at around ten-fifteen last night, gentlemen," said Mark, "at that time, in company with the maid Hannah . . . "

"That would be her own maid, Sir Mark, would

it?" interposed one of the officers, he who had introduced himself, on arrival, as Constable Ross.

"The girl Hannah is . . . was ladies' maid to both my wife and daughter," explained Mark. "We do not keep a large staff down here at the Brighton house, so the ladies' maid shared her duties between both."

"And it is this Hannah who is also missing, sir?"

"That is so. Her room was abandoned. Her belongings were taken."

"I see, sir. Please continue. Your daughter was last seen at ten-fifteen. Might I ask, was she in what you might call an upset state of mind at that time?"

Mark spread his hands toward Purity. "My dear?" he prompted.

"Far from it," said Purity, her voice calm and controlled. "Indeed, she spoke with some enthusiasm about riding out this morning. Her whole manner, the things she said to me, were most . . . warm and serene."

Ross, who had more sensibility than his looks gave him credit for, thought, she's a cool one, and no mistake. But she's near to breaking. Fine-looking woman. A Frenchy, so they say. . . .

Aloud, he said, "So she left you—Miss Landless, that is—and went to bed, ma'am? And the maid?"

"The maid went to iron my daughter's riding habit in readiness for this morning," said Purity.

"Is this riding habit to be seen, ma'am?" asked Ross.

Purity glanced at him in some surprise. "I really have no idea, Constable," she said. "The thought of it had never crossed my mind. Would you like us to find out?"

"That I would, ma'am," said the other.

"I will ring for a footman," said Mark.

A footman was summoned and dispatched to the linen room, where the flat irons and trivets were kept. He returned almost immediately with a lady's riding

50

habit: a bottle-green tunic frogged with black cord, and a riding skirt to match. Both were upon a clothes hanger. He held them out for Purity's inspection. She reached up and touched them, turning back the skirt of the tunic, lifting a sleeve.

"They were never ironed last night," she said flatly.

"You are sure of that, ma"m?" asked Ross.

"Quite sure. Apart from anything else, there is still a smear of mud on the elbow here, where my daughter took a fall from her mare when last she rode out. The maid would certainly have removed that during her ironing."

The officer nodded, then exchanged glances with his companions, both of whom looked at him more in admiration than comprehension.

"It's clear, at any rate, that the girl Hannah was engaged in other business last night," he said, "business that interrupted her while carrying out her young mistress's order to iron the garments."

"Or perhaps she never had any intention of performing the task," interposed Mark quietly, *"because she knew that the riding habit would not be required this morning!"*

Ross's unaccommodating face took on an expression of cunning. "My thought exactly, Sir Mark!" he exclaimed.

"That bitch is responsible!"

Purity's sudden outburst dismayed the officers of the law, who gaped at her in considerable dismay. Mark crossed over and laid a placating hand on his wife's shoulder.

"She will be found, my darling," he said. "Chastity will be found, never fear. I will use every influence, invoke every friendship—the duke, my connections in Parliament, the king . . . everyone."

"Sir, ma'am, everything that could be done is already being done," said Ross stoutly. "Already messages have been sent to Bow Street with tidings of Miss Landless's disappearance. By tomorrow, every officer in southern England will have been apprised."

"Find that wretched bitch of a maid and you will find my daughter!" cried Purity. "It was she who admitted the kidnappers, she who led them to Chastity's bedchamber—and she who fled with them, taking her chattels!"

"Find her, we shall, ma'am," said Ross.

"And when you do," spat Purity, her perfect countenance suffused with fury, as when a leopardess has had her cub taken from her, "if one hair of my daughter's head has been harmed, I will see to it that that bitch hangs in chains! In chains, do you hear?"

Chastity lifted her head and strained her ears to catch again the slight sound that had reached her, not so much as a sound, but as a tiny vibration against her skull while it had rested against the hard floor.

Nothing. She was tempted to call out again. Indeed, the seed of panic was already there; but she dare not call out. The last time she had done it, she had nearly driven herself mad: first the urgent, angry cries; then the edge of shrillness; finally, she had been screeching like a lunatic, with her mind out of control, her body a trembling, nerveless heap of flesh and bones. At all costs, she must stop herself from going mad.

It was pitch-black in the place—a cupboard, or a tiny storeroom?—where they had locked her. Dark and cold. And she was naked. When they had bundled her inside, blindfolded, her arms pinioned behind her by a pair of strong hands, the very last thing they had done before slamming and locking the door had been to rip from her the last rags of her night shift. She huddled closely against the corner of the wall, hugging her bare breasts, shivering. The blindfold, which she had taken off, only to find herself in darkness, now served as a brief loincloth—a scanty gesture of modesty against the next pair of eyes that beheld her.

How long had she been in the small room? One day . . . two? They had fed her twice. Twice the door had been opened, a glaring light had been shone in her face, blinding her, and something had been thrown in. The last time it was a piece of dry bread, the other time a hard biscuit. And she had early on discovered a large pitcher of brackish water in one corner and a bucket in another.

Why . . . why?

She had been kidnapped, but why *she?*

Papa Mark was rich, she supposed. He owned Clumber Grance and a London town house, not to mention the place in Brighton. A childhood and adolescence spent in what she supposed was luxury almost unparalleled in England she had always taken for granted, as if it had been her right. Of course, one vaguely knew that somewhere behind the marble facades of London town there existed places called "rookeries," where folks lived in the most appalling squalor, and sometimes even starved. Some of the lesser servants who attended to one's needs—the skivvies and the kitchen maids, the little boys who cleared away the snow from the driveway at Clumber, and who did it barefoot—must also exist in conditions more suitable to animals than to humans. She had always looked upon it as the natural order of things.

And now she—Chastity Landless—was reduced to nakedness and starvation in the dark! In a condition worse than any pauper in the land!

Money—the kidnappers were certainly after money. And Papa Mark would quickly pay them at the first demand, no matter how much they called for. He would not quibble. There would be no risking of her safety by trying to apprehend the people who had taken her. His first concern would be for her safety, likewise, Mama Purity.

But—it was puzzling—why, if the kidnappers' sole intent was to hold her for ransom, did they lock her in a darkened room? Surely because they did not want her to know in what kind of establishment she was being held, in case she was able to describe the appearance of the house to the officers of the law, after her release, and lead to their arrest. That made sense.

But, why render her naked? That admitted of no easy explanation. Perhaps they thought it would deter her from making an attempt to escape. If so, they sorely misjudged Chastity Landless: in her present state of desperation, she would run through the length and breadth of the city of London, naked as she was, to get away.

Most puzzling of all: Why, if their intent was simply to hold her for ransom, were they starving her?

It made no sense. However the kidnappers might regard her as a person, to them she was a valuable item of property. If one came across a valuable stray animal—a thoroughbred horse or fine greyhound— one would tend it well, keep it safely, and give it the best of food while waiting to locate the owner and inform him of his loss.

Perhaps . . . perhaps they were not after money at all.

She shuddered and hugged herself more tightly against a new dread that was more cutting than the bitter cold. . . .

A man like Papa Mark—rich, influential, a man who had performed many and varied services for his country all over the world—might well have many enemies, persons who would give much to do him ill.

What if she—her capture—was a means to strike at Colonel Sir Mark Landless of Clumber Grange?

What was that . . . ?

Surely, she had heard a far-off door slam. And was that not a footfall on a stair? She crept on hands and knees to the door, pressed her cheek to the cold panel, and listened.

Yes, someone was coming. There was a slow, shuffling tread approaching down a corridor outside. Someone was bringing her food. For a brief moment —though blinded by light, and gazed upon by heaven knows who in her nakedness—she was going to be in contact, however fleeting and alien, with another living being, perhaps with someone who would exchange a few words with her this time, and answer some of the questions that were dinning in her brain.

The footsteps came nearer. Instinctively, she drew away from the door so as not to be within reach of whomever opened it. She squirmed back into the farthest corner and cradled her breasts in her hands, waiting.

The footsteps reached the door . . . and continued on down the corridor without pause. Chastity leaped to her feet with a cry and threw herself forward.

"Don't go away! Please, come back—please, whoever you are! Don't leave me here!" she cried. And then: "Mama, Mama! Don't let them leave me! Not all alone here in the dark! Please—oh, please!"

She beat upon the door till rags of skin hung from her bruised knuckles. Then, weeping bitterly, she sank to the floor, defeated. And for the first time since the living nightmare when she had awakened in her bedchamber in Brighton and felt a choking pad being pressed against her mouth and nostrils, while strong arms dragged her from the bed, and her senses slipped away—for the very first time, she faced the dreaded possibility that there might be no end to her nightmare, that she would never again leave her narrow, shut-in world of darkness.

On the morning of the second day following Chastity's disappearance—they, the Landlesses themselves and the officers of the law, were studiously avoiding the use of the term "kidnap" as much as possible—Mark took Purity to London, since it was obvious that the missing girl was not in Brighton any longer. There had been house-to-house searches. Broadsheets announcing the disappearance and bearing a tolerable likeness of the victim were posted in all the public places of the town. The search had moved from the south coast to the metropolis, so to London also went the anguished parents.

They drove post-haste to their stately house in exclusive Mayfair, number 17A Half Moon Street, where Mark tarried only to establish Purity in her drawing room with the shutters closed and with a firm understanding that she would try and get some sleep on the sofa before rushing out again to make representations to certain influential friends in Whitehall in the hope of securing every possible assistance—even from the Brigade of Guards stationed in the capital—in tracking down the missing girl.

Purity had no intention, no likelihood, of sleeping. No sooner had the sound of Mark's town phaeton's wheels faded away down the street outside her window than she was on her feet and hastening to Chastity's room on the floor above.

Save for the servants, she was alone in the house. It had been decided to send Robert away. The peril had to be faced—the possibility that the kidnappers might strike again, this time against the son and heir of the Landless fortunes. They had considered the alternatives of sending him down to Wiltshire in company with a trusted footman, or to Mark's ancient but by no means senile Aunt Julia in Norfolk. They had chosen the latter course, since it was unlikely that the kidnappers' information about the family extended to details of far-flung relations. As Purity had pointed out, the accomplice Hannah had been with them for only a short while—a matter of six months—and had certainly never heard of Aunt Julia. So it was to Norfolk that the boy had been dispatched, with many tears, that same morning.

Purity entered her daughter's room and closed the door behind her, leaning against it. A wave of nostalgia swept over her, an ineffable sense of total loss. Mementos of Chastity's brief life were all around the room: those toys which, as a child, she had kept always at Half Moon Street, those that had been designated "my London children," and a rocking horse without a tail, a toy theater, a bouncing ball, and a hoop. And there were the things that told of her maturing womanhood: a vanity case with rice powder and rouge, eyeshadow for the eyes, and vanity patches in the eighteenth-century style, which were having a certain revival in fashion among the young.

Purity opened a curtain that screened an alcove containing the clothes that Chastity had kept for her use in London: ball gowns (for "young parties," for she had not yet "come out" in general, adult society); day gowns; afternoon gowns; the pretty, lacy confections that she delighted to wear over her night shifts; a severely tailored riding habit. Purity felt a tear splash down upon her hand. She met her own reflection in the pier glass that stood in the alcove.

Mark must be stopped, she told her reflection. She should have stopped him before. No guardsmen, no Bow Street Runners. There must be no move whatsoever that might put Chastity's safety in the slightest jeopardy. Instead, they would wait for whatever demands the kidnappers made upon them. Moreover, she would ask Mark to place an advertisement in the *Times* that very day, inviting—imploring—whoever held her to write to them at Half Moon Street immediately, setting forth their demands for the safe return of their victim.

What would we not give? she asked her reflection.

Let the kidnappers' terms be never so onerous, but they would not shrink, Mark and she. Let them ask for every penny the Landlesses possessed. It would be but a small exchange for the child of their hearts. She and Mark had lived in a cottage—in Spain during the war, when he had been at the front and returning only for brief furloughs—and they could do so again. She had been reared as a peasant in rural France; Mark was at heart a farmer. With their little family around them, they could do the same again.

What would we not give to have her back again? she repeated to her reflection.

All we have. . . .

She saw herself as she was: a woman in the full flower of her loveliness, saw herself dispassionately, without conceit, with the eye of truth. She was a woman with a body that was—to put the issue at its highest and purest—fashioned for the ecstasy of mutual loving, as she had experienced love with Mark Landless and with no one else in the same high, splendid degree. To put it at its lowest—and it was at this juncture that she closed her eyes and expressed a bitter tear for the memories that she had spent long months and years in trying to exorcise—her body was eminently suited for the pleasuring of a man . . . any man.

In the past—though she had never spoken of it to anyone, even to Mark, and had kept it silent, even to her own ears—she had not hesitated to give her body to save those she loved and treasured.

Would she be able to bring herself to do it again if the occasion arose?

"I will give myself willingly to anyone," she said

aloud to her reflection, "to *anyone*—if it will bring my darling Chastity back to us."

Mark was back in haste, so soon that it was obvious that he had not made the rounds of all his influential friends. Purity heard his phaeton draw up outside, heard his running footfalls ascend the steps, followed by his impatient knock for admission. He took the staircase to the upper floor two steps at a time, then burst in through the drawing room door.

"They've found the girl—they've found Hannah!" he cried.

"Here—in London?"

"Yes. I had it from the home office, which has just been informed by the office of the Bow Street Runners. She's been apprehended and taken to the Bridewell prison."

"And Chastity?"

His face was grave. "No sign of Chastity yet, my darling, but, don't you see? This is wonderful news. The girl is a mere accomplice, a cat's-paw. She was bribed for perhaps a not very considerable sum of money, to admit the kidnappers and lead them to Chastity's room. And now she has been apprehended and will be punished for her part in it. A girl like that has nothing to lose and everything to gain from cooperating with the law. With encouragement, she will tell all she knows, I promise you."

Purity was caught up in the tide of his enthusiasm and optimism.

"Yes, my darling, you are right," she said. "She must be encouraged to talk. It can be done without endangering Chastity. Once we know who has taken her, once we know where she is . . . oh, Mark, let us go and see her at once. I will plead with her, as a mother, as a woman!"

A flurry of snow was descending upon Half Moon

Street as they entered their covered carriage and were driven out into Piccadilly and eastward to the Strand and Fleet Street. It was bitterly cold outside the conveyance. As they came to the Haymarket, a small crowd of urchins, barefoot and ragged, seeing the fine lady and gentleman in the crested carriage, came running alongside, keeping pace with the trotting pair of gray horses, their pounding feet splashing up the mud and slush. Mark tossed a handful of pennies out of the window, and the lads pounced upon the coins, whooping and shoving each other aside.

Coming to Temple Bar, whose noble arches separated the cities of Westminster and London proper, they saw poor drabs crouched in the shadows, though it was scarcely mid-afternoon, and it seemed inconceivable that there were men in London so depraved as to crave their services at such an hour, in such atrocious conditions.

Down the incline of Fleet Street (and the coachman had to take care, for the churned-up snow was ankle-deep and the going was exceedingly slippery), the spire of St. Bride's church came into sight ahead —St. Bride's, with its elegantly proportioned design by Sir Christopher Wren and its over-brimming graveyard, whose charnel stench added its might to the disease and pestilence that constantly racked the capital city of the most powerful nation on earth. They turned off Fleet Street, heading for the river, and were immediately engulfed in high-walled slum alleys where the sun seldom reached, where white-faced creatures watched their passing from dark doorways, and where spavined dogs raised themselves on spindly legs and howled to see them.

The grim entrance tower of the Bridewell prison loomed out of the swirling blanket of snow. Founded three hundred years earlier as a place of training and education for homeless apprentices, its medieval cells and dank halls had come to be used for the incarceration of religious and political prisoners, vagrants, prostitutes, and persons awaiting trial or execution. The coachman's knock upon the iron-barred gateway brought a sullen face to a small wicket door, and, following a brief exchange, there followed the rattle of bolts and the grinding of heavy locks.

"Follow me. The governor be expecting you." The speaker wore rusty black and a cap of faintly military style. He carried a large bunch of keys and a heavy cudgel. Mark and Purity followed him across a snow-covered courtyard, past a row of wooden crosses that seemed to mark the last resting places of unfortunates whose misfortunes had been compounded by breathing their last breath within the insalubrious walls of Bridewell. Finally, by way of a low entrance porch and a stone-built corridor whose walls were streaked with green mold and exuded beads of discoloured moisture, they were led to a door marked GOVENOR, through which, upon their guide knocking and receiving a harsh reply to enter, they came into the presence of an individual, seated at a high desk, who rose from his stool when their names were announced. Fiftyish, incredibly thin, pale, and shifty-eyed, he instantly assumed an expression of unctuous amiability.

"Sir and Lady Landless, what an honor." He extended a large white hand to Mark and then to Purity, who took it in hers and found it to be as cold and moist as the walls of his own prison. "My name is Reeper, sir and ma'am. Nathan Reeper. Honored."

"We have called, as you will know, in connection with the prisoner recently apprehended, Hannah Wilkes," said Mark. "Can you tell us anything about her arrest—the circumstances and so forth, and then may we interview her?"

"By all means, Sir Mark, by all means," replied Reeper. He was toothless save for two yellow fangs in the center of his upper jaw, giving him a rat-like appearance. Rat-like, also, was his manner of darting dark-eyed glances from side to side when he spoke. "But, first, will you take tea? No? Perhaps a glass of brandywine? No? Then please be seated, and I will apprise you of the sad creature whom I have taken within my fold."

"She was arrested—where?" demanded Mark.

"Why, in a low tavern in Eastcheap," said Reeper, "a place that had been a regular haunt of members of her family since she was a child. Last evening, it was, and she, accompanied by her mother and father—the father is a dog-skinner and a man of bad character—and seven brothers and sisters, drank the evening through with seemingly no regard for cost. It was this circumstance, taken in conjunction with the fact that the girl Hannah was dressed in clothes of unaccustomed finery, that prompted a certain public-spirited citizen, a gentleman of excellent character who augments his slender wages, from time to time and as the opportunity occurs, by assisting the process of the law . . . "

"You mean a police informer?" interjected Mark flatly.

"Quite so, Sir Mark, quite so," said Reeper, and he looked affronted. "As I was saying, this gentleman, observing the disparity between the amount they were drinking, the girl's new clothing, and the wages of a mere dog-skinner, saw fit to apprise the Watch. And the Watch was furnished with a description of the missing ladies' maid Hannah Wilkes. Quite easily done, in the phrase of Euclid." He flashed his fangs.

"Has she yet given any information about her associates, or any indication of our daughter's whereabouts?" asked Mark.

"Has she?" exclaimed Purity. "I beg you to tell us in one word, Mr. Reeper!"

"In one word, Lady Landless, the answer to your question—and I perceive in that question the anguish of a truly loving mother, which anguish I also see mirrored in your eyes, Lady Landless—is: no. She has not." He accommodated his unpromising countenance in an expression of piety. "I have reasoned with the girl, and I have left with her a copy of The Good Book, in the hope that she may see the error of her ways and repent. I have wrestled with her soul, Sir and Lady Landless. But I fear she is far gone in the pride of wickedness."

"We should like to see her now, Mr. Reeper," said Mark.

"No, my dear!" cried Purity.

Both men looked sharply at her.

"I will see her alone, Mark," she said. "I am convinced that, appealing to her as woman to woman, I have the best chance of making her talk."

"I think you are probably right, my darling," said Mark.

The governor of Bridewell took a deep breath and then exhaled it noisily between his teeth. "Perhaps, perhaps," he said. "But, in my experience, those who have strayed far from the paths of righteousness, if they do not respond to the calls of religion, are not easily swayed by appeals to the lesser emotions. However, you have my blessing to make the attempt, Lady Landless. I will summon a woman turnkey to escort you to the prisoner."

A bell was rung, and presently an aged crone in a mob cap put in an appearance. She was smoking a clay pipe and smelled vilely of stale tobacco.

"Mrs. Grummet, I should like you to convey this lady to the prisoner Wilkes," said Reeper.

"Oh, aye?" The old woman cast a rheumy eye over Purity. "Come alonger me, Missus."

Purity squeezed Mark's hand.

"Wish me luck, and be with me in spirit, my darling," she whispered, "for the sake of our darling Chastity."

"I will be with you every living moment, my love," he murmured against her ear.

Purity followed the woman out of the door. When they were gone, Reeper cracked his knuckles loudly.

"Well, Sir Mark," he said, "in the absence of your dear lady, no doubt you would wish to accompany me to witness a flogging. 'Tis a youth who was caught stealing a sack of flour. Thirty lashes of the whip. Have you ever witnessed a flogging, sir?"

"No, sir, I have not," replied Mark coldly, "and I have no . . . "

"Not what it used to be, of course," said Reeper, seemingly oblivious to Mark's distaste. "As man to man, Sir Mark"—here he jogged the other's elbow conspiratorially—"as man to man, if I may be so bold, sir, it hasn't been the same since they abolished the whipping of women a few years ago. I could tell you of some whippings, sir. There was a pair of women, mother and daughter they were, caught picking pockets in Covent Garden. Both stripped to the waist for the flogging, of course. The daughter wasn't much, but the mother . . . " He sketched an extravagant gesture, breast-high, with both of his large white hands. And he leered.

The interior of the great central block of the prison was like the nave of a vast cathedral devoted to some demoniacal religion. Light was admitted thinly through narrow windows high up at roof level; the thin shafts of wintry day illuminated the myriad particles of drifting dust that permeated every part of the building. Galleries of stone and ironwork—three floors of them —rose from ground level; and the ascent was made by grandiose staircases set into the moldering walls. To

Purity, it seemed like ascending one of the antechambers of hell.

The first gallery comprised a line of cells whose doors were all wide open. To Purity's surprise, the first of these contained a gentleman in a flowered smoking jacket who was taking his ease in a comfortable-looking armchair and reading the day's issue of the *Times* newspaper. There was a decanter of wine and a brimming glass at his elbow. He looked up and nodded agreeably at Purity as she passed. Her astonishment was considerable, till she remembered hearing that, for a criminal with good outside contacts who had the means to bribe the turnkeys—and, indeed, the governor—there was no difficulty in obtaining the wherewithal to make his sentence quite tolerable, with supplies of food, drink, and tobacco, not to mention items of comfortable furniture.

The upper gallery appeared to be reserved for women prisoners. Again, the cell doors were all open and the inmates passed freely from one cell to another, gossiping with their neighbors, playing cards, tending to each other's hair, and trying on clothes. Most seemed to be well dressed and to have outside comforts; and most had the hard, painted look of street women. One of them, a brazen strumpet dressed only in a tight-laced pair of stays that left her nude from the navel down and rendered her breasts bare and upthrust, called out when Purity and her guide walked past. "Hello, Mother Grummet! Who's the new doxy, then?"

"Mind your own business," growled the old woman. "And a pox take you, if it ain't already!"

They ascended to the next, and upper, floor. There, men and women were mixed together, some three or four in a cell. And all of the doors were locked. Mrs. Grummet paused outside one door, and, unlocking it, she threw it open and motioned Purity to follow her inside. There were two inmates in the narrow compartment. One was a small girl—she could not have been more than six or seven—barefoot and wearing a single ragged shift, who turned a pinched and pale face, wide-eyed, to regard the newcomers, then looked back toward the wall, where she lay huddled, weeping. The second person in the cell was Hannah Wilkes.

"Lady Landless—*you!*"

The former ladies' maid had clearly not been apprehended without a struggle; there was a dark contusion over one eye, and the sleeve of her cheap, flashy dress was torn to the armpit. After the first shock of encounter, her head went up, and an expression of sullen defiance took the place of her dismay.

"How are you, Hannah?" asked Purity quietly.

"As you see me," replied the other truculently. "Those who arrested me damned near raped me, but what's that to you?"

"And what, do you suppose, they have done to my daughter, the friends of yours who took her?" asked Purity. "Was she nearly raped, also? Or, since there could have been no impediment, was she indeed raped?"

The hostile glance wavered.

"I wasn't there to see it," she replied.

"But you would care greatly—if you knew that she had been violated by your friends?"

The girl shrugged. "Mayhap," she muttered.

"Only mayhap? What harm did my daughter ever do you?"

The sullen mouth hardened again.

"She was forever giving herself airs. Looked down on me as if I were a bit o' dirt. 'Hannah, you're so clumsy, look at your great, coarse hands crumpling my gown,' and 'Don't you think I look pretty, Hannah?.' "

Purity said quietly, "And for that . . . because she is prettier than you, because she is young and thoughtless, because—and it is a fault that can scarcely be laid at *her* door—her parents are rich and perhaps overindulgent to her wants, and have spoiled her in consequence—because of these things, you sold her . . . for money. How much money, Hannah? What is the going rate to deliver an innocent young girl to possible rape and degradation?"

Hannah's eyes wavered, then closed. She bowed her head.

"They promised she'd come to no harm," she whispered hoarsely. "I wouldn't have agreed otherwise. The money—why, it was more than I'd ever had at one time, or ever am likely to have in my whole life." Her eyes snapped open again, and she looked Purity squarely in the face. "But I never would have taken it if I'd thought for one moment that they'd do her harm."

Purity, sensing that she was close to winning the girl's trust, reached out and took her by the shoulders.

"Listen to me, Hannah," she said quietly. "No harm will come to you, I promise. Any charges that have been placed against you as an accomplice will be dropped. Sir Mark will see to it. He has great influence. In return, you must tell me who are those who took her away, and, if you know it, where they have taken her. Now, what do you say?"

The girl's eyes widened with the light of hope. Purity knew that the decision rested, in her mind, upon a knife's edge. Hannah opened her mouth to speak, and then closed it and looked away sharply.

"Hannah—please! I beg you!"

" 'Tis no use!" cried the other. "Were I to tell you, were I to betray them, 'twould not matter where I went, where I hid myself. I could go to the other end of the land, bury myself in a grave. They would find me and destroy me."

Nor could all Purity's pleas and entreaties dissuade her. All the girl would agree to—and it was a half-promise delivered with a reluctant nod of the head, and Purity knew in her heart that it was only a device to be rid of her—was to reconsider the matter and send her word if she changed her mind.

Purity left her then. The small girl was still sobbing quietly against the wall, where she had been throughout the interview, all uncaring, sunk in her own misery.

And then demons began to inhabit Chastity's darkness.

They were completely substantial, fashioned by her own imagination against the blackness that filled her whole world. The walls of her narrow cell receded, leaving room to encompass an eternity of space and time. She was the sole inhabitant of a world without people, naked, vulnerable, helpless, apprehensive. It was useless to close her eyes; when the demons launched themselves out of the void, there was no shutting out the sight of them, and when she tried to run, they came at her from every avenue of escape. At those times, she screamed for help—and it was always to "Mama Purity" that she called.

On the fourth day of her imprisonment in the tiny dark room, she was awakened from a fitful, brief sleep by a knock upon the door. By the time her eyes were open, the door, too, had opened. A faint light— fainter than the glare that she had known on the two previous occasions, but nevertheless sufficient to make her cry out with pain and shield her eyes—shone in upon her.

"I have brought you food, child." The voice was soft, sibilant, feminine-sounding, but undoubtedly the voice of a man. "Also some wine. Can you see me, child?"

Chastity took her hands from her eyes. The lantern that he had brought now lay on the floor at his feet. Heavily shielded with smoked glass, the candle flame nevertheless had the power to send his huge shadow upon the wall and ceiling of the narrow room. Her night-blinded eyes, becoming slowly accustomed to the faint light, took in the vision of a towering figure clad all in black, save for a glaring white shirt front and neck cloth. His face was aquiline and pale, his hair dark.

"Yes, I can see you," she whispered.

"Here is your food and wine," he murmured. Stooping, he laid by her feet a silver tray containing a porcelain plate upon which lay some pieces of chicken. Chicken was Chastity's favorite food. The aroma of it caught her in the throat and nostrils, and her mouth instantly filled with saliva. As if from far off, she saw her hands (surely they must be her hands) reach out and take a piece of the succulent flesh.

Tremblingly, she put it to her lips, and, in her frantic haste, dropped it.

"No matter," said her companion. Stooping, he picked it up and handed it back to her. "Eat your fill. Then pour yourself a glass of wine."

"Thank . . . thank you," she whispered.

The chicken tasted more wonderful than reality, more like a repast of the imagination. Her mouth full, she laid aside the piece of bone and took up a crystal decanter that stood, along with a cut-glass rummer, on the tray. But, again, her hands, weakened by starvation and unaccustomed to use, fumbled the rummer and dropped it. The thick glass did not break.

"I will pick it up," he said.

His hand—a very slender and capable-looking hand, steady, not like her own—came down and, taking up the rummer, deftly filled it two-thirds full with the ruby-red wine.

"Thank you," said Chastity. "I am . . . very clumsy."

He made no reply.

The act of sipping the wine gave her the opportunity to steady her racing mind. What a fool she was making of herself before this tall, wise, and all-seeing creature who had come into her life, taking her from out of darkness into light, into suave indulgence. And she so mean and inept, so wrong and out of kilter.

What must he think of her? Her breasts, tiny and unformed—the breasts of a child. And the dirty piece of rag she had wrapped around her waist. She supposed that her hair was hanging in rats' tails. And, surely, she must stink.

She could faintly detect an aroma that must be eau de cologne, and it was coming from him—he of the impeccable white shirt front and beautifully manicured fingers. What must he think of her? In a wayward moment, she wished that he would leave her to her shame and ineptitude. In the instant following, she breathed a prayer that he would stay with her—naked, filthy, stinking, and uncomely as she was.

"Have you finished, child?" he murmured gently.

"Yes, thank you," she whispered. "It was lovely, but . . . but my appetite seems to have left me."

He reached down and picked up the tray. A sudden surge of panic seized her.

"You are not going to leave me?" she cried. "Not alone again—and in the dark!"

He appeared to consider the matter, looming above her, gazing down impassively upon her nakedness.

"It would distress you very much to be left in the dark again?" he murmured.

"I think I should go mad if it happened again," she

said. "Please, I beg you. I would give anything . . . anything . . ."

"You shall have the lantern," he said.

"Oh, thank you, thank you!" cried Chastity, her tear-streaked face radiant with joy.

He paused at the door and looked back at her.

"I am kind to you, am I not?" he said unsmilingly. "As kind as your mother, perhaps?"

"Oh, yes, you are kind," said Chastity. "But no one is kind like my Mama Purity."

He nodded and went out.

Purity was not sleeping, nor were she and Mark living a complete life together as lovers. After the night of the Royal Pavilion ball, when they had returned to spend those hours of abandoned ecstasy together, she could no longer bear to feel his hand upon her, but shrunk away at his touch. The image of lovemaking, in her mind, was overlaid by another image: that of Chastity being carried down the stairs in the Brighton house, drugged unconscious, past the door of their bedchamber, in which she and Mark were perhaps coupled together in rapture. . . .

Mark seemed to comprehend perfectly; indeed, it was he who suggested that it might help her to sleep if she had the room to herself. Therefore, he had a bed set up in his dressing room and exiled himself there. Purity was grateful for the gesture, and she was ashamed of herself in consequence—and in no doubt of the very real sacrifice that her lover and husband was making. Mark was a sensualist—as, indeed, in her normal state, she was a sensualist—and together they had arrived at a *modus vivendi* that was as enviable as it was unique: they knew each other's minds and bodies as well as they knew their own; there was no excess of erotic loving in which they had not been willing partners; and yet—wonder of wonders—they were

71

forever learning new delights, treading the flower-besprinkled pathways of fresh and delicious excesses. And they kept to each other—this in a bawdy and licentious era, when fidelity between married couples was a subject for mockery and lampoon.

So she lay in her great four-poster bed alone. But sleep evaded her still. Not till the thin daylight crept in through the gaps in the shutters did she drift away for a short while, worn out by sheer weariness, only to awaken shortly after, with the same questions pounding in her brain, the questions that had kept her wakeful through the dark hours: Where was Chastity? And would they ever see her again?

On the morning of the second day following their visit to see the former ladies' maid in Bridewell, there came a messenger to the house on Half Moon Street, a rough fellow who had been dispatched with a note from Governor Reeper of Bridewell.

Purity ripped it open and read the crabbed hand with mounting joy and excitement:

Dear Sir and Lady Landless,

I do not regard it of much consequence, for the minds of those far gone in wickedness are not to be trusted in matters of constancy, but the woman Hannah Wilkes did ask to see me last night and did intimate that she would be willing to divulge certain matters to you—and to you alone. As I say, her constancy may have taken another turn by this morning, so it would be most expedient to come at earliest convenience.

Your humble and obedient servant,
Dear Sir and Lady Landless,

Nathan Reeper, Governor

"Mark, we must go at once!" cried Purity. And he concurred.

They arrived at the gates of Bridewell just as the chimes of St. Paul's were sounding the hour of ten o'clock from up high on Ludgate Hill. Upon admission, they were brought straight to the governor's office, where Mr. Reeper was in conversation with a well-attired gentleman; nevertheless, the governor waved them to be seated and intimated that he would not keep them long with his present business. The present business concerned the admission, into the prison, of a pianoforte belonging to the well-attired gentleman, who, against all likelihood, turned out to be serving a sentence in the prison. The business was swiftly transacted. Reeper gave his assent to the pianoforte being brought in. The fortunate convict thanked the governor, bowed civilly to Purity and Mark, and returned to his quarters.

"Sir and Lady Landless," said Reeper, "I fear that you are too late." And he cracked his fingers noisily.

"She has changed her mind!" exclaimed Purity.

"She has done more than that," said the other gloomily. "She has departed to that place where the mind is freed of all such vagaries. *Sic transit gloria mundi*—and all poor sinners."

"She is dead?" cried Purity.

"That she is," said the governor. "Passed away. Gone before."

"But, when? How?"

Reeper's eyes looked shifty; rat-like, they flickered from side to side, as if seeking a means of escape.

"She was found this morning," he said. "Shortly after I had dispatched the note to you, your ladyship —indeed, I sent another messenger after the first, to bring him back, but the fellow lost his quarry in the press of people in Fleet Street—I was apprised that her body, dead and cold, had been discovered at the

73

foot of the main gallery, from which she had fallen from just outside her cell in the upper tier."

"But how could it have happened?" asked Purity. "She was locked in her cell."

Reeper looked, if anything, even more confused and uneasy.

"That is so, your ladyship," he said. "But, unhappily, on this occasion, the turnkey must have forgotten. Wilkes, taking advantage of the fact, and no doubt weighed down by the awful realization of her guilt—for even the most hardened sinner may sometimes be brought to repentance—cast herself over the gallery rail and destroyed her life."

Purity stared at him.

Mark said, "It is your belief, then, that she killed herself?"

"Undoubtedly, Sir Mark," responded Reeper. "In the absence of witnesses, we can assume nothing else."

"What about the child who was sharing her cell when I saw her?" asked Purity, remembering. "Was she not a witness?"

"The child in question—a creature of the most utter depravity as you would scarcely credit in one so young in years, if not in experience—was transferred to the Fleet prison yesterday morning in the hope that the more rigorous regimen of that other penal establishment will serve to break her spirit."

"And with her departure went the only witness," said Mark slowly.

"Er, quite so, Sir Mark," said Reeper, looking away.

"Then there is no more to be said or done," said Mark, rising. "Come, my dear."

They had reached the door, when Reeper, who had seemed to be wrestling with a half-digested notion in his mind, and cracking his knuckles in agitation, suddenly blurted out, "The woman may have been thrown over by one of the other convicts! I don't deny it. 'Tis possible. But 'tis no fault of mine. I cannot keep track of everything that happens within these walls, though heaven knows I do my best. I do my best."

"I am sure you do, sir," responded Mark coldly. "Good day to you."

On the way out, through the courtyard, they saw two elderly men in convict gear. One of them was digging a hole that was three feet wide and not so long as a man. The other was leaning on his shovel, watching the two passersby with lackluster eyes. Close to the new mount of grimy city earth lay a still form wrapped in a piece of sacking. It looked very small.

In the days—and sleepless nights—that followed, Purity painfully taught herself the first lessons in the long and heart-rending process of coming to accept that she might never see Chastity again, that the girl had not been kidnapped for reasons of ransom, but for other, more sinister, motives.

There was, in London, a thriving trade in child prostitution, whereby young girls of about Chastity's age—even as young as nine or ten—were enticed into brothels and houses of assignation with which the great city teemed. They were systematically debauched by the evil panderers who ran the foul trade, then hired out to old lechers for whom the deflowering of a young and untried virgin was a rich and relatively rare experience. Chastity, with the body of a developed woman, could well have caught the eye of some rich libertine who, all honor and decency forgotten in the pursuit of his lust, might have hired a gang of ruffians to carry her off. She could still be suffering this man's hateful attentions. She might (and it had to be faced, though Purity's mind screamed at the thought) have been a disappointment to her ravisher, and he, tiring of her, could have paid the same ruffians to dispose of her by the only way that could ensure his own safety:

her young body might, even at that moment, be floating, eyeless, in the cold burden of the Thames.

Such hard thoughts as these made hideous her days and nights. Into her mind, also, and for no good reason that she was aware of, came another disturbing image: the face of Captain Guy D'Eath, the notorious rake and duelist who had set his cap upon her at the ball—and worse, had even gone to the trouble of traveling all the way to Normandy to learn more about her. She had not spoken of him to Mark. There were a thousand good reasons for not doing so—not the least of them being that D'Eath was a duelist of experience, which Mark was not!

D'Eath's face came back to her time and time again —but her anguished thoughts always returned to Chastity.

It was two weeks, and more, after Chastity's disappearance—and the first signs of the new spring were beginning to show, with aconites sprinkling the lawn at the back of 17A Half Moon Street—that Purity received the letter that was to change her whole life and set her feet upon a course from which, had she known it, she should have flinched in horror. It arrived by the early morning's postal service: an innocuous-looking fold of paper lying upon her breakfast tray, neatly addressed to Lady Landless at 17A Half Moon Street, Mayfair, written in a prim, feminine-looking hand.

The contents was shocking:

If you want your daughter back, come at six this evening to the Hare and Hounds tavern in St. Giles's Court. Come alone. Do not show this letter to anyone, nor speak of it—even to your husband. To do so would be to forfeit your daughter's life. Bring the letter with you.

Purity leaped from her bed, sending the breakfast tray clattering to the floor. In great anguish of mind, she strode back and forth across the room, reading and rereading the strange missive. Was it genuine—or a cruel hoax? Notwithstanding the dire warning contained within it, her first inclination was to take it immediately to Mark and show it to him. Second thoughts counseled prudence. If it was genuine, and Mark, in his usual direct and forthright manner, put it in the hands of the law, or, what was even more likely, took the law in his own hands and raised a band of his old army friends and made a raid upon the Hare and Hounds tavern, then Chastity would be put in the most terrible peril of losing her life.

All things considered, she decided, it was best to take the letter at its face value—obey its instructions to the last detail and hope for the best. If genuine, it was likely that the sender (a woman—and that was strange!) wished to state the terms for Chastity's release. Well, she had already decided her position on that—to set Chastity free, she and Mark would give anything.

One detail remained to disturb her. She had never heard of the Hare and Hounds, nor of St. Giles's Court, but the name of the court suggested that it might be in the area of the great St. Giles rookery, the most infamous part of London's sprawling criminal slums, known to notoriety as the "Holy Land." For a respectable woman to venture within that rookery, alone and unescorted, was to deliver herself up to unimaginable perils: robbery, insult, molestation, certainly; rape, perhaps, or even murder.

But, she told her reflection in the looking glass, there was no other course—if Chastity were to be saved. She must risk all.

The day dragged past. By good luck, it chanced that Mark had made prior arrangements to pay a quick visit to Clumber that afternoon, traveling post-haste, staying overnight and returning to London the following morning. She was free to come and go as she pleased without inviting his comment.

It came to her quite suddenly: Had the mysterious sender of the letter known in advance of Mark's absence that this would leave her free to keep the strange tryst?

In matters of dress, Purity could be reckoned as something of an eccentric, and in this she followed the style of great beauties the world over, and of all times. Possessed of a stunning figure that required no artificial aids, she scorned to wear tight lacing in the then current mode, in which the bosom was thrust upward and outward in a most unnatural manner and the waist was compressed to dimensions never seen in the classical nude statuary of antiquity. Nor, while she greatly admired the current fashion of wide skirts and extravagantly large "leg o' mutton" sleeves, did she go in for modish over-embellishment in the way of frills and furbelows, of highly patterned and figured materials, or oversized bonnets with monstrous sprays of ostrich feather and artificial flowers. Instead, she contrived a subtle compromise between the fashion of the day and the fashion that she had made her own throughout her career as a society beauty: the simple Grecian look.

For her expedition that evening, she chose a day dress of plain dark green velvet, lightly trimmed with black silk cord at the edges, with a bodice that was prudently cut so as to show no trace of the cleft between her breasts, since, if she was about to step into a den of depravity, there was no profit in exciting attention. To this she added an inconspicuous bonnet and a black Merino cloak that satisfactorily masked her figure. This done, she let herself out of the front door of number 17A and walked swiftly through the gathering darkness to find a hackney carriage for hire in Piccadilly.

She secured one easily enough; not so easily did she persuade the driver to take her to her required destination. She had been corrected in her assumption about St. Giles's Court.

"What do a decent lady want in a place like that, I arsk meself?" demanded the driver. "Missus, I tell you the parish constables, even the Bow Street Runners 'emselves, never set foot inside St. Giles's rookery. Are you sure you have the right address?"

"The Hare and Hounds tavern in St. Giles's Court," reiterated Purity, feeling her courage slipping away from her. "I beg you to take me there."

"That I will not do," said the driver. "But I will do nearly as good, Missus. I will take you to the edge o' the rookery and point the way to where you must go. After that, may the good Lord defend you—for you will find no honest man in those parts who will."

Purity had no course but to agree. The drive to the edge of the rookery was brevity itself, for one of the insidious factors that made the St. Giles "Holy Land" of such value to the London underworld was its proximity to the prosperous—and highly vulnerable—residential quarters of the city. A thief could strike, then bolt for cover in one or another of a hundred alleyways around Leicester Square, the Haymarket, or Regent Street, to be lost instantly in the tortuous byways and turnings of the teeming warren. Once within the rookery, the hand of the law was impotent to ferret him out.

" 'Ere we be, Missus," said the driver at length, drawing rein and calling down to her. He pointed with his whip to a narrow alley between two tall and tumbledown buildings with dark and eyeless windows. "Go you straight down there and you'll presently come to St. Giles's Court. That'll be sixpence."

Purity paid him. The sound of the carriage wheels receding into the distance down Charing Cross Road left her with a sense of desolation and aloneness—and a terrifying vulnerability.

All was in darkness. No sign of life. But, somewhere in the vastness of the rookery, she could hear voices raised in raucous, and surely drunken, song. Nerving herself, she walked swiftly across the rutted road and into the dark alley.

She progressed into the teeming slum, and she was immediately aware of the life all around her—abundant life. From every dark window, mostly unglazed and patched with rags or straw, there came the murmurings and rumblings of many voices, of people packed to suffocation in many tiny rooms. The dense masses of habitations through which she was passing were of such an age that they seemed to lean outward on both sides and shut out the night sky above her head. And down the center of the alley through which she passed ran a reeking, open drain.

Purity came at length to the end of the dark gulley and out into a square surrounded by high-walled buildings. The unpaved ground was littered with piles of filth and discarded rubbish, and the inevitable drain ran down the center. In a few windows, the faint lights of vestigial candles burned dimly. She had still not seen a living soul move. At one corner of the square, a battered tin-plate sign pointed down a turning: ST. GILE'S COURT.

Scarcely able to believe that she had come so far without mishap, Purity crossed the square and entered the court.

And then—*they* came. . . .

They came in a torrential mass of yelling, jostling, suddenly erupting small forms; ragged coattails flying, shaven heads white in the darkness, bare feet pounding the filfth. They were a dozen or so urchin lads who must have been witnesses to her approach, who must have lain in wait for her, and who were now upon her.

They screamed all together. It was impossible to hear the burden of their remarks, save that they were all directed toward her. Fingers plucked at her cloak, ripping it from her shoulders. They snatched at her bonnet, and her hair went flying with it. Her silver-gold tresses were falling around her shoulders, unpinned and free. She fought to retain her reticule. She screamed when she felt the small hands seeking to climb inside her skirt, to knead the curves of her breasts.

They were gone as quickly as they came. A flurry and a patter of feet, and they were off into the darkness again. Purity, reeling against a wall, hatless, cloakless, but still with her reticule in her hand, marveled at her providential release.

Ahead of her, at the far end of what proved to be a cul-de-sac, was a swinging lantern set against a moldering wall. It illuminated a hanging sign: HARE AND HOUNDS.

Faint chinks of light showed through the shuttered windows, and she caught the murmur of many voices.

Smoothing down her tousled hair as best as she was able to, and composing her mind as well as she was able to (but with less success), she made her way toward the tavern, pausing at the door and endeavoring to peer between the chink in a blind that was drawn across its upper, glass panel. All she could discern was a smoke-filled atmosphere and a haze of faces. As her hand came up to open the latch, a chorus of huzzahs exploded deafeningly within, and as she entered, the occupants of the room were all on their feet, clouting tabletops with their beer mugs, smiting each other across the shoulders, embracing, and exhibiting every manifestation of jubilation. It took Purity no more than a swift glance to see the reason for the hubbub.

In the center of the taproom was a large round table, somewhat lower than an ordinary table, and set around it were three rows of seats. A red-faced ruffian in a battered tall hat was raising aloft a beruffled cockerel. Another of its kind lay in the center of the table, white featherings bedabbled crimson. Purity had happened upon a cock fight.

"Bless you, my hearty! Bless you, Jago!" cried the man with the winning bird, kissing it upon the beak. "There'll be a mash o' wheat flour, eggs, and butter for you this night, me lovely! Aye, and a cup of hot Sherry wine. Pay up, pay up, you gamesters all! And let them as wagered on Jago buy me a tankard of ale apiece."

"That we will, that we will," said one of his fellows, picking up a pile of coins from the table. Another, by his scowling mien the owner of the defeated bird, snatched up the scrap of bloody feathers and limp, spurred legs and tossed them across the room with a curse.

"Next contest!" came the cry. "Hackney Jack will set his cock Xerxes against any comer!"

Another bloody contest was about to begin. That cock-fighting being held at the Hare and Hounds was indicative of the lawless area in which the tavern was situated, for the parish authorities, regarding with grave concern the violence that the sport aroused among its devotees, had warned that all landlords who permitted cock-fighting on their premises should have their licenses withdrawn and all who were caught rioting at the table should be whipped at the common whipping post. Purity abhorred the cruel sport; but it was a lucky chance for her that it was taking place in the tavern that night, for her entry into the taproom past all went unnoticed, and she was able to hide herself away in a dark corner, at a table shared only by another woman, an aged crone far gone in drink, who lay with her verminous head pillowed in her arms and an upturned glass of gin making a puddle around her wrinkled cheek.

Purity peered cautiously around her, seeking for a sign of he—or, more likely, she—who would make contact with her.

The room was crowded, and mainly centered around the cock-fighting table. The clientele was mostly male, and of the roughest kind, but there were a few women—loose-looking baggages with painted faces and breasts shamelessly half-exposed to eye and hand, some of them seated upon the knees of their paramours for the night. A couple of wenches were serving drinks. One of them could not have been any older than Chastity, and Purity's heart melted at the sight of her unformed, yet cynical and worldly wise, little face.

"What's it to be, then?" demanded the girl. "Ale? Gin?"

"I would like a glass of brandy, please," said Purity.

"Brandy, is it?" responded the other, tossing her head and eyeing Purity down the side of her pert nose. "Lawks a-mussy, ain't *we* a fine one?"

"If you please," said Purity meekly, wishing that she had had the prudence to demand something more in keeping with the style of the establishment. The girl had a very loud voice. She was standing there before her with a hand upon her shapely hip, and she was an obvious seeker after public exhibition. Fortunately, she had no audience save Purity; everyone else was attending to the cock fight.

"Right you are, your 'ighness," retorted the girl, and she went off with her nose in the air.

After an initial encounter between the two cockerels on the table, their owners had taken them up in hand again and were about to recommence the bout. This they did by holding them, beak to beak, till the creatures were in a frenzy of bloodlust. They were then released, and rose in the air together, squawking and fluttering, lashing at each other's breasts and abdomens with their steep-tipped spurs. Blood was already flowing from one of them.

Purity averted her eyes from the scene on the tabletop, and she noticed a man who was seated in the front row of the spectators, immediately opposite her.

He was of a different style from his companions, being dressed in a decent caped riding coat, with a clean white neck cloth. He was a man in his mid-thirties, not bad to look upon, save that he had a broken nose. His hair was of dark chestnut color and curly around the ears. He watched the battling birds impassively, his fingertips drumming a rhythm on the edge of the table. And, to Purity's alarm, he looked up, almost as if he had sensed her gaze was upon him. Their eyes met across the smoke-filled room. She looked away hastily, feeling the color mounting in her cheeks.

"The challenger's down! Xerxes wins!"

The blood-crazed zealots were on their feet again, and the din was tremendous. In the middle of it all, the young serving wench returned with Purity's brandy, which she laid upon the table before her, flouncing her skirts as she did so.

"That'll be fivepence. Cash on the nob to you." She had to shout above the noise.

Purity fumbled in her reticule, extracted her handkerchief, and searched for her purse. But there seemed not be anything else within the bag. Suddenly apprehensive, she upturned the reticule, and in doing so she tipped over the rummer of brandy.

"Lawks! Now look what you've a-gorn an' done," said the girl contemptuously. "I 'spec you'll be wantin' another. Well, you can first pay me for that one, Missus. Fivepence."

"I . . . I haven't any money!" cried Purity.

"Wha-a-a-t?"

"My money . . . it's been taken. Some boys outside . . ."

In that moment, the pandemonium around the cockfighting table ceased, as the gamesters addressed themselves to the serious task of picking up their winnings or ruminating upon their losses. In the silence that followed, the girl's mean, vindictive voice rang out clearly for all to hear.

"Sam! This 'ere doxy ordered brandy, knocked it over, an' now she says she ain't goin' to pay for it!"

All eyes turned to regard the girl—and Purity.

"Says she ain't goin' to pay 'er score, does she? We'll see abaht that!" The speaker rose from his seat in the front row near the table. He was a big, sagging-gutted fellow in his middle years, with a brutish, coarse-featured face and eyes like an angry bear—small and red-rimmed. He spat out a cud of chewing tobacco and, thrusting a pile of coins into his breeches pocket, lurched across the room in Purity's direction. A large group of his fellow gamesters—men and women—surged after him to watch the fun.

"Are you the proprietor, sir?" asked Purity, striving to keep the alarm from showing in her voice. "If so, I assure you that you will be paid, but, unfortunately, not tonight. You see, I have been . . ."

"What 'ave we 'ere, then?" The man named Sam regarded Purity archly, a grin forming on his coarse lips. " 'ere's a fancy 'un, and no mistake. And a furriner, by the sound of her lingo. What are you, wench, and where from? Froggie, are you? Spaniol?"

"I . . . I was French-born," faltered Purity, not for the first time regretful of the slight, and extremely attractive, accent that colored her English.

"Frenchie, eh?" said Sam. "Well, I formed square at Waterloo again the Frenchies, and I tell you that all Frenchie fellers should be hanged and the women given to stud. That's what I think o' Frenchies. And now, you'll pay me my score, Frenchie whore, or, by the devil, I'll take it from you in kind." He glared around at his companions. "You know my ways, all o' you. You know the rules o' this house."

"That we do, Sam. That we do," came the reply. "Them as don't pay in coin pays in kind." This won a chorus of agreement, and they gazed upon him in admiration, sycophants all.

"What shall it be then, 'eh?" grinned Sam, eyeing the shrinking Purity sidelong.

"Give her a fair old beltin', Sam!" yelled one of the women, a young strumpet in a thin shift, with hair that was curled and hanging like grapes upon a bough. "Deal with 'er as you once dealt with me when I gave you some lip!"

"That's it, Sam'll!" said another. "Belt the Frenchie bitch!"

Purity backed away.

"No . . . please!" she cried. "I promise you, sir, that you will be paid tomorrow—tenfold!"

"Lay a hold on 'er, a couple o' you," said Sam. And he unbuckled from his expansive waist a thick leather belt.

Purity had an inspiration.

"You can be paid tonight, sir!" she cried. "I am to meet someone here—someone who will most certainly lend me the few pence needed to pay my score."

"She be meetin' someone 'ere tonight!" mocked one

of her tormentors. "I wonder who? Lord and Lady Muck, I shouldn't wonder."

"Or the Archbishop o' Canterbury," said another. "The old feller comes here often."

"Enough o' the shilly-shally. Get 'er across the table and let's see the beltin'!"

"Please!" cried Purity, looking around her in desperation. "If any one of you is the person who was to meet me here tonight, I beg you to declare yourself. . . . Ah!" she cried out as two grinning brutes laid hands on her, one on each of her arms.

They dragged her, struggling and screaming as she was, across the room to the cock-fighting table. In doing so, one of them made a snatch at the bodice of her green velvet gown, so that the hooks and eyes were pulled apart, and her bare breasts were made available to the intrusion of a licentious hand. One of them was still kneading her breasts when, with her face downward upon the table, someone else dragged up her skirts and petticoats high above her waist, presenting her thighs and buttocks to the general gaze. Apart from stockings of black silk gartered with ribbons, she was nude from the waist down.

"Hold 'er fast, lads," said Sam, flexing the belt between his huge hands. "I've a mind to use the buckle end, but 'twould be a cryin' shame to mark that fine rump, 'specially since I've the notion to give 'er the handy-dandy when she's had 'er beatin'."

"Zounds! And I'll follow after you!" cried one of the brutes who held Purity. "I've a great feelin' on me to mount this Frenchie!"

"You did mount _me_ only an hour ago!" cried one of the strumpets. "Hark to the fellow's boastful talk!"

In the general laughter that followed, the cruel belt whistled down and cut Purity's bare buttocks with a stinging welt that made her scream out anew. Another, then another, quickly followed, with the tavern keeper warming to his work, and the cheers of his cronies and clients urged him on. At somewhere about the tenth cut, Purity must have fainted away with the agony.

"She's had enough, Sam'l!" called one of her torturers. "Let it be quits, and on with the handy-dandy."

Purity opened her eyes. She was still being held across the table by the wrists, but the agonizing assault of the belt had ceased; only a constant, throbbing pain remained. She half-turned her head to see what her tormentor was doing, and she was horrified to observe that, having unfastened the flap of his breeches, the huge tavern keeper was advancing toward her unprotected nakedness. The onlookers were cheering him on, the shameless women louder than the rest, clapping their hands and commenting admiringly.

"Have done! Leave 'er be!"

A deep and commanding voice silenced the raucous din. Purity looked to the direction from which it came, and she saw the man with the broken nose standing at the far side of the table. His hands were in the pockets of his riding coat, his whole demeanor relaxed and nonchalant. But there was power of command in every line of him.

"Mind your business, Jack Moonlight!" growled the tavern keeper. "I'll 'ave no man cheat me of the handy-dandy when I'm in my pride."

"I have made it my business," replied the other. "And I say leave her be. The woman has paid her score. She'll not be raped in the bargain."

"And how shall you stop me?" sneered Sam.

"With this!" said the other. "Take one step nearer to her and I will blow your head from your shoulders!"

Purity found herself almost looking into the twin muzzles of an over-and-under pistol that the man with the broken nose had taken from his pocket. There was a click as he thumbed back the hammer to full cock.

The two ruffians holding Purity hastily released their grips. She squirmed aside, found her footing, pulled down her skirts, then drew the edges of her bodice across her bared bosom. And her eyes never left the broke-nosed man who had been addressed as Jack Moonlight.

"Now, now, Jack!" The tavern keeper's voice was wheedling, ingratiating. "You've taken women aplenty in your time. Would you deny an old friend 'is pleasures?"

"I have not recently taken a woman against her will," said Jack Moonlight, "though frequently against her inclinations. And no man will ever rape a woman in my presence if I have the means to prevent it. And you are not my friend. Now, button your breeches and forget it." Coolly, he eased back the hammer of the pistol and placed it back in his pocket. "Wench, bring me two glasses of your best brandy, and be quick about it!" he ordered.

The serving wench (the same hussy who had caused the trouble for Purity) hastened to do his will. Moonlight looked at Purity and pointed to the empty seat beside his own. "Sit you down," he commanded. And, with a wry grin, he added, "If the pain in your leathered backside will allow you the luxury."

Purity obeyed—gingerly.

"Thank you for what you did," she whispered with a fearful sidelong glance at her recent tormentors. She need not have worried; the incident was past and seemingly forgotten. The tavern keeper was still scowling, but everyone else had gone back to discussing the next pair of cockerels to be set against each other.

"Why are you here?" asked Moonlight. "This is not your sort of place."

"Nor yours, I would have thought," countered Purity.

That seemed to amuse him. "Why so?" he asked.

"It would seem that you are . . . a gentleman," said Purity.

"That I am," said Moonlight. "To be more precise, a gentleman of the road."

"A highwayman!" Purity reacted in wide-eyed alarm to hear the familiar euphemism for the small band of mounted thieves who were the terror of the main roads leading into the capital, and whom the officers of the law, even the efficient Bow Street Runners, seemed powerless to stamp out—though many of their number ended their days upon the Newgate scaffold, cheered to the echo by the London mob whose popular heroes they were.

The serving wench brought two brimming rummers of brandy and Moonlight paid her. He handed one to Purity.

"Drink it down," he said. " 'Twill steady you after your ordeal. And I wager 'tis the first time you have taken brandy with the likes of Jack Moonlight. Why are you here?"

"It was true, what I said," replied Purity. "I am here, by appointment, to meet someone. Would it be you, perhaps?"

He shook his head. "No. Would that it were." His eyes fell—quite candidly and without any shiftiness—to the smooth, peach-tinted skin of her imperfectly covered bosom. "I would greatly wish to be the other half of your mysterious assignation."

Before Purity could reply, two men came forward to the table with cockerels fluttering in their hands, and there was a general move to be seated again. Realizing that she was in the front row of chairs, and not wishing to be close witness to the next bloody contest, she excused herself from Jack Moonlight and left him. The highwayman seemed scarcely to notice her departure; his gaze was fixed intently upon one of the squawking cockerels, and his hands were counting guineas upon the table. . . .

She returned to the seat from which she had been so rudely taken. The drunken crone had gone. In her place sat a sly-looking individual dressed in seedy black, with a slouch cap pulled low over his brow. He rose at Purity's approach.

"Lady Landless," he whispered in a hoarse undertone, close by her ear, "you will come alonger me."

Chapter Four

He took her out of a door at the back of the establishment, and the bloodlusting cries of the gamesters
followed them across a high-walled courtyard and into
a tunnel that was pierced through the building opposite. Emerging from this, her guide led her down a
flight of steps and through an archway. They then
crossed a low bridge that spanned a stinking ditch,
where the debris of the rookery floated slowly beneath. Immediately in front was a many-storied house,
isolated from its near companions, with the two end
walls propped up by massive wooden piles. A solitary
light burned in an upper window.

The man in black knocked softly upon the door,
and they had not long to wait before it creaked open.

"Follow me," said her guide.

Immediately in front of her was a steep flight of
stairs that rose to a landing where there hung a gut-
tering lantern. By its light, she picked her way upward, at the heels of the black-garbed man. Reaching
the landing, he took down the lantern and proceeded
on up the next flight of stairs, and on up the next, till

93

they came to. the termination of the staircase, which was announced by a door immediately in front of them.

There followed another knock, and her guide opened the door. He stood aside and beckoned her to enter.

"Madame awaits you, my lady," he croaked hoarsely, and he was racked by a spasm of coughing that marked his progress all the way back down the stairs.

Purity found herself in a darkened room that was faintly illuminated by a shaded candle set upon a table at the far end. By its light, she discerned the figure of a woman seated facing her. A hand reached out, unmasking the candle and throwing its beam upon Purity.

"Yes, you are indeed Purity Landless," came the woman's voice, low, husky, sensuous. "Come over here and sit down. We have much to discuss, you and I."

But a stubborn resolve was forming in Purity's mind. After the degradation she had suffered at the hands of the brutes in the tavern, after the long days and nights of anguish she had gone through since Chastity's disappearance, her native grit and fortitude had reasserted themselves. She stood her ground.

"Damn you, who *are* you?" she cried. "And what have you done with my daughter?"

"Another outburst like that will cause your precious daughter two days of starvation," came the harsh answer. "Do not waste your time by venting your hatred upon me, Lady Landless. You are here to listen and to obey. Be seated—and, firstly, listen."

The threat, and the implacable tone in which it had been uttered, rudely reminded Purity of the peril in which Chastity stood, and of her own impotence. The woman was right: she had no course but to submit to whatever demands were made upon her. It was useless —and dangerous—to show anger.

She crossed the room and sat down. At closer quarters, she saw that the other woman was of about her own age, and well formed, with a pile of bronze-colored hair and a magnolia complexion. One thing, only, marred the perfection of that cold and lovely countenance: she wore a black velvet eye shade over her right eye. The other stared out at Purity in deep brown clarity from under long lashes and an imperious eyebrow. She was dressed in black, with a gold medallion worn on a chain across her fine, high bosom.

"My name," said the other, "is of no importance to you, or to the matter between us. Call me, if you will, Madeleine. It is not my real name. I will address you as Purity. It is important, in view of our future relationship, that we should have a fair degree of . . . intimacy. Did you, by the way, suffer any molestation in the tavern?"

"I was nearly raped," replied Purity coldly.

The fine eyebrow rose archly. "Were you, now?" said Madeleine. "I had not thought you would attract such dire attentions in so short a time. You are to be congratulated. My apologies for making the tavern the place of assignation, but it would have been quite impossible for you to have found this house within the rookery." She paused. "Now, to business. First, you will give me the note I sent you. You have it, of course?"

The note in question had survived, together with her handkerchief, the rifling of Purity's reticule. She took it out and passed it to Madeleine, who, after treating it to a brief glance, deliberately held it over the candle flame before her, then watched while it was entirely consumed, then dropped the ashes into the base of the candle holder.

"What passes between us shall be a secret," she said. "And I refer particularly to your husband."

"Why is that?" asked Purity.

But the other was not to be drawn out. She smiled a small, private smile, then resumed. "You and you alone will negotiate for the return of your daughter," she said. "I do not doubt that there are questions you would like to put to me. You have already demanded to know what I have done with the girl. I will tell you. She is alive and well. Will I tell you where she is? The answer is no. How can you win her freedom? Quite simply, you must obey my orders—and you must obey them to the letter and without question."

Purity experienced a chill of foreboding.

"What orders are these?" she asked.

"First, you must bind yourself to the group of personages of whom I am merely another member," said Madeleine. "Together, we form an exclusive and highly secret society. In order to serve us—which is what you are required to do as part of the conditions for securing your daughter's release—you must be inducted into that society. The ceremony will take place tonight—immediately."

"What form does this . . . ceremony take?" asked Purity.

"The form of dedication," replied Madeleine. "You will be required to submit yourself to our rules, of which the cardinal rule is obedience to the society. You will note how I constantly return to the subject of obedience. Keep it in the forefront of your mind, Purity. Disobey—and you will never see your daughter again. Do you understand?"

Purity had flinched to hear her name on the woman's lips.

"Yes," she whispered.

"Very well."

Madeleine rose and crossed the room to where there

96

stood a cupboard in fine inlaid mahogany. Purity, who had an eye for quality furnishings, recognized it as the handiwork of the great cabinetmaker Thomas Chippendale, and this prompted her to glance around at the other appointments of the chamber: finely wrought chairs and tables; a Venetian scene by Canaletto; exquisite silk Oriental rugs. The disparity between the richness and elegance within the gaunt old house and the seamy life without was a paradox that struck her most forcibly.

Meanwhile, the woman had taken from the cupboard a black silk robe, which she held out to Purity so that the latter was able to see that the garment was of the academic, or monkish, sort, with a hood of scarlet and gold.

"You will wear this at your induction ceremony, Purity," said Madeleine. "I will leave you while you put it on, for I, too, have to prepare myself." She laid the garment over a chair back and walked to the door, her black skirts making a frou-frou. There, she paused. "Before you robe yourself, you will strip naked—completely naked."

An enigmatic smile . . . and she was gone.

Madeleine was identically robed (and was she also naked underneath? thought Purity) in the flowing black with the gold and scarlet hood, which in her case was drawn over her hair of dull flame. Candle in one hand, she had taken Purity's hand in the other and was leading her down the stairs to a door on the floor below that silently opened at their approach. It was dark in the chamber beyond, and Purity caught the sweetly cloying odor of incense. Madeleine's candle dimly sketched the interior: a bare room that had a kind of altar at one end, and a pentacle—the five-pointed star associated with the dark arts—painted in the center of the floor. From some distance, and muffled, as if by heavy curtainings, came the eerie music of a solitary flute.

Laying the candle in the center of the pentacle, Madeleine motioned to Purity to stand with her inside the five-pointed figure. This done, she gently clapped her hands.

A moment later, Purity gave a sharp intake of breath upon seeing a strange trio emerge from the shadows behind the altar. The central figure commanded her first, and horrified, attention, since it wore upon its head and face what could only have been a mask: the mask of a goat, with curved horns. Accompanying the goat-headed creature, in the roles of acolytes, each holding an end of the black cloak that entirely covered its body, were a youth and a girl of exceeding comeliness of face and body—the latter being clearly observed because they were both entirely nude.

Without preamble, the horned figure proceeded to recite the Lord's Prayer backward, raising on high his arms as he did so, an action that caused the edges of the cloak to fall apart and revealed his male nakedness beneath.

The profaned prayer now finished, he slipped into a gabbled mumbo-jumbo that was meaningless to Purity, so that her attention wandered to the beautiful nude figures flanking him. Both young creatures' eyes had the somnambulant, lackluster stares of the heavily drugged. Both stood perfectly still, like pale statues the only sign of life being the gentle rise and fall of their breasts.

A touch of Madeleine's hand upon her arm prompted Purity to give attention to what the goat-headed creature was saying. With something of a shock, she realized that he was addressing her.

"Are you ready to take the binding oath?" he repeated. Then he added in a harsh tone, "If there is any doubt in your mind, I command you to go from this unholy place and speak to no one of what you have witnessed."

There was a pause, and Purity replied, in a voice that sounded quite unlike her own, "I . . . am ready."

"Approach me!" commanded goat-head.

When Purity hesitated, Madeleine's hand tensed on her arm.

"Remember!" whispered the woman in her ear.

Purity left the pentacle. Three paces brought her face to face with the hideously masked figure. She could see the eyes framed in the hairy covering of the face-piece. She shrank from him, from his slender white hands as they came toward her, and, unfastening her robe, she drew it slowly from her shoulders till it fell in a pool around her bare feet, rendering her nude to his gaze.

"Before I administer the oath," said the voice behind the mask, "I will bestow upon you the four unholy kisses."

A shudder ran through Purity's frame, and she closed her eyes. In so doing, she was spared the sight of that hideous mouth approaching hers. She suffered only a spasm of horror at the touch of alien lips upon her lips. But a morbid curiosity prompted her to watch the horned head bow over each of her breasts, first the left, then the right, and deposit a kiss upon each proud, coral-tinted peak. A sob of anguish burst from her lips to see him kneel before her and bow the great goat-head upon her shrinking loins in the fourth, and final, embrace.

Somehow, she restrained herself from screaming, Somehow, she was able to keep the image of Chastity's sweet face before her—and that of Mark, who loved her dearly, and who would have killed to prevent her from experiencing the monstrous indignity to which she had been subjected.

Goat-head was standing again. His acolytes had taken hold of each edge of the long black cloak, drawing the garment aside to expose the length of his nude body.

In an instant of great dread, she knew what was to follow.

The words of protest were framed in silence upon her lips, but they never spoken.

"You will now bestow the four unholy kisses, in return, upon me," came the stern voice from behind the mask.

Shame . . .

She would never be clean again, surely. The lips that had tasted the salt taste of that man's body could never again accept the kisses of the man she loved, never touch the lips of her adored children, never again truly be part of herself, but an area of her own body that was forever defiled.

The hideous mockery of a religious ceremony over, Madeleine had escorted her back upstairs to the room where she had left her clothing. Madeleine was watching her at that moment, seated, chin in hand, gazing at her—appraisingly? with mockery? what did it matter?—while she dressed herself, drawing the garments over her defiled flesh.

"You will not forget the words of your oath, Purity," said the woman.

"As if I ever could!" replied Purity bitterly. "As if, for my sins, I could ever be so blessed as to have them wiped from my mind."

The oath-taking had immediately followed the exchange of kisses—after she had repeated the ritual upon his masked lips and his body. The vow, wrung from her in agony of mind, tearful, entreating, had been specific in content, admitting of no ambiguity:

100

Let any member of the society, be they male or female, approach me and make themselves known to me, and I shall respond without hesitation to their lightest demands upon my body, forsaking my marriage vows and all other allegiances. This I swear.

In return for Chastity's life, she had delivered herself up to be a whore!

One vital thing remained to be settled.

"When will you return my daughter?" she demanded of Madeleine. "When?"

"Later, when you have proved the sincerity of your intentions," came the reply. "When you have shown to us that it was not a hollow oath that you took tonight."

Purity thought for a moment, pausing in the act of making what shift she could of fastening her bodice, which had been torn during her encounter at the tavern, and she said, "And after Chastity has been freed, shall I be released from the oath?"

"When your daughter is freed, the oath will continue to be binding," said Madeleine, "for such an oath, given under such circumstances, would put your very soul in jeopardy in the breaking. However, when that time comes, it is not likely that you will be required, any longer, to fulfill the terms of the oath."

"You mean . . . I shall be released from my whoredom!" retorted Purity bitterly.

"Put it that way if you will," said Madeleine without anger. "When the time comes for Chastity to be freed—and I promise you that it will not be long—the society will have no further use for your services. And now I shall answer no more questions. The reasons for your being inducted into the society, the reasons for our taking Chastity—these things may be revealed to you one day, but not now. It remains only for me to give you . . . this."

She took from around her neck the chain with its suspended medallion, which was circular in shape, somewhat the size of a golden guinea, and quite plain. However, when Madeleine turned the chain between her fingers and presented the reverse of the medallion, Purity was shocked to see a head engraved upon it: the head of a goat, with curved horns, and eyes that blazed out with the brilliance of two tiny emeralds of which they were composed.

"It is a representation of . . . *him!*" cried Purity with distaste.

"Take it," commanded Madeleine. "Wear it always, with the goat's head showing, so that all may see it plainly. Any member of our society who comes up to you and shows you a companion to this medallion will have established himself—or herself—as coming within the compass of your oath."

Obediently, Purity took the chain and placed it around her neck. She shuddered when the cold disc of precious metal touched the bare skin of her bosom.

It was her badge of whoredom.

That same guide who had brought her from the Hare and Hounds to the tall, dark house took her from there, by a tortuous and circuitous route which for the life of her she never could have retraced, to the edge of the rookery. He waited with her till she had hailed a passing hackney carriage and then returned from whence he had come.

It was past midnight when Purity arrived back at 17A Half Moon Street. Despite the late hour, she summoned her maid to prepare a bath for her. Other servants were aroused—sleepy-eyed and grumbling among themselves at the vagaries and whims of those who did not have to rise and begin work again at four o'clock in the morning—and carried jugs of hot water from the copper boiler that was kept forever filled and simmering in the basement kitchen to her ladyship's dressing room, where there stood a handsome bathtub of beaten pewter, in which her ladyship presently luxuriated in total misery of mind and weariness of body.

She had to clean herself as best as she was able to. Her buttocks, still striped and throbbing from the whipping she had received, must be symbolically purified with clean water. Her breasts and nipples, too, must be thoroughly soaped and sponged; likewise, her loins.

Her lips—the lips that had performed the vile honors upon *him*—were beyond all cleansing. . . .

The watchman passed below her window, calling out the hour of one o'clock when she finally dragged herself wearily to her lonely bed and tried, with no success, to compose herself for slumber. This she attempted, first, with thoughts of Mark and the children in better days: days when they had hired a boat to take them down the Thames in the summertime, with picnic hampers, bat and ball, laughter and joy unexamined, unquestioned; or of Christmases at Clumber, all under snow, when they harnessed the horses to a fine big sleigh that would carry all four of them and drove across the wide parkland, where antlered deer stalked among the oak trees that had been mature when Sir Francis Drake sailed around the world. Such thoughts brought no ease or sleep; they only served to increase her misery and apprehension.

One comfort, only, she was able to take: the thought that, by her acts that night, by her endurance and her suffering, she had possibly (how could she be entirely sure, considering the quality of the people with whom she had made the compact?) made the first move that would unlock the door to Chastity's imprisonment—wherever, and in whatever circumstances, that might be.

Holding tightly to that thought, and keeping Chastity's young, innocent, and unformed countenance before her, she presently drifted away into sleep—and the demonic nightmares that awaited her there.

Chastity, in her narrow room, rapidly moved from terror and living nightmares to total dependence upon the softly spoken man in black who brought her food and provided her with light. Then she moved toward a feeling that she must in some way win his approval —show him that, though clumsy, stinking, and naked, she nevertheless had the desire to better herself in his eyes.

The candle inside the lantern had all but burned away. She had been trimming it with scrupulous care, burning her anxious fingers in the process, fearful of extinguishing the flame with her clumsiness. He came in just as she was steeling herself against the threatened darkness, when the last sliver of wax would be consumed.

"I have brought you another candle," he said.

She felt her eyes prickle with tears.

"Thank . . . thank you," she whispered tremulously.

"Later on," he said, "not tomorrow, I think, but perhaps the next day, I will bring you something to wear. Would you like that? And would you, perhaps, like to have a bath? That might be arranged. Yes, I don't see any difficulty there."

"A bath! That would be heavenly!" she said.

He looked down at her coldly from his daunting height.

"Why do you cover yourself with your hands?" he demanded. "Is it because you know yourself to be ugly and unpleasant to look upon?"

"Yes . . . that is . . . I . . . " She let her hands fall from her breasts. There was no longer any use in hiding herself—what remained to be hidden of herself—from his all-seeing, all-knowing gaze. He saw through her, outside and in. She had offended him; she could see that from his face. In doing that, she had possibly destroyed the frail bond that had almost taken shape between them. Not for the first time, she was searingly aware that his kindness in providing sustenance —the food of her choice, that she most doted upon, and life-giving light, without which she would surely have gone mad long ago—was entirely dependent upon his whims. Let him be affronted by her stupid and inadequate behavior and he would be stern and unbending toward her. He had promised her the unimaginable delights of a bath, of clothing to cover her ugly nakedness; by another whim, he could well deny her food and life-giving light.

She must hasten to retrieve what she had lost in his eyes. . . .

"Get up," he ordered. "Get to your feet and stand over there by the wall." He said it very quietly, but in tones that brooked of no disobedience. Nor did she disobey, but hastened to do his bidding. She stood with her back to the cold stone wall.

"That filthy rag you are wearing around your waist," he said, "take it off—it offends me."

In frantic haste, her trembling fingers fought with the knot that secured her makeshift loincloth. It seemed to her the most natural thing in the world, and entirely in accord with her ineptness, that the thing would not come undone. In the event, she was reduced to ripping the material. It fell to the floor, rendering herself to his disapproving gaze, before which she dropped her eyes in shame and confusion.

"I am not pleased with you," he said presently. And for all the sternness in his voice, there was a hint of sorrow and regret, as when a strict father contemplates punishment of a loved child, but more in sorrow than in anger. "I am not pleased with you. Do you hear me? Answer."

"Yes, you say you are not pleased with me," she whispered.

"Are you not sorry?"

"Yes, I am very sorry."

He shifted his stance. Glancing up, she saw that he was preparing to take his leave, his hand upon the door.

"Regret—sincere regret—is halfway to contrition," he said. "Do you know what is meant by 'contrition'?"

"No," she said fearfully.

"Contrition is the state of realization of sin," he said, "so that one is free of all false pride, and truly penitent. It is a state you must cultivate. I will leave you to think about contrition."

The door shut behind him. Chastity was alone.

Alone, she sank with a sob to the hard, cold floor. She was overwhelmed with a sense of guilt for wrongdoings uncounted and uncountable, none to which she could put a name, but none the less real for that. Still sobbing, she put her thumb into her mouth and took some comfort from sucking it.

The new day brought Purity to the need for preparing herself for Mark's return. She rose early from her uneasy bed and dressed herself with great care in the gown that was his great favorite: a pretty thing of striped candy-pink-and-white silk. Her glorious silver-gold hair she had sculpted into the Greek chignon that had always been her own personal style. That done, she went into her drawing room, chose an easy chair that commanded a view down Half Moon Street as far as the corner with Piccadilly, took up her embroidery frame, and waited.

The embroidery was soon forgotten; even the simple, undemanding task of *petit point* had no magic to soothe her mind and make the time fly. Her mind must instantly return to the horrors of the previous night, to the awfulness of the oath that she had solemnly sworn (albeit against her will, but none the less binding, in her own mind, for that), and, most of all, to the hideous goat-head medallion that lay upon her bosom. And the morning dragged past like a funeral cart.

Mark must have left Clumber before the first light, for it was not long after lunch (Purity had not eaten any lunch) that his fast phaeton swung around onto Half Moon Street with him at the reins.

She watched him alight from the box, then saw the groom take the horses in hand. She heard her husband make his entry into the house. She was on her feet to greet him when he came into the drawing room.

"My darling, is there any news?"

She gasped. "Any news—of what?"

"Why, of Chastity, my love. Is there any word, any sign?"

Of course, it would be the first thing he would ask. Strange that, guilt-ridden as she was, the thought had never crossed her mind. And now she must instantly mar their reunion with a lie for which she was entirely unprepared.

He took her by the shoulders. "Well, *is* there any news, Purity?"

"Nothing!" she blurted out. "No—no news at all!"

"Oh, my dear." He folded her in his arms, held her close to him, so that she smelled the familiar male scent of him, clean, wholesome. And her heart melted for a sudden and wayward desire to be taken by him.

Holding her then at arm's length, he said, "You must have been through hell this last day and night. I should never have left you, but the matters requiring my attention at Clumber simply would not wait. Why, my dear, that's rather an odd thing you're wearing around your neck. Wherever did you get it?"

Her hand flew to the medallion—her badge of whoredom—to cover it from his gaze, or at least to turn it over, so that he should not see the vile face upon it. But he gently pried it from her fingers and examined it.

"I . . . I bought it some time ago," she said hastily, "on . . . on Bond Street. I . . . I think it's rather unusual, don't you?"

"Ugly-looking fellow, isn't he?"

"Oh, I think he's rather appealing." Another lie. How many lies so far, Purity?

Mark dismissed the medallion from his mind. Crossing to the console table, he poured himself a glass of brandy and took a sip.

"Mind you, I haven't entirely wasted my time with estate business alone," he said. "On my way back here, I called in upon Charlie Strachan—that's the Marquess Strachan, you know—and he received me very civilly. Briefly, my darling, I wrote to him last week, enlisting his aid. He is brother-in-law to the Home Secretary, you know. I had hoped that, with Strachan's good graces, the Home Office might be persuaded to intensify the search for our darling Chastity. . . ."

"But that would be dangerous!" she cried. The words were out before she could consider their import.

Mark frowned in puzzlement. "Dangerous?" he repeated. "How so, dangerous, my darling?"

"It's simply that . . . well . . . it seems to me, Mark, that we must wait for the kidnappers to approach us and demand certain terms," she said. "With the officers of the law searching everywhere, might Chastity not be put in jeopardy?"

"That agrument might have had some weight a couple of weeks ago," he replied, "or even one week ago —though I myself have never subscribed to it. But,

108

really, my dear, in all this time we have not heard a word from them, have we? Not a word."

"No," she whispered.

"In any event," resumed Mark, "Charlie Strachan has promised every aid. Furthermore, he has invited us to dinner on Thursday to meet several of his influential cronies. What do you think of that?"

Searching in her mind for words—any words—Purity said, "I don't think I have ever met Lord Strachan in society. What manner of man is he?"

Mark laughed shortly. "To be honest, Purity, he's an odd one—as odd as they come. For one thing, he has some very odd political views. Has a bee in his bonnet about the royal family and the succession to the throne, with which he bores anyone whom he can contrive to hem into a corner to listen to him. I am very much afraid, my dear, that we shall have to pay for our dinner in coin of boredom. But it will be well worth it if he agrees to lend his weight and influence for Chastity's sake."

"Yes, indeed," murmured Purity.

"Oh, and he's also got a rather odd reputation with women," said Mark, "though it's nothing that should alarm you, Purity. As you will see, he is brusque and belligerent, particularly when he's filled up with brandy, which is quite often. But the poor man is frightened to death of the ladies. Not that he doesn't fancy the ladies; quite the reverse. My aunt Julia tells how he took a very attractive young person of her acquaintance into his picture gallery—alone—on the pretext of showing her his fine collection of Gainsboroughs and Reynoldses. Once there, after much huffing and puffing, Charlie Strachan managed to pluck up courage to steal a kiss from the lady. Whereupon, he turned around and fled for his life and wasn't seen again all evening." Mark laughed.

How handsome he is when he laughs, she thought.

Most men's faces come apart when they laugh; Mark's takes on a new humanity. Poor Mark, he's had precious little to laugh about in these last awful weeks. And the prospects . . . not to think of the prospects ahead of him. Oh, my poor darling!

She said, "If he invites me to see his pictures and steals a kiss from me, I will try to be kind to him and assure him that one stolen kiss is no cause for him to ruin the rest of his evening. However, if he chances to take any further liberties . . . "

"Further liberties! My darling, you are speaking in jest. I had it from Aunt Julia that he never so much as laid a finger on the lady. One quick peck to the cheek and my lord marquess was off as fast as his feet would carry him."

Purity smiled. "I think I will not succumb to such a frail attempt at seduction, Mark." And then, an imp of perversity brought a question, all unbidden, to her lips. "You trust me, don't you, my dear? You don't believe that I could be seduced by the blandishments of other men?"

He looked at her in mild surprise.

"Of course I trust you, my darling," he said. "Could you ever doubt that? Why, my love, you are well named. You are Purity, indeed."

He embraced her. She caught the reflection of her face in the looking glass over his shoulder. And she saw—or thought she saw—the hard, street harlot's look there.

Charles Edward Montague Frederick, fifth holder of the title of the Most Honorable Marquess Strachan, had never married, and he had devoted his life to the pursuance of political power, which, by reason of his eccentric views (he was a High Tory of the deepest dye, but most English Tories shunned his company), he had never directly achieved. Nevertheless, by reason of his family connections, he had the ear of the most powerful men in the land, and it could truly be said that, while seldom venturing into the House of Lords (where it was quipped that, within five minutes of Charlie Strachan rising to his feet to address his peers, the chamber would be empty of all save those already asleep), he really did possess the political power he had always strived for by his own efforts. In the days before the king had deteriorated, under Lady Conyngham's baleful influence, into a pathetic sot, Strachan had even had the ear of his sovereign. One man of power, alone, never gave an ear to the well-connected marquess and held him in flat contempt—and that man was the Duke of Wellington.

In their town phaeton, the following fine Thursday evening, Purity and Mark drove down to Kingston-upon-Thames, that pleasant rural hamlet on the Surrey bank of the river, to Kingston Manor, the seat of the Strachans.

The manor, built in the reign of Mary Tudor for a Catholic ecclesiastic of the Strachan family who was afterward executed in the reign of Queen Elizabeth, was frankly medieval in looks, in size, and in total lack of comfort. A vast great hall comprised over half of the interior space, and it was in this commodious apartment, where former lords of the manor had dispensed summary justice to their tenants and underlings, that the principal meals were eaten. An oak and elm refectory table occupied the entire length of the hall, with a shorter table at one end, forming the letter T, where the marquess and his guests of honor sat.

When the Landlesses arrived and were announced by a sonorous-voiced butler, the early arrivals were taking champagne in the solar, a small anteroom off the hall. Their host came forward to greet them, and Purity was immediately alerted to the would-be libertine hidden behind the marquess's pouched, pale eyes and ruddy, outdoor complexion. Nor did she miss the covert glance he cast upon her bosom when he bent over her hand to implant a token kiss upon her extended fingertips.

"Vastly pleased to have made your acquaintance at last, Lady Landless," he said in a booming voice, the voice of the bluff, no-nonsense English gentleman that was his stock in trade. "And I'm terribly sorry to have heard of your daughter's disappearance, ma'am. A bad business, ma'am, but have no fear. I will see to it that every effort will be made to search out the scoundrels who have taken her. Depend upon it."

"Thank you, my lord marquess," murmured Purity.

Another sly glance at her physical attributes and then he turned away to continue the conversation—it was more of a monologue—in which he had been engaged at their entry.

"I have never been able to understand why Charlie Strachan always shouts so loudly," murmured Mark into Purity's ear.

"To keep up his courage," she replied, *sotto voce,* "because he is frightened of the intensity of his own secret passions."

"How do you know that?" Mark asked, surprised.

"Any woman would see it in his eyes," she said.

There was an elderly maiden lady, a relation of the marquess's, who effected introductions in a hushed voice. Purity knew some of the people present. All of them were either titled, members of Parliament, high-ranking officers, or big landowners from the shires —all who were powerful and influential in England, and all were listening to Charlie Strachan holding forth, while drinking his excellent champagne.

"The king is approaching seventy," boomed their host, "and if drink and bloodletting don't finish him off soon, the Conyngham woman will. Then we'll have his brother Willie as king, and he won't last us for long, being only a couple or so years younger than George. What follows then?"

"The Kent gel, Princess Victoria, will succeed," said one of the womenfolk. "She is a very nice gel. Not pretty, but what can one expect with her parentage? That abominable mother!"

"The Kent girl! The Kent girl!" The marquess spat out the words, his rheumy eyes sweeping the line of watching faces around him. "My friends, I tell you, all of you, that that is a recipe for disaster! If a woman—a young woman, such as she will be, for she is barely eleven years of age now—were to ascend the throne of England in this century, in this nineteenth century, we are done! Finished! I tell you, my friends, that all the bright promise of Trafalgar, of Waterloo, would be brought to nothing. The colonies would go—the way the Americas went. India would go. Scotland would secede, Ireland also. England would be finished!"

His vehement declaration caused a stir of interest, and some amusement.

"Charles, dear fellow, I think you are putting it rather high," said one of his listeners. "The Lords and Commons will rule the country, as they've done since we kicked out the Stuarts. Little Victoria will do as she's bidden, and she'll scarcely make any difference to the outcome of the nineteenth century. Besides, what alternative do you propose, pray?"

"A man!" snapped Strachan. "Let George be succeeded by another king—*by his own son!*"

"His *son?*"

"The king has no son!"

"What *are* you saying, Charlie?"

"I tell you he has a son," declared Strachan, "by Mrs. Fitzherbert."

Mention of the king's former—and most renowned —mistress, said by some to have been the only woman he ever deeply loved, to whom he had returned time and again, and who still lived, an old lady in her seventies, silenced the hubbub. There were things that could be said about the king and Mrs. Fitzherbert that carried the stink of high treason.

"Careful, now, Charlie," cautioned someone. "Mind what you say, though you are among friends."

"Mrs. Fitzherbert bore a son," said Strachan. "Furthermore, the lad is no bastard, since, as everyone here knows, George married the woman when he was Prince of Wales!"

The declaration, which was an open secret in high society, even though the king had denied it to Parliament throughout all the years, brought another pall of awkward silence upon the gathering.

Presently, one stalwart, less awed by high treason than the rest, said, "Marriage or no marriage, such a succession would fail on two counts. First, Mrs. Fitzherbert's a Catholic, and second, George married her without his father's permission. Both these conditions should have put *him* out of the running, let alone any child of the union."

"An act of Parliament can change all that!" shouted the marquess. "I tell you . . . "

"Take it easy, Charlie!" cautioned someone.

"Give it rest, Charles," said another. "We'll have our little Victoria, whether you like it or no."

The marquess scowled and muttered to himself. As many of his guests commented to each other quietly, it had been a typical Charlie Strachan performance: full of sound and fury, but lacking in any real depth. Still, there was no denying that the fellow had a lot of "pull" in high places. If anyone could put in his oar and prevent a woman from succeeding to the throne, it would be Charlie Strachan—not, mark you, by his own efforts, but simply because he was *related* to so many of the people who *really* ruled the country. And it was odd, was it not, what a scorn he had for women

114

generally—considering his inclinations? But no more of that here. Ha-ha!

Purity and Mark exchanged glances.

They were unwilling eavesdroppers to another bit of conversation.

"Tell me, do we still hang, draw, and quarter for high treason?"

"I suppose so."

"Not for the aristocracy, of course. Only commoners are half-hanged, have their innards drawn out before their very eyes, and are cut up into four pieces and stuck on the gates of London. If Charlie persists in this enterprise, he will, as a peer, simply be hanged with a silken rope."

"There are tremendous advantages in being a peer —as one has always found. Where is that feller with the wine?"

Laughter . . .

Purity glanced again at Mark, this time sidelong. It was to be hoped that, in return for Strachan's assistance in helping to recover their daughter, Mark was not called upon to participate in the marquess's hare-brained conspiracy—if, indeed, his crazy ideas were so advanced as to be graced with the sobriquet of "conspiracy." For all his eminence, Colonel Sir Mark Landless could be hanged, drawn, and quartered for high treason. The accolade of knighthood does not ennoble an Englishman; he remains, still, a commoner.

Dinner, which was to be comprised of fifteen courses with changes of dishes, was due to begin at about six and would certainly last till ten or eleven. It was still an hour before the guests were summoned to the table, and a very great deal of champagne and brandy had been consumed when Strachan, excusing himself from the group to which he had been attached, sidled across to Purity, who was conversing with the marquess's maiden lady relation. The latter immediately made herself scarce with an unconvincing excuse.

"My dear Lady Landless, how well you are looking tonight. Tell me something, please, of your place in Wiltshire. Clumber Grange, isn't it called?" The pale eyes were probing at her bodice, and they slid away to the depths of his champagne glass almost immediately. "Is it of considerable architectural merit?"

"It is very fine, sir," said Purity. She had him placed now, she decided. With his shaggy bulk, his coarse features, the Most Honorable Marquess of Strachan, given another bedroom in which to have been born, would have made a convincing street sweeper or builder's laborer. So much for aristocratic birth.

"Of the last century?"

"Palladian, sir, by Mr. William Kent," said Purity.

"So distinguished!" cried Strachan. "And, tell me, ma'am, do you possess any art treasures of note? I speak myself as a collector and cognoscente. You have, no doubt, heard of my exceedingly fine collection of Gainsboroughs, Reynoldses, and Stubbses, not to mention my Rape of the Sabine Women, attributed to Rubens."

"We cannot boast such artistic richness at Clumber, sir," said Purity, knowing in her mind what must follow. "But there is a fine Dobson portrait of one of my husband's ancestors of the Civil War period. And we have a Romney . . . "

"Lady Landless, ma'am," interrupted the marquess, "I see in you a fellow devotee of the arts. You must instantly allow me to escort you to the picture gallery. We have ample time before dinner. Your arm, ma'am."

Purity acquiesced, though she would have preferred not to, for to be the object of a stolen kiss from such as the marquess was something that, given her state of mind, she could well have done without. But it seemed churlish to refuse, and, anyhow, the thought that

116

Strachan was willing to lend his influence for Chastity's sake was a source of considerable comfort to Mark, if not to herself.

They passed close to Mark on the way out of the solar. He observed them, and, from the slight raising of an eyebrow and a quirkish grin that creased the corner of his lips, it was obvious that he divined the reason for their departure. Purity was tempted to wink at her husband, but there were too many other people in a position to observe such an inelegant gesture.

The great hall, which they passed through, was crowded with liveried servitors putting the finishing touches to the loaded tables, and all of them bowed at their master and his beautiful companion. Her hand still upon the marquess's arm, they ascended a sweep of fine staircase with richly carved banisters in the Jacobean manner to the gallery that ran the entire length of the mansion, and which contained the renowned Strachen picture collection.

They paused by the first painting in the seemingly interminable line of dark canvases framed in heavy gilt.

"Moira, Marchioness Strachan," intoned her guide, "wife of the fourth marquess. And my own mama. Painted by Reynolds in '82."

"Charming," murmured Purity dutifully, "quite charming."

The face in the portrait spoke volumes for the sitter —and explained a very great deal about her son. There, if Purity had ever seen one, was a Gorgon. A harridan. A vinegar-avised shrew and a scold. There was no line of love or tenderness in the pinched, almost lipless, mouth, nor was there an iota of humanity in the cold, pale eyes that stared down at her in smoldering malevolence. Small wonder that Charlie Strachan had grown up to hate all women and to fear them as creatures—though still desiring them, and incapable of

117

satisfying those pent-up desires. One could almost feel it in one's heart to be sorry for the man. Purity resolved that when the time came—as come it must—to be the object of his stolen, nervous kiss, she would receive it with good grace.

"We now move on," said the marquess, "to a portrait of my father's stallion Bucephalus, painted by George Stubbs in '78 while still a colt. Though the nag never actually won the derby, he . . . "

The booming, rotundate voice rolled on and on. Purity let her mind wander at will, while still retaining an expression of lively attention, a trick one learns from dealing with the chatter of small children and the ramblings of the elderly. Her mind wandered—as well it might—to the problems that beset her, to speculations about Chastity's health and well-being. Was the darling girl being adequately fed and looked after? Did they make provisions for the changing of her linen and her bedclothes? Would the woman Madeleine not permit her to send Chastity some changes of clothing: a few of her favorite day dresses, perhaps; some pretty underclothing and night attire, to cheer her up?

The marquess was still droning on. They had gone some way down the long gallery, but there was still an interminable distance yet to go. When was dinner?

"And now," said Strachan, "we come to the gem of the collection. Not an undoubted Rubens, I concede, ma'am, but certainly painted by one of his finer pupils, under the master's personal guidance, when he was in England at the invitation of Charles the First. And the main figures have certainly known the touch of the master's brush. This way, ma'am. As befits its quality, the picture has a room all of its own."

He opened a door, admitting them to a small, square room that was furnished with a sofa—and an enormous figure composition that covered the entire wall opposite the door. The subject of the painting was, as Strachan had said, the rape of the Sabine women by the Romans, done after the sweeping Baroque manner of Rubens. A swirl of draperies and naked flesh, of prancing horses, gesticulating men, and screaming and abandoned women stretched from one end of the canvas to the other. It was a feast of nudity: of pearly buttocks; swaying, cherry-nippled breasts; deeply naveled bellies.

"Well, what do you think, eh, ma'am?"

"It is . . . very powerful, sir," murmured Purity, who disliked Rubenses intensely, and the particular example before her was not even a good Rubens. And it was blatantly lewd. Small wonder Charlie Strachan kept it out of sight in a room of its own. Mostly locked, no doubt.

She turned to see him cross over and quietly shut the door. As he met her gaze, the pouched eyes wavered and fell. There was a rim of sweat around his mouth. His tongue came out and licked dry lips. The moment had come.

Purity sighed inwardly and looked away, toward the appalling picture, presenting him with her cheek. Let it be over and done with quickly, she prayed.

His heavy breathing came close to her. She smelled tobacco and brandy on his breath. It grew stronger. The moist, slack lips met her cheek briefly and then were withdrawn.

Assembling a false smile, she turned to look at him.

"I thank you for the compliment, sir," she said mildly. "And, since no harm is done, we can still be friends. Now, shall we resume the tour of your collection, or shall we join the . . . "

She broke off, seeing the expression in his eyes. She was aware that—unbelievably—his stubby forefinger was reaching out to the bodice of her gown, was probing the edge of it, was—horrors—dipping low within the deep cleft of her breasts.

"It is not finished, ma'am," he said softly, throatily.

And the sweat was now running in rivulets down his high-complexioned cheeks. "And I regret that there *is* harm, still, to be done."

Purity shook herself free of the insinuating finger. She stood back a pace from him.

"What do you *mean?*" she gasped.

He pointed—to her bosom.

"I mean . . . *that!*" he replied.

She glanced down at herself. Suspended across her so recently defiled bodice, lying in the cleft of her breasts, was the hateful medallion, with its green eyes winking wickedly.

She gasped with horror, then looked up to see him, as, grinning, he withdrew something from the fob pocket of his pantaloons. It was not a watch. . . .

It was an exact copy of her own medallion, her badge of whoredom!

"No-o-o-o!" she cried.

"Yes, indeed," said Strachan. His grin was nervous, and he was still sweating profusely—but he was gaining assurance with every passing instant. And the medallion in his hand seemed to be acting as a talisman— a badge of courage.

"What . . . what do you want?" asked Purity in a voice that did not sound like her own.

"Need you ask?" The grin was more assured.

"Please . . . no . . ."

"You will not refuse," he said. "You cannot. I know the rules of our society. You have sold your soul in an oath. To break it will mean eternal hellfire for you. You will give yourself to me by every means I demand—or burn in hellfire."

He crossed over and seated himself upon the sofa, the medallion still held between his fingers.

"Go and stand over by the picture," he commanded, "close by it, as if you were . . . one of the Sabine women."

She obeyed, numb with shock as she was, and quite incapable of further protest.

He lolled back on the sofa, and he very deliberately unbuttoned the flap of his pantaloons. There was no nervousness in his manner any longer; he was as brash and blustering in his attitude toward her—a woman— as he had been earlier in the solar when laying down the law about the royal succession.

"Now you will strip naked!" he said, rolling the words around his mouth like vintage port wine.

Her fears directed her will, and her numbed will directed her shrinking hands. They unfastened the bodice of her gown and drew the silk material down over her smooth shoulders. She felt the hated medallion swing on its chain across her bared breasts.

"By thunder!" grated the man on the sofa. "You're not wearing stays! 'Tis all your own, that shape of you, egad! On with what you're doing, woman! Don't tarry!"

She bowed her head so that she should not see the expression on his face—nor the fact that he had uncovered himself—as she removed the remainder of the gown, allowing it to fall around her feet."

"Retain the stockings," said the marquess. He added with a lewd snigger, "They will serve to distinguish you from the ladies in the picture, who do not enjoy such modern fripperies. And now you will approach me, woman."

She obeyed, shuddering. She shrank within herself when he reached out to touch her. Every inch of her bare skin was prickling with the pain of anticipation. He remained seated, with her standing before him, her body open to his importuning hands and gloating eyes.

And then—horror piled upon horror—he was first inviting her, then cajoling, and finally demanding that she sit down upon his lap.

Dinner at Kingston Manor that evening began promptly at six o'clock, when his lordship's butler announced the hour at the door of the solar. By this time the marquess and Purity had rejoined the others, and the former—much invigorated and in high good humor —was holding forth about politics.

Purity, pale and quenched, drew forth an anxious question from Mark. "My darling, do you feel faint? It is appallingly hot in here with the candles blazing and all the windows shut, but I'm sure it will be cooler in the great hall. Would you like to go outside?"

"I shall be all right in a moment," she whispered.

"What happened in the picture gallery?" he asked quietly, with a note of good humor. "Did his lordship try to kiss you?"

She was saved from answering, but at great cost, by the booming voice of their host.

"Gentlemen, I bid you to take your partners for dinner! I have the honor of Lady Landless's company. Your hand, ma'am."

The pouched eyes were upon her all the way to the table—gloating, triumphant. To Purity, it was like the walk to the scaffold. In such a manner must her aristocratic French ancestors have ascended the steps of the dreaded guillotine to meet their end. She remembered to keep her head high; it was all she had left—her inherited ability to suffer with dignity.

She was placed in the seat of honor, at their host's right side, at the center of the head table. Mark was somewhere down at the far end of the long table, next to the marquess's elderly maiden relation. In the light of what followed, Purity counted it a blessing that he was out of sight and sound; but her whole being screamed out for his help.

There was a large and stupid-looking gentleman at her right side. For reasons best known to himself, he had on an evening tailed coat of hunting scarlet, with the engraved buttons of the famous Strachan foxhounds. His first attempt to engage Purity upon the subject of fox-hunting was thwarted by having imbibed too much of his host's champagne, with deleterious results upon his utterance, and by the marquess's intervention.

"M'lady, am I c'rect in s'posin' that you've a pack o' hounds at Clumber?"

"Lady Landless," interposed Strachan, in a very loud voice, to no one in particular, "is a tremendous admirer of the painter Rubens and his followers. And she particularly admires the major work in my collection entitled The Rape of the Sabine Women. Is that not so, Lady Landless?"

"Yes," murmured Purity, grateful, if for nothing else, that the general hum of conversation must have prevented even Strachan's voice from reaching all the way down the length of the hall to Mark's ears.

"Is tha' so?" commented the drunken fox hunter on her right. "Tha's terribly interestin'."

"Lady Landless, indeed, was quite carried away by certain aspects of the composition. Were you not, ma'am?"

When she hesitated in her reply, his hand crept under the table and along her thigh. She nearly screamed aloud when his fingers bit cruelly into her tender flesh.

"Were you not, ma'am?" he repeated, with an edge of menace that only she could have detected.

"Yes. Yes . . . I was," answered Purity.

"Terribly interestin'," said the man on her right, addressing himself to a brimming glass of claret.

"In fact, Lady Landless clearly identified herself with some of the personages in the picture. Did you not, ma'am?" demanded her tormentor.

"Yes," she said. There were at least a dozen people within earshot, and some had ceased their own conversations to listen to Strachan's remarks, many of them with expressions of faint puzzlement.

"Do you recall the figure in the center, ma'am?" asked the marquess. "The handsome lady with the golden hair?"

The fingers resting upon her thigh began to scrabble at her skirts, drawing them up, inch by inch. Her own hand reached down to prevent him, but hesitated as his other hand moved across the tabletop and laid something before her.

The hateful medallion! A prompting to obedience. . . .

"I would say you greatly resemble the lady with the golden hair. Would you not, ma'am?"

"Yes."

She closed her eyes, but the image remained before her: how he had forced her to adopt the abandoned pose of the wanton-eyed creature in the lewd picture as, naked, she had knelt to plead for the life of her young lover, offering herself, her body, to the brutish Roman soldier who held her lover by a knot of his hair and raised aloft a sword with which to butcher him. The pose, the cloying sentiment, rendered by the brush of a third-rate imitator, had put Purity in mind of the salacious engravings whose sale in the streets of Paris nothing—not even the height of the Revolution's terror —had ever prevented. She had been forced to put herself into the position of the creature in the picture. And when her tormentor was satisfied with her pose, he had obliged her to render him a service so licentious, so vile, that her mind, thanks to the blessed workings of nature, was already beginning to shroud it in the merciful wrappings of forgetfulness. . . .

"Will you have a larded guinea fowl, m'lady, or will you have a boiled knuckle of ham?" Her right-hand neighbor, fortified by claret, was making tremendous inroads into the third course, which the servitors had just laid before them, together with its platters of tempting alternatives that would have inspired even the most jaded palate.

"Thank you, no, sir," said Purity.

"As y'please, m'lady," responded the fox hunter, dousing his enormous knuckle of ham with a generous libation of red wine from his glass. "Most 'stonishin' state o' affairs. I see Charlie Strachan ain't eatin', either."

On her left, Strachan had waved aside all food, and he was devoting himself exclusively to the grape, swallowing copious potions of claret and Burgundy, Madeira, Port, and nips of brandy to clear the palate. And all the time his restive right hand was engaged upon toying with the bared thighs of his lady guest of honor. In such a manner—in such a hedonistic and self-indulgent manner—had Charles Edward Montague Frederick, fifth marquess of Strachan, celebrated, in the private room off his picture gallery, his liberation from a lifetime of wanting and wishing. Like a greedy boy in the high branches of an apple tree in a forbidden orchard, he had gorged himself upon Purity Landless's loveliness, had choked himself with her soft flesh, and all the time calling upon his dead mother to witness that he had come into his manhood at last.

Later, much later, during the eighth or ninth course, the fox hunter on Purity's right dropped his fork. Stooping to retrieve it, his befuddled gaze encountered her shapely legs bared to the thighs and above. Forgetting the fork, he righted himself and passed a hand across his brow.

"Egad! I must have had a drop too many," he gasped. And he slid slowly to the floor.

It was past one o'clock in the morning before Purity could prevail upon Mark to depart. He was in high good spirits when they settled down in the phaeton and the coachman drove back to Mayfair.

"By George! You made a fine impression upon Charlie Strachan, my darling!" he cried. "He told me that he would go to see his brother-in-law first thing tomorrow and endeavor to bring every available officer into the search for our darling Chastity. Said he: 'I will not have dear Lady Landless unhappy for one day longer than is necessary, for I esteem her above any lady of my acquaintance.' Now, what do you think of that?"

"His lordship is most kind," said Purity flatly, remembering how her tormentor, having satiated his initial lust, had made her crawl around the floor on hands and knees—nude as she was—in order that the sight might stimulate him to new endeavors.

"Did he . . . er . . . steal a kiss up in the picture gallery, my love?" asked Mark. "A mere peck on the cheek, I'll wager. And then he ran like a frightened rabbit, I shouldn't wonder."

"As you say, a mere peck on the cheek," replied Purity.

"Poor fellow. One could feel almost sorry for him."

"One could. Indeed, one could."

Silence. The river was like beaten silver in the moonlight. Thank God he could not see the tears that coursed down her cheeks—the tears of shame, of utter degradation. Oh, my darling Chastity, I did not bear you in my womb, nor suckle you at my breasts, but I have paid for your life, for your safe return, in bitter coin—and I am likely to go on paying for a while yet.

"However," said Mark, "I think we may now hope that Chastity will be found and the miscreants who took her will be properly punished. You must be greatly relieved, my love."

"Oh, I am. I am," she replied.

His hand was insinuating itself around her waist. At any moment now, his cheek would be pressed against hers, and he would find it streaked with tears. That would have been bad enough, but when his fingers laid a tender caress upon her bosom, she thrust them aside in revulsion.

"Damn you, why can't you leave me alone and stop mauling me?"

He stiffened, then withdrew his arm and hand as if it had touched hot iron. Purity, instantly appalled by the violent intensity of her rebuff, was contrite upon the instant. She seized hold of his hand and squeezed it passionately.

"Mark, darling! Forgive me—I beg you. I can't understand what came over me that I should speak to you so—you of all people. . . ."

His face was a shadowed mystery in the darkness of the covered phaeton. She had only the tone of his voice to guide her to his true feelings. His voice was in a minor key.

"It was nothing, Purity, nothing. You are tired, that's all. It has been a tiring day for you. And all your worries . . ."

His hand somehow contrived gently to slip out of hers. His face turned away from her; she could see his striking profile against the moonlight beyond. She should say something else, she told herself, offer more tangible tokens of her love and devotion to him . . . even—remembering what had passed during their short drive back from the ball at the Royal Pavilion— to the point of offering her body, there and then.

The very thought of it revolted her.

She was soiled, unclean.

She had nothing to offer the one man in the whole world whom she loved.

That night and the aftermath in the conveyance on the way home set the tone for the break between Purity and Mark. They had both supposed—it had been an unspoken agreement between them—that the arrangement begun in Brighton, and continued in London, whereby he slept in his dressing room, was only of a temporary nature: a convenience to help her over a period of sleeplessness brought on by the shock of Chastity's abduction; something that would have a termination in the near and foreseeable future. The day after the marquess's dinner party, Purity chanced by the open door of Mark's dressing room—which was on the same floor as her bedroom, formerly *their* bedroom —and saw Mark's valet and one of the footmen carrying in some more furniture: an armchair, a writing desk, and a console table. With a pang of anguish, she realized that he was settling himself in permanently.

And she could do not a thing about it. For all her love, for all her anguish, she could not have brought herself to set his mind at rest—and give herself to him, mind and body. She was the captive of an unholy vow that had destroyed the whole heart and center of her existence.

She and Mark met at mealtimes—those meals at which he presented himself; he took to having luncheon more often at his club—but seldom at any other time. Her life became bounded by her favorite chair in her drawing room, with the view down the elegant facades of Half Moon Street, her embroidery, and her bitter tears. Only one topic of conversation remained a bond between them: the speculations about Chastity's return.

Strachan had been as good as his word. His brother-in-law, the Home Secretary, had been prodded into extending the search for the missing Landless girl. Every available magistrate officer had been thrown into the fray. Thus far, no trace of Chastity had emerged, but the officers had uncovered the disturbing fact that no fewer than twelve young girls had been missing in the environs of the metropolis during the previous twelve months, all of them disappearing without a trace and seemingly without cause. However, the abductions in question (if abductions they were) were not connected with the missing Chastity Landless, for, though like her, the other twelve were all young and attractive in face and form, they were all of the lower classes, and most of them were amateur whores who augmented slender wages as tavern girls and skivvies by selling their bodies for a few coppers at a time.

Another occasion when Mark had shown any interest and animation in her company was the day upon which was announced the appointment of the Duke of Wellington as Prime Minister. Mark was triumphant, not only for the success of his old army chief, but also because, as he said, "With the Home Office on our side, and now the Prime Minister, it can only be a matter of weeks, even of days, before Chastity is brought back safely."

Purity nodded agreement—and kept her own counsel.

The days dragged by. The view from the drawing room window grew increasingly irksome, and she longed to go out. Only the risk of meeting someone who might present her with the hateful medallion, and make some unspeakable demands upon her body and her spirit, kept her pent up indoors, receiving no one, communicating with no one. Young Robert sent her a letter from far-off Norfolk, but he was no correspondent: four hastily penned, poorly spelled lines informing *"dahling Mama"* that he was *"oright and hop you are to,"* notwithstanding which, Purity read and reread the slender missive a hundred times, then put it away next to her heart and wrote a ten-page letter in reply, pouring out all her love and misery, her passion and her loneliness. When she read it through, she realized the letter could never be sent. She was so French, so volatile, throwing her heart before her head, always. Poor little Robbie—a very ordinary, matter-of-fact English boy of the upper class, who had been taught from the cradle to keep a stiff upper lip and not display his emotions—would have been embarrassed to read such a diatribe from his own mother. She threw it in the fire, all ten pages. And she wept anew.

But she had to get out. How to contrive it so that she would not meet anyone, or, if she did, she would be in no position to accede to any licentious demands?

It came to her in a flash of inspiration as she chanced to look at an equestrian portrait over her mantlepiece: she would ride out in Rotten Row!

Certainly, she might meet someone, for all society rode out in the Row. But she would ride fast—at a gallop, stopping for nobody, nor responding to any greeting. Let any medallion-carrying lecher try to catch Purity Landless in full flight!

Quickly warming to the idea, she bade her maid to lay out her riding costume of peacock-blue velvet trimmed with black braid, and she put it on, together with a tall hat and veil. Thus attired, she went down to the mews behind the house, where the under-groom had already saddled up her favorite chestnut gelding, Rupert of the Rhine, and cupped his hands for her tiny booted foot to help her up into the saddle. Splendidly erect, perched sidesaddle with effortless elegance, she urged Rupert into a brisk canter out of the mews archway and down the rutted length of Half Moon Street to Piccadilly—all in the glorious sunshine of a spring morning. She rode past Regent's Park, to Hyde Park Corner, and to Wellington's splendid Apsley House, which faced the high garden wall of Buckingham Palace. The palace had been renovated a few years previously by Mr. John Nash, and at tremendous cost, giving the king's subjects yet another stick with which to beat their unpopular sovereign.

The beginning of Rotten Row lay immediately ahead

of her. She checked Rupert's pace, all ready to make a hasty retreat if she espied any possible danger.

There seemed to be no danger. Two Household Cavalry officers in blue "patrols" were cantering side by side in the distance, going away from her. No one else was in sight. Purity shook the reins, tapped Rupert lightly in the flank, and sent him into a smart canter, rising to a gallop.

Five minutes later she flashed past the two officers, who gazed after her in considerable admiration. The end of the Row came into sight. Her mount was going well, and she decided to turn him and gallop back at least as far as the officers, then slow down to a canter.

She had brought Rupert to a walk and was turning him when, from out of the line of trees on the Knightsbridge side of the Row, there emerged a tall black horse and a tall rider.

"Good morning, dear Lady Landless. What a very pleasant surprise. May I accompany you for a while?"

Purity's heart gave a treacherous lurch.

A pair of ice-blue eyes stripped her naked. Full lips were pursed in a sensuous smile. There followed a bow and a raising of his tall hat that were part civility, part mockery—the way a gentleman will greet a whore of the better, more expensive, type. Purity felt at once cheapened and strangely aroused.

"Good morning, Captain D'Eath," she murmured.

Accepting her lack of answer as consent to his request, D'Eath brought his black stallion alongside Purity's mount, and together they walked back down the Row the way she had come. Not a word passed between them till the two officers had passed and saluted them civilly in passing, which they both acknowledged.

And then it was he who began the conversation. "I think you are a little less frightened of me than on the previous occasion."

She cast a glance down at her bosom and became hideously aware that the medallion, which she had tucked within the tunic of her habit, but which had emerged during her gallop and was now lying against the peacock-blue velvet and plain to his gaze.

As surreptitiously as she could, she turned it over so that the hideous head and eyes were hidden; it would have drawn his attention if she had attempted to tuck it back out of sight.

He said, "Am I not correct that you find me less daunting today?"

"Sir, I cannot lie to you," replied Purity simply. "You continue to terrify me."

"Because I desire you physically, or because— though you will not admit it to yourself any more than you will admit it to me—you desire me also?"

"Will you leave me alone!" she cried.

"Why should I?" he replied blandly. "The attraction of opposites—and we are vastly opposite in all things: in gender, in temperament, in our philosophies of life —is a curious alchemy that permits of very intense connections. If I were to bed you once, my dear Lady Landless, you might well never wish to be bedded by another in your whole life." He regarded her with his ice-blue eyes half-hooded. "Has that occurred to you, perhaps? And is it for that reason that you hesitate to become my lover?"

"Leave me be!" cried Purity. "If you do not, I will . . ."

"You will do what?" he interposed. "Will you, per-haps, complain of my conduct to your husband, the excellent Colonel Sir Mark Landless?" He laughed, throwing back his head so that the muscles of his powerful neck tautened. "By heaven, Lady Landless, if that is your intent, I sincerely trust that your spouse is a good pistol shot. Do you know that I have killed men?"

"Yes," she murmured.

"Do you then have ambitions toward early widow-hood?"

"No."

"Not so? You surprise me."

"What . . . what do you mean?" she asked, puzzled.

His fingertip slowly stroked the corner of his eye—a gesture she remembered. He cocked an appraising glance at her full bosom, rounded beneath the well-fitting habit of peacock-blue.

"Oh, come, come," he said with a mocking inflec-tion. "Let us not be naïve—not *you*, of all people."

"I don't understand what you are trying to say," in-sisted Purity. "You are just playing with words."

"I will put it bluntly," said D'Eath. "Would not the state of early widowhood greatly suit your present style of living?"

"My . . . style of living?"

"Your predilection—I might say your most surpris-ingly indiscriminate partiality—for what vulgar persons allude to as the handy-dandy!"

She gave a sharp, involuntary intake of breath.

"The . . . handy-dandy?"

"With Charlie Strachan, for one," said D'Eath. "And any woman who'd give herself to *him* would allow her-self to be tumbled by anything in breeches."

"The . . . the Marquess of Strachan has said that about *me*?" asked Purity. "To *you*?"

"He's told all and sundry, anyone who will listen—and I assure you that everyone is only too happy to listen—that he has had the beautiful Lady Landless in every possible way that a man may take a woman. Does he then lie?" responded D'Eath cheerfully.

"Yes, he lies," said Purity, dropping her gaze.

His hand came out and took her, not ungently, under the chin. He forced her to meet his mocking, ice-blue gaze.

"We will test who is lying," he said. "Charlie

133

Strachan was most precise and particular as to details
—to everyone who cared to listen, as I have told you.
Let me recapitulate some of the more sensational of
those details. First of all, he says that he persuaded you
to strip naked before him—everything save your stockings."

"Please . . . " begged Purity.

"After that, my lord marquess took you upon his
lap," continued her tormentor. "And then you . . . "

"No-o-o-o!"

"And after that . . . "

Purity, blinded by sudden tears of shame, tugged at
Rupert's rein and kicked with her heel. The spirited
gelding, responding instantly to her command, went
into a full gallop within a few strides, leaving the sandy
track that constituted Rotten Row and heading out
across the greensward of Hyde Park and the banks of
trees beyond, where sheep and cattle grazed in the cool
shade.

D'Eath's taunting laugh followed her, but it soon
faded away in the distance. He made no attempt to follow.

Purity did not draw rein till she reached Park Lane,
by which time she had dried her tears and was facing
the appalling realities of her situation.

Strachan had told all—and would continue to tell.
That—considering the man, considering his hatred of
women, the imaginary humiliation he had suffered from
them in their protracted thwarting of his passions—was
to be expected. Charlie Strachan—thanks to the convenient arrangement of the medallions, which cut
through to the nub of the matter and disposed of such
embarrassing niceties as persuasion and seduction, not
to mention rape—had had his way with the beautiful
and desirable Lady Landless, the half-legendary Purity.
That much would soon be common knowledge throughout society—if it was not already.

But would it reach Mark's ears? That was the problem. Let that not happen, and she would suffer all the rest, gladly.

Fortunately, there was an established code in such matters. One laughed behind the back of a cockold; but half the sport with cuckoldry lay in the fact of the victim's ignorance. It was considered a tremendously smart move, for instance, to tumble one's mistress while her husband was near at hand and innocently unaware (as Strachan had taken her). Such games became pointless if the poor fool was aware of his continual betrayal, and, as was so often the case in society, was making what shift he could of turning a blind eye to his wife's infidelities.

No, taking it all in all, she decided that the chances were better than even that, gossip as gossip might, news of her humiliation at Strachan's hands would not reach Mark's ears—not unless an enemy decided to inform him anonymously, for spite's sake. And try as she would, Purity could not think of anyone who could possibly have hated Mark as much as that.

One small consolation she took from the encounter with the disturbing Captain Guy D'Eath: he had had ample opportunity, surely, to have seen the fateful medallion. If he had been one of that persuasion, one of the ubiquitous members of the strange society, the owner of a similar medallion, he would surely have declared himself. Good God, he had tried hard enough to seduce her by conventional means!

D'Eath was not a problem, no more than any other persistent would-be seducer. And she had had plenty of experience with those gentry, and she had learned a hundred ways to fend them off.

Only, D'Eath was not *quite* like all the others. . . .

She shook off the disturbing thought. She turned Rupert into the slow-moving, mid-morning traffic of busy Piccadilly. She went at a walking pace behind a

135

line of slow-moving cattle that were being driven by swiftly darting dogs and by barefoot farmers' lads. Purity moved among the high-stepping carriage horses, the drays, the town phaetons, crested coaches, the great stream of foot travelers, all of which were wending their way, to and fro, back and forth, through Westminster's principal highway.

Too many people, she thought. Too many opportunities for holders of the medallion (how many of them were there?) to challenge her. She must not go riding out again, not after what had happened. D'Eath might easily have been one of *them,* or one of them could have accosted her as smoothly as he had done.

Best to stay at home. Receive no one. Invite no one. Write to no one, except darling Robbie.

There was a carriage standing at her door. She saw it as soon as she reached the corner of Half Moon Street. Two men, a groom and a coachman, both in dark blue livery, were lolling by it. They eyed her covertly as she went past, expertly appraising the qualities of the nag, then of the woman atop him.

Having given Rupert a bit of fuss and affection and having handed him over to the under-groom, Purity went into the house by the mews door. The butler was awaiting her in the hallway.

"Milady."

"Yes?"

"A gentleman called. I showed him into your drawing room, milady. A Mr. Hardcourt."

"Hardcourt—*Hardcourt?*" She shook her head in puzzlement. "Do we know a Mr. Hardcourt?"

"Here is the gentleman's visiting card, milady."

She looked down at the piece of pasteboard, at the name, address, and the hand-written message scrawled beside the primly flowing copperplate engraving:

To see Sir Mark on a personal matter.

Chastity!

The thought sprang instantly to her mind. The personal matter must concern Chastity. What else? Hardcourt was obviously sent from the Home Office, or perhaps by the duke himself. Purity took the stairs two at a time, with the butler gaping after her.

She paused at the door of the drawing room, her hand hesitating over the latch.

Supposing . . .

Supposing that he was the bearer of evil tidings?

She had blithely assumed (such is the natural, buoyant optimism of the human mind) that this Mr. Hardcourt, from the Home Office, or wherever, was a harbinger of good tidings. What if it were otherwise? What if, in their valiant and expert searchings, they had tracked down Madeleine, but she and her accomplices had had time to destroy their innocent victim?

Summoning up every remaining scrap of her fortitude, Purity opened the door.

A smallish, dark-complexioned young man in gray rose from her favorite easy chair by the window. He bowed low over her hand, as, extending it, she approached him.

"Lady Landless, it's an honor."

"Mr. Hardcourt, I do not think I have had the pleasure."

"Ma'am, I am the member of Parliament for Stoke-by-Zouch, and I'm a very old acquaintance of Sir Mark's."

Purity was struck with a sudden sense of loss. Hardcourt's eyes were shifty, certainly, but not with the agonized unease of a person who is the bearer of evil tidings—or of any tidings touching upon matters of life or death.

"So you have come to see my husband, sir?" she said flatly. "I regret to have to inform you that he is taking luncheon at his club today. Perhaps, if the matter is so urgent, you may wish to contact him there. The club, as you may know, is . . . "

She froze into silence on the instant as Hardcourt produced from his breast pocket a shining, small disc of gold that he then presented to her suddenly appalled gaze. The hideous, shimmering-eyed goat's head stared out at her.

"I am aware that your husband is absent today," he said, and his voice was now breathless, excited. He moved closer to her, and his questing fingers were searching for her. "I saw you, Lady Landless, a few days ago, being driven in your phaeton along Bond Street. You did not see me. Why should you? For I am not known to you—was not known to you at that time. But I observed . . . "

His fingers reached out and took hold of the telltale goat's-head medallion that was suspended across Purity's breasts, and his dark-avised, young, savagely lusting face took on an expression of a vile hunger.

She closed her eyes.

She submitted.

Chapter Five

Chastity's change of circumstance, when it came, was as abrupt and unannounced as it was total. For uncounted and uncountable days and nights (in fact, she had lost all idea of the difference between night and day), she remained within her narrow, empty room. She was naked, filthy, alone, empty in mind and spirit. Only the occasional visit from her keeper and guardian gave her a hold upon life. To say that he became the focus of all her thoughts is not to overstate the case. He became mother and father to her, guide and exemplar, the object of her affections, even of her love.

One day (or night), he entered, unannounced, as always, and, instead of bearing a tray of food or a fresh candle, he had in his hand a silken shift, which he tossed at the crouching girl.

"Put it on, Elizabeth," he said mildly. "You are going to leave this place."

"To . . . leave?" She stared at him wonderingly.

"That is so. Hurry now. Don't keep me waiting, or it's possible that I may change my mind."

The rebuke, the bland threat, jolted her into activity. She opened the garment and put it on. The very unfamiliarity of clothing, after her protracted nudity, rendered the normally simple feat a difficult piece of manipulation; she was like a small child who is asked, for the first time, to fasten her shoes. In any event, it was done. When she stood up, she was wearing a thin silk shift whose white transparency clearly delineated every part of her body.

"This way, Elizabeth," said her mentor, indicating the open door.

She preceded him through the door. He followed after and closed it behind them. They were on a half-landing of a staircase that rose on high into darkness and into a Stygian gloom below. By the light of a single candle that he carried, they proceeded upward. One floor. Another. A door faced them at the top. He tapped upon it.

"Come in, Quintin," a female voice called out.

Entering, they faced a woman seated at a writing table. She had bronze-colored hair and an incongruous black patch over her right eye. She was dressed in a peignoir of wispy black silk that scarcely concealed the secrets of her voluptuous body. She rose and extended a welcoming hand to the dazed girl.

"Hello, Elizabeth," she said. "I am Madeleine, and I am your friend."

"Hello," said Chastity, nervously approaching. The hand was warm and dry in hers.

"You have met Quintin," said the woman, indicating the man. "He is also your friend, as, indeed, he is mine. Quintin has been very kind to you, has he not?"

"Oh, yes," said Chastity. "Very, very kind. He brought me candles and food, and he came to see me often." She looked around into the man Quintin's aquiline, yet curiously womanish, countenance. "He has been a true friend."

There was a tap upon the door. Upon Madeleine's summons, there entered a young girl of about Chastity's age. She was, in face and coloring, so much like Madeleine that they were quite clearly mother and daughter. She wore nothing but a shift, and she was barefoot.

"Elizabeth, this is Cornelia. Cornelia, dearest, I should like you to look after Elizabeth, please. See that she has a bath and then put her to bed."

"Yes, Mama." The girl briefly touched Chastity's hand. She smiled sidelong at her from under long-lashed eyelids, with full lips parted to show very white, sharp teeth. "Hello, Elizabeth."

"Hello," responded the other.

"*Au revoir,* my dears," said Madeleine. "We will meet again later, after you have slept."

The door closed behind the two girls, Madeleine gave a short laugh, and, taking from a carved box a long cigar, she lit it from the candle before her, then drew deeply and luxuriantly from the aromatic cigar.

"Well, my dear?" she murmured.

"It goes well," replied Quintin. "She is ours—or nearly ours."

"Did she question the new name we have given her?"

"No. She will question nothing."

"Nothing?" The solitary eye gazed at him quizzically from under a raised brow.

He frowned. "Only in one matter—the matter of the mother. In her sleep, many times, I have heard her calling for her mother. When that bond is severed, as severed it will shortly be, she will be all ours."

"A puppet upon a string," mused Madeleine. And she drew again upon the cigar. "You are very clever, my dear."

"I am merely . . . a servant," said the other, his pale lips primly pursed.

"And do not ever forget it, mind you," said Madeleine severely.

The bath was not merely a bath, but a revelation. One felt like a sea-nymph disporting oneself in some sun-kissed ocean of antiquity, with dolphins and tritons for company, and mermaids playing sweet music upon conch shells.

Indeed, the bath itself was luxury beyond all belief: not the solidly utilitarian English bath of one's experience, but a sunken pool of glazed porcelain set in a tiled floor. Tiled, also, were the walls of the chamber. And, as in every room and passageway of the house that Chastity had seen so far, the windows where shuttered and bolted.

She leaned back in the soapy, perfumed water and luxuriated. Cornelia was sitting, cross-legged, on the floor nearby, her back against the tiled wall. Her eyes never strayed. It was curious to have another girl seeing one in a state of undress—she who had never bared herself before a soul except her own mother, and that not even recently, except that she had been nude in front of him—Quintin. But, then, Quintin was special. . . .

"When you have finished, we will go to bed," said Cornelia.

"Bed—that will be nice."

"Are you sleepy, Elizabeth?"

"A little."

The other girl stretched herself. "Do you think I'm pretty, Elizabeth?" she asked. Again came that sidelong, long-lashed look—like a kitten.

"I think you are very pretty."

"People admire my feet." She slid forward one bare, pink foot for inspection. "Do you think my feet are handsome? Do you find them so?"

"Oh, yes, I do."

"And my shoulders—my shoulders have been commented upon." The girl shrugged her arms free of her shift so that it fell to her waist. "Would you say they are rather fine, Elizabeth?"

"Oh, I would."

"And my bosom—do you admire my bosom?"

"Yes." An impulse drove Chastity to sink lower into the water.

"Not too large, my bosom, do you think?"

"No."

"I think it's rather larger than yours. Let me see you again, Elizabeth. Sit up, do."

The girl had a perfect right to make the demand, for she was a friend, and without her friends Chastity was lost. It was simply the shame of her own inadequacy, her own ugliness, compared with the radiant, copper-haired beauty whose violet-shaded eyes perused her so critically.

"Mmmm. Your breasts *are* rather tiny, Elizabeth."

"I . . . I'm sorry."

Cornelia stood up, then stretched herself again. Unsupported, the flimsy shift fell in a silken pool around her feet.

"Get out of the bath, and I'll help you to dry yourself," she murmured.

The Turkish towel was as soft as lamb's wool. Soft, also, were the hands that directed it over her body, smoothing her flanks, her rump, and her loins. She gasped for sudden breath when they lingered at the small of her back.

"Are you sensitive there, Elizabeth?" asked the other, amused.

"Yes," she admitted.

"How curious. Everyone has a sensitive spot, don't you know? Mine is . . . here, give me your hand."

Gently holding the other girl's hand at the wrist, Cornelia directed it to the peak of her own left breast and brushed the nipple with the fingertips. She closed her eyes and gave a small moan.

"Mmmm—such a delicious sensation. Do you not find it so, whenever someone touches you there?"

"I . . . I don't know."

"Then let us see." The violet-shaded eyes were alight with mischief, like those of a playful kitten. "Ah, I can see—it is perfectly obvious—that you have yet another ticklish spot. Just look at the darling little thing coming to life. Do you know that you are trembling all over?"

"I . . . I can't help it. . . ."

The bedchamber was adjacent to the room with the bath. It was decorated with dusky-pink hangings, and the walls were covered with the same material. A large four-poster bed dominated the center of the room; it was curtained in cloth-of-gold. The sheets were of the softest satin, white as swansdown.

Cornelia led Chastity by the hand to the bed, and her whole body was afire at the other girl's touch. Together they mounted the three steps to the dais, and Cornelia drew back the sheets for them to enter.

It was another world. Forgotten were the long days and nights in the dark and stinking hole that had come to be all her life. With her head back against the yielding, soft pillows, she watched her friend's slender hand and arm reach out to the candlestick. There came a flashing glance in her direction, a smile that promised unimaginable delights, and the flame was snuffed.

Alone together in the warm and soft-scented darkness, Chastity felt herself being enveloped in Cornelia's arms. She felt the whole length of Cornelia's body pressed against hers. Breasts, bellies, thighs, flanks, and feet were entwined. And she gasped anew when the questing fingers touched the small of her back.

"Shall I do it again?" said the smiling voice against her ear.

144

"Yes . . . please."

The walls of the room had receded, and Chastity was with Cornelia in their own eternity of darkness, with a million stars looking down. Like the first notes of a great concerto, she experienced the early promise of a rapture almost beyond endurance.

"And now, do the same to me, darling Elizabeth—just as I showed you."

It was a delight to pleasure her, to savor her sweet moans, to sense her soft flesh coming alive at her fingertips, and, later, against her lips.

In giving, and in receiving, Chastity was led out of their world of darkness into a new sunlight—she and her friend together, their bodies joined with feverish lips and hands. It was over all too quickly: her first, blinding ascent into the new world of ecstasy. All too soon she was back in the warm darkness once more, lying, spent and breathless, in her lover's arms, her cheek against the other's breast, Cornelia's fingers stroking her tumbled hair.

"Was that the first time for you, Elizabeth, darling?"

"Yes. Oh, yes."

"Have you never been to bed with a man?"

She gasped at the thought of it. "Oh, no, Cornelia. No!"

"Nor yet with a girl?"

"Nor yet with a girl. Not before . . . now."

"How was it for you, Elizabeth?"

"It was . . . beautiful beyond belief." She caught her breath sharply as Cornelia's hand moved from her hair and began gently to stroke her breast.

"It is always beautiful," whispered Cornelia, "when there is love between two people. In the beginning, we were friends. Now we are lovers."

"Lovers." She repeated the word, savoring it upon her lips.

"Mark you," said Cornelia, "there are some who do it for lust. That is an abomination."

"Oh, yes! That would be dreadful—dreadful!" Cornelia's hand moved from her breast to her belly, gently stroking, descending with every stroke. Sublimely contented, she relaxed in the other's embrace and felt herself opening out, like a lily flower in the summer sunshine.

The sun was all around her. Before that there was only darkness, and far-off memories of places and people in another time, another existence.

The moment she was living, the place she was in— they were reality, and everything else was a dream.

She was Elizabeth. And Cornelia, once her friend, was—miraculously—now her lover.

She was becoming hardened by experience, she decided. She already had her story prepared when Mark came into the drawing room to give her what had by then become a customary peck upon the brow (formerly it had been an embrace, and frequently of such passion that they ended up in bed together, at whatever time of day!).

She had heard him address the butler in the hall— no doubt upon seeing Hardcourt's visiting card on the hall table—and had heard the manservant's reply.

She looked up from her embroidery at his entrance.

"Good afternoon, my dear."

"Hello, Mark." She closed her eyes as his cold lips brushed her forehead. "Have you had a good day at the club?"

"Useful," he replied. "I wouldn't put it any higher than that. I took luncheon with Grayson, from the Home Office. I detected, from his attitude, an indication that they despair of ever finding our girl. You may be assured that, by the end of the meal, I had stiffened Grayson's resolve. The search will continue."

"I am relieved to hear that," murmured Purity.

"I gather we have had a visitor," said Mark. "Hardcourt, M.P. What did he want, pray?"

"He brought his commiserations," replied Purity, "and those of his constituents in Stoke-by-Zouch. By the way, where *is* Stoke-by-Zouch?"

"Somewhere in the midlands, I believe," replied Mark. "One of the shires: Leicestershire or Derbyshire. That was very civil of him. Anything else?"

Anything else? thought Purity. Yes, my darling husband, there was very much else!

Aloud, she said, "He offered his . . . services—in the search for Chastity, I mean."

"Hardcourt," said Mark, rubbing his chin thoughtfully. "Yes, I remember the fellow now. Little fellow who always looks as if he needs a shave. Not a front-runner by all accounts. Never seems to be able to make up his mind. Still . . ."

Oh, my sweet, my darling spouse, she thought. Mr. Hardcourt knows his own mind and makes it up very firmly, I can assure you. He knew what he wanted of Lady Landless, and he made no bones about getting it. She closed her eyes and shuddered. On that same Persian carpet that Mark was now crossing to get himself a brandy from the drink table, she had coupled with Hardcourt, and she with her skirts around her waist and he scrabbling at her like a rutting stag. And that selfsame table, where Mark was standing, had been a pillory across which he had made her lie to take her again. In the violence of his assault upon her, they had overturned a glass. . . .

"There's a broken glass here," said Mark.

"I will ring for the duty footman," murmured Purity.

"Don't bother, my dear," he said. "I can pick it up. What else did you do today?"

"I rode in the Row," she said.

"Which nag?"

"Rupert. He went very well."

"Meet anyone you knew?"

A moment's pause. You must learn to be quicker, Purity. . . .

"No," she said.

Oh, my cuckolded darling, what am I going to do? The sanctuary, even, of my own house offers me no protection from them. They will rape me in my own drawing room. Next they will demand to have me on our own marriage bed, my Mark. I think I would rather kill myself than suffer that.

What use is there in trying to hide from them? I had as lief walk the streets like a common whore, for that is what I've become—a strumpet for any man who shows the right coin. Even the cheapest dockside whores are paid—and I am not even paid. They take me without so much as a thank-you. That swine—that Hardcourt, who represents the interests of the enlightened inhabitants of Stoke-by-Zouch—having slaked his lusts upon me no less than thrice, left me lying there with my skirts still in disarray. He stepped over me as if I had been a dog on the hearth rug and went out without a backward glance. Is it to be wondered at that women hate men—some men?

No more hiding, my Mark, my poor, cuckolded Mark. Purity Landless shall walk abroad, with head held high. She will not wait to be taken in the sanctity of her own home.

"Mark, dear," she said in a very cool, bright voice, "I find myself getting rather bored. Of course, it is impossible to return to Brighton or to Clumber while we hourly await news of our darling Chastity. Would you mind greatly if I did some charitable work?"

He looked at her over the rim of his brandy glass, from the other side of the room.

"Of course not, my dear," he said. "What sort of charitable work have you in mind, pray?"

"I thought . . . mmmm . . . visiting the sick. The vicar of St. James's Church will surely furnish me with a list of those of his parishioners who are ill and abed. I could take them nourishing soup and some fruit perhaps, read to them a little, make bright conversation. What do you think of that?"

He smiled at her fondly, and her heart gave a treacherous lurch. If he had crossed the room to her there and then, she told herself, and taken her in his arms, a great weight of guilt and self-loathing would have slipped from her shoulders. But he did not.

Instead, he said, "Purity, my dear, the sick are always with us. You and I have a problem much nearer home. I refer to our darling Chastity's continued disappearance. If you find the waiting irksome, I can furnish you with a list of people to visit—not the needy sick of the parish, but men, and women, of influence and position, whose support will become vital when the efforts of the Home Office begin to slacken, as slacken they must, if much more time passes before our darling is returned to us. What do you say?"

"I will do it!" she cried, clenching her fists so that the fingernails all but pierced the palms of her hands.

It was inevitable, of course. She had known it from the first moment that Mark put his suggestion to her. The woman Madeleine had told her that the ubiquitous society was composed of an exclusive group of personages. In such a category, the unsuspecting world would place the Marquess of Strachan and the member of Parliament for Stoke-by-Zouch. Persons of that ilk figured prominently in the list that Mark gave her.

She made her first visit the following day. By the end of the week—having canvassed two peers of the realm, a high court judge, a dowager countess, someone who was supposed to have the ear of the royal favorite Lady Conyngham, and the master of an Oxford college—she was rudely brought face to face with another of the hated medallions.

She had not dared to hide her own for fear that the transgression would be brought to Madeleine's attention by one means or other. When she entered the room in question, it lay upon her bosom—her mark of whoredom.

He was the Honorable Gervase Browninge, young (younger than she), handsome as a Greek god, rich as Croesus, and heir to a viscountcy. He had civilly received her in his elegant house in Upper Brook Street, bidding his butler to convey Lady Landless to him immediately. He had provided her with tea and buttered griddle cakes, cucumber sandwiches and seed cake. At the end of a very civilized tea, after he had promised, in response to her carefully assembled arguments, to speak to his uncle, who was Lord Chamberlain, he took from his fob pocket a disc of bright gold, which, having tossed it into the air, he caught in his palm and then held out for her inspection—goat's-head side up, the emerald eyes winking.

"Oh, no!" cried Purity.

"Oh, very much yes, ma'am," responded the Honorable Gervase Browninge cheerfully.

He must have her aboard his yacht. His yacht was moored at Gravesend, on the Thames. To Gravesend they went together in his smart coach with four matched grays, all through the pleasant water meadows, with the gray river sliding past and a pair of navy frigates going seaward on the tide and all plain sail.

He was dressed in a frock coat of dove-gray, with an enormous beaver top hat in the same shade, a lemon-yellow cravat, and cream pantaloons. Purity was all in blue taffeta and as lovely as the summer's morning. He held her hand throughout the journey, and he did not attempt to do anything other than kiss her—very tenderly and with palpable sincerity and enjoyment—just behind her left ear.

After the humiliations she had received at the hands of Hardcourt, and remembering the shameful antics that Strachan had put her through, here was a gentle seduction, indeed—scarcely to be reckoned as rape.

His yacht was half the size of an East Indianman and was possessed of every luxury that a bottomless purse can provide. They took luncheon together under an awning on the poop deck, while a string quartet played airs by Bach, Handel, and Mozart. The menu consisted of a white soup, cold lobster, a soufflé of rice, lobster pudding, meringues, and fruits. All the time, her host—seducer? rapist?—engaged her in the most agreeable discourse upon all things imaginable: upon yachting, the latest scandals concerning the king and Lady Conyngham, and how the king was rapidly slipping into his dotage. (The pall of lunacy that lay over his family had led him to the delusion that he had actually fought at Waterloo, and it was quipped that, upon his appealing to the Duke of Wellington to confirm this curious claim, the duke had replied: "I have heard your majesty say so before.")

Despite herself, Purity found herself laughing at the fresh-faced young aristocrat's sallies. He really was a very far cry from Strachan and Hardcourt.

His discerning and civilized behavior extended, even, to the manner in which he made his carnal demands upon her. There was no unseemly haste, no inelegant fumblings, no embarrassing vulgarities. When they had finished luncheon, he suggested—as a man might suggest to his wife, or his lover—that a short rest and nap might be an agreeable way to spend the early afternoon. With less feeling of apprehension than she would have believed (and it must be added that she had not refused the quite considerable amount of sparkling rosé wine of Burgundy that young Browninge had gently urged upon her, keeping her glass forever filled), Purity allowed herself to be led to his superbly appointed stern cabin, with its galleried windows that presented fine views of the river and the shoreline. The cabin contained priceless French furniture of the Louis XV period, which included a *papier mâché* bed shaped like an upturned scallop shell, with porcelain figures of nude cherubs and nymphs cunningly arranged to appear to be flying above it and supporting the silken canopy. Upon this bed, Browninge laid her, and he unself-consciously divested himself of all his clothing in her plain view. Purity, a sensualist and a Latin, could not but admire the slender perfection of the young man's beautiful body, which could have been likened to that of a Hellenic statue. Nor did she flinch away when he gently divested her of her attire. He marveled aloud as he did so at the sights and sensations that were revealed to him with each discarded garment. He spent half an hour playing with her breasts, fondling them with his hands and lips, and he made merry sport of lightly slapping her dimpled rump.

When finally he took her, it was with a gentle consideration for her sensibilities that entirely disarmed Purity's resentment at his intrusion. She did not respond in kind to his passion, nor did she play the whore and simulate a counterfeit passion. But she lay gently submissive, with a long, slow tear on each velvet cheek, as she thought of other afternoons of tender ecstasy that she had known with the only man she had ever loved, or would ever love.

When Browninge was spent, he slept in her arms, and she lay holding him, as one might hold a child.

She watched the reflections of sunlight on water making shifting patterns of light and dark upon the ceiling of the cabin, and she listened to the river sounds of the rushing tide and the call of water birds.

In the late afternoon, she almost drifted to sleep, and she might have done so had not Browninge stirred in his slumber, tensed his body against hers, and commenced to mutter. Clearly, he was having some sort of nightmare, and he seemed much distressed. Purity was about to awaken him when he stiffened, shuddered, and called out in a clear, loud voice, *"No! No! We shouldn't be doing it!"*

And: *"We shouldn't be slaughtering those poor girls like sheep!"*

He awoke almost immediately after, and he seemed to be in no way downcast by the disturbing content of his dream. He smilingly devoted fresh attentions to the beautiful female with whom he discovered himself to be lying, slipping easily from play into earnestness, taking her yet again with all the vigor and energy of youth.

As before, Purity gave herself freely, but she was not caught up in the running tide of his passion. And all the time, the strange and disturbing words ran through her mind—the astounding declaration that he had shouted from out of his nightmare: *"We shouldn't be slaughtering those poor girls like sheep!"*

Mark took a lively interest in her canvassing of the personages on his list. He actually apologized for Browninge. Browninge was a pleasant but rather stupid young man whose life was given over entirely to pleasure, he explained. But, nevertheless, his uncle *was* Lord Chamberlain, and he in a position to exert tremendous pressure in the House of Lords and at Court. Purity must have found the young fop appallingly tedious, he said. But she had extracted the promise of help, and that was all to the good.

Purity made no comment.

Some days passed. It seemed to her that even Mark's buoyant optimism seemed to be wearing thin, his energies flagging. On the few occasions when they met, his thoughts appeared to be far away and cast in the deepest gloom. The only topic of conversation between them remained that of Chastity and Chastity's return. He came to speak of this event, more and more, as a possibility—whereas he had formerly referred to it in terms of certainty. Purity, who knew that (unless Madeleine had been lying to her) the girl was alive and presumably well, suffered from no such fears. She fervently believed that, by her sacrifices, their daughter would be returned to them. It was not a piece of solid comfort that she was able to offer Mark.

The sacrifices continued. . . .

She met Mr. Arthur Davenport at Lady Mary Laurence's home. Lady Mary, a faded society beauty who had been the toast of London before the Napoleonic wars, figured high on Mark's list. She had invited Purity to tea, had listened to her requests with every appearance of intelligence, but had immediately changed the topic of conversation to that of the theater, of which, it appeared, she was a devotee—particularly of mime and ballet. Lady Mary, as Purity was discreetly informed by her fellow guest, was stone deaf, had been for years, and never acknowledged the fact to a living soul. The fellow guest was Mr. Arthur Davenport.

Davenport was well-known for being, arguably, the richest man in Europe, having made his fortune with the East India Company and in shipping, and, formerly, in the slave trade. Possessed of a London mansion, a country seat, estates in Scotland and Ireland, as well as extensive plantations in Jamaica and Barbados, he now devoted himself to the acquisition of a title, preferably that of viscount or better, but he would have settled—for the while, at any rate—for a simple knighthood. Regrettably, by vastly overplaying his hand—by heavily subscribing to the Tory party shortly before it fell from ascendancy in the country, thereby incurring the contempt of the Tories—Davenport was able to extract no honors from either of the great parties, and he remained plain Mr. Davenport.

He dearly loved a lady, particularly when she was the daughter of a duke, as was Lady Mary. By the same token, it seemed, he was willing to make himself most agreeable to Purity, the wife of a plain knight. Or so it seemed that way to Purity, who had heard tell of the fawning Mr. Davenport, whose snobbishness was the laughing stock of society. While their hostess prattled on about the theater, deaf to all else, he engaged himself in impressing Purity with stories of his wealth and possessions.

It was not till they had both taken leave of Lady Mary and were about to ascent into their respective carriages that Davenport revealed one of the hated medallions lying in the palm of his hand. . . .

"My carriage will call for you at eight o'clock this evening, my lady," he murmured in a voice that was thick and hoarse with desire.

She watched, appalled, as the stocky, middle-aged figure entered his conveyance, assisted by the hand of a giant black servant in purple livery.

Mark dined at his club that evening. Purity ate alone. She toyed with her food, pushing it around her plate and finally abandoning it for the wine decanter. Not a heavy drinker, or even fond of drink, she felt herself drawn toward oblivion, and she was certainly tipsy when she rose from the table and prepared herself for her ordeal.

Davenport's carriage was outside number 17A, and a black postillion was knocking upon the door as the chimes of St. James's church tower were striking the hour of eight. Lady Landless, the beauty with the hair of miraculous silver-gold, was borne to her appointment with degradation.

It was a drive of no great distance. Davenport's town mansion was close to Pall Mall. But apprehension and shame had quite dispersed the effects of the wine by the time Purity alighted at his ornate door. She was presently shown into a suavely lit room, where the grinning millionaire rose from a sofa and gestured to her to approach him. He was fully dressed, wearing a velvet jacket and smoking cap with a tassel.

Still grinning, he took from her shoulders her velvet cloak, motioned her to be seated, and pulled a bell cord.

Purity waited, a treacherous moistness forming in the palms of her tightly clenched hands. Moments passed in silence between them, measured out by the ticking of a long-cased clock in a corner of the room, and by the man's heavy breathing.

Presently, there came a tap-tap upon the door, and, following Davenport's summons, two menservants entered. Both were in purple livery, with powdered white wigs, jabots, and knee breeches of the previous century. One was a massive brute of a fellow, with the complexion of a country yokel, who peered at the woman on the sofa with brutish lewdness and licked his coarse lips. The other was coal-black, as powerfully built as his companion.

"My lady," said Davenport, "I should greatly like to present these two excellent footmen by name, Josh and Henry. Henry is the blackamoor. As you can plainly see, both are well endowed by nature for the purposes of stud work. And I can heartily recommend . . .

"No-o-o-o!"

She was on her feet in an instant, clutching for her cloak, which was resting on the back of the sofa. Davenport's hand forestalled hers.

"You are not leaving, my lady," he said smoothly.

"Let me go!" she cried.

"In good time," he replied, "after I have watched the pleasantries that I have devised for you and these excellent fellows. You will be well served, my lady, of that I promise you. There are serving wenches in this establishment who will testify to the prowess of Josh and Henry. I know it well, for I have often been witness to their willing sacrifices upon the alter of Hymen."

"You are . . . a monster!" she cried, backing away, her fearful glance turning to the pair of giants in the purple coats.

"Mayhap," admitted the millionaire without rancor. "But I prefer to think of myself as a harbinger of delight. You perchance will not find the rest of this evening entirely to your aristocratic tastes, my lady. But I assure you that what you have to offer will greatly warm the hearts of these two simple fellows. And now, my lady, if you will kindly divest yourself of your garments."

"No!" she whispered.

"As you please." He shrugged. "I am sure that Josh and Henry will be more than happy to do the honors." He pointed to Purity, addressing the two footmen. "Strip her ladyship, and be not too gentle with her in the process, for she must be taught the sharp lesson of obedience."

Purity's options were few, and she scarcely had time to make a choice. The grinning giants were almost upon her, their hands outstretched to take hold of her garments. It was too late now to acquiesce to Davenport's demand and undress herself. She could stand and submit with what dignity she could muster. She could close her eyes and put up no resistance when they stripped her. Or she could fight.

Fear—the fear engendered by the looks in their eyes, by the grins of bestial lust upon their faces—drove her to fight.

She backed away from them till she could go no farther, till her shoulders came up against the hard wall. And there she made her stand. The first one to make a snatch at her wrist she clawed in the face with the fury of a wildcat. He howled with pain and anger. The other—the black—seized the neck of her bodice and pulled it down to the waist, bearing her breasts.

The odious Davenport settled himself in an easy chair to watch his minions strip and deflower a woman of quality: one of that breed whom he both hated and envied. He hated them for their easy assumption of superiority to him and the remainder of the lower orders; he envied them because, for all his riches, he knew—come coveted title or no—that he would never be able to counterfeit their unmistakable air of aristocracy.

It pleased him that Purity struggled. He called scorn upon the men when they flinched from her raking fingernails. He lusted when her breasts emerged. He settled himself more comfortably in his seat when, having torn off the last bits of her gown, they carried her, still kicking and flailing, to the sofa.

His breathing became more labored when, finding that they were unable to so arrange her limbs that the first of them could take her, they resorted to brutality. Teeth bared with bloodlust, one of them pummeled her with his bunched fists, hammered at the soft flesh of her torso, and struck a blow to the side of her head that rendered her unconscious across the sofa back.

And there, while she lay prone, he took her with savage force; after he was done, the other followed.

And when they had repeatedly had their ways with her, and their lewd master wearied of the spectacle, they threw her cloak to her and bundled her roughly out into the night, as if she were some paid-off and discarded strumpet.

Stumbling homeward, her head throbbing, every drawn breath an agony from her cruelly bruised ribs, naked and violated beneath the concealing cloak, it was, nevertheless, her spirit that was the more deeply wounded. And a resolve had formed in her mind, which she repeated, over and over again through clenched teeth: "I'll not submit again! No man shall use me like that—not for the whole world!"

Chastity's love for Cornelia had all the innocence of a first love. To catch Cornelia's eye and attention was everything. Failing that, she would furtively spy on her through her fingers and see her moving, speaking, touching things. She longed, above all, for the brush of her hand, accidentally, perhaps, across her own hand or cheek.

At night—or, rather, the times when they went to bed together, for there was neither night nor day in the shuttered old house—after they had made love and Cornelia was asleep, it was the most exquisite pleasure for Chastity merely to lie there in the darkness and listen to her breathing. Perhaps she would put out a hand to caress her hair or her cheek—but gently as swansdown, so as not to awaken her. And she treasured the warmth and sweetness of lying side by side, to know her soft body was so near.

Wakefulness brought fresh delights. Chastity greatly enjoyed seeing Cornelia in beautiful clothes and pretty colors. And it was a special pleasure for Chastity to wear something that her loved one had just cast off, with the warmth and scent of her body still in it.

And then there were the small intimacies, made rare and beautiful by her love for Cornelia. There were such things as brushing each other's hair, buttoning garments for each other, or dabbing scent on a satin cheek or between her breasts. It was delightful, also, to watch Cornelia bite into an apple, unbraid her hair and shake it free, stand admiring herself in front of a pier glass, naked perhaps, comparing her shape with hers, wishing she were lovelier for her sake.

Such was the innocent quality of Chastity's love for Cornelia.

They ate *en famille,* in a dining room on one of the upper floors. Madeleine sat at the head of the table, with Cornelia on her left and with she who now answered to the name of Elizabeth on her right. There was always a cover laid at the far end of the table, together with a fine, masculine-looking "carver" chair —but the place was never occupied, and no allusion was ever made to the absent one.

Quintin served at the table, and this seemed right and proper to the girl Elizabeth, who, now that Cornelia had replaced him in her needs and affections, was able to look upon him as merely a friendly servant.

With Madeleine, she always felt a certain constraint. It stemmed from the fact that Cornelia addressed her always as "Mama" and encouraged Elizabeth to do likewise—but the latter found she could not. Her first quarrel with her lover was brought about by this shortcoming on her part. It took place during a meal.

Madeleine said, "Are you happy with us here, Elizabeth?"

"Yes . . . yes, I am," responded the other timidly.

"Yes, *Mama!*" snapped Cornelia. "Heavens, girl, I've told you time and again to call her Mama."

"I . . . I'm sorry." Tears were welling in the girl Elizabeth's pansy-dark eyes and her delicate lower lip was trembling.

"Don't apologize to me," said Cornelia. "Apologize to Mama, and say the word, like I told you."

"Please, Cornelia." The tears were falling fast. "Please, I . . ."

"Please! Please! Please-Cornelia-this, and please-Cornelia-that! I'm tired of your whining ways from morning till night, forever making cow's eyes and pleading for my attentions!" Cornelia's mouth was a thin line, and red spots of anger appeared on her cheeks.

"Cornelia!" Madeleine's single eye flashed fury at her daughter.

"Ooooh!" Bursting into uncontrollable sobs, choking into her napkin, the girl who answered to the name of Elizabeth rose to her feet and, with a despairing cry, ran to the door, threw it open, and went out. They heard her footfalls rapidly descending the stairs.

"Now look what you've done, you little fool!" blazed Madeleine. "Get after her. Calm her down. Make up with her."

"I'm sick of that creature," responded Cornelia, her face sullen and truculent, and she seemed in no mood to obey her mother. "Why do I have to be cooped up in this hateful old house, day and night, with *that* stupid creature following me with her eyes everywhere I go, in everything I do? Do you know that she always carries around one of my stockings with her? I spied her yesterday, stroking it against her cheek and cooing like a baby. She's mad, that's what she is—mad, I tell you!"

"Not mad, merely . . . *persuaded*." The interjection came from Quintin. He was leaning back against the serving table behind Cornelia, his neatly shod feet crossed, arms folded, a study in elegant and unruffled repose that complemented the quiet sibilance of his tones. He addressed the girl with mild patience, as one addresses a promising pupil who has made only one small error. "With very great care, we have persuaded her that we are the only friends she has in the world and that without us she will swiftly return to cold, naked darkness. You, Cornelia, are a very important extension of that persuasion. Do you not understand?"

"Well . . ." Cornelia's mouth was still truculent, pouting.

"Damn you, little bitch!" Her mother's open hand took her full across that mouth. "When I think of how we've worked and schemed for this! When I think of what there is at stake—and all to be put in jeopardy by a selfish, troublesome creature whom I had the misfortune to bear and suckle!"

"Aaaaaw!" wailed Cornelia, clasping her hands to her mouth and wailing again when she saw splatters of bright blood upon her fingers. "Look what you've done to me!"

"On my word, I will kill you with my own hands if you do not obey me—and instantly!" cried her mother, pointing to the open door. "Go after her and patch things up. You know how to do it—there's no one better, you debauched little bitch. It may well be that your foul temper has ruined everything, that we have lost her trust and will have to begin the whole process all over again. I hope not—for your sake! Now—get you gone!"

Cornelia might still have defied her mother, but Quintin's soft hands came down upon her shapely shoulders.

"Do as Mama says, my dear," he said. "There will be all the time and all the opportunities in the world for you when this matter is brought to a conclusion. These four walls are your prison now, you may think. Think of them, rather, as an antechamber to a splendor beyond all your imaginings."

The girl softened immediately—and Madeleine bit her lip in chagrin to see it.

"I'll do it for you, dear Quintin," she said, and she immediately rose and ran out of the room, slamming the door behind her, and with not so much as a glance toward her mother.

"Bitch!" grated Madeleine. And again: "Bitch!"

"You are too harsh in your judgments, my dear," said Quintin, pouring himself a glass of wine over by the serving table. "Always striving for perfection. The complete perfectionist. You were ever thus. One must learn"—he held the brimming glass up to the candlelight and squinted up through the ruby redness of the wine—to work with imperfect, intractable material. By the way, I think we should offer some encouragement and consolation, however small, to Lady Landless."

"Why so?" demanded Madeleine.

"My information is that she was brought, the other evening, to Davenport's house," said Quintin. He took a sip of the wine and rolled it around his palate appreciatively. "Considering Davenport's proclivities, I would not suppose for an instant that Lady Landless found the experience tremendously—how to put it?—*congenial.*"

"Davenport!" The single eye flashed with contempt. "I sometimes wonder if we really need that swine!"

Quintin drained the last drop from his wineglass and wiped his thin lips with a cambric handkerchief.

"With respect, my dear, we shall possibly stand in need of his fortune when the time comes," he said. "As to the man . . . well . . . the fortune having been handed over, we can speedily dispose of the donor. I

163

really must remember to order another dozen cases of this excellent claret."

Madeleine laughed.

"You were speaking of consolation and encouragement," she said. "What form do you have in mind?"

"I thought . . . a letter," said Quintin, musing, "a short note from the beloved adopted daughter, informing Mama Purity that she is in good health, is being well looked after, *et cetera, et cetera*. After all, it won't come amiss. The more times that Lady Landless, convinced that her adulterous conduct is furthering the girl's benefit, makes free of her no doubt manifold favors"—here he wrinkled his aquiline nose in distaste—"the better for our advantage."

"You are right—as always," said Madeleine. "And there remains one other question to be decided between us, Quintin."

"About . . . *him?*"

They both looked to the far end of the table—to the empty place laid there, to the empty chair.

"Soon, I think," said Madeleine.

"You are right," said Quintin.

"Is it safe, is it prudent, to bring them together?" demanded Madeleine.

Quintin pursed his lips and stroked his smooth chin thoughtfully.

"There are . . . hazards," he ventured.

"Indeed, there are!" cried Madeleine. "What if he should . . ."

"We shall have to ensure that he does not," said Quintin.

"In any event, it's not yet necessary that they should meet," said Madeleine.

"Quite so," Quintin agreed. "We will take care of that when the time comes. By the way, I shall be seeing him tonight."

She looked at him in some surprise.

"So soon again? How the months do fly past. How many meetings have been held up to now?"

"Twelve," replied the other. "Tonight will be the thirteenth." He smiled thinly. "Considering that there are thirteen participants, there is a certain . . . rightness in the number, don't you think?"

One's whole world was broken apart, and one was back in the chill darkness, alone, naked, stinking, frightened, haunted by demons that came out of the blackness and devoured one's flesh. . . .

"Elizabeth! Elizabeth, darling, where are you?"

That beloved voice, the voice that had once only murmured words of sweet endearment. She opened her eyes, peered through the chinks of her fingers, and blinked away her tears.

"Elizabeth, darling, how silly of you to hide in the cupboard. Come out, do. Oh, my dearest, you are all covered with cobwebs, all in your lovely hair. I will brush them off with my hand. And you've been crying. Let me wipe your eyes. Oh, you silly, silly, darling girl. What shall I do with you?"

Wonder of wonders, Cornelia's arm was around her, and her hand was gently dabbing her cheek with a handkerchief. And now Cornelia's soft lips were seeking hers. A moist, soft tongue was flickering playfully between one's lips, tantalizingly.

"How could I ever have been so cruel to my darling little goose?"

"Cornelia . . . Cornelia, how I love you!"

"Yes, my darling girl, yes."

Her hands were pulling the shift from one's shoulders, cupping both of one's breasts, gently squeezing, teasing the nipples till one's breath was robbed clean away and one was sobbing. And then the hand that stole to the small of the back! The divine excitement!

165

"Cornelia!"

"Yes, my darling. Yes! Now!"

Hand in hand, they stole to the bed. With trembling fingers, she divested Cornelia of her own shift, rendering her nude to one's hands, one's lips.

"Snuff out the candles," whispered Cornelia. "It's so much more exciting and mysterious in the dark. We can make believe so beautifully. What game of make-believe shall we play tonight, my Elizabeth?"

"Anything . . . anything . . ."

"Let us be . . . dancers. That's it. We are dancing nude for some Oriental potentate—the caliph of Baghdad of the *Thousand and One Nights*. We are dancing for his pleasure, because we are beautiful and nude. What he doesn't know"—she paused to place a kiss of ineffable tenderness upon lips as moist and eager as her own—"what he doesn't know, my darling, is that we are *lovers*."

Cornelia began to hum snatches of a languid, dreamy melody, and she felt herself become caught up in the rhythm. Lying side by side, arms entwined around each other, they swayed their hips in time to the music, loins pressed to loins. Then Cornelia speeded up the tempo so that their swaying became a frenzied threshing. And then they broke apart, each seeking the other in a different embrace; kissing, touching, moaning; borne high on a great tumbling wave of passion.

She was Elizabeth, and in love. All doubts and all fears were gone. She was locked in her lover's embrace, shamelessly accepting and giving without shame in return.

And now Cornelia was mounting to a peak of ecstasy, and one must guide her there, forgetting for a while one's own body, and taking pleasure in the act of giving; coaxing her on, subtly and with infinite gentleness. Gentleness as soft as eyelashes. Tenderness that could scarcely be felt, but which was carrying Cornelia to a paradise beyond imagining. . . .

The door was flung open!

A blaze of light from a four-branch candlestick flooded the room with the dusky-pink hangings and mercilessly picked out the two sprawled figures lying upon the four-poster bed with its curtains of cloth-of-gold.

"What goes on here? Not that I need to ask!"

Two pairs of eyes looked out at the newcomer. Cornelia's glance was slack, satiated, uncaring; the girl astride her was staring in horror and shame.

"Hello, Mama," drawled Cornelia.

She who answered to the name of Elizabeth, hastily disentangling her limbs from those of her companion in shame, hastened to cover up her breasts and her exposed thighs from the woman's single, regarding eye.

"Elizabeth . . . Elizabeth," said Madeleine softly, as if more in pain than anger.

"Please, I . . . that is, we . . ." She glanced in anguish to Cornelia for guidance. The other girl had scarcely moved; she lay with her arms behind her head, her breasts upthrust, her long and elegant legs shamelessly sprawled out, regarding her mother questioningly.

"My girls—my dearest girls," said Madeleine brokenly. And then, unbelievably, she was weeping tears of pure joy and, laying aside the candlestick, had moved forward and taken the girl called Elizabeth around her bare shoulders and was pressing the flushed young cheeks to her shapely bosom. "Oh, my darlings, how happy you have made me."

Madeleine's arms were comforting, her soft breasts reassuring. She looked up into Madeleine's face, seeking to read there the meaning of the woman's words.

"We have made you . . . *happy?*"

"Yes, my dearest. Happy." The tears continued to flow, and she was smiling through her tears. "Happy, with all my heart and soul that you have both found love. For it is written in your eyes, both, and in your adorable faces that you have been blessed with the most wonderful gift on earth—the gift of perfect love."

"And you are not angry with us?"

"Angry, child? Why?" She touched the smooth young cheek.

"You don't think that what I was doing to Cornelia was . . . evil?"

"Evil?" The single, startling eye was closed, as if in mortal anguish, and the finely wrought brow was furrowed. "Oh, my poor, innocent, darling girl. What do you know of evil? I will tell you of evil, my Elizabeth, and you will judge for yourself if the things you were doing to your beloved Cornelia, the tender acts of devotion you were bestowing upon her, could ever be described as evil. Sit down, my sweet child—there, beside Cornelia. Hold her hand if you will. Embrace her. You need feel no shame or embarrassment before me, nor attempt to cover your nudity. My heart overspills with love and understanding for you both."

"Are you going to tell us a story, Mama?" Cornelia asked primly, her face expressionless.

"Yes, my darling," replied her mother, "for both your sakes, but mostly for Elizabeth's sake—she, who is so innocent that she cannot distinguish beauty from evil."

"Please continue, Mama," said Cornelia.

"How to begin?" said Madeleine. She rose and, pressing a hand to her brow, commenced to pace the floor before them. "Shall I tell you how I was introduced to evil? I think you must hear it—though it will destroy your innocence forever."

"I was born in one of London's worst rookeries. I

was the fifth child out of a brood of eight, and six of them died in infancy. My father they hanged at Tyburn for stealing a handcart. On the day he was tried, another wretch was transported for life because he killed a man. English justice has more regard for a man's property than for his life. I watched my father die. He did not even have a penny to pay the hangman so that the fellow would pull on his legs and shorten his agony. How the crowd laughed. I was six at the time. "When I was eleven, my mother sold me into whoredom."

"Oh, no!"

Madeleine nodded gravely. "Into whoredom, my dear Elizabeth. I cannot find it in my heart after all these years to lay any blame upon her for what she did. She and my young brother and I were all starving, and our home was an archway. Along with all the rest of London's teeming outcasts, we slept outdoors, winter and summer. I was—by some miracle—pretty and well-formed for my age. She wept when she let me go, my mother did. She begged me to forgive her for what she had done. She told me that I should never starve again. I never did.

"The whoremaster's loutish son, it was, who took my maidenhead. For that his father whipped him, for there are rich old men in London who will pay up to fifty guineas to deflower a young virgin, and the younger the better. Strange, how old men crave to slake their lusts upon the young. It seemed to me that as I grew older, the men who lay atop me grew younger. By then I had grown hardened to the game. But, oh! I shall never forget the first time that I, a frightened child of eleven, was bundled into a room where there awaited a grinning old man with a great belly and . . ." She buried her face in her trembling hands.

"Don't say anymore! Don't upset yourself further, I beg you!" cried the girl called Elizabeth.

Madeleine drew a deep breath. "I must finish it," she said. "For your sakes, I must show you what evil is about, so that you will know the quality of the beauty that has touched your own lives.

"I have spoken of evil. Lust is evil . . . the lust that drives a man—or a woman—to the most foul sin of all: the sin of hypocrisy. Some of the men I have spoken of, the men who slaked their lusts upon my unwilling young body, were personages of high respectability: fathers of families, good churchgoers, chairmen of this and that. There was once a clergyman, and I will not sully your ears by telling you of the act I was obliged to perform upon him. And there was . . . a woman . . ." Her voice faltered and broke.

"Please don't go on! Not for our sakes! Beg your mother not to go on, Cornelia. We can't let her torture herself like this!"

Cornelia said nothing. She lay with her arms pillowed behind her head, watching her mother with unwavering eyes.

Presently, Madeleine said, "There are none so vile, so steeped in lust and hypocrisy, as your rich, idle women of quality. I met one such. Her name was a household word twenty years ago, for her charitable works, her great virtue. Virtue and charity—hah!

"I tell you, that woman—and there were many like her in what they please to call 'high society,' and there still are—would go to bed with any man who cast an eye upon her. Nor was she content with men.

"The whoremaster took me to her, to her fine house in the country. Money changed hands. I was left alone with this woman. Handsome, she was, with a body like the Roman goddess Juno when she was stripped. Beneath all the beauty was a vileness that belies description. The things I was obliged to do! They bore no comparison, my dears, to the sweet and tender tributes you two have paid to each other's loveliness.

"I recoiled from her. I pleaded to be spared. She would have none of it. When I persisted in my refusals, milady took a whip—it was a hunting whip—and hit me with it, lashing my buttocks and my thighs, my budding young breasts, my face . . . "

"Oh, no! *No!*"

Madeleine's hand went up and pulled aside the black patch that marred her otherwise perfect countenance.

She who answered to the name of Elizabeth screamed in horror.

There was a scar across what had been Madeleine's right eye, and the eye itself was dead and opaque, white—like the eye of a dead fish.

"This was done to me," said Madeleine, "because I would not satisfy that women's lust. She—who lusted after every man who looked her way—did this to a young girl for hesitating to pander to her lewd caprices, this woman of virtue and charity!"

"Horrible—horrible!"

"Yes, Mama, it is rather horrible," drawled Cornelia. "Cover it up, do."

"My dears," said Madeleine, replacing the black patch, "I will tell you this: throw not a stone at a poor whore, for a whore gives herself in order to eat. The evil ones are those who give themselves for lust, or who procure the bodies of others to serve their lust. And the worst sinners of all are those who hide their lusts behind a veneer of hypocrisy. Will you remember that always, my darlings? Will you, Elizabeth?"

"Oh, yes—yes!" responded the other fervently.

"And you, Cornelia?"

"Yes, Mama."

"Then I have not recalled all those bitter memories

171

in vain," said Madeleine. She reached down and touched both girls tenderly on their smooth cheeks. "And the end of my story is a happy one, as Cornelia will confirm. I was saved from my life of degradation by the love of a splendid man—a man who took me to himself, despoiled as I was, disfigured as I was, and raised me up with his great love. That man, Elizabeth, is the father of your beloved Cornelia, and you will meet him one day soon."

"That is a beautiful ending," whispered the girl Elizabeth. "Beautiful!"

"And that is why, my dears, I tell you that the discovery of your love for each other has brought me great happiness," said Madeleine. "For, unlike me, you have not had to pass through evil in order to find love. Love has come to you, in all its truth and beauty, while you are still young and innocent. Love each other, do. You have my fondest blessing."

She stooped and kissed both girls' foreheads.

"And now, Elizabeth," she said, "there is something I want you to do for me."

"Anything—anything!" said the other fervently.

"I should like you to write a short letter," said Madeleine. "Now. Tonight. Will you do that?"

"A letter? Of course."

"That's a good girl. Now, put on your shift, my dear, and go up to my sitting room, where there is pen and ink and paper. Go now, my dear. I have something to say to Cornelia, and I will join you in a few moments."

"Yes, of course."

Madeleine's single eye covertly watched the girl as she put the thin shift over her head and covered her nudity. She followed her progress across the room to the door, till it shut behind her.

A moment's silence—and then she laughed: a full-throated laugh; a sensual, self-regarding laugh; her head was thrown back, her splendid bronze hair falling around her shoulders.

Cornelia shifted her position and stretched her lissome limbs luxuriantly.

"Mama, you never cease to astonish me," she said. "The stage lost a great actress in you."

"You liked my performance, daughter, dear?" asked Madeleine, seating herself down upon the bed and stroking Cornelia's hair.

"Wonderful," responded the other. "I particularly enjoyed the part about you being saved from a life of degradation by the love of a splendid man. Really, Mama, when one thinks of the man in question . . . "

Her mother's self-satisfied smile died on the instant. Then she shrugged.

"No matter," she said. "The story served its purpose. We almost have her now. One more push, one more rude awakening, and she will be ours. Kiss me, dearest."

"Of course, Mama," responded the other. Sitting upright, she put her arms around the older woman and kissed her full upon the mouth. As the embrace grew more protracted, her small hand stole across Madeleine's shoulder, then down the neck of her bodice. Her fingers slipped between material and soft flesh, busily probing. . . .

Madeleine's breathing became labored. Parting her lips, she took in the tiny, darting tongue that was offered.

With a pert smile, Cornelia drew apart from her.

"Time's a-wasting, Mama, mine," she said brightly. "And you have business upstairs with dear Elizabeth."

"You are a bitch, Cornelia!" cried the other. "A vile, licentious little bitch!"

"I take after you, Mama, dear," was the cheerful retort. "And you taught me all I know."

173

At about the same time, Quintin let himself out of the front door of the many-storied house in the St. Giles's "Holy Land." It was nearing midnight. The full moon hung over the rookery, painting its grimness with a silvery light and mercifully shadowing the stinking ditches and the eyeless hovels. From the distance, through a low arch, came the sound of voices raised in drunken song. They were indulging in another night of revelry in the Hare and Hounds.

At Quintin's sharp whistle, a small covered carriage drawn by one horse emerged from the shadows. Perched upon the driver's box was the same sly-avised fellow in seedy black and a slouch cap who had guided Purity Landless to that place.

"Where to, guv'nor?"

"Try one of the taverns on Charing Cross Road. Not one we've been to before, mind you."

"Right you are, guv'nor," was the hoarse response.

Quintin entered the carriage, which rattled off, over the bridge, through the archway of the tunnel, and out into the heart of the rookery. Huddled in a doorway, a group of urchins watched its passing, but they made no move to molest it; both driver and carriage were well known—and feared—in the "Holy Land."

They were soon out of the rookery and into a rutted road lined with cheap theaters and alehouses, with colored lanterns picking out crude posters that advertised Chinese jugglers, performing dogs, strong men, a wild creature from Borneo, *poses plastiques* and—incongruously—*Hamlet,* by Mr. William Shakespeare. Quintin scanned every tavern and alehouse they passed. Presently, he tapped on the partition.

"That will do—the Black Dog."

"Right you are, guv'nor."

He alighted, and with an injunction to the driver to wait there, he entered the tavern and was immediately assaulted by a fury of sound, bright lights, and the stink of stale ale, sweat, and powder. He elbowed his way through a press of men and women who drank, caroused, kissed, and mauled each other's bodies till he found a table alone in an alcove.

His narrow eyes scanned the crowded room, taking in all the women and young girls. He rejected those of unpleasing face and figure, those whose looks and bearing lacked the certain wantonness that he sought. He was all but despairing, and he was about to rise and take his leave when his glance lit upon a young chit of a thing in cheap finery of soiled taffeta, bows, and furbelows, whose over-generous bosom all but overspilled her bodice. She made a half-jesting slap at the hand of a roisterer who sought to paw her —and met Quintin's eye.

Instantly, her hand went up to pat her side curls, and a false smile broke out across her vulgar, pretty face. Though plainly clad in his habitual somber black, Quintin was possibly the best-attired man in the tavern. Furthermore, he was looking at her with more than special interest. Giving her bodice a smart, downward tug, she approached him through the crowd with a complicated, hip-swaggering walk. She placed her none-too-clean hands upon his table and leaned forward, the better to show off her considerable wares.

" 'Ello, loved one. Goin' to buy a gel a drink, are you?"

Quintin signaled a passing servingman.

"Sit down," he told the girl.

"Eeooow! You're a bully, an' no mistake!" complained the girl, but she sat down nevertheless. "I can see I'm goin' to 'ave a lot o' trouble wiv you—I 'ope. . . ." She fluttered her painted eyelashes at Quintin, who busied himself by ordering two brandies from the servingman.

"Brandy!" cried his new friend. "Ain't you

a-frowin' your money around, loved one? Wassit—your old dad popped 'is clogs an' left you a fortune, eh?"

"Do you want to earn five guineas?" said Quintin.

She had large, prominent, and rather watery, blue eyes. They opened wide.

"Garn!" she jeered. "Pull the other leg, it's got bells on! Five guineas—garn!"

Two gold coins fell upon the table before her, rolled a little way, spun around together, then stopped by her fingers.

"Two in advance," said Quintin. "The remainder will be yours when you have carried out your side of the bargain."

"And wassit, eh?" Her native, slum-bred caution asserted itself. "Wassit I gotta do for five guineas, eh? I'm a decent gel, I am. . . ."

"You are a whore," said Quintin flatly, "and an amateur at that. For a pint of ale, you will let any man squeeze your boobs. For sixpence, you will handy-dandy up against a wall in the pouring rain."

"Eeooow!" cried the girl, affronted.

"I was gravely mistaken in you," said Quintin. "However, it is not too late . . . ." His hand reached out for the two guineas.

"Oh, don't let's be 'asty, mister. No, don' let's be 'asty!" she cried, scooping up the coins and slipping them deftly into her bodice. She smiled coquettishly. "Wassit I gotta do then, loved one?" she asked. "What's your pleasure, then?"

Quintin winced. "I am not concerned—directly—in this transaction," he said. "You will be required to perform a certain service for my master."

"You a servant, then?" said the girl.

"I am a servant," said Quintin. "And I propose to take you to my master's house, which is not far—just out in the country—at once. There is a carriage waiting outside, and you will be returned here when the transaction is finished."

The girl grinned. "Why didn't you say so at first?" she said, "instead of all the beatin' around the bush. You wants me to go an' have a handy-dandy wiv your master, who's a fancy gennleman wiv plenty o' guineas to throw around. What are we a-waitin' for?"

"What, indeed?" agreed Quintin. "Here is the brandy. Drink it up and let's be gone."

The girl raised her glass, toasting him.

"Wish you a long life!"

"And yourself," murmured Quintin, peering into the amber depths of the spirit and smiling thinly to himself.

Minutes later, they went out into the night . . . and she was off to her last journey on earth.

Chapter Six

Purity took to sleeping late. The fears that haunted her wakeful nights did not grow less oppressing in the dawn; but in that hour when human resistance is lowest, and when the graveyard beckons the sick, she would slip into an uneasy slumber for a few hours.

One morning, a few days after the shocking events at the house of the millionaire beast Davenport, she awoke to see bright sunlight streaming in through the cracks in the window shutters. Her clock told her it was past ten. She rang for the maid to bring her coffee, toast, and marmalade.

With the breakfast tray came a letter.

She instantly recognized the neat, feminine hand that had penned her name and address on the outside of the letter.

The woman Madeleine had communicated with her again! Could it be, could it mean, that she was planning to return Chastity? Had her dreadful sacrifices finally found their reward? With trembling fingers and prayers upon her lips, she ripped open the letter.

Her heart turned over to see only three short lines

within. But, wonder of wonders, before she read even a word, she was able to recognize Chastity's round, girlish writing:

> *I am safe and well. Please*
> *do not let anything change,*
> *or I shall be very unhappy.*

There was no more: no "darling Mama Purity," no "Your ever-loving and adoring Chastity." Nothing.

But still her heart rejoiced. The child was safe and well. Her sacrifices had not been in vain. Furthermore—the cryptic message, which might mean nothing to an outsider, written clearly for her to see—she was being warned that on no account must she cease her efforts to obey Madeleine's instructions and she must continue to play the whore with all who presented the hated goat's-head medallion. Nor would she disobey! Forgotten was the resolve that she had formed during her agonized return to her home after her ordeal at the hands of Davenport's lackeys, when she had had to steal into her own house like a thief in the night, naked as she was, bruised and disheveled as she was, lest one of the servants noticed the mistress's condition.

Purity leaped out of bed. While bathing and dressing, she reread Chastity's brief communication a score of times, weighing every word and phrase, as one will dissect and devour a love letter, seeking to find a fresh nuance, a hidden meaning.

No, there was no doubt about it. Chastity was safe and well. And she must continue. That was the plain and unvarnished content.

She regarded herself ruefully in a pier glass, stroking her painful side, where the footman's big bunched fist had bruised her: three large and unsightly patches of discoloration were under her left breast and beneath her arm.

What would her next unwanted lover think of that? She shuddered. . . .

Mark had taken to being out most of the day. She knew that all his energies were directed toward keeping the search for Chastity going at full strength. He took luncheons and dinners with any person of influence and position, scorning the company of no one, however distasteful to him personally, in order to secure his ends. And the strain of his efforts was beginning to show. On the few occasions that Purity had seen him since he had given her the list of names, she had noticed that his face had grown haggard, with worry lines down each cheek and telltale pouches beginning to form under his eyes. Furthermore, she gained the distinct impression—from his unsteady footfalls mounting the stairs when he returned home late at night—that he was drinking heavily.

She would have given the world to have been able to comfort him with her love. But, as the weeks wore on, as her guilt increased, it became more and more out of the question. Her guilt, her remorse, her sense of being unclean—all these erected a barrier that she was unable to surmount. And Mark remained in his own room, and he avoided her eyes as much as he was able to.

She continued to introduce herself to personages on the list. It was indirectly through this activity that she met her next partner in licentiousness.

It happened this way: she was going to leave her calling card with a retired general's wife—a lady of impeccable credentials who lived just around the corner from Half Moon Street, in Berkeley Square. The day was fine, so Purity resolved to get some fresh air and walk. On the corner of the square, she was accosted by a gentleman of good appearance who, pointing to the medallion that hung across her bosom, claimed her favors as a member of the society. And he claimed them immediately.

He was, he told her, a Mr. Rupert Steadman, a gentleman of leisure, with interests in London. His Mayfair house, to which he took her, spoke volumes for the owner's wealth. The bed upon which he possessed her—and with commendable gentleness—had been imported from France and had formerly been owned by Napoleon Bonaparte's favorite sister, the alluring Princess Pauline Borghese. She remained with Steadman till dusk, by which time he had enjoyed Purity's peerless body in ever conceivable manner that lay within the bounds of civilized sensibility. And at the end, he obliged her to join him in an act so monstrous, so at variance with the manner in which he had previously used her, that she formed the opinion that there was insanity in the mind of Mr. Rupert Steadman.

Returning to Half Moon Street by hackney cab (for even elegant and fashionable Mayfair was no place for a woman after dusk), her mind and body shamed and degraded, it occurred to her that, save for young Gervase Browninge, all her passing paramours had been tainted with a certain vileness, a cruelty of spirit. And even Browninge dreamed of slaughtering girls; she had not forgotten his crying out during his nightmare.

Purity's next encounter followed hard on the heels of the last. Angus, Lord Houghton, left his card at 17A Half Moon Street and called himself the following day. He was another of those who had become aware that the beautiful Purity Landless was available to members of the society. Indeed, he frankly admitted that she had been highly recommended by a fellow member, though he did not give that gentleman's name.

Silencing Purity's protests, Lord Houghton declared that he would take his pleasure of her in her own bedchamber; nor would her frantic declarations that Mark might return at any hour, that the servants could not fail to be aware that she had taken a strange man up to the third floor, shift him from his resolve. Together they climbed the stairs, with Lord Houghton bearing with him a small leather case, which, upon opening in the sanctuary of her former connubial bedchamber, was revealed to contain a whip.

Ten stripes did Lord Houghton lay across Purity Landless's bare back and shoulders, and he was with difficulty restrained from also flogging her breasts. He finally settled for a markedly vicious attack upon her shapely rump. This done, and he having aroused himself to a high tide of passion, he threw himself upon the trembling, tearful woman and brutally raped her. And through it all, through the cruel flogging and the violation that followed, Purity was unable to utter a sound; she lay with her teeth gritted and with a silent scream echoing and reechoing in her temples.

That night she made a pile of all the clothes that she had worn during, or prior to, the occasion of her ordeals, beginning with the silk evening gown that she had herself removed for the delight of the Marquess of Strachan, and ending with the simple hostess gown that Lord Houghton had ripped from her shrinking shoulders a few hours ago. This done, she summoned her maid and told her to have them burned.

Tomorrow, she told herself, she would begin anew, with a fresh wardrobe that had not been defiled.

Unlike her body. . . .

In later years, the events of the following day became—like a design scratched upon a copper plate by the limner's needle point and then bathed in acid

—more deeply etched upon Purity's mind, with no diminishing by time's benign erosion.

It began like any other day in that dark period of her life—that is to say, with anxiety overlaid with remorse, with guilt tinged by anguish. Only one circumstance lightened her spirits: she was going to start her life afresh—at least in the sartorial sense—with a new wardrobe.

She had ordered a carriage for ten-thirty, and the footman who came to inform her that it was ready seemed overcheerful in a sly sort of way. There was a sidelong twinkle in his eye when he bowed and addressed his mistress; and it seemed to Purity that he had some trouble in preventing himself from laughing aloud. However, she dismissed the incident from her mind, telling herself that he had obviously heard some jest or other down in the servants' hall. She had forgotten the matter by the time she got into the carriage. The coachman was not grinning; he was a dour fellow who would have made an excellent driver of a funeral hearse.

Madame Dupuis's dressmaker's shop on Bond Street had been patronized by Purity ever since she came to London. Madame herself had died a few years previously, but the establishment had been taken over by her younger sister, Mademoiselle Hubert, who continued the tradition of fine workmanship allied to the Parisian's touch of sophisticated elegance.

The arrival of Milady Landless, the shop's most esteemed customer, always caused a stir. There might be customers of more exalted birth and title, wealth and distinction; but Milady Landless was one of the acknowledged beauties of her generation, and there was not a seamstress, a *vendeuse,* or a pale little apprentice from the workshop downstairs who did not steal an opportunity to creep up to the showroom and peer through the curtains at the legendary Milady Landless.

On this occasion, the stir was even more remarkable. News that Purity had arrived swiftly brought the entire establishment to look; nor was it done surreptitiously, as was customary at that discreet emporium. A row of ogling eyes greeted Purity's progress to the upstairs showroom where models of Madame Dupuis's latest "creations" were displayed, bolts of fine silks, satins, taffetas, laces, trimmings of all kinds, together with pattern books and engravings of the latest styles. And Mademoiselle Hubert herself—a prim little woman who dressed always in black bombazine, favored by French dressmakers and Parisian restaurant keepers—was there to greet milady, as always, with a deep curtsy, which was echoed by the line of fitters, under-dressmakers, and *vendeuses* standing behind her.

Purity did not notice a slight, almost imperceptible chill in Mademoiselle's greeting—at first. But she did observe that some of the women with her—principally the younger ones—bore upon their countenances the same look of suppressed mirth, of sly amusement, that she had observed on her footman's face. And, in a curious way, Purity found it somewhat disturbing.

She made her wants known to the proprietress: a couple of evening gowns, a day dress, an afternoon gown, something pretty to wear around the house. It was a substantial order that would keep Mademoiselle's seamstresses plying their swift needles for many weeks to come, and it would add greatly to the shop's profit. Why, then, did Mademoiselle Hubert receive the tidings with so little enthusiasm?

And, when it came to choosing styles, the woman flipped through the pattern books with almost an off-handed air—as if she believed in her own mind that the proposed garments would never be made, and

185

that they were merely playing out an empty charade. By that time, Purity had become quite seriously concerned about Mademoiselle Hubert's manner, and she had half a mind to ask her what was amiss. With her late sister, the old Madame Dupuis, nothing would have been easier; she and Madame had been the best of friends, always chatting away in their native French, exchanging the gossip and scandal of the town. Madame, a cheerful, bawdy body, forever used to urge Purity into necklines that bordered on the indecent, telling her that it was a sin against humanity for the most admirable *poitrine* in London to be hidden from sight behind silks and satins, and that Purity would not keep her elegant figure forever. Madame's younger sister, in those days, was seldom allowed in the showrooms, but was relegated instead to the supervision of the workroom. "A miserable soul," Madame had frequently explained. "Never touches a drop of drink, and would run a mile if a man so much as laid a hand on her spinsterly bottom. Religious. Heaven save us from religious women!"

No, decided Purity, it was out of the question for her to take Mademoiselle Hubert to task. Best to get the business over with quickly and make her departure. Something she had said, or done, had offended the woman. Well, then, if she could afford to let it interfere with her trade, the more foolish was she. One thing was certain: after the present order was completed (if it *was* ever completed, for she had no desire to present herself for fittings), Purity Landless would never darken the door of Madame Dupuis's dressmaker's establishment again.

She and Mademoiselle parted company with frigid politeness. Mademoiselle curtsied (but not very deeply), and her assistants did likewise. Every eye in the establishment followed Purity out of the door and into sunlit Bond Street, where her carriage waited.

Her coachman was talking to the liveried door-keeper of Madame Dupuis's establishment, and there was something slightly distasteful about the manner in which they were sniggering together, head to head. They sprang apart when Purity came out. The door-keeper helped her into the carriage obsequiously enough, but he did not bother to wipe the grin from his face. As for her coachman—the normally sour-visaged individual—he was shaking with suppressed laughter.

It seemed to Purity, on her way back home to Half Moon Street, that the world had gone strangely awry that morning.

She took luncheon alone, and she paid particular attention to the demeanor of those who served her: two footmen and a housemaid, with the supervising butler. The butler would not have shown, by any expression upon his impassive countenance, if his nearest and dearest were to have been hanged that day. Nothing to learn from him. The footmen, whether to hide their true feelings, or from some secret sorrow, both scowled throughout the proceedings. Only the maid betrayed herself; when her back was turned on one occasion, she emitted a distinct giggle.

"What is amusing you so greatly, Alice?" demanded Purity loudly.

The girl spun around as if she had been shot in the back.

"No-nothing, milady!" she stammered.

"Come here!" ordered Purity. "Come and stand by me."

"Yes, milady." The other hastened to obey.

As she did so, something slipped from between the bib of her apron and her bodice, where it had been hidden. It was a folded piece of pink-colored paper, which, having fallen to the floor, unseen by the girl, was instantly snatched up by the butler, who thrust it hastily into his pocket.

"What is that?" demanded Purity.

"Milady?" The butler's countenance remained impassive, as ever. But he had no control over the rush of blood that tinged his cheeks with the bright redness of acute embarrassment.

"The thing you put in your pocket—give it to me!" ordered Purity.

"Milady, it is nothing. This stupid girl . . ."

Purity extended her hand imperiously. Her head held high, marvelous eyes blazing, she reduced his bluster to silence.

"Give—it—to—me!"

Slowly, reluctantly, perhaps living in the hope that the piece of paper had lost itself within his pocket, the butler groped and grew redder. From somewhere beyond Purity's range of vision, the housemaid gave a choked sob. The two footmen were looking on in slack-mouthed horror. Purity felt a cold finger of apprehension trail its way down the length of her spine.

"Milady, please, 'tis nothing." The man was making a last, desperate attempt. "Give me leave to throw it in the fire. . . ."

Purity's hand remained outstretched, her expression bidding of no compromise. He gave her the piece of paper, which she unfolded.

What she saw there brought a cry to her lips. That done, she pressed it against her bosom, as if to prevent the others from witnessing what was printed there. Then she realized that they had probably been laughing at it all the morning—or longer, as had the rest of the servants' hall . . . and the entire staff of Madame Dupuis's (small wonder that Mademoiselle Hubert had been so frigid with her—she a religious woman!). And heaven knows who else—perhaps all London.

She drew in a shuddering breath.

"Leave me, all of you!" she commanded in an unsteady voice.

"Yes, milady."

The butler bowed, and his assistants followed suit, and the maid curtsied. The girl was in tears.

Only when the door had closed behind them, only when their footfalls had faded away, did Purity bring herself to gaze upon the vile obscenities printed upon the lurid pink sheet.

It was a caricature—a lampoon—the likes of which had been rife in the previous century, but which had all but died out through public decency. The king, when Regent and earlier as Prince of Wales, had been a favorite butt of the caricaturists and the lampooners. What bitter, sardonic sport they had made of his lechery, his gluttony, his spendthrift ways—and most of all, of his mistresses. Even popular heroes had not escaped the satirists' gravers and pens; Lord Nelson, England's darling, had been vilely lampooned for his love affair with Lady Hamilton.

The thing in her hand was in that same vile tradition. If anything, it was even worse.

The central figure in the crude engraving was—herself. The likeness was unmistakable: the blonde tresses gathered up in her characteristic Greek chignon, by which she was recognized in society and amongst the general public of the capital; her alluring figure, made more extravagant in slenderness of waist, fullness of bosom and buttocks, length of leg. They had represented her in one of the Greek-style gowns that she favored, with her breast bare and ludicrously accentuated, with nipples sticking out like chapel hat pegs. If that were not enough to point to the subject of the caricature, the ill-printed title at its head told everything to all who had doubts:

TO THE IMPURE, PURITY IS ALL THINGS
—TO *ALL* MEN!!!

The cruel pun was echoed elsewhere, in such literary perversions as—mocking *Hamlet*—"*Be thou chaste and nice, thou shalt not escape calumny. To do this, thou needs to be—Purity!!!*" There were other twisted allusions to the word "purity," gleaned from the ancient classics, even—scabrously—from the Bible. Some of them emerged, in bubble-shaped excrescences, from the mouths of a collection of males who peered in upon the central figure from doorways and through open windows. They numbered six in all and were labeled: "*The Marquess S——; Mr. Thos. H——, M.P.; The Hon. Gervase B——; Mr. Arthur D—— port; Mr. Rupert S——man; Lord Hou——n.* And all bore passable likenesses to the six members of the detestable society with whom Purity had been obliged to couple herself in shame.

The caricatured lampoon, taken all in all, was a complete exposure of her shame.

Seated in her dining room, with expensively prepared foods growing cold and uneatable all around her, with a servants' hall doubtlessly buzzing with excited speculation, with half of London, perhaps, doing likewise, Purity had only two thoughts fighting for supremacy in her mind.

The first concerned Chastity's continued safety. She speculated that since her role of amateur whore was exposed to all and sundry (And by whom, and for what reason? Did she have an enemy in London who would do such a thing? She must have!), her compact with the woman Madeleine was, in a sense, broken. Madeleine had made a great thing about obedience and secrecy. She, Purity, had obeyed to the letter. Would Madeleine believe this? Or would she suppose that, by her indiscretion, by her wagging tongue, Purity

Landless had brought the lampoon down upon herself? And how would that affect Chastity?

She recalled Chastity's plea: " . . . *do not let anything change, or I shall be very unhappy.*"

Would the lampoon bring down a terrible retribution upon Chastity's innocent head?

"Oh, my darling Chastity!" she cried aloud.

And then: "Oh, Mark—my Mark!"

He was somewhere in London, perhaps even at that living moment returning to Half Moon Street, in all haste, to confront his faithless wife with the evidence of her vile antics.

A rattle of carriage wheels in the street ouside sent Purity rushing to the window, her heart turning sick within her. It was a delivery van going past.

But he must come, sooner or later.

What to do?

Flight was her first, instinctive answer. But to where would she flee, and to what advantage? What use would it be to poor Chastity if she was nowhere to be found—if and when the woman Madeleine tried to communicate with her again? The only advantage of flight, she ruefully admitted to herself, was that she could evade the hurt in Mark's sea-blue eyes when he confronted her. . . .

Another carriage was coming down the street. She closed her eyes and willed it to pass.

It did not pass, but halted outside the door. She glanced out of the window and she saw the top of Mark's hat and his broad shoulders under a dark blue coat as he bounded up the steps two at a time and hammered for admittance.

He had seen the obscene lampoon . . . !

Not for the first time in her star-crossed existence, Pruity craved for death and oblivion in that instant, telling herself that if she had the means immediately at hand, she would have put an end to herself with a leadened pistol ball or a sharp knife. No such escape was available.

Mark flung open the door. Their eyes met. With a lurch of the heart, a harking back to days almost forgotten—days when there had been no doubts, no fears—she saw only one emotion displayed in those marvelous, sea-blue eyes . . . *love*.

"My poor darling!" he cried. "I prayed, I hoped—but I can see that you have already had that filth brought to your notice!"

The next moment he had rushed forward and taken her in his arms, and she was crying against the rough, male bulk of him, smelling his familiar, beloved odor of well-kept leather and Macassar oil.

Wonder of wonders! Splendor piled upon splendor! Mark had no thought of her guilt. All would be well. He had seen—but he had not believed. She should have known that love such as theirs does not doubt or question; but trusts unswervingly to the end. . . .

She closed her eyes, ecstatically content merely to cling to him and to be held there; all her terrors were forgotten.

He was speaking. The words intruded upon her suddenly peaceful world. "It is monstrous—monstrous! My poor darling, how could they have done such a thing to you? I will stop it, of course. The evil shall be nipped in the bud. For all that the filth is being peddled at every street corner in London for one halfpenny a time, the damage to your reputation can be restored."

She sought his face and gazed up at him through tear-misted eyes. His fine countenance was grave, determined.

"What . . . what are you going to do?" she whispered.

"Do, my darling? Why, I shall call upon all the men mentioned in that vile calumny. From each I shall demand a public admission that the innuendo in question is a foul libel and that they join with me in a condemnation of the libeler—whoever he may be."

She caught her breath in alarm. "You . . . you will do that?" she asked in shock.

"That I will," said Mark. "And should any of those gentlemen be tardy in complying with my demands, I shall demand satisfaction for your honor, and I will challenge any such man to a duel. As to the perpetrator of the calumny, he who caused the libel to be printed and disseminated, whoever he may be, I shall challenge him also—be he a gentlemen, or what passes for a gentleman. If he is one of the lower orders, I shall horse-whip him to within an inch of his life."

"Oh, no, Mark . . . *no!*" she cried. Her thoughts flew to Chastity and to Chastity's safety. It was enough that she had brought the lampoon upon herself—presumably by some indiscretion—thereby breaking her compact with Madeleine. What might follow if Mark further aggravated the situation? Imagine him demanding a denial from, say, the marquess!

Mark smiled down at her, a brave, reassuring smile, and he touched her cheek gently as he did so.

"Trust me, my darling," he murmured. "I shall do what is for the best."

"Please, Mark," she pleaded, "please, let's forget it!"

He was patient with her, understanding. "I know full well how you feel, my love," he said tenderly. "You have no wish to be filthied further by this affair, but would prefer to put it out of your mind. In your innocence, you feel that you have been sufficiently hurt already. But, my darling, it will not serve to ignore this calumny, for that would be taken, by society and by all London, as an admission of guilt. You must fight. We must both fight to cleanse your fair name.

Oh, you may say that some of the filth will stick. But the passing of time will wash away the last traces. What is important is to strike back immediately. I came home only to tell you this. And now I am going immediately to see Charlie Strachan." So saying, he kissed her gently on the mouth, then crossed the room in three swift strides.

"Mark ... I ... " she faltered.

"Yes, my darling?"

He paused at the open door, looking back across the room at her with an expression of such love and devotion as must now last her all her lifetime. She remained silent for a while to protract the glory of bathing in the splendor of his gaze. But all must have an end. . . .

"Don't go," she whispered. "Any interference on your part will only do further harm."

He was still for a few moments. Then he quietly closed the door.

"What are you trying to tell me, Purity?" he demanded in a flat voice.

"I ... "

"To whom will further harm be done if I pursue these inquiries?"

Think quickly, Purity Landless. Do you tell him everything? Do you risk Chastity's life further by revealing Madeleine's name? Answer quickly, for time is running out fast!

"To whom will further harm be done?" he repeated. "To ... *you?*"

She nodded. "Yes," she whispered.

"I see."

His face quite expressionless, he crossed over to the console table, where there stood a tray of decanters and glasses. Pouring himself a bumper measure of brandy, he gulped it down in two mouthfuls and refilled the glass. He did not invite her to join him in a

194

drink. Purity watched him fearfully. She knew well the signs and portents. Mark was about to explode with fury; only his breeding and his steely self-control was holding him back—and this he was seeking to break with the aid of the strong spirits.

She said, "Mark, I wish I could explain, but . . . "

"You *will* explain!" he snapped. "Oh, yes, you will explain, of that I promise you! Every last word! To begin at the beginning, is there one iota of truth in this . . . this filth?" He produced a copy of the lampoon from his pocket.

"Yes," she said.

"My God!" He downed the last of his brandy and poured another. "Well, let us proceed. Let us examine the gentlemen concerned, taking the estimable Marquess of Strachan, that woman-shy nobleman, with whom we dined the other week. What congress have you had with him, pray, *madame?*"

"He . . . " She could go no further, but instead lowered her gaze from the contempt in those wonderful blue eyes, already glazed with drink.

"When did he . . . whatever?"

"On . . . on the night of the dinner party, when . . . when he invited me to see his pictures," she said.

"I see. He took you up to the picture gallery and made some advances toward you, doubtlessly. Perhaps having had a little more to drink than usual, my lord marquess was emboldened to—what?—pat your *derrière?* Squeeze your admirable breasts? Tell me!"

"He . . . " She gazed at him pleadingly, her eyes streaming with tears of bitter agony.

"Oh, my God!" He threw the empty glass from him. It smashed against the far wall, and the pieces fell, tinkling, to the parquet floor. "Not *that!* You are not telling me that while I was exchanging pleasantries with my lord marquess's guests downstairs, you were upstairs having . . . " He reached her in two swift strides,

seized hold of a handful of her hair—her miraculous silver-gold hair—and forced back her head so that she was obliged to look into his eyes, to smell his brandy-ladened breath. "You are not telling me, woman, that you were upstairs having the . . . *handy-dandy?*" He spit out the common vulgarity.

"Yes," she whispered.

"By all the devils in hell!" He flung her from him, and she fell in a bruised heap in the center of the floor, where she lay, fearfully watching him as he strode over to the drink table again, picked up a fresh glass, and filled it. Nor did he turn to address her again till he had consumed the liquor. And his voice was calm, almost matter-of-fact.

"So, you have now admitted to adultery with Strachan. What next?" He referred to the pink sheet of paper that he had laid out on the console table. "Next on the list in order of presentation is Mr. Thomas Hardcourt, M.P. What congress, *madame,* have you had with him? The same?"

"I . . ."

"Answer me!"

"Yes."

"The handy-dandy?" he demanded.

"Yes."

"Might one ask when . . . and where?"

"On . . . the day he called here," she replied.

"Ah! You are telling me that you pleasured your-self with the estimable Mr. Thomas Hardcourt, M.P., here in your admirably appointed drawing room?" There was a mock smile on his face as he gestured around him. "How convenient. Upon the well-upholstered sofa, perchance?"

His taunt stung her as something almost akin to de-fiance.

"No!" she cried bitterly. "He didn't think me worthy of the sofa but he took me here, upon the floor, and across the table against which you are standing. That was the treatment I had at the hands of Mr. Hardcourt!"

"But he did not rape you? You gave yourself willingly? You did not cry out for help from the servants?"

"I did not cry out," she whispered, lowering her gaze, the thin spark of defiance dying within her like a snuffed-out candle.

"So . . . let us proceed," said Mark implacably. "The next actor in order of appearance would seem to be that young fop Browninge. Well, at least you had the pretext of his youth and undoubted masculine beauty. How was this . . . alliance . . . effected?"

The interrogation dragged on. He spared her—and himself—nothing, and he tore an admission from her lips on every score. He had to know where, when, how, and for how long. Purity answered him, haltingly at first, but, as her guilt became spread out between them, as so much filth displayed to their mutual gaze, it became less important to hesitate or prevaricate. She gave him the true and unvarnished facts about each and every one of her encounters, omitting only the fact of the hateful goat's-head medallion, which was the key to the entire shameful business. By doing so, she told herself that she was protecting Madeleine and, through Madeleine, Charity. For herself she gave not a thought; her life had ended with the dying of the love light in Mark's eyes.

When he had finished, when he had heard it all, he carefully folded up the sheet of pink paper and placed it in his breast pocket.

"I have been most con-considerate to you of late, have I not, ma'am?" he demanded, demonstrating by his slurred speech that the brandy had now taken a firm hold on his wits. "Con-contingent upon the upset of our darling Chastity's disappearance, I have not —how to put it?—demanded my conjugal rights. In short, ma'am, I have not tumbled you of late. Correct?"

"Correct," she repeated. And a slow tear fell down her cheek and upon her hand.

"Yet I have been mistaken all this while," he said. "While I have been keeping myself chaste within a chaste and lonely bed, *madame*—my wife—has been tumbled by everything in breeches. Tell me, ma'am —*look at me when I address you!*—have I kept you short of money of late? You have enough to pay the housekeeping bills? Ample for your clothes, jewels, gewgaws, and so forth, eh?"

"You have been very generous—as always," responded Purity.

"Ha! So it was not for money that you played handy-dandy with all those excellent gentlemen? You have not played the whore for whorish reasons— stealing the very bread from the mouths of the professional strumpets? Answer me!"

"I have taken no money," she said bitterly. No, whores are paid; Purity Landless scarcely received a thank-you for her body.

"Then it was for *lust* that you did it, eh?" His voice was thick with barely suppressed fury. At any moment, she knew—and feared—that the bonds of reason and breeding would break, and he would explode.

She gave no answer.

"Look at me!" he shouted. Answer me this: Is there any reason, a single extenuating circumstance, any possible excuse, pretext, half-truth, white lie, pretense, subterfuge—anything that could earn you a degree of forgiveness, however slight? Answer me!"

It was her last opportunity to unburden herself of the dreadful secret. But to share it with this now violent and intemperate man might be to destroy Chastity within the hour. She visualized him gathering together his friends, his old army comrades, taking the law into his own hands, scouring the St. Giles rookery in search of Madeleine and her prisoner.

She saw, before her mind's eye, Chastity's pathetic note: *"Please do not let anything change, or . . ."*

"Well?" he demanded. "Do you have any excuse, or was it simply lust that drove you to take your pleasures elsewhere than in my bed?"

She drew in a deep, shuddering breath, then closed her eyes.

"It was . . . lust," she whispered.

When she awoke, it was nearing dusk. From where she was lying, she could see a line of starlings gathered on the eaves of the house opposite and the last pink glow of sunset.

She raised her head and winced with pain. Her temples throbbed unbearably, and the skin of her elbows hung in shreds from rough contact with the parquet floor. Her gown—the same day gown that she had worn (it seemed like another lifetime!) on her visit to the dressmaker that morning—lay in three heaps nearby, just as they had been ripped from her, rendering her naked, as she now was.

Painfully, Purity raised herself to her feet, picked up her torn skirts, and made some attempt to cover herself. The clock on the mantelpiece told her that she must have slept for several hours after having cried herself into a state of utter weariness and merciful oblivion.

After *he* had . . .

Shut out the thought!

Crossing to the door, she opened it slightly and looked out, fearful of seeing some of the servants lurking outside to catch a glimpse of the mistress. A servant does not often have the vicarious entertainment of hearing his mistress being raped by her own husband in her drawing room, nor to feast his eyes upon the wretched creature afterward. It is an experience that compensates for a lot of servitude.

There was no one in sight. Hugging the torn rags to her bosom and thighs, Purity hastily ascended the staircase to her bedchamber, went in, and locked the door behind her.

She met her reflection in the mirror. Her right eye was already darkened with a bruise. Mark had not struck her purposely. Not even half a decanter of brandy would make him so completely forget his good breeding; but in his drunken frenzy, in his pent-up lust, he had accidentally elbowed her in the face while fighting to pinion her threshing limbs and ravish her.

She had fought him, but not to resist his importunities; rather, she did so to plead with him to take her gently and lovingly, so that she could receive him in a like manner.

He had not listened to her pleas, but had raped her in the manner of a drunken soldier from a victorious army, in a city given over to sack and pillage, violently and without consideration, rutting like a male animal upon the gentle, helpless thing beneath, heedless of her tears. He had been exalting in his rampant maleness. And, when he was spent, he cast her aside and left her to weep for what was lost.

His last words came back to her, the words that he threw in contempt as he stood framed in the doorway in his shirtsleeves, unconcernedly buttoning up the flap of his pantaloons: "Now I go to salvage what is left of my honor, not, I hasten to point out, *your* honor—for *you* have no honor left! There is, however, a means by which even a cuckold may recover some few shreds of the dignity that has been stolen from him!"

With that—ice-cold, contempt-filled and hating, and completely sober—he had walked out of the house and out of her life.

"Mark, oh, Mark. How could you have done that to me, no matter what my sin?"

She molded her bruised and violated body with her hands: her breasts, which he had mauled so brutally, and her roughly used thighs. And she thought of the interminable, unforgettable hours of sweetness that he had lavished, in the past, upon those tender fruits of his delight. And she wept anew at the remembrance.

Presently, recalling his parting words once more, she was stricken with a great fear. Even at that moment, Mark might have put himself in terrible jeopardy. Things had greatly changed since the war; but the male code of honor was still deeply rooted in the eighteenth century and earlier. To "salvage one's honor" was a euphemism for "demanding satisfaction," which, in its turn, was a euphemism for the "gentlemanly" practice of dueling. Mark, to her knowledge, had fought two duels in his life. In the first he had suffered a wound, and in the second he had killed his man. The latter result may or may not have been a fluke; Mark was always the first to admit that he was a less than good shot with a pistol.

So what if . . . what if his idea of "salvaging what was left of his honor" meant that he was going to challenge *all* of the men with whom she had cuckolded him?

Purity was already snatching the first gown that came to her hand before she had answered that question in her mind. . . .

On his past record, Mark had showed a fifty-fifty chance of success. It was not a performance that augured well for his surviving—how many?—*six* duels!

She was dressed and out of the house (fortunately without encountering any of the servants) within minutes, and, since she found it impossible to secure a hackney cab in the busy evening hour, she ran all the way up Piccadilly to St. James's Street, in whose stately environs was situated Mark's club. She had toyed with the notion of going in the other direction, to Apsley House, to throw herself upon the charity of the Duke of Wellington. But wiser counsel prevailed. It was better to find Mark first, plead with him, if he would listen to her, beg him not to throw his life away upon a male caprice. And where else to find him, or to obtain any news of his likely whereabouts, but at his club?

The ancient in powdered wig and knee breeches, who guarded the hallowed portals of the Senior Cavalry Club all but succumbed to a fit of apoplexy at the sight of a person of the "inferior sex" setting foot over the threshold of this "holy ground." It had happened before, but only once in the memory of the ancient doorkeeper. This had been when Queen Caroline, estranged wife of the present sovereign (who was patron and president of the Senior Cavalry Club), had demanded admission to confront her husband, as she had similarly demanded admission to Westminster Abbey, on his coronation day, so that she might be crowned alongside him. Poor Caroline had all but talked her way into the Abbey; she had not gotten within a mile of getting into the Senior Cavalry Club!

Besides, the ancient had heard all about Lady Landless the whore! Did he not have a copy of that pink note that they were selling like hotcakes around town? Randy cow! Not that he would have said no in his prime, nor scoff at the idea of getting his hands on those fine breasts here and now. Bur Sir Mark—now, there was a fine officer and gentleman to be cuckolded by that loose mare. Nor had she gotten away scot-free with her handy-dandyfying, not if that fine black eye was any witness. Good for Sir Mark!

No, he told her sullenly, Sir Mark was not at the club. He had been in earlier, but now he had gone. Was there any gentleman who might know as to Sir

Mark's present whereabouts? ('Pon me word, woman, are you after another black eye to match the one you already have?) Well, there was Major Prendergast, with whom Sir Mark had had a long conversation. Would he bring her to Major Prendergast? No, he would not. But if Lady Landless would care to take a seat—there —and if Lady Landless would remain seated—there —he would presently fetch the major.

Purity meekly obeyed the tyrant of the Senior Cavalry Club's portals, and the latter shuffled off to find Major Prendergast.

Upon presenting himself to Lady Landless, the major stiffly informed Lady Landless that, yes, he had had some talk with Sir Mark that evening, but Sir Mark had now departed.

"Departed? To where, Major?" asked Purity.

"To . . . several destinations, ma'am," responded Prendergast.

"Upon what errand, sir?" asked Purity.

The other raised one elegant eyebrow, a gesture for which he appeared to have a facility.

"Need you ask, ma'am?" he drawled.

Resisting a surge of her Latin blood that instructed her to smack the man across his sneering mouth, she replied, "Tell me honestly, Major, is my husband intent upon issuing challenges to duels?"

"That he is, ma'am," replied Prendergast. "And he has asked me to act as principal second in all cases. I, in my turn, have delegated the responsibility of assistant second to an officer of my own regiment. He is presently accompanying Sir Mark in his round of issuing challenges—to make the detailed arrangements," he explained with an air of masculine condescension.

"When, Major, is the first duel to take place?" asked Purity. "And where?"

The officer gave it some thought. Finally, with a shrug, he replied, "Tomorrow, at dawn, in Hyde

Park. Sir Mark issued the challenge here, in the club. The other party"—he gave Purity a searching, sidelong glance—"is a member, and he was fortuitously present at that time."

"His name, sir?" asked Purity.

"Lord Houghton, ma'am," replied her informant.

The hum of bees early to work and the cawing of rooks in high branches were the only sounds to disturb the stillness of the pristine morning in Hyde Park as the first of the coaches began to arrive. Though it was early summer, there was a touch of frost; the men were not averse to a nip of brandy. There was some consultation among them, some glancing at watches.

A covered carriage turned off one of the driveways and came bounding across the frosty grass toward the group, whose eyes were directed toward it, and who exchanged knowing glances when, the window blinds of the carriage having been raised, there was revealed the face of a woman—a perfect, oval-shaped face framed in a black bonnet—gazing out at them, searching, and searching in vain.

"It is . . . her!" murmured one of the men.

"One would have thought . . . I mean, there are limits to what good taste permits. . . ."

"She is French, you know. What can one expect of a nation that spawned a damned fellow like Bonaparte?"

"Quite, quite."

As one, they turned their cloaked backs upon the covered carriage and its occupant.

Some time passed till a subsequent arrival—a tall figure on a tall horse—stirred the group to excitement.

" 'Tis Houghton! Will my lord's seconds please attend to him?"

"And here comes Landless. Sir Mark's seconds,

forward, please. Are you ready in all respects, Doctor? Where are the sabers? Excellent. Be so kind, please, to unsheath them and lay them upon the ground, side by side, both pointing in the same direction."

It was to be with the blade, and not the leadened bullet, that the duelists were to be matched. And that was to be expected, since both were cavalrymen and long experienced in the art of the saber. The two weapons lay there on the ground: beautifully fashioned killing knives with thick blades forged in sweeping curves of blue steel chased with gold and with inlaid ivory handgrips. The surgeon, who was laying out the tools of his trade, had equipped himself quite differently from the manner in which he would have prepared himself for the more conventional pistol duel; instead of scalpels and probes for extracting deeply placed bullets, he had tourniquets and staunches to stem the excessive bleeding that results from the butchery of sword slashes.

Purity had eyes only for the horse and rider approaching through the mist from the direction of Park Lane. . . .

She was out of her carriage and racing to greet Mark as he handed the reins to one of the seconds. Their eyes met. He frowned, then looked in anger and with some embarrassment toward the men, who were muttering together, some of them sneering quite openly.

"I had not thought to see you here, ma'am," he said coldly. "Be so kind, please, as to be gone—and at once."

She knew that her chances of success were slender, knew that she had intruded upon a man's world in which she was no more than unwanted chattel. But there was no escaping her need to fight to the hideous end to save the life of the man she loved.

"Please, Mark, I beg you to withdraw!" she cried.

"Withdraw . . . *withdraw?*" He stared at her blankly. "What are you asking, ma'am?"

"Mark, I have sinned," said Purity. "But I beg you not to let my sins accomplish your death. Abandon this madness. What will it profit you? If you were to succeed in your enterprise, if you were to kill all those men, their blood would not be enough to wash away my sins."

He looked down at her, head erect, blue eyes freezing her very soul.

"Ma'am, as I have said before, it is not your honor that is at stake," he declared. "You have no honor remaining. I am fighting—and I am willing to die—to prove my own."

"Mark! On my knees, I beg you!" And she fell upon her knees before him.

His revulsion was total; he backed away from her, beating aside her hands, which clutched at his coat-tails.

"*Madame,* compose yourself!" he cried. "Have you no shame?"

The men around her were openly contemptuous.

"Damned Frenchie!"

"By God, Landless has my sympathy!"

"The creature must be insane!"

Wild-eyed and frantic, Purity looked around for succor, and she saw Lord Houghton regarding her. His lordship had stripped off his coat and was rolling up the immaculate sleeves of his white lawn shirt. He was sneering at her—like the rest.

"My Lord!" she cried. "Please . . . I beg you!"

"By all the devils in hell!" exploded Mark. "Is there no limit to the shame you will bring down upon us both, woman?"

Purity paid no heed to her husband's remonstrations. Rushing to Houghton's side, she laid a hand upon his arm and recommenced her entreaties. He looked at her in amused contempt—he who had flogged and ravished her to gratify his own dark lusts.

"Lord Houghton, I ask you to withdraw from this duel!" she pleaded.

"My dear lady, that is quite impossible," he retorted.

"Why . . . *why?*" she demanded. "Why do you men do such things to each other? Your cruel and absurd customs! Your so-called honor! Lord Houghton, you have had your sport with me. Why not let that suffice? Why do you have to take up a sword against my husband? Why can you not walk away from here and refuse to have anything further to do with the matter?"

"I would draw your ladyship's attention to the facts of the case. . . ." It was the insufferable Major Prendergast speaking at her elbow. Prendergast was clearly enjoying his brief moment of glory as principal second. "The manner of Sir Mark's challenge precludes any withdrawal by Lord Houghton. Sir Mark did not invite an apology from his lordship, but struck him across the face in full view of the gentlemen in the club's smoking room. It is Lord Houghton who is the challenger, not your husband. As such, he could not withdraw even if he so wished."

Purity was not to be put aside so easily.

"Words . . . words!" she blazed. "You men have all the words! Is there nothing that I—a woman—can say to bring you to your senses?"

"No, there is not!" Mark was speaking to her. "Get back into your carriage, ma'am, and leave us!"

"Do that, ma'am," drawled Lord Houghton. "There is no cause for you to repine, you know, no cause at all." His cynical, worldly wise countenance bore an expression that was almost pitying. "You have only yourself to blame. You broke the seventh commandment . . . well, no one thinks much of that. A married lady may commit adultery here and there. We are living in an enlightened age. But it has to be done with discretion. You, ma'am, committed the cardinal sin of breaking the *eleventh* commandment: 'Thou shalt not get found out.' "

A chorus of laughter greeted his lordship's sally, and Mark Landless flushed angrily.

"Lord Houghton is pleased to waste time in jesting!" he cried. "May we now get down to the business at hand?"

"Take up your sabers, gentlemen! ordered the seconds.

"Stand clear, all!"

"This way, Lady Landless!" A firm hand on her arm prevented any further protest. Purity allowed herself to be led to her carriage, assisted into it, and the door was firmly shut after her.

She was witness to all that followed—watching, her whole life held in limbo, through the open window.

The two principals were of much the same height and build: tall, straight, and lean. Mark was as dark as a raven; Houghton was sandy-haired. They faced each other, their sword arms outthrust.

"Commence!"

Blade clashed on blade. The sound had homely overtones: like the sound of a kitchen scullion sharpening his carving knife upon steel, in preparation for slicing a joint of beef.

Purity bit deeply on her knuckle to prevent herself from crying out.

Houghton was taking the initiative. He was advancing upon his adversary, cutting to left and right shoulder, to the head, then thrusting to the hip. Both men's feet made patterns of lines upon the dew-spangled grass. Purity could hear their labored breathing. The onlookers stood like mutes. The surgeon knelt by his instrument case where lay his tourniquets and staunches, his needles already threaded with gut.

Houghton's fury being spent, Mark went into the assault, and there was a cold anger in his sword-play, a controlled fury that was fearful to look upon, as, with a set countenance and an unflinching glance, he directed his flickering blade to dance lights around the body of his opponent. He scored the air within inches of the vulnerable flesh, meeting only defending steel.

Back and forth they went, sometimes with one on the retreat, sometimes the other. To the trained observer, it was apparent that the men were evenly matched and that both knew their business. To Purity, for whom every lunge of Houghton's blade was like a cut to her own heart, it seemed that Mark was always on the defensive and losing badly.

The end, when it came, was lacking of any high drama. And Purity saw little of it, by reason of Mark's broad back obscuring his opponent from her view. But she saw Houghton drop his saber and lurch sidelong, clutching his sword arm just below the elbow.

As the surgeon and the others came rushing forward to the aid of the wounded man, a thick stream of dark, arterial blood spurted like a fountain from between Houghton's clutching fingers, and the stricken nobleman sank to his knees.

Mark Landless stuck his saber point into the ground, snatched his coat from a passing second, and was astride his horse and away without so much as a glance in the direction of the woman in the coach, who watched him go with tears of mingled relief and anguish coursing, unchecked, down her smooth cheeks.

Madeleine was alone in her sitting room when Quintin entered. She was not engaged upon any time-consuming occupation; needlework, embroidery, and the reading of books played no part in her life. When time lay heavy upon her, she simply closed her eyes and looked around inside her head for hour upon hour.

Her eyes snapped open at his entry.

"What news of Houghton?" she demanded.

"He may lose the arm," said Quintin, "but he will live."

"A pity," said Madeleine.

"Quite," agreed the other. "Houghton is one of those whom we have marked down to destroy, in any event. There would have been a certain . . . rightness . . . if Landless had performed the task for us—instead of the public executioner."

"I had not thought," said Madeleine, "that Landless would have gone so far as to challenge all six of them. He must love that woman very much."

Quintin shrugged. "It is to be hoped that, before one or the other of them puts an end to the career of the gallant Landless, he does not kill one of those who will be useful to us—the unspeakable Davenport, for instance. Would it not be prudent to suggest to Davenport that, for his own sake, he should go abroad? No, on second thought, he is almost the last opponent on Landless's list. My information is that the duel between them—with pistols—is set for Thursday. It is certain that Landless will either have been killed or incapacitated by then. My dear, you are not looking well."

Madeleine raised a slender hand to her temples. Her single eye closed, and the eyebrow arched painfully.

"Nor am I," she said. "This business is a trial to the nerves. I have not slept well for the last few nights, and my head aches abominably."

"It is time for your treatment," murmured Quintin soothingly. Stepping behind her chair, he commenced to massage the muscles at the back of her neck, driving his fingertips deeply, yet with infinite gentleness, into the firm flesh of her shoulders.

"Mmmm, what should I do without you, my dear?" murmured Madeleine. Then, unbuttoning the neck of her shift, she allowed it to fall to her waist. She was nude underneath.

"Lie down upon the sofa," said Quintin.

She obeyed, shedding her shift as she did so. She lay face down, bared to his healing fingertips. He worked in silence for some time, kneading her magnolia-shaded flesh from neck to ankle.

Presently, he said, "Does this make you desire me?"

"I have never felt any desire for you," she replied.

"Nor I for you," he said blandly, "even when we were children together and you used to creep into my bed in the dead of night and try to tempt me by asking me to feel how handsomely your breasts were budding."

"It was done in complete innocence, with no intent to seduce you," she said. "There was no passion on my part, only a certain curiosity about the nature of men. I learned precious little about men from you, Quintin, dear. For that I had to go elsewhere, where I learned plenty—to my cost. Do you think that our friends have any idea that we betrayed them by publishing the lampoon?"

"I am sure the notion has never entered their heads," said Quintin.

She laughed. "If they knew, they would be angry with us, would they not?"

"I doubt it," he said. "Lady Landless's reputation is irrevocably ruined—that is the unhappy state in which a woman stands. Conversely, however, her paramours' reputations are, if anything, enhanced by the cachet of having tumbled she who is arguably the outstanding beauty of her generation. Would you like to turn over now?"

She turned over on her back, relaxing with her arms pillowed behind her head, while he resumed his gentle ministrations. He probed her firm belly, breasts, thighs . . .

"When do we totally destroy her?" asked Madeleine presently.

"Lady Landless? Soon, I think—tomorrow or the next day. Perhaps it would be best to wait till Landless has either been killed or badly wounded in one of his encounters. Yes, I think that would leave her in a state in which she would be quite incapable of dealing with the *coup de grâce*. She would be without the will to fight for her adopted child."

"And then Elizabeth will be ours—all ours!" cried Madeleine.

"Where is she now?" he asked.

"In bed with her beloved Cornelia," replied Madeleine carelessly. "Where else? That randy little bitch has quite besotted her, so that she can think of nothing else but tumbling under the sheets with her loved one. Quintin, I am worried about . . . you know. . . ."

Quintin paused in his work. He gazed thoughtfully into the middle distance, gently rubbing together the smooth palms of his slender white hands.

"About bringing Elizabeth into contact with . . . *him?* Yes, I am also viewing the prospect with grave concern."

"What if he . . . interferes with her?" asked Madeleine.

"If he does that to any degree," said Quintin, "if he uses her as he has used so many others, yourself included—then I think we have lost her."

"Must they meet?" she asked. "Surely it is not necessary to our plans."

"He asks about her," said the other. "We have already delayed too long, and he constantly demands to know why she has not been brought to him. To deny him any longer would be . . . *dangerous!*"

The house on Half Moon Street was a desert to Purity. Already some of the servants—with the unerring instinct for the need of self-preservation that is brought about by listening at keyholes and keeping one's eyes and ears open when serving at the table—had hastily left for other employment, guessing that the Landless marriage was finished and that the London house would be closed. Without a ladies' maid, Purity had to do things for herself. It was fortunate for her that her early, austere upbringing well qualified her for the task of dressing her own hair, tending to her clothes, and bathing herself. Most women of her position, if reduced to such straits, would scarcely have had the enterprise to get out of bed in the morning.

She drifted on through the empty days, hardly noticing that, with the departure of the cook, the meals became execrable, the service tardy, and the servitors sullen and insolent. All her thoughts were for Mark, all her prayers for Chastity.

Mark had not set foot in the house since his raping of her. He had sent a servant from his club to collect some of his belongings. Upon an impulse, Purity had dashed off a note for the fellow to deliver:

> My Dear Mark,
>   You will not wish to hear from me, but in pity's sake I beg you to put me out of my misery and let me know what you intend to do with
>
>   your erring,
>   but eternally loving and devoted, wife

And she instantly regretted the impulse when the messenger disappeared around the corner of Half Moon Street.

For all that day and the wakeful night that followed, she waited in fear and trembling for a reply to her message. Of course, she told herself, he would not reply, for his intentions were quite clear: if by chance he survived the awful hazards of the five remaining duels, he was finished with her. Living or dead, he wanted no more of the woman who had betrayed him so assiduously.

In the mid-morning of the following day, a hammering upon the front door not having summoned a footman, she herself ran to open it. A man in the livery of the Senior Cavalry Club handed her a letter that she immediately opened—there, upon her own doorstep, with the man looking on.

Madam,

I thank you for your letter. As regards yourself, I have arranged for my solicitor immediately to transfer the title deeds of 17A Half Moon Street to yourself entirely, to revert to the Landless estate upon your demise. Nothing else needs to be arranged. Upon my own demise, the entire estate (save Half Moon Street) will devolve upon our son. In the circumstances, any question of my instigating divorce proceedings against you is purely academic. But I have to say that, even if I should survive the next few weeks, the prospect of terminating our marriage by process of law would be totally repugnant to me.

> I remain, Madam,
> Your Obedient Servant,
> M.L.

When she pressed the letter to her bosom, when, in a paroxysm of choking tears, she swayed and fell against the door and clung there, sobbing heartbrokenly, the club servant, greatly embarrassed, essayed to comfort her. But, his mumbled and inept condolences gaining no reply, and he not having the breeding and assurance to persist, he crept quietly away and left her alone in her misery.

That night her butler—who alone of all the servants continued to treat his mistress as if she had not become the most notorious adultress in London—discreetly informed her that his master Sir Mark was engaged to fight a duel on Blackheath the following dawn. His opponent: the Honorable Gervase Browninge. The weapons: pistols.

In her dream that night, she relived all of the most poignant and disturbing experiences of her youth: a medley of sights and sounds, tastes and touches; ecstasy counterpointed with horror, laughter with bitter tears. . . .

. First, in a wonder of revelation that always had the power to move her to tears of a strange bliss, she saw Mark nude, as she had seen him for the first time aboard his yacht the morning when he brought her out of Revolutionary France: high blue skies and flying spray; a man, straight, brown-skinned, and tall, in the splendor of his vigorous youth, laughing to the morning sun while a sailor threw a bucket of cold water over his triumphant nakedness. It was a vision that had illuminated her life; in her dream, years after, it lit her still.

In the way that dreams have, the image cracked, crazed, and fell apart, and she was standing in the blinding sunlight of the slave market of the Algiers Casbah, awaiting her turn to mount the auction block and be sold like an animal: stripped, prodded, probed, mauled, slobbered over—like the frightened, trembling young girl who had mounted the block before her and who was being led away to unimaginable soiling at the hands of the old lecher who had purchased her soft flesh. She, Purity, was next upon the block. The grinning slavemaster's assistants were prodding her forward with their whips, pushing her toward the sea of faces and the multitude of eyes that widened in wonder at the sight of the French woman with the miraculous hair like spun silver and gold. Reaching the block, a strange and wayward defiance fired her will. Ripping the few remaining rags from her back, she screamed her defiance: *"I am Purity Landless, and nothing that you do to me—nothing!—shall touch me! For I am free! Free!"*

The sea of faces pressed forward. Their voices were raised in laughter. She had rendered herself nude to their eyes and their clutching fingers. She shrank away, screaming. . . .

The image changed. Again, the sun. This time it was the sun of Spain, with the serried heights of a blue-gray mountain range in the distance beyond the valley, and the Ebro River snaking its way below the vineyards. There was the house—*their* house, which she and Mark had made an island sanctuary in a tormented sea of war. He was beside her, stooping low over their vines, picking out the weeds that had become entangled there through long neglect. Her whole body stirred to regard him: the way his thick, dark hair curled behind the ears; his way of pursing his lips in a silent whistle when totally absorbed in a task; his lean brown arms, strong and capable.

He became aware of her regard. The wonderful sea-blue gaze was directed toward her, first in quizzical amusement, and then, when he saw the desire in hers, the wonderful eyes reflected all that was burning within her. He lowered his bundle of ripped-out weeds to the ground. Then, taking her by both hands, he pulled her gently down to the warm earth. Their mouths met in a kiss of passion. Feverishly, they dragged at each other's clothing, mutually baring the other to hands and eyes and adoring lips. Under the searing sun of Spain, out on the vineyard slope, with the distant heights of the Sierra de Cantabria looking on, and with the Ebro River snaking down to the sea, they gave and received in love and passion. And then they lay, spent and contented, till the slanting evening sun cast the shadows of the vines upon their naked bodies, whereupon they gathered up their clothing and walked, hand in hand, up the hillside to the old farmhouse. . . .

The sun ruled her dream. Its last evening rays pinkly touched the high-pitched roofs and turrets of the old château in whose shadow she, the adopted daughter of a good peasant and his wife, had been raised. Its vestigial light masked the true intent of the procession of roisterers who crowded through the archway and swept past below the bedroom window from which she watched. Then their nearness revealed that it was bloodlust, not gaiety, that made them sing and prance, and it was not turnips they carried atop their long poles, but severed human heads. They were the Revolutionary mob from the Paris slums, hellbent on murder, rape, and pillage. Later that evening, she was destined to see things that colored her life forever after, things that set her to screaming, and, screaming still, awoke her in her beautifully appointed bedchamber in London's elegant Mayfair district.

It was ten o'clock in the morning. Thanks to the brimming glass of brandy spiked with laudanum that she had imbibed upon retiring, she had slept through the dawn that might well have been Mark's last dawn on earth. She, at least, had been spared the agony of living through the rising of the sun. Her agony was still to come—the agony of waiting.

She remained in her room, summoning no one. With the departure of her maid, no one but the butler ever answered the summons of her bell—and not always he.

At twelve midday, she decided, she would walk to the Senior Cavalry Club, where surely by then they would have heard the outcome of the duel. In the meantime, the two hours stretched before her like an eternity of wasted life.

The floor of her bedchamber became, in those waiting hours, a *via dolorosa,* which she paced, back and forth, in a turmoil of dreadful apprehension. A score of times she imagined Mark dead, and in a score of hideously cruel ways: maimed, agonized, ebbing out his life by inches and screaming for oblivion. At other times she tried to picture his safe return to her: bounding up the very stairs beyond her door, hastening back to her side, forgiveness shining from his wonderful eyes and understanding filling his generous heart.

At eleven-thirty, just as she was about to put on her bonnet and shawl and set off for St. James's, the butler announced a visitor.

She descended to the drawing room, where the visitor had been shown. Not knowing what to think, she allowed her mind to drift into an oblivion of unfeeling.

The visitor was a shortish, fuzzy-haired man of middle years, with a nearsighted squint. He was vaguely familiar to her, but from where or when she could not recollect. His first words set the image in her mind.

"My lady, I am Dr. Johnson—army surgeon."

"The surgeon who attended the duel!"

"Quite so, ma'am. And I also attended the affair of honor at Blackheath this morning."

She felt, quite distinctly, the blood drain from her cheeks, and she reached to support herself upon a chair back. She knew why this man had come. . . .

"Doctor, I beg you to tell me immediately," she gasped. "Has he . . . is my husband . . ."

The man was nervous. He licked his dry lips.

"Ma'am, your husband—that is, Sir Mark . . ."

"Yes . . . *yes?*"

" . . . is wounded, ma'am."

"Wounded!" Relief—a blessed washing away of terror—was her first response. And then a fresh horror struck her. "How badly is he wounded?" she cried.

"Quite . . . badly, ma'am."

"Ah!"

"But not fatally. Gravely, yes. But, given time and the best of attention, he will recover."

Hands pressed to her eyes, she fought with dreadful images of Mark's wounding: blinded, perhaps; disfigured, his wonderful countenance scored and scarred. And even more horrible wounds . . .

"Tell me . . . more!" she whispered. "Tell me everything!"

"The ball—which I was fortunately able to recover—entered the region of the left hip," said the surgeon, "severely lacerating the *quadriceps femoris* muscle, though happily missing the femoral artery. The femur bone, however, was much scored and I had fears for the entire leg." Safely launched upon his professional opinions, the man was more at ease—cheerful, even. "The prognosis, in my view, is very favorable. Given time, Sir Mark will be able to resume a normal, though somewhat more circumscribed, existence."

"He will be lame, you mean?"

"Slightly lame, ma'am. A previous leg wound sustained during the war has, as you are aware, left him with a perceptible limp. The limp will be somewhat more noticeable now."

Her mind was made up on the instant. "I must go to my husband at once, Doctor," she declared. "It was most considerate of you to bring me the news immediately. Both Sir Mark and I are exceedingly grateful. To where has he been taken, pray?"

The man was completely put out of countenance by her request. His nearsighted eyes probed hither and thither, as if seeking a source of inspiration . . . or, perhaps, a place to hide.

"Ma'am . . . your ladyship . . . "

"Yes? What's amiss, Doctor? Surely you know where, and in whose care, your patient now is."

He took a deep breath and blurted out his reply. "That I do, ma'am. But I am not at liberty to divulge it."

A strange chill enveloped her entire body.

"Why so, sir?" she asked in a small voice.

"Because Sir Mark, your husband, expressly forbade me, ma'am," he replied. And there was compassion in the myopic eyes. "He expressly ordered that you were not to be informed."

"I see," she said. And she remembered to hold her head high. Then, seeking a grain of comfort, she said, "But, nevertheless, he requested that you come here and bring me news of his welfare?"

The surgeon shook his head. "I wish I could offer you that small consolation, ma'am," he said, "but I regret that I cannot. I am here, ma'am, entirely of my own volition."

"I see." And now the tears were starting. She looked away.

"I observed you at the previous duel, ma'am," said the surgeon, "and I was stricken with sorrow at your plight. Because of that . . . "

Her back was now turned to him. She addressed him without looking around. "You are very kind to be sorry for me, sir. And now, will you please . . . leave me?"

"Of course, ma'am. Good day to you, ma'am."

"Good day, Doctor. And, again, thank you."

"It has been an honor, ma'am. I only wish that I . . . good day, my lady."

When the door was safely closed behind him, Purity gave in to the bitter tears for a chapter in her life that was now shut and sealed up forever: cut off, destroyed, purged and abandoned—and at the behest of the man she loved.

Later that day—much later, for she was by then dry-eyed—there came the sound of a conveyance pulling up in the street outside the house. Peering from her window, she saw that it was a fine coach with liveried coachmen; with flunkeys perched on the rear, who descended to lower the steps and open the door for the occupant.

Purity's visitor was a lady—a young lady. She was clad in a rich gown of oyster satin, with a long feather necktie draped, snake-like, around her slender shoulders. A large-brimmed bonnet trimmed with summer roses hid her face from the watcher at the window above. But when she reached the foot of the steps leading to the door of number 17A, she glanced upward—and Purity saw her clearly.

It was Chastity!

Chapter Seven

Between laughing and crying, Purity was seized with the quite inconsequential notion that she must look a fright, that the child would see her, after all those long and agonizing weeks, with a shiny nose and eyes swollen with tears; furthermore, she was wearing an exceedingly unbecoming gown.

Her feet, her trembling legs, would not see her even to the door of the drawing room; she merely stood, clinging to a chair back, waiting, her heart pounding enough to rouse the dead, as Chastity's footsteps ascended the stairs. It was absurd, she told herself—after all that had happened, all she had gone through: the disasters that had followed after Chastity's disappearance, and she could not even summon up the strength to rush to meet her and enfold the beloved child to her breast.

The door opened.

"Chastity—my darling!"

Purity made a move to approach her, reaching out her arms. But the strange and alien expression in the girl's dark eyes stopped her. So did her unbelievable words, delivered in a voice of such hatred that one could almost have reached out and touched it. "Get away from me—*whore!*"

"Chastity!" Purity backed away before the loathing she saw in the beloved face.

"Whore! Hypocrite! I know all about you!"

From her reticule, Chastity took a folded sheet of paper . . . pink-colored paper.

"Oh, my God!" cried Purity. "Not you, also. . . ."

"Yes, me!" Chastity spit the words at her. "I can read. I'm old enough to understand what you've been doing all these years."

Purity made a move toward her again. Why was she so concerned about what Chastity was saying? she asked herself. It was so ridiculous. If only the child could be made to understand. . . .

"My darling . . . " she began.

"Don't call me your darling!" screamed Chastity. "Don't touch me! I don't want to be soiled by the filth that drips from you! Oh, I'm old enough to know what all this means!" She tapped the paper in her hand. "The handy-dandy— I know what that entails . . . all the things you did with these men, *are* still doing with any man in breeches."

"No, Chastity—no!" cried Purity. "Never again! I . . . "

"Liar! What's to stop you?"

"You are home," said Purity simply.

"Home!" The word brought forth an expression of bitter mirth from the girl. She threw back her head and laughed. This done, she eyed the older woman smolderingly. "I will tell you why I have come home," she said. "I have come home—as you are pleased to call it—to unburden myself to my feelings toward you —you, who I have looked up to all my life as the very embodiment of all the female virtues. Do you know that I used to feel inadequate in your very presence? I worshipped you—but at the same time I was conscious that I should never, ever, come within a world of being your equal in virtue, in sensibility, in sweetness of character—not to mention beauty and sheer splendor."

"How wrong you were," said Purity brokenly, "how very mistaken."

"Was I not!" cried Chastity. "As, apparently, were many others—including the poor dupe whom you married. I understand that he has now left you. I must say I don't blame him, cuckold though he is!"

"Don't speak like that of your father!" blazed Purity, taking an angry pace toward the girl, who backed way with an expression of sudden alarm. "Say what you please about me, but I will not stand here and listen to you uttering a word against your father!"

The fear that her outburst had inspired in Chastity was gone with the brevity of a struck flint's tiny spark. She tossed her head arrogantly.

"He is no father of mine!" she declared. "Any man who has lived all these years with a creature of your sort—and nothing on earth would convince me that he hasn't been turning a blind eye to your disgusting carryings-on all this time—deserves nothing but contempt. For him I have contempt. For you—loathing!"

Purity's anger was gone. She had no resolve to sustain it. There was nothing she could do to silence the girl, nor to alter her feelings. It was out of the question, of course, to explain everything. Chastity's mind would be incapable of encompasssing the knowledge that it was for her sake that her adoptive mother had descended to the acts that so disgusted her. It could even drive her mad to be presented with such a searing truth.

She, Purity, must suffer, and endure. . . .

"Is there more that you have to say, Chastity?" she asked quietly.

"Only this," replied the other, "and this is the reason for my coming here today. I have learned much since I have been away. I have learned that there is worse evil than that of a poor drab who sells her body to stay alive. There is the evil of hypocrisy that conceals lust—and that is *your* evil!"

Purity shook her head desperately.

"No, Chastity—no!" she pleaded. "You mustn't believe that of me. I am not like that!"

"Liar!" The girl's voice rose in a scream. Her face close to Purity's, she threw the denunciation straight into the other's eyes.

"No!"

"I say you are a liar! A liar and a whore! Worse than a whore, for a whore gives herself in order to eat! You give yourself for . . . lust!"

"Lust?" Purity's gorge rose. "My God! You can say that of me—*me?*—after all I've been through for you! You . . . *you little bastard!"*

It was not her own will that directed her hand, but the instincts of a hundred generations of proud aristocrats of Latin blood. The blow took Chastity full across the mouth. She screamed, then fell back.

Eyes wide and unbelieving, she stared at Purity, whose passion turned instantly to anguished remorse.

"Chastity, my darling, I didn't mean it. Please . . . "

"Yes, you are right," said the girl. "I am what you called me—a bastard. My own person. No one owns me, so I can give myself to anyone I choose—to anyone who is kind to me and offers me love and understanding, to anyone who will look after me and cherish me as one of the family. And that I have done!"

Then she was gone, out the door, before Purity could raise a hand to prevent her. She heard the girl's footsteps clattering swiftly down the stairs. Shaking off the sense of hopelessness that kept her rooted there, she raced after her.

Purity arrived at the front door, which was standing wide open, just as one of the coach lackeys was folding up the steps and climbing back up to his perch. As the driver shook his reins and urged the horses forward, Purity caught sight of Chastity's flushed, hate-filled face, directed toward her.

The girl was not alone; others had waited down below while she had delivered the *coup de grâce* to Purity Landless, and Purity knew them both. . . .

There was the woman Madeleine, her single eye fixed upon the tragic figure standing in the doorway, a triumphant smile upon that almost perfect, magnolia-complexioned countenance.

And the third passenger in the coach was Captain Guy D'Eath!

Mark gone. Chastity gone. . . .

There was a pistol in a locked drawer of the library: a useless little thing, scarcely more than a toy, which Mark had insisted upon her taking into her charge—for her defense, he had said. She unlocked the drawer and took it out, case and all. The muzzle looked very small, but the leadened balls, of which there were six provided in the case, together with a brass flask of powder and some linen wads, looked adequate enough for the task of ridding Purity Landless of her unwanted life. She weighed one of the small lead spheres in the palm of her hand, trying to imagine the sensation of its being driven through the roof of her mouth and into her brain. A kindly bringer of oblivion.

If only one had more courage . . . or, perhaps, a little less courage. If only one did not have the instinct to hold on to life, however unwanted, tasteless, and suddenly without meaning that life had become. With a sigh, she put the pistol and its appurtenances back into their neat case, then shut them in the drawer and locked it.

Robbie . . .

Robbie, her son, was the clue to her continued existence. With all else gone, there was nothing to keep her in London anymore. She would travel to Norfolk at once, that very day. She would collect Robbie from Aunt Julia and take him away somewhere, to a place where they could make a fresh beginning together. No matter about the details of where and how—all that she could decide along the road. She had plenty of money, for Mark had never stinted on her, and the size of her bank account had become something of a joke between them in recent years.

They could even go abroad. To France. To Château Feyelle. How Robbie would love that!

The resolve made, she wasted no time. She packed a few things in a valise—light enough for her to carry without assistance—and quietly let herself out of the front door of the house without a word to any of the servants.

It was out of the question to travel to Norfolk in one of her own conveyances, for that would mean she would have to endure the company of the sour-faced coachman—that same individual who had driven her to Madame Dupuis's on that never-to-be forgotten morning when her whole world had begun to go crazy and break apart.

She would travel by public stagecoach, like the teeming and unprivileged masses of England. If the going was good, she should reach Aunt Julia's village of St. Peter's-by-Wymondham within two days.

A hackney cab brought her to the George Inn in Southwark, where the coaching office sold her a ticket for the stagecoach that was departing that evening for Newmarket. An onward posting to Wymondham could be made at the Rutland Arms in Newmarket, she was informed.

The stagecoach set off at the stroke of eight o'clock

on that summer evening. It clattered out under the archway of the George's yard to the raucous blasts of the post horn and the huzzahs of those who had come to see off their friends and relations. The stage-coach proceeded through the narrow streets of Southwark and out past London Bridge, with the swift river below and kipper-brown sails of long barges plying with the tide down to Greenwich and Barking Creek, Greenhithe and Gravesend.

There were eleven fellow passengers seated within the coach, placed six on each side. And as many were riding outside on top. The windows were shut, and Purity was immediately assailed by the smell of humanity combined with that of hot meat pies, ale, cheap perfume, and a particularly unkempt dog sitting and scratching itself upon the floor of the coach near her feet. No one else appeared to find the combined odors amiss. No one suggested that the windows be even partially opened, and Purity could not bring herself to assert herself and make the request. Truth to tell, she was not feeling well, and the odorous interior of the coach only served to aggravate, and was not the direct cause of, a malaise that had lain upon her all day since rising that morning. It was a sense of physical illness that had no connection, so far as she was aware, with the terrible problems that had beset her. Her head ached and her nose and throat felt raw-edged and uncomfortable. In short, she had the symptoms of a summer cold. Moreover, she felt feverish. To add to her dismay, she found herself to be *vis-à-vis* a coarse-looking young man, in a cheap and flashy hat and absurdly over-large neck cloth and spike-ended collar, who was ogling her with smoldering, insolent eyes. She pretended not to notice him.

Atop the coach was a party of Cambridge undergraduates. These young gentlemen enlivened their journey through the northern suburbs of the city by chorusing songs of dubious provenance, and by breaking off to whistle and to shout extravagant compliments, in Latin and the venacular, to each pretty woman they passed along the way. And so, the stagecoach rolled through the last of the narrow streets and by the rural tranquility of Bethnal Green to the windmills of Stratford-atte-Bow, with the green smudge of Epping Forest a promise to the northward.

Purity dozed off soon after. Her feverish dreams were disconnected images of vague unease, from which she awoke with a start as the rhythm of movement changed from the steady lumbering of the wheels over hard-packed earth to the brisk clatter of cobblestones.

A shattering blast of the post horn announced that they had arrived at their first stop. Now there would follow a change of horses, the opportunity for the passengers to have a pint of ale and some supper, or even, for those with leisurely tastes and ample purses, the option of taking a room for the night and resuming the journey on the morrow's coach. Purity was not hungry, but her parched throat craved a cup of tea or coffee. She alighted with the rest of the passengers.

The inn yard was ill lit. She followed the straggling line of passengers heading for the lighted windows of what, from the sounds of song and merriment emerging, appeared to be the taproom. One glance into its packed, smoke-filled interior sufficed to tell her that it was no place for a woman with a headache, a sore throat, and a craving for a drink that was both bland and warm. She turned aside and went in search of another, quieter part of the establishment, where she might satisfy her needs.

Halfway back across the yard, she paused as someone closed a shutter behind a lighted window in the gallery above, plunging that part of the yard where she stood into sudden darkness. Ahead lay pitch-blackness; behind was the streak of light from the taproom—and the choice was obvious. She turned to retrace her steps.

And then she saw . . . him.

A tall, silhouetted figure stood against the light from the taproom window. The tall hat was worn askew, and the ends of an absurdly large neck cloth were sticking out in long points. It was the man who had spent the whole journey ogling her with his loutish, insolent eyes. And he was walking with slow and very deliberate steps toward her.

She backed away. Then, as his pace quickened, she turned and walked more quickly. The swift pitter-patter of his heels on the cobblestones spurred her to increase her pace. She was running, and with a sudden and desperate sense of urgency that was rapidly rising to panic, when she collided with the hard wall at the far end of the yard, was knocked half-senseless by the contact of her temples with rough brickwork, and fell to the ground with every ounce of breath driven from her body.

And then she was back in her own, suavely comfortable bed. It could have been at Half Moon Street, Clumber Grange, or at Brighton. A cloying and persuasive warmth was enveloping her. And, though her head ached intolerably, that must surely soon pass. Someone—Mark, and who else?—was trying to comfort her. Mark, my darling, be not so rough with me, please. Why must you rip my night shift? My love, you are too eager. . . .

Mark, you're hurting me. . . !

She came to her senses with a jolt. She was lying on damp cobblestones. A blinding pain in her head all but shut out the horror of the fact that a man was astride her. He was clawing, groping, thrusting at her, and her skirts had been dragged above her waist.

Purity fought. She raked an unseen face with her fingernails and felt blood start to drip beneath them.

231

Her resistance did not in the least impede the bullish fury of her assailant, who continued to wrestle with her nether extremities, fighting like a man possessed to so position her that he could effect his designs upon her body.

With the whole weight of him upon her, with a parched and painful throat that rendered her incapable of screaming for assistance, Purity might well have suffered a violent raping in the darkness of the inn yard; indeed, with her strength flagging, and her senses slipping away, she could feel the instant of defilement almost upon her, when . . . deliverance . . .

Another shape loomed up behind her attacker, who gave a strangled cry and released the vise-like grip in which he had taken her hips. There came sounds of a scuffle, the dull smack of fists against flesh and bone. A muffled curse. And then came the clatter of running footfalls receding across the yard into the distance.

A hand on her arm. She peered up into the darkness, seeking to identify her rescuer.

"Are you all right? Did the brute harm you?"

"No," she whispered. And then she fainted dead away.

Her head ached abominably, and her skin was all afire. Opening her eyes, she saw a black-beamed ceiling, very low, so low that she could have reached up and touched it. Somewhere a candle flickered and sent a shifting pattern on the white plasterwork beneath the beams.

"I've brought you a warm drink of broth. Do you think you can sit up?"

She turned her head—it was a quite painful effort—to see the face of a young man, his countenance half-thrown in shadow by the candlelight.

She said, "Yes, I . . . I think so."

He helped her to sit up in bed. He carefully arranged the pillows behind her, folded the sheet, and arranged the bedclothes around her as tenderly as any nursemaid. Seeing him more clearly, she became aware that he was even younger than she had surmised: no more than nineteen, surely.

"Comfortable?" He smiled, and it was a wide, eager smile that showed white teeth that contrasted with the healthy, ruddy tan of his cheeks. His hair was blond, almost as blond as her own, and curly.

"Yes . . . thank you," she murmured, suddenly and embarrassingly aware that she was wearing only her shift, which was of the sheerest black silk, and vestigial at that. Looking down her front, she could see everything she had—and he could scarcely do less.

"Hot broth," he said encouragingly. "Shall I hold it, or can you manage?"

"I . . . I can hold it," she assured him hastily, pulling together the neck of her shift as well as she was able to.

She took the cup from him. He smiled and nodded. Seating himself unconcernedly on the edge of the bed, he watched her lift the vessel to her lips and take a sip.

The broth was good-tasting, rich and clear, and its comforting warmth did wonders for her sore throat. With the mists of unconsciousness rapidly receding, and her head paining her somewhat less, Purity fell to speculating about her young friend. Certainly it was he who had saved her from the brute who had tried to rape her. Who, then, was he? And where had he brought her?

Other questions intruded themselves. . . .

"Is that good?" he asked.

"Very," she assured him.

"Can you talk now, or would you just prefer to listen?" He smiled again, looking absurdly young. With a sudden lurch of the heart, she saw something of her son, her own Robbie, in him.

"Tell me who you are," she said. "My name is Purity Landless. I believe—I think—I have to thank you for a very gallant act on my behalf, Mr., uh . . . "

"Martin Eccles, ma'am," he said, "of Trinity College, Cambridge, where I was bound this evening, on the same stage as yourself. I and my colleagues were riding atop." He grinned. "You may have heard us. 'Twas the end of a last wild spree in London before the university closes for the long vacation."

She looked around her. "We are at the posting inn?" she asked.

"Indeed, we are, ma'am," he confirmed. "The Blue Boar at Epping. Not a bad hostelry, as hostelries go, but the landlord is mightily disobliging. I had to make the most extravagant pretexts for securing this room."

"What pretexts, Mr. Eccles?" she asked.

He looked serious. "To put it bluntly, ma'am, for a start, I said no word about . . . about what took place out there in the yard. An episode like that, why, landlords don't stand for such a thing. It gives an establishment a bad name. I merely told him that you had been overcome by the heat of the journey and needed to rest overnight. He was not over-mightily pleased, but he grudgingly gave us the last room he had."

"*Us?*" Purity glanced at him sharply. Her new friend blushed to the very roots of his curly blond hair.

"Ma'am, I have a confession to make," said he, "which I fancy is not going to please you overmuch."

"You must try me, sir," responded Purity, "and see how the confession fits upon me. Sir, why do you tarry? I am all agog."

He said, "Well, you will understand that it was quite out of the question for me to leave you here on your own, considering the state you were in. Futhermore, it is certain that our friend the landlord would have refused to accept the responsibility for an unattached lady who had needed to be carried upstairs in my arms. So I told him we were together."

"Ah, I see," said Purity. She smiled at him. "That was very astute of you, Mr. Eccles."

"I am mightily relieved you think so, ma'am," said Eccles. And he looked it.

"You represented us as mother and son," she said.

The young man's brow furrowed in puzzlement. Then a smile broke out across his lips—the smile of a fellow who is not slow to notice that someone is trying to jest with him.

"Ah, indeed I did not, ma'am," he said. "For that would have been absurd, would it not? I mean, the fellow would have thrown us both out into the night for such a patently obvious untruth. Why, I said that we were man and wife—what else?"

"Man and . . . *wife?*" She stared at him, wide-eyed with appalled speculation. Then, remembering the state of undress she was in, she pulled the neck of her shift more closely to her bosom. "And he—the landlord—accepted that without demur?"

"Indeed, he did," said Eccles casually. "Why should he not?"

Why should he not? Even Purity—overburdened with grief and beset with troubles uncounted, newly escaped from violent rape, and ill from a bad cold in the bargain—could not but thrill at the implied compliment. The youth before her—and the landlord of the Blue Boar—accepted her as some young slip of a girl-wife!

"Very astute of you, Mr. Eccles," she repeated. "But what of your onward journey to Cambridge? Were you not intending to continue toward there to-night?"

He shrugged. "What matter, ma'am? I can as lief take the morning stage."

"But . . . your colleagues have gone on?"

"That they have, ma'am," he confirmed. "Yes, indeed."

"So you are, as it were, stuck here with me."

He grinned broadly: a guileless grin, like that of a youngster who has all unexpectedly found himself the lone inhabitant of an apple orchard in full fruit.

"That is so, ma'am," he said complacently.

"I hope you will be comfortable on yonder armchair, Mr. Eccles," said Purity flatly.

The complacent grin slipped somewhat askew and became a trifle less complacent.

"Quite so, ma'am," he said.

Purity's next comment was cut short by a paroxysm of coughing, which, in addition to being protracted, was most painful to her chest. When she had finished, she lay back against the pillows, quite exhausted.

"Ma'am, you are not well, not well at all," said Eccles with concern.

"A summer cold, that is all," said Purity. "I shall be as right as rain tomorrow. The broth has done me a lot of good already, so my condition cannot be all that serious."

He looked relieved. "Quite so, ma'am," he said. "However, you have a very high fever. When I brought you up here and laid you upon the bed, your clothing was quite soaked through."

She gazed at him steadily. "And it was because of that that you stripped me to my shift and laid me between the sheets, Mr. Eccles?" she asked.

He reddened again. He did it very readily, she decided.

"It was done with perfect propriety, I assure you, ma'am," he declared. "If the word of a scholar of

236

Trinity carries any weight with you, you have my promise."

"I would never doubt the word of a scholar of Trinity, sir," said Purity. She relaxed against the pillows. "What hour is it, Mr. Eccles?" she asked.

"It is past ten o'clock, ma'am," said Eccles.

"Then I will bid you good night, sir," she said. "You had best take this eiderdown to lay atop you. I hear it raining outside and it will surely be none too warm in here during the early hours."

"I shall be fine enough, ma'am," he said somewhat stiffly. "Thank you, all the same. Good night to you."

"Good night, Mr. Eccles."

She closed her eyes. Moments later, she heard him sink his weight into the leather armchair that stood against the wall beyond the foot of her bed. Next, she felt a slight movement as, very carefully, he rested his booted heels on the bed end. He shifted position, then grunted. Moments later, she smelled the acrid tang of a snuffed candle. No sound then, but the sluicing of the rain outside the window. She fell asleep.

A lightning flash and a crash of thunder awoke her with a start. She sat up in bed. Another blinding and protracted glare revealed her roommate seated bolt upright in his chair, chin in hand, hair awry: the embodiment of a young man who has not slept, who will not sleep, and who knows he will not sleep.

"Come and lie upon the bed, Mr. Eccles," she said resignedly, "between the eiderdown and the top blanket," she added.

"Yes, ma'am. Thank you." He leaped up with alacrity and, lifting up the eiderdown, laid himself by her side. Another flash of lightning and a rumble of thunder—this time from farther off—was followed by a renewed downpour of rain. Purity closed her eyes and composed herself for slumber again. The pain in her temples had abated, but she found breathing difficult and her throat was like fire; nevertheless, she was able to drift into the first portals of sleep, when, at that time between waking and dreaming, when dreams and reality become so blurred at the junction as to seem one and the same, she thought—it seemed to her, and she felt it quite distinctly—that a hand stole past her shoulder, brushed the edge of her shift, and closed around her bare left breast. Without emerging from her half-sleeping condition, she pushed aside the importuning hand.

Her last recollection, before total sleep closed in around her, was of the return of the hand upon her breast. Or it may have been the beginning of her dream. . . .

The fever-induced dream, experienced in that most profound sleep that comes only to a sick body, was of astonishing vividness. She and Mark were lying together upon the shore of a tropical island, with the roar of great combers crashing upon the shingle not far distant, so that they were both damp and slippery with the flung spray. They lay side by side. His hand, which had been cupped around her left breast, moved with loving stealth down her smooth flanks, pausing at her belly, then descending to her awaiting thighs. With a sob of desire and ineffable contentment, she rolled over to face him, mouth to mouth, arms embracing, and their bodies joining. To the sound of the great waters thundering upon the shore, she soared with her lover to heights unimaginable and to an ecstasy that was infinitely protracted through the entire length of her strange dream.

She awoke with the sun streaming in through the unshuttered window. Eccles was standing by the window and looking down into what must have been the inn yard, for she could hear the clatter of hooves and the rumble of coach wheels on cobblestones.

He turned as she stirred and smiled across at her.

"Good morning," he said. "Did you sleep well?"

"Thank you, yes," said Purity. "And you?"

"Admirably well." He smiled and looked back out of the window.

He was fully dressed. She looked down at herself; she was still wearing the shift. The bed was undisturbed; indeed, considering that two people had slept upon it, the sheets and blankets were in a remarkable state of tidiness—almost, she thought, as if the bed had been remade with her in it. . . .

She fought to find a question that might settle her growing unease, one way or another.

"I . . . I think I must have been feverish during the night," she said. "I trust I didn't disturb you?"

He turned and smiled at her blandly. "Not in the least," he said.

"My dream," she said, "was extremely vivid. It occurred to me that I may have cried out."

"You may indeed have cried out," he said. "But you didn't disturb me in the least."

He returned to his inspection of the scene below.

Later, after he had left the room in order that she could get dressed, they breakfasted together in the coffee room of the inn. Purity sipped a cup of hot chocolate, nibbled at an oatcake, and regarded her companion thoughtfully as he manfully ate his way through a piled plate of boiled ham and pea pudding, followed by a huge slice of veal-and-ham pie and some broiled kidneys from the buffet table. He washed it all down with a foaming tankard of ale. He gave Purity a running discourse upon his life at Cambridge, his tussles with his tutor and the university authorities, and his hopes for the future. He was, it appeared, destined for a place in the East India Company.

Never once, by word or gesture, by covert glance

239

or by innuendo, did he hint at an answer to the question that was uppermost in Purity's mind.

They parted company in the yard. The Cambridge coach was the first to leave. He climbed up onto the top seat, throwing his valise in front of him. She reached up her hand for him to take in his.

"Thank you for what you did," she said.

His eyes—he had wide-set and very guileless gray eyes—never faltered.

"My thanks is all to you, ma'am," he said. *"Adieu."*

The coachman cracked his whip and shook his reins. The post horn blared. As the conveyance rattled out through the archway, Martin Eccles turned and gravely raised his hat to her.

She never saw him again—that scholar of Trinity who could keep his counsel, one way or the other.

Newmarket lay far behind, and they were journeying through the flat, cloud-hung landscape of Norfolk, with Wymondham soon passed, and Aunt Julia's long, rambling barn of a house was a promise beyond the next belt of hedgerow. Purity's heartbeats quickened and her pulse raced. The anticipation of being reunited with Robbie, to feel his strong, wiry arms wrapped around her, and to press her cheek against his tousled hair and weep tears of joyous release was almost unbearable.

"Here we be, ma'am!" The local carter, who had driven her from the posting inn at Wymondham, pointed with his whip. "That be Miss Landless's."

"I know it well," murmured Purity.

She had half-hoped that Robbie's slight figure might have come racing down the driveway to greet her, whooping as he came, waving to her. But she was greeted only by Aunt Julia's ancient dog, which barked at the front door steps and was reduced to a joyful wagging of its tail when it recognized her voice.

Aunt Julia came out soon after, as fast as she was able to. She was crippled with rheumatism, but, as ever, too stubborn and proud to resort to the aid of a cane. As soon as Purity saw the old woman's set, thin-lipped expression, she knew that she had been forestalled.

"You're a mite too late, my gel," said Aunt Julia. "Mark has been here before you and has taken your chick with him. Both birds have flown away. Come in and have a cup of tea."

Later, in the fussy, overfurnished sitting room off the long hall of the ancient house, full of knickknacks and ferns and the family paraphernalia of a dozen generations of Landlesses, the old woman told Purity how Mark had arrived two days previously in his own carriage, accompanied by two powerfully built lackeys who had carried the wounded man into the house and laid him on a sofa. He had departed the same evening, Aunt Julia told her, taking Robbie with him, and, no, she did not know where they had gone.

"Did he look very ill?" asked Purity tremulously.

"As ill as I ever hope to see a man look and still live," replied the other woman, a red patch of anger showing on each cheekbone.

"He . . . he fought a duel . . . for me," said Purity, looking down at her hands.

"Mark did not tell me as much, but one of his men was more forthcoming," said Aunt Julia coldly. She made no more comment. It was clear that she knew little, but speculated plenty. A lady of strict upbringing, a devoted church-goer, and a lifelong celibate, it was not to be wondered that her feelings toward Purity were ambivalent. She had always been fond of her nephew's beautiful wife. But Mark was her nearest and dearest—indeed, her only surviving— relation. And she doted upon young Robbie. Whatever had caused Mark to take away the boy and abandon his wife could only have been a matter of exceeding gravity, a sin that was beyond the comprehension of an old maid such as she.

"You don't look well yourself," she said gruffly. "I had best send for Dr. Forsythe to bleed you of a few ounces."

"It is nothing," said Purity, "only a summer cold. It will be better by tomorrow. Tell me, do, how was Robbie when he left you? Was he well? Has he put on some weight in the country?"

"Never saw him better," responded the other fondly. "Ate me nigh out of house and home—as his father before him did many times when a lad. My gel, I think that you have made a big mess of your life. Am I right?"

Purity nodded. A tear fell upon her hand.

"I would give the world to see Mark again," she said, "to put things to right. But I doubt if he would agree even to speak with me. And what I have to say could never be written in a letter."

"I'm sorry for you," said the old woman. "But you have made your own bed, Purity, and now you must lie in it. I spoke the truth when I told you I did not know where Mark and the boy have gone. But this I must add: when I recall the hurt and misery in Mark's face as he lay there on yonder sofa—and, I assure you, he spoke not one word against you all the time he was here—I have to admit that, even if I knew their whereabouts now, I would not tell you. To my mind, gel, you have hurt him enough."

"You are right," sighed Purity.

Aunt Julia had offered her a bed, which she declined. With no clear object in mind, save that of escape, she took a coach back to London. And where else should she go? Clumber was out of the question,

Brighton also. The house on Half Moon Street was hers for life. Just as well to end the long span of empty days there as anywhere else.

Her fellow passengers were looking oddly at her. They muttered among each other about the ravishingly beautiful creature with the high complexion of fever and the hacking cough. They opined, one to the other, that she must be a victim of the consumption. They edged away from her as if she had been a leper.

Somewhere along the way, the coach pulled into a posting inn yard for a change of horses. Purity remained where she was, and she did not open her eyes and respond when a hostler thrust his head through the door and announced that there would be an hour to wait. By the time the coach resumed its journey, the fever had taken hold of her and she sat with her head lolling, her chest rapidly rising and falling, and her mouth open. Her fellow passengers gave her an even wider-berth.

Inside her head, she was back again in Clumber in the summertime, in the great house on the escarpment overlooking the rolling landscape of parkland. The children were young, innocent and adoring her. Mark was as he had always been. . . .

Her fellow passengers saw her smile in her delirium, for, though it was now dark, they had lit a small lantern within the coach. They nodded to each other and commented that the woman was perhaps crazed. The sooner they reached London the better, and be rid of her. Epping was behind them, and Hackney Downs was not far ahead. It was damnably dark outside.

The coach stopped its onward pace, brakes screaming on iron tires. A horse whinnied wildly. Those facing forward were all but thrown onto the floor.

"Stand and deliver! Your money or your lives!" It

243

was the traditional cry of the highwayman, a command that struck terror in every traveler.

There was much frenzied activity within the coach: much hiding of rings and other jewelry; the concealing of gold watches within boot tops. One gentleman even took out a set of gold teeth on a plate and slid them surreptitiously behind the seat cushions. No one took the slightest notice of the unconscious woman with the miraculous silver-gold hair as she slipped slowly sideways and lay along the seat.

"Open up, there! Get down, all of you! Step lively, or I'll make an example by blowing off someone's head!"

The door was flung wide open by the coachman, anxious above all to do the highwayman's bidding and escape with a whole skin. He cursed at the passengers to hurry. They all got down. By the light of the coach lamps, they could see the tall figure on the large horse, pistol in hand, bright eyes glinting behind a black face mask, brow shaded with a slouch hat.

"Is that everyone?" demanded the robber.

"All 'cept a lady, sir. She's a-lyin' in there."

"Very poorly, she is. Taken o' the consumption, I shouldn't wonder."

The highwayman urged his horse forward, bent low in the saddle, and peered into the coach. By the light of the lantern within, he discerned the slender figure stretched out there, one hand and arm trailing to the floor, and a wealth of silver-gold hair unbound and flowing free.

He cursed under his breath.

And then: "You there, coachman, and you, the fellow standing next to him, lift her out. Look sharp about it, do you hear?"

Wonderingly, they obeyed, carrying the limp form between them, out of the coach door.

"Give her to me!"

244

They handed the unconscious woman up on high, and the masked rider took her in his arms and laid her across the saddle bow before him, supporting her lolling head against his breast. The awestruck passengers, men and women both, stared in breathless speculation as to why the thief should have need of a sick woman, and for what dark reason he was taking her.

And taking her he was! Without another word or sign to the onlookers, the highwayman wheeled around his rangy black and, setting his heels to the big mount's glossy flanks, went off at a clatter into the gloom.

They listened and watched in silence till the horse and its burdens had gone from sight and sound. And still they continued to stare, amazed at their deliverance, for the highwayman had taken not a thing save the woman with the silver-gold hair.

It was the coachman who broke the silence. "He be a strange one, that," declared the man. "I know him well by sight, as well as that stallion he do ride. That be Jack Moonlight."

There was a part of the Essex shore of the Thames, marshland like most of the remainder, that had escaped the ministrations of the seventeenth-century Dutch engineers who had reclaimed wide tracts of sedge and reed prairie from the domain of river and sea. It was the haunt of wild geese, curlews, and herons, ventured into only by oystermen and wildfowlers—and they seldom braved the inner fastnesses of the marsh, which was known to notoriety as "The Devil's Hundred."

It was to this forbidding tract of wilderness, by way of the southern edge of Epping Forest and the outskirts of Hackney hamlet, that the highwayman headed that night after he had taken Purity Landless from the Newmarket stage, arriving at the entrance to the marsh—a tributary of the Lea River—shortly after midnight. There he urged his mount down the steep bank and into the slow-flowing stream till it was wading knee-deep, its four hooves firmly set upon hard shingle. They progressed in this manner, through many loops and bends of the stream, till they came at length to a fallen willow tree of great age, whose gnarled trunk completely overhung the water, and whose tortuous branches formed an archway through which horse and riders were able to pass. Once beyond the willow, the steed was wading in chest-high marsh water through reed thicket whose feathery tops were swaying in the night wind high above the man's head. With seemingly no mark by which to guide him, he headed in a straight line across the marsh, straying neither to the left nor to the right, till presently they emerged into an open mere, where a flight of mallard ducks, which had been driven before them, rose in a noisome chorus of cries and flapping wings and took the night air across the mere.

The man lightly touched the stallion's flank and directed the mount along the fringe of the open water, to where a narrow inlet snaked away into shadows. This marked the beginning of "The Devil's Hundred," in which, by reason of the treacherous quicksand and mire of which it was largely composed, even the hardiest wildfowler never set foot. The highwayman entered it without fear, for he, and a few others, were privy to a secret pathway: a ridge of hard-packed claysoil that meandered like the spine of a giant snake into the heart of the forbidden land. Here it broadened out into an islet upon which was set an ancient stone keep that had stood within "The Devil's Hundred" since the days of King Alfred the Great, who had caused it to be erected there as a defense against the longships of the marauding Danes in their forays up the Thames to London. Little of the fortress remained; half a dozen courses of limestone blocks, each the size of a handcart, formed a rough circle that had been open to the sky for generations. Now it was neatly thatched with a bonnet of reed, and a stout oak door filled the rounded archway, which provided entrance and egress to the keep. And there was a stable and outhouse built of logs, with a thatched roof in the same manner. It was there that the highwaymen led his horse, where, having carefully laid the unconscious woman upon a bed of dry straw, he untacked the mount, provided it with a bale of hay and a tub of water, then took up the woman and carried her through the massive door and into the ancient keep.

The interior, when he had lit an oil lamp, was revealed as a single, oval-shaped chamber of roughly dressed stone, with a stone floor that was strewn with Oriental rugs of fine quality. The Spartan harshness of the walls, also, was softened by rich tapestries of the seventeenth century depicting scenes of the chase, with ladies and gallants riding amidst improbable landscapes peopled with exotic birds and animals. In the center of the floor was a small refectory table and bench. In one corner was a canopied bed. The whole ambiance, with its air of austerity mingled with opulence, betrayed a mind of markedly contrasting qualities. This fact was underscored by the disparity between the personal possessions that were scattered about the chamber; beautifully bound volumes of abstruse philosophical, medical, and scientific works lay cheek by jowl with fine handguns—pistols, smoothbore muskets, and a superbly chased Kentucky rifle —and swords and sabers of every description.

He carried Purity Landless across the chamber and laid her upon the bed. This done, he unhooked the bodice of her dress and carefully drew it down over her hips and legs. The shift followed, and then the slippers and stockings, rendering her entirely nude. The highwayman then covered her over with a lambskin rug of unbelievable softness and warmth. Then he heated a pannikin of water over a spirit stove, testing it with his hand from time to time till he was satisfied. And then, removing the covering from the unconscious woman, he proceeded to wash her all over with a flannel cloth soaked in the warm water. He did so tenderly, devotedly, the way a mother will bathe her infant child. Afterward, he dried the smooth, rounded form with a Turkish towel.

When he had finished the ablutions, he carefully examined her: lifting both eyelids and gazing into the unseeing eyes; probing the chest and back; feeling the pulse and heartbeat; running his fingers inside the mouth and peering down the throat. What he found appeared to give him cause for some disquiet, for he regarded the silent, prostrate figure for some little while, chin in hand, his broken-nosed profile bowed in somber thought.

Presently, coming to a decision, he brought from out of a locked cabinet a case of surgical instruments from which he took a lancet, holding the keen-edged sliver of steel against the light and squinting to test its keenness. Then, unwinding his own neck cloth, he bound it around Purity's right arm, slightly above the elbow, drawing the knot tight till the veins of the lower arm swelled up. He selected one which, just below the bend of the elbow, sent a branch inward and outward. It was to the outer branch that he speedily directed the point of his lancet: one thumb was pressed gently below the point of entry, the tip of the instrument went into the vein, and then he cut in a gentle curve.

The bright blood flowed freely into a basin on his lap. When it was half-filled, the surgeon laid his thumb firmly over the tiny cut and held it there till all the bleeding had ceased, and he finally secured it with a small pad held in place with a handkerchief.

He stood up and regarded his handiwork. Some of the feverish heat appeared to have gone from Purity's cheeks, but her breathing was still labored and quick, and her heartbeat—which he again sounded by laying the palm of his hand under her left breast—was alarmingly rapid.

A brass carriage clock on the bedside table told him the hour was half-past two. He rose and poured himself a glass of wine, which he sipped, watching his patient from a chair that he had drawn up by the bed.

He remained there the livelong night, not stirring, save occasionally to renew his wineglass, and from time to time to lay a cold compress upon the woman's fevered brow. When the first light of dawn filtered in through narrow arrow-slits high on the rough stone walls, Purity thrashed from side to side and murmured in delirium. He leaned forward to catch the words while laying a fresh compress upon her sweat-streaked brow.

"Not Robbie! Don't take my little boy from me! I've nothing left— nothing!"

His strongly chiseled, pleasantly ugly countenance took on an expression of grave compassion.

Purity's recovery began abruptly with a crisis, at which he feared for her life. But this was swiftly followed by a rapid end to the feverishness. On the fourth day after her arrival at the ancient fort in "The Devil's Hundred," she was able to gather together in her mind the sights and sounds around her in some sort of order and coherence. But she was so weak, so spent in mind and body, that even the effort of connecting the face that looked down at her with a memory of the recent past was almost too much to bear.

"I . . . I know you," she whispered. "You saved me that night—in the rookery."

"Jack Moonlight," he said, nodding.

"Jack Moonlight . . . "

He laid his hand gently across her eyes. When he removed it, they were closed in sleep—the first quiet and undisturbed slumber she had enjoyed since her arrival there. While she slept, he bled her once again, then applied a cold poultice of linseed meal, bran, and bread to her chest in order to excite an increased circulation on the skin. It was the last medical attention that was necessary for him to render to his patient.

The following day, Purity was well enough to lie propped up against a couple of pillows, where she watched from under her unbelievably long lashes as the man moved about his tasks in the oval-shaped chamber that had unaccountably become their shared abode. She saw him prepare an invalid's gruel of groats, mixing the crushed and powdered grain with cold water in a basin, adding boiling water, stirring the brew over a spirit stove till it was cooked, then adding a dash of Sherry. He was stripped to the waist, for it was hot in the airless chamber, though the door was open to the sea of reed and sedge that shimmered in the baking sunlight outside. His thickly pelted torso was well muscled and powerful, like that of a prize-fighter; but he carried himself with a tigerish grace and elegance of movement, and his strong hands performed the task of preparing the gruel with great dexterity and economy of effort.

"You . . . strike me as being a very capable person," she murmured as he brought the basin of gruel over to her and, having tied a napkin around her neck, began to feed her like a child.

"Robbing stagecoaches in defiance of the gallows is not my sole accomplishment," he said. "Open wide." He spooned a mouthful between her lips.

"I was taken ill on the coach," she said presently. "And it was there that you found me and presumably recognized me as the woman you had saved on a previous occasion?"

"How could I forget you?" he said. And his eyes were directed in frank appraisal of her bare shoulders and arms and the delicate structure of her perfect breasts, lightly veiled from his gaze by the napkin he had tied around her neck.

Purity was unaware, or uncaring, of his appraisal. The mention of the stagecoach had set in motion a series of connected images that ended in the desolation of the terrible loss that she had suffered at the end of her journey to Norfolk. Refusing the next mouthful of gruel, she turned her head away from him, and he saw a tear fall from between her closed eyelids and descend her satin cheek.

"Is it Robbie you weep for?" he asked gently.

"You . . . know?" she whispered.

"You spoke his name in your delirium," he said. "Your son?"

She nodded. "Yes."

"Taken from you . . . by whom?"

"By my estranged husband."

"It is sometimes of great help to unburden oneself," he said. "Feel free, by all means, to share your grief with me if you are so inclined."

"I wouldn't wish to burden you," said Purity. "You've done enough for me already. I shall never be out of your debt. I know you tended me through my illness. I was aware of you—a shadowy, gentle figure who held my hand and guided me out of the valley of the shadow of death."

He shrugged. "It was little enough. You had an attack of lobar pneumonia, fortunately without complications, and with the advantage of an excellent constitution."

"You are very knowledgeable on matters medical," said Purity.

He avoided her gaze for a moment.

"I was not always a hunted thief," he said.

"You were, perhaps, a physician?" she suggested.

"Briefly, yes," he said. "Leastways, I attended classes in anatomy at Edinburgh under the renowned Alexander Monro *tertius,* afterward proceeding to a degree in medicine at Leiden University. But I never did practice my craft. Other . . . things . . . intervened."

"I see," murmured Purity sympathetically.

He smiled. It was a quirky, self-deprecating smile that carried a great burden of sorrow behind its frail facade.

"No, you do not see, dear lady," he said quietly. "But it doesn't matter. Nothing matters—now. By the way, I don't even know your name, though you are familiar with the *nom de guerre* I use to protect from disgrace that with which I was born and baptized. What are you called, pray?"

"Purity Landless."

"Mrs. Purity Landless." His gaze fell to her left hand, and to the wedding ring there.

"Lady Landless, wife of Sir Mark," said Purity. Then she added bitterly, "I am surprised you have not recognized me."

"Why so?" asked Jack Moonlight. "I do not much mix in high society, save when I have the great good fortune to come upon a private coach owned and occupied by my well-heeled betters."

"I was recently the subject of a lampoon," said Purity, "a scurrilous cartoon that unmasked me as a fornicating adulteress of the very worst type."

"Falsely, of course," he ventured.

"It was vilely, cruelly done," she said, "but, nevertheless, true in substance."

"I see," he said.

"No, you do not see, Dr. Jack Moonlight," responded Purity. "But it doesn't matter."

He said, "And it was for your fornication and adultery that your husband became estranged from you and took the son. I see."

"And I also was bereft of a daughter at the same time," said Purity, "an adopted daughter, but no less dear and loved for that. And it was in connection with her loss that I went to the St. Giles rookery that night —when first we met."

Jack Moonlight unfastened the napkin from around her neck. He carefully lifted the edge of the bedsheet so that her alluring breasts were shielded from his gaze.

"Your gruel is cold and uneaten," he said. "Might I suggest, if you feel strong enough, that you continue with your story and unburden yourself, after all? I promise you that I am a mighty good listener."

"I think I will," said Purity.

So she told him everything, beginning with the hideous discovery of Chastity's disappearance at Brighton, then telling of her summons to the woman Madeleine's house in St. Giles rookery and what befel her there. Her voice faltered and she looked away when touching upon the more shameful details of her cohabitings with members of the hated society. But she did not skip anything, however distressing to her, that was germane to the true account. And when she was finished, she lay back against the pillows and searchingly regarded her companion's pleasantly ugly face for signs of contempt, distaste, or even prurient enjoyment. And she saw nothing but understanding and compassion.

"I wish you had come to me before," he said at

length. "I wish you had presumed upon our earlier acquaintance and sought me out, for I can help you."

"You can?" she queried. "But how . . . *how?*"

"I have never heard of this woman Madeleine," he said. "But the fellow known as Captain Guy D'Eath is known to the criminal world of the metropolis, though, mark you, I do not say he is a member of that world."

"He is evil!" cried Purity. "Evil! And to think that my darling, my Chastity, is associating with that creature!"

"Something is afoot," said Moonlight. "And I will discover what it is, and how, if at all, it concerns your Chastity. I want you to go to sleep now. No protests, I beg you, the physician knows best. Presently, I shall have a visitor, a spry young fellow whom I describe as my 'runner.' He it is who acts as my eyes and ears in the rookeries and along the highways and byways of the city and its environs. Not an event of importance takes place without it coming to young Barney Bates's attention. I will tell Barney your story —as much as he needs to know—and set him to discover what lies behind your daughter's unholy liaison with D'Eath and the woman Madeleine. Sleep now. Sleep as much as possible. Every time you wake up, you will feel better and stronger."

He laid a soothing, cool hand on her brow. Before he had taken it away, Purity had succumbed to the suggestion contained in his deep, gentle voice, and had relaxed into a deep and untroubled slumber.

The day passed, the following night, and then another day.

She assumed that he slept beyond the confines of the oval-shaped chamber, for once on awakening in the dark she cried out in sudden and unbidden panic, and it was some little time before he put in an appearance, bearing a lantern. He slept naked. Naked, but unashamed, he tended to her needs and gave her a few sips of barley water, afterward bedding her down again and smoothing her brow, as if she had been a child.

He was never far from her once in all that time. He prepared food for both of them over the spirit stove and washed her from head to foot thrice daily, and always with the most tender, yet totally impersonal, circumspection. His own ablutions he carried out in the clear waters of a stream that surrounded the islet. And he would re-enter the oval chamber nude, as he left it, goosefleshed, and covered with a million diamond droplets, which he proceeded vigorously to towel away.

On the second day of her convalescence, he picked her up and carried her in his arms out into the sunlight, laying her down in a shady spot by the ancient walls of the keep, where he had made a daybed of rugs and lambskins, with silken pillows for her head. A family of mallards—the drake leading, his beldame behind, and a line of half-grown ducklings trailing like a squadron of navy frigates to the rear—came out of the rushes at the far side of the stream and clustered at the shore of the islet, honking stentoriously for sustenance. Moonlight produced a haunch of bread, which he and Purity proceeded to break into pieces and feed to the ducks. The last piece they broke between them, hand to hand.

Faces close to each other's, their eyes met. She shut hers as, with infinite tenderness, he kissed her full upon the lips. When she looked again, he was squatting at the water's edge, tossing the last of the bread to the nearest duckling.

"Barney Bates will be here tonight," he said. "He will have all the news. A good lad is Barney."

Purity made no response. She had just received—

and was striving to come to terms with and absorb —a realization that no woman, however otherwise committed in her heart and in her affections, is ever able to accept with any other than the most profound and disturbing reverberations.

She was loved. That strong, yet curiously gentle, man was in love with her. His kiss had betrayed him.

Barney Bates arrived shortly after sunset. He came astride a fat pony. He was a diminutive Cockney sparrow of a youth in a suit of clothes many sizes too large and in a tall hat perched so far on the back of his close-cropped ginger stubble that he had constantly to incline his head forward to maintain its balance.

" 'Evenin', all," he said, his dark, boot-button eyes swarming over the beautiful woman with the silver-gold hair who was seated in an armchair at the head of the refectory table.

Jack Moonlight effected a brief and cursory introduction between Purity and his "runner," not mentioning her name.

"What news, Barney?" he asked. "What are they whispering in the rookeries about you-know-who?"

"Do you 'appen to 'ave a drop o' the old mother's ruin by you, guv'nor?" was the other's response. "Or, conversely, a tot o' Nelson's blood, for to wet the whistle an' cut the phlegm? 'Tis a long ride from Mill Hill, where I 'ave presently come from."

"I have no gin, but there's a double tot of rum for you, and welcome, Barney," said Jack Moonlight. "Mill Hill, you say? And what have you been up to in Mill Hill, of all places?"

Not till the youth had taken a gulp of the proffered spirit, then rolled it appreciatively around his mouth and swallowed it, did he make a reply. "Why, guv'nor, 'tis in Mill Hill that this feller Cap'n D'Eath do 'ave 'is abode," declared Barney, "which is a great barracks of a place as would house the Brigade o' Guards, the Irish parliament, an' 'alf the whores in Whitechapel ... beggin' the lady's pardon."

"The name of this abode?" demanded Moonlight.

"Jermyn Abbey, guv'nor," was the reply. "Called an abbey by reason of it once bein' an abode o' monks in popish times long ago. This I learned from a scullery wench employed there at Jermyn Abbey." He looked pointedly at Moonlight. "For this information, an' more, I did 'ave to bribe 'er with ten shillin', not to mention a stand-up handy-dandy in the kitchen gardens behind the stew ponds ... again beggin' the lady's pardon."

"The ten shillings will be reimbursed," said Moonlight. "As to the handy-dandy, you must regard that as a gratuity ... and may you be spared of the pox. What others news?"

Barney took another gulp of his rum, then said, "Accordin' to my little piece of handy-dandy, Cap'n D'Eath has recently been joined, at Jermyn Abbey, by a lady cousin accompanied by 'er daughter. This latter, who D'Eath do claim to be his niece, may well be the lass you did instruct me to inquire of, among others, guv'nor. Her name—Elizabeth."

"Elizabeth?"

Their informant cocked a shrewd eye at Purity for her outburst, took another swig of his rum, and resumed his discourse. "D'Eath, now 'e 'ave been a-livin' at the abbey this last twelvemonth, it bein' 'is family home, like. The lady cousin, who be named Madeleine somethin', the daughter Cornelia, an' she who is called Elizabeth—they did arrive only a few days ago."

"Where is Chastity, then?" cried Purity. "Where is my child?"

The youth's boot-button eyes regarded her dispassionately.

"This one you call Chastity, ma'am," he said, "be she dark as to hair an' eyes? A regular beauty, I might add."

"Yes, yes, that is she!"

"About your own 'eight, I would say? A way o' carryin' 'erself like she might be a queen? Young, but well-hung-about for all that, with trim little boobies that would knock your eyes out?"

"You describe her exactly," said Purity. "To the last detail," she added coldly.

"Elizabeth," said Barney Bates firmly.

"What are you saying, man?" demanded Jack Moonlight.

"She do now answer to the name o' Elizabeth, no matter what she was called afore," said Barney. "What's more, though I 'ave it from my bit o' handy-dandy that she ain't no such thing, she do address the wench Madeleine as 'Mama.' "

"Oh, no!" cried Purity. "No . . . that!"

Barney glanced to Moonlight as if for guidance. The latter waited for a few moments while Purity buried her face in her hands and appeared to pass through a state of shock. Then he said, "What more of D'Eath? What's his business, if any?"

"You may well ask, guv'nor," replied the other. "My wench knew nothin' in that regard, as you might imagine. For that, I 'ad to go back to the rookeries. Indeed, I did 'ave to consult them right at the very top. Guv'nor, did you ever 'ave any dealin's with Blind Archie?"

"Owned a string of young thieves and child prostitutes in Whitechapel," said Moonlight. "Before that, he was a prosperous banker on Threadneedle Street —till the auditors went through his books. I knew him slightly before they hanged him at Newgate. What of him?"

"Them as took over Blind Archie's dealin's told me

that D'Eath used to bank with Archie in 'is Thread-needle Street days," said the informant. " 'E was left a million pounds by 'is father an' gambled it away. Two other fortunes 'e's made an' lost. An' now 'e's on the way to makin' another—or so they say."

"By what means?"

Barney hunched his shoulders and spread his hands.

"No one knows—or no one's tellin'. But this I gather—there's more to it than thievin'. There's more to it than a-knockin' some party over the head. It's big stuff."

"Big? In what way?" demanded Moonlight.

"Politics, maybe. There's members o' Parliament involved. Big fellers in 'igh places. Nobs. Fellers with 'andles to their names. An' that ain't all. . . . " He looked down at his now-empty glass.

Jack Moonlight refilled it for him. "What else?" he asked.

"There's a move afoot to organize a private army in the rookeries. I don't say it concerns whatever D'Eath's up to, but it do 'ave the same kind o' smell about it."

"A private army? For what purpose?"

"No one's tellin'. But money 'as changed 'ands, an' more's promised. An' the fellers who've been approached are all the sort as would sell their poor old mother for cats' meat if they so minded: the real rough-an'-tumble, the bully-boys army an' navy deserters, escaped convicts, that sort."

"I see," said Jack Moonlight. "And is that all?"

"I'll keep me eyes and ears peeled, guv'nor," said Barney, his gaze turning to Purity, who still sat with her face covered with her hands. "In the rookeries, an' likewise from my piece o' handy-dandy at Jermyn Abbey."

"I would be obliged to you, Barney," said Moonlight. "Be assured that you will not go unrewarded."

Barney Bates rose to take his leave, grinning up at the tall highwayman who towered over him by a head and a half.

"No need for reward from you, guv'nor," he declared. "But for you, I'd 'ave danced my last jig in the air on the three-legged horse long ago. Good day to you guv'nor, an' to you, ma'am. An' I wish I had brought you better news."

Purity lowered her hands. She had not been weeping, but there was all the tragedy of womankind in her eyes and written large upon her perfect countenance.

"It is no fault of yours, Mr. Bates," she said. "You have played your part well. And I thank you."

She watched him leave, then watched Jack Moonlight see him off the islet and set off across the stream astride his fat pony. And then she broke down. When Moonlight re-entered the stone-built chamber, she was bowed over the table in a helpless fit of grief that was terrible to behold. The highwayman gazed down at her in compassion. He reached out his hand to lay it upon the slender shoulder so convulsed with racking sobs, but he thought better of it and let her be. He went over and busied himself at the spirit stove. Later, when Purity had brought her emotions somewhat under control and was drying her eyes, he pushed a steaming mug across the table toward her.

"A drop of tea," he said. "And one for me—the cups that cheer, but do not inebriate. I am very sorry, Purity. There, you see, I have called you by your first name at last."

"You understand, don't you?" she said. "You really are a most remarkable man, Jack, aren't you? You understand my feelings perfectly."

"About Chastity?" he said. "Who is now called Elizabeth and addresses that woman as her mama?

Yes, I can understand why that has cut you so deeply to the heart.".

Purity looked down into the mug of straw-colored brew.

"I have not had an entirely untrammeled life," she said. "I have lived through war and revolution. I have suffered, and been witness to, most of the evils that human beings heap upon their fellow creatures. As regards my associations with men, I can tell you that there is nothing a man may do to a woman's body—be she willing or unwilling—that has not been done to mine, and many times by force. Add to that the fact that I have suffered the loss of my husband, my son, and now my daughter. But I think that the tidings that your fellow brought today, the news that Chastity has finally and utterly cut me off, is addressing that woman as . . . " She hesitated. Moonlight said nothing, but waited till she had regained control of herself, of her trembling nether lip. "I'm sorry, and I have always prided myself upon my fortitude in adversity."

"It is no weakness to bow before the storm," said Moonlight. "Fatal, I fancy, to stand firm till one breaks beyond all mending. Yes, I can see why your being abandoned by Chastity has come as such a blow."

"It is like the slamming of a final door in a long corridor that represented my life," she said. "I am now standing outside. Abandoned. Alone."

"Not quite alone," he said, eyeing her over the rim of his mug of tea.

She reached out her hand across the table and laid it upon his arm.

"That I am not, Jack," she said tenderly. "Indeed, I am very mindful that I possess a new, and very dear, friend, one who saved me, first from shame, and afterward gave me back my life."

He leaned forward till their faces were close.

261

"I would be anything that you wished me to be, Purity," he murmured. "For I have to tell you that I am . . ."

She placed her fingers lightly over his lips.

"You can tell me nothing, Jack, that I have not already discovered for myself," she said softly. "But I beg you to hold your peace—at least for a while. I am not a whole woman, Jack. I am still married to a man whom I have loved since the first moment I set eyes upon him. I have always said that I should love him to eternity. But I am no longer a girl in the first flush of a new passion. I have grown older and more wary. One learns, by experience, that all things pass. The experiences of these past days have so lacerated me, so shaken my firmest convictions about the nature of perfect love—blind, all-suffering, all-understanding, and forgiving love—that I can no longer believe with total and unquestioning conviction that my love, also, will not pass and be forgotten."

"If that should ever come about, Purity," he said, "I beg you to remember Jack Moonlight." And he took her hand in his, bent over it, and planted there a most tender kiss.

They supped late together. She, who with every passing day was growing stronger, cooked the meal. They had rabbit stew—the rabbit he had shot on the edge of the marsh the day previously—and vegetables, which had been brought—as were most of his provisions—by his "runner." With no mention of the delicate topic they had discussed earlier, they made some attempt at small talk while they ate the stew and washed it down with a flask of quite tolerable claret from Moonlight's well-stocked cellar.

But Purity's mind had been all the time revolving around a question that burdened her greatly. Finally, she could keep it to herself no longer. "Jack," she said, "what can those people want with Chastity? Why did they take her? And how and why have they made her one of themselves?"

"As to how it was done," he said, "there are many ways in which a person—particularly one who is young and untried in the nuances of life—may be altered out of all recognition. Take the case of your bright-eyed young fellow who, full of patriotic fervor, takes the king's shilling and enlists in the army. Give him but a twelvemonth of the army's brutalities—with the rotten food, the cheap liquor that's all he can afford, bullying sergeants, long marches, blood, pain, and the eternal threat of the cat-o'-nine tails to drive him on and dull his sensibilities—and what have you got? An unfeeling brute who will kill, or be killed, an animal in a red coat whose vision of paradise is a city given over to sack, with more loot than he can ever carry, more women than he can ever rape. I do not say that those people have subjected your Chastity to such a dire regimen—the idea would be absurd. I merely use the example to illustrate how persons—particularly the young, the easily manipulated—may be turned away from their normal mode of life, even from those they have loved."

She nodded doubtfully. "Allowing that they devised a means to influence her so profoundly," she said, "what reason could they possibly have to lure her away and draw her into their circle, as if she were a member of their family?"

"Tell me more about the girl," said Moonlight. "She was adopted by you when an infant, so I understand. What of her antecedents? Do you know who either of the parents is?"

"We know nothing of her parents," said Purity. "Nor did we probe too deeply, not wishing to have secrets that might, for the sake of the child's happiness, best be kept from her. She was a foundling of the Marylebone orphanage, and she was recommended to us by the wife of one of my husband's army comrades, herself a member of the orphanage's governing board. Jack, you don't think that something connected with Chastity's antecedents may lie behind her abduction at the hands of those people!"

"It is a possibility that must be taken into account," said the highwayman. "But, since she was, as you say, a foundling, it might be difficult to trace her parents —or even her mother—for we may safely assume that the child was born out of wedlock. I will set inquiries afoot immediately. There is not much that the criminal world of London does not know—or cannot uncover. But"—he looked at her very steadily—"is it your wish, Purity? Further knowledge might well bring you further hurt. Do you really *want* the truth?"

She drew in a deep, wavering breath, then said, "I think I can bear to know why she—the child I did not bear and suckle, but whom I have loved as my own—could turn her back upon me, fornicator and adulteress though she found me out to be, and bind herself to a woman who threatened her life and made me play the whore. I think I could bear to . . . "

Overcome with bitter tears, Purity bowed her head.

"No more," said Jack Moonlight quietly. "You have tortured yourself enough for one day. The physician prescribes a sound night's sleep. To bed with you."

"Yes," said Purity, rising. "You are a good, kind friend, Jack. Where would I be now without you?"

"I am your friend," replied Jack Moonlight, "but what you are pleased to call my goodness and kindness are only manifestations of the esteem in which I hold you. I have not been notable in the past for such qualities."

"Little Barney Bates might think otherwise," she said shrewdly. "He dotes on you. You are his hero and he would do anything for you. Only men of real quality inspire such sentiments in other men."

"Barney Bates is not a man," said Moonlight. "He is a boy. Moreover, he is incurably sentimental concerning me. I have warned him many times to leave me be, to quit London and find honest work in the country from whence he came. But he will not. And his absurd devotion to my service will inevitably bring him to the gallows. And, now, good night, Purity."

"Good night, my dear friend."

She kissed him upon the cheek, as one might kiss one's beloved brother, fondly. And she felt his breath quicken. For an instant, she thought he was going to embrace her. For a moment she hesitated, half-hoping that he would do so. And then she turned away.

The moment passed.

But in the dark, a great yearning came upon her. She, neglected and bereft of the loving attentions that are a woman's right, spurned and discarded by the man to whom she had long since given her all, lay and hungered for solace, her whole body afire. Trembling, fearful of what she was about, shrinking from the very passions to which she was submitting herself, she slipped the flimsy shift from her shoulders, baring herself to her own caressing hands.

She caught her breath as the merest touch of her fingertip upon a taut nipple sent a path of flame searing like a lightning flash from breast to loins, and she felt her whole body open up like a flower in the benison of the summer's sun.

Her thoughts flew to . . . *him.* . . .

Not a stone's throw from where she lay, she knew, he was bedded down upon a couch of straw, upon which he had spread sheepskins and his riding cloak. He slept naked—that she guessed, for he always bathed in the stream before retiring, and he went back, still naked, into the outhouse next the stable, where he had shifted his sleeping quarters since her arrival on the islet.

Perhaps he, too, was lying awake in the darkness and thinking of *her*. He, who loved her. For love her he certainly did. She had not needed the beginning of a declaration that she had checked upon his very lips to tell her that. One kiss—one unbidden and unexpected kiss—had betrayed him earlier.

So he would certainly be thinking of her. Imagining her. Yearning for her, perhaps. And she knew what it was to yearn for love unrequited.

It was strange that she, who had been the victim of so many men's dark lusts, should be living in such a secret and remote place in company with a man and yet feel so safe and secure. Never once (save for the impulsive kiss) had he imposed upon her. He, who had probed the secrets of her body with his hands and eyes, who had stripped and washed her thrice daily, had never taken advantage of her helplessness. Nor had he sought to seduce her with male wiles, and it was well-known among men that there is no woman so easily seduced as a woman who had been cast off by an old lover. Such a woman needs consolation. More, she needs reassurance. The man who lay awake in the outhouse next door had offered her both, but in the pure and unselfish form of friendship. He had never imposed himself upon either her body or her will, nor had he taken her for granted.

Yet he loved her. It followed, therefore, that he desired her. For he was a man, if she ever saw a man.

And here, she told herself, lies the chaste and beautiful Purity, Lady Landless, all opened out like a flower, with a great yearning upon her, with hands that can be better employed than in the discovery of her own body, lips that will get scant consolation from kissing her pillow, and a lonely heart in dire need of simple and uncomplicated love.

She slipped out of the bed, hastening, in case she changed her mind before a sudden assault of conscience came over her. The bright moonlight from the arrow-slits on high guided her to the oaken door, which creaked open to her touch.

She paused, suddenly appalled. If asleep, the sound must surely have awakened him; if awake, he would certainly come to discover the cause of the sound.

Hard upon the heels of one decision, she was faced with another. She had been presented with another option—her last—which was either to go on—and quickly—or to rush back into bed, and be there, feigning sleep, if and when he came to investigate the sound of the opening door.

The night breeze gently caressed her nude body, prickling her skin. Seduced by its suave caress, she was lost to all reason, all self-doubt.

She went on.

He sat up when she flung open the door of the outhouse. The moonlight behind her presented the breathtaking contours of her body in strong silhouette. She saw him as she had imagined him: lying upon the bed of straw and sheepskins, with his riding cloak but vestigially draped across his nude form.

"My God!" he gasped in awe and wonder. "Purity!"

It seemed an absurdly unsuitable time to make a speech, and her voice was betraying her as being near to tears, but she said, "I . . . I told you earlier that I was not a whole woman. But I have found that I am wrong. I have found that I am, in a very real sense, still a complete woman. This may be because I am what they say I am: libertine, whore, adultress. I do not know. I offer no excuse. I only know that I need you very badly, as I hope you need me."

"Purity, my angel!"

Then she was running to him, to his waiting arms. Her lips, eager, open, closed upon his, and their tongues entwined. His powerful arms enfolded her body in all its slenderness, its subtleties of the lissome and the voluptuous. And he moaned with the pure pleasure of discovery, he who knew that lovely body so intimately, but never before in the surrender of passion.

For her part, Purity had abandoned herself utterly to the experience. All doubts and scruples were far gone. She was led only by the siren call of desires that burned her very mind, that echoed every touch of his hands, every moist motion of his questing lips.

"Yes!" she said. "Now, my lover—*now!*"

She was mounting ahead of him, confident that he was at her hastening heels, rising up into the clouds of ecstasy that she knew and loved so well. So surely did she know the path to the illimitable stars that it required only the gentle coaxing of his lips and hands to effect her elevation to those pure and pellucid places. High in the glory of eternal sunlight, she paused in her ascent and waited for her lover to join her. She waited indulgently, with the serene confidence of her own beauty, her singular ability to entice, allure, coax, persuade, seduce. . . .

And then, with a jolting pang of distress, Purity was brought to the sudden and unnerving realization that she was alone in the clouds of ecstasy, and that her lover would not, could not, join her.

"Jack!" she cried. "What is it? What have I done wrong? Oh, my dear! In what way have I failed you?"

He leaped from her as if she had become a searing fire, as if her very touch had become repugnant to him. She watched from the tumbled heap of sheepskins—nude, dismayed, her own lush desires already disappearing like water draining away between the fingers of cupped hands—as he strode to and fro in the moonlight.

"You have failed me not at all!" he finally declared in a voice of anger.

"Then why . . . why . . . "

"You have eyes to see, woman!" he blazed. "I am impotent! Is that not clear? Jack Moonlight, terror of the highway, fawned upon by all the doxies of the London rookeries—those who have not tried him in the lists of Venus; and they are mighty few, I promise you, for a self-declared stud cannot risk his reputation with a blabber-mouthed whore—is no better than a eunuch!" He bowed his head.

All Purity's Latin passion and forthrightness asserted themselves. Leaping from the bed, eyes flaring, breasts a-jounce, she pointed to him.

"You are no eunuch!" she cried. "You are all man, as is plain to any woman who is a woman!"

"The failure is here." He smote his brow. "Do you understand? These ten years and more, I have not been able to pleasure myself with a woman. And, as I live, I have desired you, Purity, as I have never desired another woman."

"Why?" she screamed at him. "For pity's sake, *why* can't you?"

"Purity, what is the worst crime known to mankind?" he demanded.

"I lose patience with you with every passing moment!" she blazed. "Now must come a catechism! I come to you in the night—I grant you, not the most comely woman since time began, no Cleopatra, no Sheba, no Pompadour—for, let it now be frankly stated, the handy-dandy. But, though not numbered amongst those distinguished ladies of horizontal persuasion, I am deemed—I have been deemed in my time—a not inconsiderable performer of not inconsiderable attributes. What follows? I am left high and dry, and when I make an inquiry as to why and how, I am treated to a catechism, a question-and-answer roundelay."

"Answer me!" persisted Moonlight. "What, in your opinion, is the worst crime known to mankind?"

She shrugged. "Murder," she said. "Well . . . no . . . in my opinion, there is a fine finality about being killed. For a woman, especially, there are ways of being alive that are quite insupportable. I would opt for rape. Yes, for a man to rape a woman, I think that is the most heinous crime of all."

"And what would you think," asked Jack Moonlight, *"of a man who raped his own mother?"*

"No-o-o-o-o!" she cried.

"I see the answer in your eyes," he said. "There is no hope for me, and that is my just dessert."

"Jack . . ." Her eyes were brimming with tears.

"All unknowingly, I swear it," he said. "Not that it mitigates my sin in the slightest degree, but I didn't know . . . I simply didn't know. . . ." He pressed his hands to his brow.

"Oh, my dear!" cried Purity, reaching to embrace him.

He struck her arm aside—violently.

"Leave me be!" he cried. "Can't you see it's no use?" He gestured toward her, to her ravishing body, flaunted before him in its tempting nakedness. "Even you can't turn a eunuch into a whole man. Ten years ago, I brutally raped my own mother, and I have paid the price. Never once since that time have I been able to pleasure any woman."

Purity was not to be thrust aside so easily. Braving another brutal rebuff, she again reached out and laid a hand upon his.

"Tell me, Jack," she said. "Unburden yourself—as I unburdened myself to you. Tell me *everything.*"

Chapter Eight

She had been quite correct in her first summation of him: he was, indeed, a gentleman in the literal sense, gently born and gently reared. His father, so he told her, had been a Leicestershire squire, owner of rolling acres, a mansion, held a Lord-Lieutenancy of his country . . . and had a mistress whom he kept in suitable style in Ashby de la Zouch. It was his partiality for the latter—and, indeed, for any woman of reasonable attributes who was willing to go to bed with him —that led to his downfall. His lady wife—a gentle soul of Puritanical upbringing, who possessed the fatally disparate attributes of a delicious body and a complete lack of sensuality—found out about the charmer in Ashby de la Zouch and about some of her husband's more temporary attachments, and she left him, taking their infant son.

Jack was reared by his mother till the age of eight, when he suffered the fate of other English boys of his class and was sent to boarding school, from which system he emerged at the flowering of his manhood and proceeded straight to the commencement of his medical studies in Edinburgh. During that time, his mother had remarried (the father having died of drink and debauchery) and, after the manner of such ladies as she, had chosen badly yet again: Jack's stepfather was a brute and a bully. On occasions when the boy was on vacation from school, he was regularly beaten and abused. From the age of eighteen, when his academic brilliance had won him a bursary and a degree of financial independence, he never saw his stepfather again . . . or his mother.

Until . . .

"Don't stop now," counseled Purity. "Tell me all. You promised."

Jack Moonlight ceased his pacing up and down the chamber. Out of some prompting of modesty—or shame—he had put on his breeches. Purity, too, had had the delicacy of feeling to cover most of her nakedness with a sheepskin. She reclined upon the bed, regarding him gravely.

"You really want to hear the worst?" he demanded.

"I told you the worst of my doings, Jack," she responded. "Did you think it was easy for me, a woman, to admit to the things I did with those men?"

He nodded, acknowledging the truth of her statement. And he resumed his frenzied pacing. Purity bided herself with patience.

Presently, he resumed his tale. "For three years I read and practiced anatomy under Professor Monro," he said. "After that, knowing my circumstances, and regarding me as his star pupil, the professor was instrumental in obtaining for me a free place to study medicine at Leiden. The four years I spent in The Netherlands were by far the happiest of my life." He ceased his pacing. He pointed at Purity, adding vehemently, "Four years. Mark that! Four years at Leiden, plus three at Edinburgh, and the best part of a year before that—call it eight years in all—and in all that time I had never set eyes on my mother.

"Yes, the best years of my life. It was at Leiden that I first fell in love. And I continued to do so at irregular but continuous intervals. I also drank rather a lot, I seem to remember. Purity, must I go on?"

"You know you must go on," she said quietly.

"Back in London," he said, "I took lodgings in the Inner Temple together with a couple of newly appointed barristers, fellows like myself: young in the splendor of arrogance; confident that the world not only owed us a living, but a damned good living at that; convinced that the women of England were only too willing to lay themselves down for our delectation; and poor.

"God, we were so poor. They, my roommates, were without clients, but at least they made a guinea here and there by slaving for some idle Jack or other who couldn't be troubled to prepare his own case. I, a physician without a practice, was reduced to living on my wits, and my wits being what they were, more frequently going hungry than not. And we took our vicarious pleasures. . . ."

"Go on," said Purity implacably. "You can't stop now."

He drew in a deep breath. "You have heard of the Mohocks, those idle sprigs of the upper classes who used to terrorize the streets of London after dark before the war. I and my friends and a few others of our sort banded ourselves together as latter-day Mohocks. The original gentry of this persuasion did it out of boredom. They had everything; all that remained was vandalism and brutality for its own sake, for excitement. We robbed, beat, and bullied, out of frustration, to repay the world for reducing us to what we were: overeducated, unemployed paupers. Do I seem to protest too much?"

"Please continue," said Purity.

"In addition to beating and robbing innocent passersby," said Moonlight, "we also raped. To give us our due, it was not so much rape as it was nonpayment for services rendered. We would be accosted by some cheap drab, tumble her in a dark doorway, and run off laughing when she screamed for her shilling. But it was a kind of rape.

"Then one night we raped in earnest. It happened in the Haymarket. We were drunk, some of us more so than others, but I don't offer that as any excuse for what we did. There was a hackney cab that had lost a wheel. Its passenger—a lady of uncertain years, but quite comely, so far as one could make out in the dark, and befuddled with drink, as we were—was trying to secure another cab in which to continue her journey. Our ringleader, a barrister named Forrester, doffed his hat and very civilly invited the lady to accept us as her escort till we had procured a cab for her. On the corner of the Haymarket, when we were out of sight and sound of a soul, when that innocent, unsuspecting woman who had confided her safety into our hands was far from any help, we . . . raped her.

"It was Forrester who ripped the shawl from her shoulders and threatened to cut her throat if she screamed. Two of the fellows took her by the arms and held her up against the wall while Forrester tore open her gown from neck to hem. He it was who took her first, rutted her like a stallion. The others followed, one after the other. I was next to the last one. When I came to her, she was all but insensible, but trembling, as if with the ague. I discovered her body to be soft, pleasing. Her bare breasts . . . "

"If you stop now," said Purity, "you will never unburden yourself of it for the rest of your life."

Moonlight passed a hand across his face. "When I had had my way with her," he said, "when I had

274

spent myself upon the body of that . . . total stranger, who had reposited her trust in us, I took my turn to hold one of her arms while the last of our companions unbuttoned himself for the fray. By that time we were having totally to support her against the wall, for she had swooned completely away. The last fellow—his name was Smythe, Jacob Smythe—complained loudly that he had gotten the worst of the bargain and called upon me, a physician, to rouse the woman, for, as he said, 'Twould otherwise be akin to having the handy-dandy with a corpse.

"Her head was bowed upon her breast. Taking her by the hair, I lifted it up and smacked her smartly across the cheek. And in that same moment . . . "

He broke off, ceased his frantic pacing, and stared down at his hands, turning them over. He examined the palms, the knuckles, the fingernails, all done with the air of a man who was regarding them for the first time. Purity said nothing, offered him no further prompting, but lay still, watching him with breathless horror.

Presently, he continued. "My 'tender' ministrations bore fruit, for I aroused the woman from her swoon, and my good friend Jacob Smythe was mightily grateful and proceeded to pleasure himself with great abandon. It was then that the moon came out from behind the clouds, where it had been hiding all during our lusty adventure.

"I saw clearly, for the first time, the face of the woman.

"And she saw me!

"The instant of recognition was immediate—and mutual.

"She called my name aloud. It was the last utterance of any humankind ever to pass from her lips. Looking into her eyes, still holding her wrist so that my friend Smythe could have his way with her, I saw my mother go insane upon the instant!"

"Oh, no!" gasped Purity.

"I lost all control," said Moonlight. "They shouted to me to desist when I took Smythe by the throat and dragged him away from her. They were still shouting and hitting me about the head when I felt Smythe choke to death between my fingers. And then they ran off, leaving me alone with the man I had killed. He was dead, and there was a mad woman who sat upon the ground, naked and defiled, babbling and grinning like a child."

At the termination of his terrible tale, Jack Moonlight slumped down upon the bed and buried his face in his hands. Purity was swift to offer him comfort. She wound her slender, bare arms around his broad shoulders and laid her head against his.

"Jack, Jack, what can I do for you?" she asked.

"My mother never recovered," he said. "The merciful insanity that washed the horror of realization from her mind has kept it so all these years. She still lives—if the state in which she exists can, indeed, be called living. She is in Bethlehem Hospital. I visit her often. They have many visitors to Bedlam, you know. Fashionable folk go there for the entertainment of seeing the lunatics cavort like Barbary apes. For a small fee, the attendants will tickle their charges with a hot iron to encourage their amusing antics. Perhaps, when I am not there, my mother is . . . "

"Be quiet! Stop it, Jack!"

Sobbing, she pressed her hand against his mouth and her forehead to his, mingling her tears with his. Together, they slumped sideways upon the bed, held each to each, and lay there in stillness, silently. Finally his breathing became more regular, and he slept with his cheek against her uncovered breast, like a babe. Purity remained staring into the darkness till dawn finally crept over "The Devil's Hundred," and out in the sea of reed and sedge a heron called to its mate.

The next night, by unspoken and mutual agreement, Jack Moonlight left the outhouse and shared the bed in the oval chamber with Purity. He slept naked, as always, and she wore her thin shift. There was no carnal congress between them; they lay in each other's arms with the bland innocence of two small children huddled together for mutual warmth and comfort. And all her beauty and softness were incapable of arousing his manhood. They never again referred to his dreadful secret.

A couple of days later, Jack left the islet, and he was absent most of the day and all the night following. Purity busied herself by cleaning and tidying up the interior of the keep and tending the two horses, which, together with the highwayman's black gelding, occupied the stable adjacent to the outhouse. One of her new charges, a handsome roan mare, developed a great affection toward her, and it was this that put an idea into Purity's head. She told it to Jack Moonlight the following morning, after they breakfasted together upon his return.

"Jack, next time you ride out, I want to go with you."

He eyed her askance. "Purity, do you know what you are asking? I don't ride out for pleasure, you know. Nor am I a country physician making the rounds of his patients—much as I would prefer such a way of making my living. I am a hunted outlaw, my dear, a thief, with every man's hand against me. I rob to stay alive, and since, as you know, I prefer to live in a certain style and comfort, I perforce have to work hard at my thieving trade. It is no pastime for a woman, I can assure you."

"Nevertheless, I wish to accompany you," she said, "and share your dangers, if only on one occasion."

He regarded her searchingly for a few moments, then asked, "Why, Purity? Why this sudden caprice?"

"It is more than a caprice," she said. "I am quite sincere and serious. You saved me from rape, and now I know the reason why you did that. You also saved my life. What is more, you continue to feed and shelter me. It seems only right, therefore, that I should make a token sharing of the dangers that you have to endure in order to keep me here in comfort and idleness. Add to that the fact that I feel restless and at odds with myself."

"You are still pining for the life you have left behind?" he asked.

"Not left behind, but lost," she said. "It is gone forever. No, Jack, I have finished pining. Something has died within me. I think it perished in the telling of it, the day you persuaded me to unburden myself to you. I am left with an emptiness that I must now fill."

"I do not think that highway robbery will adequately fill the emptiness in your life," he said dryly. "But you are welcome to savor the experience, Purity."

They left the islet together the following night, after resting together upon the bed throughout the afternoon. Jack outfitted her out in a pair of his buckskin breeches, which fit where they touched. An old riding cloak and a spare hat of his, which she made fit by padding it out with paper, completed her slender disguise. And they both carried masks.

With Jack leading on the black and Purity following on the roan, they traversed the hard spine that was the causeway through the treacherous swampland and traveled by devious and twisting paths till they

278

emerged from under the archway of willow into the tributary of the Lea. An hour later, after a hard canter through moonlit countryside, avoiding the lights of scattered hamlets, they came to a rutted highway and a gnarled signpost that pointed to London.

Jack indicated a line of hawthorn bushes that stood back within hailing distance of the road.

"We'll take cover behind there," he said, "and have a look at anything that passes. If we fancy what we see, we ride in pursuit. And, mark you, keep well behind me, Purity. And if we run into any trouble, ride like the wind, keeping the moon on your left shoulder. Don't draw rein till you come to the river, and wait for me there. Is that understood?"

"Yes," said Purity, for whom the whole adventure had taken on a curious excitement that was compounded half of fear and half of a breathless feeling of anticipation.

They rode over and took their places behind the bushes, over which they commanded a view up and down the highway. Save for the occasional restless shifting of a horse's stance or a chomping at a bit, there was silence between them. Somewhere far off an owl hooted, and it was answered by another.

"Someone's coming," murmured Jack, "on foot."

Purity heard the footsteps soon after. Presently, a lone figure came within sight down the road toward London. As the figure drew closer, the newcomer was revealed to be an elderly man in a battered tall hat and a flapping, tailed coat, which, even at that distance, they could see to be patched and threadbare. Under his arm he carried a violin.

"A traveling fiddler," whispered Jack Moonlight. "Not worth powder and shot."

The old man went on his way, unscathed. A hard knot of tension that had formed in Purity's stomach relaxed itself. She smiled up at the broken-nosed profile beside her.

"A talent for patient waiting is of tremendous benefit in this profession," he said. "More highwaymen die of boredom than ever Jack Ketch hoisted on a rope's end."

"You make light of it," said Purity. "You jest. But there is danger, surely? The Bow Street Runners?"

"The Runners have made inroads into the profession," he admitted. "But the public purse does not run to the kind of nags that your successful highwayman can afford to provide himself with. Black Harry, here, could hold his own with a derby winner over five furlongs and more, and your little mare, Alice, is nearly as neat-footed. Add to that, we gentlemen of the road have the advantage of surprise, while the Runners have to stretch their slender force to cover every mile of every road leading into London. I tell you, Purity, the crowd that cheers a highwayman at his hanging is applauding a fool who has only his folly or incompetence to blame for the plight he's in. And that's the truth of it."

"You greatly reassure me," said Purity.

They fell silent. Despite her nervousness, Purity felt curiously at ease with herself, and she was surprised to realize that, since leaving the islet, she had thought of nothing but the immediate tasks at hand: riding Alice through the swampland, keeping pace with her companion, attending to her surroundings, watching out for likely danger. She gave no thought to the misery that had closed in upon her life. Abandoned wives and mothers should turn highwaymen, she thought ruefully.

"Something coming!" exclaimed Jack. "A coach, by by the sound of it. A four-in-hand. Mask yourself, Purity. I think we may have a client here."

Obediently, Purity took her black face mask from

out of the pocket of her overlarge breeches and put it on. Jack did likewise. Next, she saw him draw the two long horse-pistols from the holsters fixed to his saddle. She heard the click-click of their hammers being pulled back to full cock, then saw him carefully replace them. And then she heard the coach.

The tight knot formed itself in her stomach once more, and with it came a feeling of lightness in the head, a sense of unreality. What was she—a lady of society, wife of a highly respected knight of the realm, and mother of two—doing out at this hour, in company with a thief and murderer who had the temerity to be in love with her, yet whose manhood was not equal to the task of tumbling her in bed?

"Stand ready," murmured Jack. "If I break cover after our client, follow behind me, but not too closely."

"Yes," she whispered.

The coach and horses were coming from the London direction, and moving at a trot, with all the attendant creaking and jingling of a large and cumbersome conveyance being driven over a hard and rutted road in dry weather. Moments later, they saw the twin, winking pinpoints of light from its lanterns.

"'Tis a big one," said Jack. "A regular stage. The Harwich stage, I shouldn't wonder, bound to connect with the packet for the Hook of Holland. There'll be diamond merchants from Amsterdam aboard her, with their baggage stuffed with uncut sparklers. I think you have brought me luck this night, my dear Purity."

She did not reply. Now she could make out the humped bulk of the oncoming stagecoach, the silhouettes of the tall-hatted menfolk riding atop, the curve of the driver's whip, even a plume of steam from the laboring horses as it swirled within the loom of the coach lamps and was briefly illuminated.

"We'll take her!" said Jack. "Remember what I

said, Purity. If there is any trouble, ride like the wind with the moon on your left shoulder."

Purity essayed to whisper acknowledgment, but her throat was too dry to utter a syllable.

The stagecoach drew slowly abreast of them, then went past.

"Now!" exclaimed Jack. "Ride, highwayman!" And, clapping his spurred heels into his mount's flanks, he thundered forward in a long, curving path that would bring him abreast and ahead of the slow-moving coach. Purity urged Alice to follow.

There was a wild exhilaration in her blood. Danger and possible death were prospects that action—now that it was upon her—had entirely banished. Instead, she experienced a sense of power and achievement, of overwhelming superiority. Well-mounted as she was, armed as her companion was, the faceless puppets who rode within and upon the lumbering stagecoach were entirely at their mercy, mere onlookers to a drama in which they could only play the role of victims.

Jack Moonlight was riding at full stretch now, hunched high over his mount's neck, his coattails flying. Their curving path had brought them fifty yards ahead of the coach, and they were now cutting in toward the road. The highwayman had gauged it nicely; he would be drawing rein twenty yards in front of the oncoming vehicle.

By now they must have been spotted by someone atop the coach. And the presence of two careering riders coming out of the darkness of a lonely highway spelled only one thing. Purity experienced a momentary pang of compassion for the unknowns in the coach, but dismissed it from her mind when, seeing Jack Moonlight bringing his horse to a slithering halt, she was obliged to follow suit, or collide with him.

"Stand and deliver!" The highwayman yelled the traditional command.

The stagecoach did not stop its onward pace; instead, the lead horse swerved violently to one side, the others following, so that the big vehicle was brought abreast of the two halted riders and heading for the verge of the wide highway. In that same instant, Purity saw a blossoming of orange flame come from the rear, upper part of the coach. It was instantly followed by a thunderclap of sound. And then . . . something plucked the hat from her head.

"Zounds!" cried Jack Moonlight. "They have a guard who's hellbent to earn his shilling! Are you all right, Purity?"

"Yes!"

"Stay here. I'll close in on them. Unless the fellow's carrying another gun, his bolt is shot."

It was then that Purity saw *them* and screamed the warning to her companion. *"Jack! Look! Behind you!"*

They, too, were approaching the scene in a long, curving path, across almost the same ground that Jack and Purity had ridden. Six of them, at a glance. Caped coats flying. Rising in the stirrups. They meant business.

"Runners!" shouted Jack. "It's a trap! Ride for your life, Purity!"

"Jack, what about you?" she cried.

"Do as you're told, woman!" he bellowed, and, suiting the action to the command, he reached and slapped Alice full across the rump. The mare whinnied, reared, and set off at a standing gallop, with Purity hard-put to retain her seat. Behind, she heard the dull crash of a pistol discharging—that would be Jack's. It was immediately followed by an answering fusillade. The Runners really did mean business!

A hedge loomed up out of the darkness ahead of her. Purity scarcely had time to gather up her mount in readiness for the jump before they were over and plunging on across a stretch of plowed land. The going was heavy and she had to swerve to avoid a pond that lay in the middle of the field, which gave her the opportunity to look back the way she had come. There appeared to be no one pursuing her. She wondered how the highwayman had fared in the shooting. . . .

The far hedge came in sight, and she was over it in a trice, the mare tittupping into a tree-lined lane. Left or right presented no problem, but two horsemen were thundering down from the left. There was a crash, and Purity distinctly heard a ball scream past her bent head. And then she was setting Alice into a breakneck gallop along the lane, in and out of the moonlight, with the trees slipping past like palings of a long fence. And all the time, in counterpoint to Alice's drumming hooves, she could hear the hoofbeats of her pursuers.

Trapped like a rat in an alley, with no chance to leap out of the narrow, hedged-in lane, with armed men in pursuit and heaven knows what in the darkness ahead, (perhaps a gate that was too high to jump, in which case she was doomed), Purity had no recourse but to keep going—and hope.

Another pistol shot. The Runners were well armed to be able to burn powder so freely. It was likely that they had a pair of pistols apiece, and double-barreled ones at that. She bowed her head more closely to the flying mare's streaming mane.

Suddenly the lane ended, and she was out in the open, thundering across a seemingly boundless meadow of rich grass. Alice, appearing to like the going underfoot, increased her pace to a long, easy stride. Purity took the opportunity to snatch a glance back over her shoulder. The pursuers were in sight—just: twin shapes rising and falling in the shadows. And they were dropping back: fifty yards away, at least. She remembered what Jack had said about the inadequacy of the Runners' mounts, and she blessed her good fortune to be riding a highwayman's steed.

It was shortly after—and just about the time that her pursuers had fallen out of sight—that disaster befell the galloping mare. In mid-stride, she caught her forehoof in a rabbit hole and plunged forward on her front, rolling over in a spectacular tangle of flying limbs. Purity had the presence of mind to kick free of the stirrups. The next instant her head connected with the soft turf, her whole world dissolved into a sea of blinding lights, and she rolled, over and over, down a gentle slope and came to rest, half-conscious, in a narrow drainage ditch. Opening her eyes, she was just in time to see the two Bow Street Runners riding past over the crest of the low hill—in pursuit of, did they but know it, a riderless horse.

The hoofbeats faded away in the distance. It was very quiet. She moved her limbs and found them to be unbroken. Indeed, apart from a sore head, she had emerged extremely well from the very spectacular tumble, and she hoped that the mare had done likewise.

The thought of her runaway mount alerted Purity to the danger of her situation. At any time, Alice might slow to a halt and betray that she was riderless. It followed, then, that the Runners would retrace their steps in search of their quarry. She must get well away from the path along which they would be returning. But which way?

The moon was high. Climbing out of the ditch, she put it on her left shoulder, as Jack had instructed her, and began to run. Before she had reached the hedge at the far end of the meadow, the Runners had returned. She heard their mounts' hoofbeats quite clearly in the darkness behind her, and then they faded away. She had given them the slip—just.

The moon was setting behind a bank of trees that sketched the shape of a hill. It was still on her left. A dog barked in the distance, and she saw the light of a dwelling. Dawn could not be far hence, she decided; the farm workers were already rising.

How far to the river? And what should she do when she reached it? What if Jack had been caught?

She plodded on, dragging one weary foot after the other, willing herself to forget a pain that had developed in her side. She had shed her cloak, and the shirt she wore was plastered to her shoulders and breasts with her own sweat. In the interests of comfort, she had also disposed of her shoes and was walking barefoot. The going was sometimes hard, since, in guiding herself by means of the moon, she had to take whatever terrain offered itself: crossing streams and ditches, crawling through hedges and undergrowth, traversing farmland and grassland.

As the first pale glow appeared above the eastern horizon, she saw the silvery sheen of the river ahead of her. She covered the last fifty yards at a stumbling walk, then fell, face downward, on the bank, dipping her hands and arms into the cooling benison of its flow, splashing her throbbing brow, sucking in mouthfuls, letting her silver-gold hair trail into the water.

"Rise to your feet with your hands above your head, or I will shoot you where you lie!" The command came from behind her.

She rose, her heart leaping.

He came out of the shadows of a copse twenty paces distant: tall, cape-coated, hatless. The last of the moonlight had gone, so she was nothing to him but a shape in a white shirt.

But she had heard his voice . . . and had rejoiced.

"Jack!" she cried.

"Purity! Oh, thank God, my blessed, blessed girl!"

286

He was running to join her, and she to him. He held her at arm's length for a few moments, gazing upon her as if for the first time ever.

"I kept the moon on my left shoulder," she murmured.

"I thought you were dead," he said. "I've been waiting here all night. But you're alive and well, my Purity, my dearest."

He held her in his arms, pressed her softness to him, drank of her lips as if he were supping at the very cup of life. And all the time he was murmuring his adoration of her, of the wonder and delight to have her alive and in his embrace. And as he held her close to him, she became aware that a miracle had been wrought in Jack Moonlight during his long and anguished vigil and that her return had brought that miracle to full and splendid fruition. Half-laughing, half-crying, she drew him down with her upon the grassy bank. There, with the music of the flowing water close by and the rosy fingers of the new dawn painting the eastern sky, she helped him remove the last of her clothing, and likewise his, till they were nude together.

On that, her second ascent into the clouds of delight, they rose together, hand in hand, joined in ecstasy, with no impediment to their flight into the glory of everlasting sunlight. And dawn broke to find them lying, still locked in each other's embrace, nude, sleeping, satiated.

"You have a mole under your right breast. May I kiss it?"

"Of course."

She ran her fingers through his dark chestnut hair, marveling at the way the tight curls sprang back when she released them. The kissing of her mole having become a more protracted and extensive exploration, she then lay back, closed her eyes, and yielded to his gentle ministrations of lips and fingertips.

"Am I a good lover?" he asked presently.

"You know you are a good lover," she murmured, "and you are merely fishing for compliments, as all men do."

"You have known many men?"

"Don't question me, Jack," she admonished him gently. "Take me for what I am and resist the temptation to pick me to pieces, the way a child will take a flower apart, petal by petal, to discover how it is made. Yes, I have known many men. But few men have known me. They have *used* me, but they have never been aware of the woman within. And, though I have been often used, I have not given myself to many men, and when I have, it has always been out of love, or compassion, or simply because the man in question had a grave and pressing need."

"You have given yourself to me," he said, "totally, as no woman ever has before. And I have known women. I assure you—ten years ago, before . . ."

She silenced him, her finger on his lips.

"Never speak of that again," she said. "It is over, finished. Your sin has been forgiven. You have paid the price. You are now exorcised."

He said, "I was going to ask: In what category do I stand? Was it out of compassion, or because of my great need, that you abandoned yourself—continue to abandon yourself—with me?"

Purity traced a fingertip down his breast, then watched his nipple pucker and harden to her touch.

"You stand in a unique category," she said. "What we have done together, and what I hope we shall continue to do together, is because of my *own* need. Does that sound brazen, Jack? Are you one of those men who think it is whorish of a woman to confess to her needs? If so, then I am a whore. I can only say that I never felt less like a whore."

"We have not spoken of love," he said quietly. "Can I presume to ask you something? Was it not also for love that you gave yourself?"

She shook her head. "I cannot lie to you, Jack. No, I have no love to offer, for I gave it away to one man a very long time ago, and all that remains in its place is a very deep and sincere affection, which is all yours."

"And this need of which you spoke," he said, "is it the need that follows your loss—the loss of the man you love?"

"You are on dangerous ground, Jack," she whispered, looking away. "I asked you not to pick me to pieces."

"You have answered me," he said. And he gave a sigh.

"Jack, Jack!" She put her soft arms around his neck, looking closely into his eyes. "Don't be aggrieved. I am not yours, nor ever will I be. Rest content that I gave myself to you without hesitation, without reserve. Be assured that you have filled my need, as I hope and trust that I have filled yours." She gently drew him closer to her so that their breasts touched. "And now I think that I should like you to take me again," she whispered.

The mare Alice was gone for good, he said, taken, without a doubt, by the Runners. He still had Black Harry, though. They dressed in the warm sunlight, kissed lingeringly, and set off through the swampland, she nestling in his arms.

Returning to the stone keep was like returning home. The events of the night, plus the delirious aftermath, had cleaned Purity's mind of many specters, many bitter regrets. Never more clearly had she realized that a chapter in her life was ended and that it was useless to repine. Best to bury the past, and wait for the future to materialize itself. Meanwhile, she had a home. And she had the love and devotion of a man who—though the world might brand him a criminal—was a good, true man whom, to her great joy, she had made whole again.

Watching him move about the oval chamber, as he busied himself with the small tasks that devolve upon the male half of a *ménage,* she told herself that she had chosen well; being a woman incapable of living alone and celibate, it had been inevitable that, given time, she would have turned, sooner or later, to some man's bed and company. That she should have chosen a hunted outlaw was in some ways providential; they were both alone in the world, cut off both by the barriers of his calling, and also by the sea of rush and sedge that surrounded their tight little haven. In their shut-off state, she would never suffer reminders of her former existence, never have to endure the sly glances and whispered innuendos whenever she and her lover appeared together.

She was, in a word, secure.

Their only visitors were Barney Bates and, occasionally, his younger brother, who rejoiced in the name of Wilfred. Diminutive like his sibling, Wilfred also came on the fat pony, and always to deliver a verbal message from Barney. Two days after their night encounter with the Runners, he brought news that the mare Alice was indeed in the law's possession and that notices had been posted throughout the city announcing that the new accomplice of the highwayman Jack Moonlight—described as a short, slightly built youth of a violent and dangerous temper—was deemed to have a price of seventy-five guineas on his head, to be paid to any person or persons who might accomplish the villian's capture. Jack smilingly advised the shocked Purity that seventy-five guineas was a very handsome price, and that she should be proud to have achieved such a notable distinction after only one foray.

She never accompanied him on another night ride. He went out on one or two nights in the weeks when the moon was full, or nearly so. The rest of his time he spent with her. No longer did he spend nights drinking and attending the cock-fighting in the taverns of the rookeries, as had been his wont. Purity provided his every need; she was wife and lover, confidante, helpmate, and friend. They made love at any hour, in bed and out in the sunlight, or in the shadow of the keep's ancient walls. She gave herself unstintingly, refusing him nothing, withholding no part of her; but all the time she was aware that what he most desired—her love—was unavailable.

On the few nights when he was absent, she existed in a limbo of emptiness. No matter how she protracted the few small tasks that needed to be done around the place, there came a time when she was thrown back upon her own thoughts.

Thoughts of . . . Mark. No matter how she tried, he obtruded upon her and was not to be shut out by any effort of will. And when she used the most outrageous means—when she interposed the image of she and Jack making love together—her only reward, and it was a bitter reward, was to recall the times when the man in her arms had been Mark Landless. It was then that she had to admit to herself that, no matter how ecstatic her experiences with Jack were, they were not to be compared with the otherworldly rapture that she had shared with the man to whom she had given her heart. And then the tears came.

If not Mark, it was her beloved Robbie who came to haunt her loneliness.

And if not Robbie, it was Chastity. . . .

She was Elizabeth, and in love.

She and Cornelia no longer shared a bed. Cornelia slept in a room on the floor below. It had been her, Cornelia's, idea. She had said that if they were forever in each other's arms, it would grow stale. Better that they should sleep apart, said Cornelia, and that she should come in the night, from time to time and all unexpectedly, and creep into bed with her darling Elizabeth.

Elizabeth had wept at the idea—the very notion that the wonderful, delirious things that darling Cornelia did to her body and that she did in return to Cornelia's could ever grow stale was unthinkable. But her lover was quite firm, and the arrangement stood.

It was dark, and she had just snuffed out her candle. There was a light in the corridor outside, which caused a strip of brightness to show at the foot of the door. When Cornelia came—and she had not come for so long that her whole body ached with desire—her lover always betrayed her presence in that strip of light at the foot of the door as she paused for a moment before creeping in.

Elizabeth's eyes never left the light at the foot of the door. Surely, darling Cornelia would come tonight. They had exchanged glances across the dinner table, and she had felt herself coloring with a sudden onrush of emotion, a kindling of a desire that suffused her whole body, beginning at the pit of her stomach and radiating outward to her breasts, her loins, her toes, and her fingertips. Cornelia had looked so beautiful tonight in that striped dress, which hugged her bosom and made much of her lovely shoulders and arms. She had wished to communicate her feelings to Cornelia, but it had been difficult with the others looking on. A touch of a hand, if that had been possible, might have been sufficient to let Cornelia know how much she ached for her.

Perhaps, in the miraculous way that lovers have, Cornelia had sensed it, anyhow. Perhaps, even at this moment, she was preparing to come to her: plaiting her long, silky tresses into a single pigtail, putting on her flimsy peignoir, dabbing musky perfume on her cheek, her wrists, in the cleft of her bosom. . . .

Elizabeth remembered the times when they had slept together always. That was before they took the ride in the coach with drawn blinds and arrived at this rambling old house in the country, where she was able, for the first time in what seemed like an eternity, to look out of unshuttered windows. Not that there was anything to see: only a thick bank of dark trees.

If only darling Cornelia came to her more often, she would be happy in the house . . . happy with Mama Madeleine, with dear Quintin, even with the forbidding man who sat at the end of the table—he whom she could not *quite* bring herself to address as Papa.

She was sure that Cornelia was coming. Her skin prickled at the idea, and her breathing quickened. She closed her eyes, willing her lover to hasten. She pictured Cornelia leaving her own room and closing the door behind her, climbing the stairs to the upper floor, gliding, barefoot, down the long corridor to the door at the far end. She would pause there for a brief time, savoring the moment when, having stepped out of her night shift, she would slip between the silken sheets and reach out to take . . .

Elizabeth's eyes snapped open at a sound from beyond the door, and her heart turned over, her loins moved, and her whole being hung in eternity to see that the strip of light was part-obscured by the shadow of her lover standing on the other side of the threshold.

Hurry, my darling. Why do you tarry?

The door handle rattled slightly. The latch creaked.

Elizabeth closed her eyes in an overpowering flux of wanting and needing.

The door opened, then was quietly closed. And now her lover was tiptoeing over to the bed. A pause, and now her peignoir was slipping to the floor. The night shift, falling from those perfect shoulders, over that superb bosom, had joined the peignoir. Cornelia, nude, was stepping over to lift up the edge of the bedsheet.

"Dearest, you came!"

Elizabeth could wait no longer. The brief moment was too long and had to be circumvented. With a sob of relief and release, she reached out for her lover.

Her hand closed around a wrist . . .

. . . a thick, muscled wrist, heavily pelted with coarse hair!

And then she was screaming. The screams were cut off when a clenched fist hit her full in the face. Next, her arm, with which she tried to fend off the hand that was ripping away her night shift, was taken in a vise-like grip and snapped like a carrot.

Silent, breathless, swooning, she felt the whole weight of her attacker descend upon her. A thrusting, agonizing intrusion. A violent threshing. Then merciful nature intruded upon her agonies and she knew no more.

The day it ended was like every other day on the islet that summer's brief idyll. It began with the dawn chorus of marsh birds: the honking of the every-importuning ducks that clustered in the shallows close by their doorway; the far-off crying of the herons; the pigeons calling in the willows that fringed the marsh.

Jack Moonlight was up early. He awoke Purity with a kiss and a mug of tea. The tea went almost unregarded when the kiss became protracted, the caresses more urgent. Finally, Purity thrust aside his importuning hands and frowned at him with mock severity.

"I will not let your excellent tea go cold and to waste, sir. First the tea. After that—and it be your pleasure, sir—will come the handy-dandy."

"It is an arrangement, not to say a contract, ma'am, upon which I enter with the greatest pleasure," declared Moonlight. "Your tea, ma'am. And I bid you to drink it down with all dispatch. I, in the meantime, will sit on the edge of your bed and tap my feet with some impatience."

"I never thought that a man could look so handsome with a broken nose," she said over the rim of the mug, "nor with his hair sticking up all around in silly curls."

"You are trying to find a quick way to my heart," responded the highwayman. "Get on with your tea."

The tea was finished. She lay back, pillowed her arms behind her head, then composed herself to receive, and joyfully accept, his tender and passionate ministrations. His hand was advancing upon her breast, and his lips, seeking the softness behind the angle of her smooth jaw, were murmuring blandishments that would have turned the heart of a vestal virgin.

And then . . . an interruption.

"Hallo!"

Jack Moonlight jerked upright and cursed under his breath.

"It's Barney, damn his eyes!" he growled aloud.

"Sounds more like Wilfred," suggested Purity. "In any event, my dear, you will have to wait for your handy-dandy till he's gone. But I thank you for a most excellent mug of tea."

She ducked under the edge of the blanket as he mimed a smack at her. She watched him step into his breeches, buckle on his belt, and stride over to the door.

He was not gone for long. When he returned, the expression on his face caused her to catch her breath in sudden alarm.

"Jack! What is it? What's happened?" she cried.

He avoided her eyes. He snatched up his shirt and pulled it over his head.

"It's young Wilfred," he said. "Barney sends bad news."

"How bad?"

"Bad enough—as bad as it could be."

"Concerning what?"

"I'll speak of it later, when I return, Purity," he said, picking up his coat and hat.

"You're leaving?"

"With Wilfred, yes. But I will be back—as soon as I can." He leaned over and kissed her full on the mouth. "Such a pity—about the handy-dandy," he murmured. "I think it might well have been . . . a truly memorable experience."

She did not reply, but simply watched him go out of the door, shrugging his broad shoulders into the coat as he left.

An involuntary shudder shook her slender frame, as if someone had walked across her grave, and she experienced a sense of sudden deprivation, as if his departure had marked the end of yet another chapter in her turbulent life, another door slammed in the long corridor of experience, an idyll banished in the morning sun.

He was back in mid-afternoon, his face grave.

"Purity, you must flee the country," he said. "Is there anywhere you can go?"

"Why—*why?*"

He took her hands. His ugly-handsome face was expressing a sweetness of compassion that brought tears to her eyes.

"My dear, it's your daughter," he said. "Chastity—she has been hurt."

"*Hurt?*" Purity screamed the word. "You mean . . ."

"In her body—only superficially," said Moonlight. "I have already tended to that, and she is sleeping peacefully at Barney's place. As to her mind . . . well . . . I'm no judge of what may have happened to her mind. I return to the question I just put to you, my dear: Is there a safe refuge for you outside the country? What about that château in Normandy where you were reared? Is there a place there for you and Chastity?"

"The Château Feyelle?" Purity hunched her shoulders and spread her hands, the mere mention of the grass roots of her existence summoning up her latent Gallicism. "How do I know? There is a community of people living and working on the old De Feyelle estate. Most of those whom I knew well are dead and gone. The younger ones, those who do not know me . . . maybe it is possible that they would take us in. But why must we flee, Chastity and I? Tell me, Jack. By all that's holy, you owe me that!"

"Purity, Purity, my dear, you have got to be very brave," he said, and he took her gently by the shoulders. "You are in danger. And not only you— Chastity, also. It has happened this way: Barney received a summons from his doxy, the scullery wench at Jermyn Abbey, home of D'Eath. Upon arriving there, the wench led him to a barn, where she revealed Chastity lying unconscious and hurt."

"Oh, no! My poor, darling girl!"

"Yes, gravely hurt, but as I have said, not fatally. The wench, as you might imagine, was not able to say much, only this, and I have her very words of warning, which she made Barney repeat twice, so that he should have them correctly. She said: '*Tell them as care for this child to take her far away from here, as far as*

297

*they are able—or worse will befall her, or any who
try to protect her.'* That was the warning, Purity,
straight from the mouth of an ignorant little slut who
could not be expected to be privy to whatever devil-
ment is taking place at Jermyn Abbey between D'Eath
and his accomplices. But I am convinced that you
should act on it, for you see, my dear, though I have
some small influence in the criminal world, I do not
have the weight to oppose the likes of D'Eath and
his ilk—not to mention the army of cutthroats that
has been raised in the rookeries. Now, what do you
say?"

"I will go, Jack," she said. "I will take Chastity and
throw myself upon the charity of the good folk who
work the De Feyelle estate. I think they will not turn
me away."

He kissed her forehead.

"Spoken like my own true Purity," he said. "We
leave tonight, as soon as the sun is down. I have arranged a rendezvous with Barney on the Dover road."

"And Chastity?"

"She will be with him, my dear. You will be
reunited with her this night. Tomorrow, with every
good fortune, you will be in France."

Reunited with Chastity! Her mind slipped back—
and with some reluctance—to the last parting with her
adopted child: the hideous day at Half Moon Street;
the lovely, flushed, hate-filled countenance spitting
words of loathing and denounciation at her. She closed
her eyes and shuddered.

She gathered together her few belongings, to which
was added a gold locket on a chain that Jack Moonlight presented to her.

"It belonged to my mother," he said gravely, "a
relic of happier days. I think that she, if she were
capable of knowing, would wish you to have it, since
your kindness and affection, not to mention the love

you have inspired in my heart, have served to make me whole again." He put the chain around her neck. She murmured her thanks. They kissed.

At sunset, she took one last look around the oval room where she had felt so secure and content. It was the end of a chapter in her life.

"Good-bye, old place," she murmured.

Jack had made ready Black Harry and his remaining spare horse, into the saddle of which he lifted Purity. They set off across the swampland in the dying evening, and they were at London Bridge as the city watchmen were calling out the hour of eleven. They progressed through the narrow streets of Southwark and Deptford, with Jack leading. They rode over the dark hump of Blackheath, where herds of sleeping sheep lay dotted, then skirted Shooter's Hill, and joined the Dover road just beyond, near by an ancient oak, from which was suspended on high a gibbet. And it was there that Jack Moonlight drew rein.

"This is our rendezvous point with Barney," he said. "I apologize for the wry turn of humor that prompted me to make Dead Man's Oak our meeting place."

Purity glanced upward and shuddered. The coffin-shaped iron cage that swayed gently upon its chain in the night air contained the mere skin and bones of something that had once talked and laughed, eaten and drunk, made love.

"Would he have been . . . a highwayman?" she ventured.

"Like as not," answered Jack carelessly. "One of the foolish and incompetent sort I told you about—the kind that get's caught."

Purity thought back to their joint encounter with the Bow Street Runners, to her own nightmare chase across country in the dark. And she made no reply.

It was Jack, as always, who first heard the oncoming conveyance, and he signaled to her to ride forward with him to meet the newcomer. Her heart pounding, dry-mouthed, she did so.

It came out of the gloom: a small covered carriage pulled by a single horse, and with two escorting riders, one of whom she immediately recognized, by his over-large, tall hat, as Barney Bates. The other horseman was a stranger to her. The side of the carriage was emblazoned with the legend: H. POTTS—CARTER AND CARRIER—ORDERS TAKEN—BERMONDSEY.

" 'Evenin', all," was Barney's cheerful greeting. "Reckon as 'ow it might rain afore mornin' if the wind don't change."

"The girl?" said Jack.

The Cockney jerked his thumb. "Inside, guv'nor."

"How is she?"

"Right as a trivet, guv'nor, an' sleepin' like a babe."

Jack laid a hand on Purity's arm, then gave it a reassuring squeeze when he found that she was trembling and obviously near tears.

"There is room for two inside," he said. "You travel in there with her to Dover. We will ride guard. Good night, my dear. It will be morning when we arrive, and I have hopes of getting you a place on a France-bound packet in the forenoon."

She dismounted, full of dread for the condition in which she might find Chastity to be. Jack Moonlight, with his usual sensibility, knew exactly how she felt.

"Pay no undue heed to her injuries," he murmured. "As I have said, they are superficial, though cruel. The hardest part to heal will be her mind. That will be your concern, my dear."

The driver opened the door and she climbed into the small conveyance.

"Onward, lads!" cried Jack Moonlight. "To Dover! I want to see the white cliffs in the dawn light."

It was dark in the carriage. Slumped along the rear seat was a still form wrapped in a blanket. Purity, settling herself upon a small, facing seat, reached out to touch the sleeping girl, first her hair, which was damp, as if with sweat, then one soft cheek, then the curve of an eyebrow, which flickered as her fingers brushed against it, then one delicate shoulder. There were no injuries that she could detect by touch, and there was nothing to see.

She sat back in her seat and composed herself for a long night of loving, sleepless vigil over the beloved girl with whom she had so unexpectedly been reunited.

They clattered into Dover at dawn, then proceeded straight down to the quay, with its forest of masts and rigging, where the sea gulls swooped and screamed. The chalk cliffs looked dingy in the early light, like a string of dirty wash stretched out to South Foreland. Jack Moonlight dismounted. Handing the reins to Barney, he peered inside the coach. Nothing stirred in there. The young girl was still beneath her concealing blanket; nothing showed but one pale cheek and a sweep of raven hair. Purity was also asleep, her head with its glorious crown of silver-gold bowed on her breast.

"We'll leave her be," muttered Jack. "There's time enough for her to see what that animal did to the child. Stay here, Barney. I'll search for a packet that's leaving for France this morning."

"Right you are, guv'nor."

Barney and his companion—who was a large, taciturn individual with a villainous squint and a mouth as gentle as a woman's—tethered their mounts and went to sit on the harbor wall with the driver of the conveyance. They had scarcely begun to enjoy some chewing tobacco when from the carriage came a sharp cry of horror, then was instantly cut off, as when a hand is pressed against the mouth.

"Reckon she 'ave seen what was done to the young

maid," vouchsafed the big man with the squint, biting hard upon his haunch of tobacco.

Jack Moonlight had the good fortune to secure a most providential berth for Purity and her charge in a ketch named the *Arrow,* which was leaving on the morning's tide for Le Havre. This French port, lying as it did at the mouth of the Seine River, was no more than fifteen to twenty leagues from the Normandy château that was their destination. Accordingly, they went aboard: Jack leading, followed by Purity, carrying a small bundle that contained her few belongings, with Barney and his comrade bearing the limp, blanket-wrapped figure of the girl.

Jack had secured a tiny, two-bunk cabin near the stern, into which the precious burden was brought and laid upon the lower of the bunks. Barney and his comrade then withdrew, leaving Purity and Jack together with the injured Chastity. Purity was in tears, and she was white-faced with shock and horror.

"I have given her a draft," said Jack, in as matter-of-fact a way as he was able to. "And that should keep her sleeping till late this afternoon. The passage to Le Havre, of course, is far longer than a straight crossing to Calais, but you will have a shorter distance to travel along those appalling French roads. Now, there are some instructions I must give you regarding the patient. Do you think you can bear the ordeal?"

She nodded. "Yes."

"Well, then, as to the face . . . " He reached out and drew back the blanket.

"Oh, my God!" Purity cried out, but she forced herself not to look away.

Chastity's face, turned toward them in sleep, presented a hideous contrast, one side with the other. The left side—the one that Purity had lightly touched in the carriage the previous night—was unharmed; but the whole of the right cheek and brow, the eye included, was swollen to twice its size, bruised a livid green and sullen brown, with the eye no more than a dark slit, like a slash in the skin of an orange.

"It looks a sight worse than it is," said Jack. "I have drawn off the morbid blood and the contusion will subside quite rapidly. I have been able to determine that the eyeball itself is undamaged." He uttered a forced laugh, which he immediately changed into a cough. "It is . . . ah . . . a fortunate matter that, in addition to my predilection for the cock-pit, I am also an enthusiastic supporter of prizefighting, and I have rendered medical assistance to many such injuries as this one, which is, in essence, no more than a bad black eye—such as is inflicted by a blow from a fist."

"What manner of creature," asked Purity, "inflicts such a blow upon a young girl in the flower of her loveliness?"

"You may well ask," said Jack. "Indeed, you may well ask." He took a deep breath. "Ah . . . to continue. The left arm, as you see, I have put into a splint, after having set the broken ulna and radius. Again, I foresee no complications here. She is young and healthy. The bones will knit quite comfortably and the splint can be removed in a month's time. So much for that." He licked his dry lips and appeared to hesitate.

Purity glanced at him sharply.

"What else?" she inquired nervously. "You are not going to tell me that further injury was inflicted upon my darling?"

Jack nodded. "Again, you will have to summon up all your fortitude, Purity," he said. "This is worse— far worse."

Someone had provided the injured girl with a coarse flannel shirt many sizes too big for her slender torso. It had been ripped at the left sleeve to allow for the splint and bandages on the arm. Gently, so as not to arouse the patient, Jack unbuttoned the shirt to the waist and laid it open, disclosing Chastity's right breast, which was small and well-formed, rising delicately to a point, pinkly nippled . . . and disfigured by a double row of teeth marks.

"Merciful heaven!" cried Purity. "Who . . . what insane monster . . . could have . . ."

"The madman who raped her," said Jack Moonlight flatly. And, when Purity's agonized glance sought his for confirmation, he said, "Yes, I found her to be *virgo non intacta* upon examination. She has been most brutally outraged, during the course of which her ravisher savaged her with his teeth, like a wolf. You may be sure that the injuries inflicted on her face and arm were made during her defense of her chastity. Chastity—she was well named."

"Will the marks heal?" asked Purity.

"I think so," said Jack, "provided there is no mortification of the blood, which will cause the tissues to scar. Furthermore—and this has to be faced squarely, Purity—such a development could bring about fever, a general mortification of the blood . . . and death."

"No-o-o-o!" cried Purity.

"You must bathe the wounds thrice daily," said Jack, "with cold water. That drives the blood from the surface to the center, and it also reduces the pulse. If you detect the slightest signs of mortification on and around the wounds, manifested by inflammation and discoloration, you must immediately apply leeches."

"Leeches!" Purity exclaimed, appalled.

From the pocket of his caped riding coat, he produced a stoppered bottle in which a cluster of tiny, writhing forms swam in water. He laid it down on the small table, which, together with a chair, and the berths, formed the only appointments of the narrow cabin.

304

"Apply ten or a dozen leaches to the affected part of the breast," he said. "When they have gorged themselves with the morbid blood, they will fall off of their own accord."

Gently, he covered the girl again. Then he turned to face the woman who had shared his life and his bed in the last idyllic days.

"It will be high tide within minutes, Purity," he said. "The captain will wish to set sail on the first of the ebb. It's time for us to kiss and part." He took her in his arms.

"I shall never forget you, Jack," she murmured against his mouth. "You took me in, made me well, and filled my empty life with your love. Without you, I might have despaired utterly and slipped from sickness into oblivion."

"We shall meet again, my dear," he said. "I think it is written in the stars."

"Look after yourself," she said, remembering the thing on the gallows tree hard by Shooter's Hill that had once been a man.

"Have no fear," he said. "A gypsy once told me that I was not destined to hang. Good-bye, my Purity, my love."

"Rather . . . *au revoir.*"

One last kiss, and he was gone. Blinded by tears, she heard his booted feet mount the companionway and cross the deck above her head. She heard him call out a farewell to the skipper of the ketch as he crossed over the gangplank onto the quay. Scarcely had he gone than a shrill whistle and a shouted order brought other, barefoot, patterings onto the deck, and she heard the squeal of block and tackle, the creak of ropes, and a splash as something hit the water. And then the *Arrow* shifted under her feet, heeled slightly as the newly spread sails caught the wind, and the ebbing tide caught the stout vessel in its grasp.

Casting a glance at Chastity to assure herself that the girl was still sleeping peacefully under the influence of the draft, Purity put a shawl over her head and went up on deck.

Gulls circled over the moving ketch, mast-high, shrieking as they followed her out of the arm of the harbor. Shielding her eyes against the sun's glare, Purity searched the quayside for Jack's tall figure, and she saw him clearly at the very end of their harbor, by the lantern that guided incoming craft to their safe anchorage.

He took off his hat and waved it on high. She waved back. The *Arrow* nosed her way toward the lantern, with the wake hissing at her sharp stem as the wind took the kipper-brown sails. And Jack Moonlight was standing right on the edge, clinging to the lantern, leaning out, one hand extended.

Rushing to the bulwarks, she, too, held out her hand, stretching as far as she could.

An instant later she was swept past him; their hands failed to touch only by mere inches. But they were already a whole world apart.

Chapter Nine

Folkestone was a smudge of white-painted houses and a church tower behind them, and Dungeness headland was a menace on the starboard bow. The skipper of the good ship *Arrow* was busily trying to claw her away from a lee shore and get out into mid-Channel. Down in the little cabin, Purity sat watching her beloved charge, and she felt the stirrings of queasiness as the ketch took a white-capped wave on her bow and heeled in a fountain of flung spray. A cook had earlier knocked on the door and asked her if she wanted any food brought down to the cabin; she was glad that she had declined.

Three hours of beating back and forth in the East Road finally brought the *Arrow* clear of Dungeness, where a more favorable wind directed her farther out to sea. The skipper was able to steer a course that set him fairly for the bay of the Seine. This done, he went to his cabin and got drunk, leaving charge of the vessel to his mate.

Purity watched and waited. The sleeping girl's face was mercifully turned so that her hideously contused side was hidden. She was breathing evenly, lips slightly parted, long eyelashes brushing the upper cheek, a curling lock of her long black hair looped across her brow most becomingly. She could have been lying peacefully in her bed at Clumber, or on Half Moon Street, or Brighton, with another day of innocent, carefree activity ahead of her. Instead . . . what? She was a fugitive from an evil force that had snatched her from the arms of her loved ones, had destroyed and dispersed her family, and, after heaven knows what manipulations of her naïve and unsophisticated young mind, had brutally outraged her tender flesh.

Why . . . *why?*

The question burned in Purity's mind.

What ill had Chastity ever done? Or she herself? Or Mark? (It was scarcely possible that little Robbie could be involved.) Why was it that those people should have chosen the Landlesses upon whom to practice their foul machinations? Mark and herself, she decided, had enemies by the score, for the Landlesses had lived dangerously, amidst war and revolution: stormy petrels in a violent age. But all of those enemies were dead or dispersed, surely. Who, then, was so determined to destroy the Landlesses?

The woman Madeleine? But one had never set eyes on Madeleine till the hideous night in the St. Giles rookery.

The disturbingly handsome and enigmatic Guy D'Eath? Surely there was no reason for him to encompass such a thing. Had he not admired her, pursued her? And, though he must have some connection with the hateful society to which she had been bound by ties of whoredom (since he had been with Madeleine in that same coach which had taken Chastity away from Half Moon Street), he had not produced a replica of the medallion (and, surely, he could have done that easily enough) that would have commanded her unquestioning obedience.

It was all very puzzling and disturbing.

As the wind shifted more favorably to the *Arrow's* aspirations, the skipper's mate edged the vessel a couple of points to windward, and the low-cast sun no longer shone through the tiny green glass window that provided the only light in the cabin. The shift to gloom, coupled with the slight movement of the vessel and the attendant creaking of timbers, aroused the blanketed figure in the lower bunk. Purity held her breath, then saw a slender, white arm emerge from the sleeve of the overlarge flannel shirt. Then questing fingers made a painful probe at the contused face. The girl gave a small, piteous cry of pain at the contact.

"Chastity, my darling!"

Purity hastened to her side, fell on her knees by the bunk, and gently eased the arm and hand away from the ruined face.

Chastity's single, beautiful eye was directed upon her. Puzzlement and fear fought together for dominance, but they were finally overcome by realization.

"Mama Purity . . . "

"Oh, my dearest, my only girl!"

Laughing, weeping, with infinite care, so as not to hurt the tender, injured body, she embraced the girl-child who, though not the fruit of her womb, was as dearly beloved, and who had been returned to her in body and in mind.

The good vessel *Arrow* made fast alongside the quay in Le Havre the following morning, and the skipper of the ketch, by then sober and obliging, secured for his lady passengers the hire of a diligence that would take them down the snaking road that ran abreast of the Seine and on to Château Feyelle. The driver of the diligence, with typical Norman prudence,

309

not to say parsimony, demanded his payment in advance. Purity, who besides having ten guineas left of what she had had in her reticule when Jack Moonlight had taken her under his care, had had that amount augmented by the gift of an additional twenty from him. ("I will brook no argument, my Purity; 'twas stolen from the fat and idle rich, who would otherwise have squandered it on gluttony and lechery." Those had been the words that had reduced her from protest to laughter.) So Purity was able to comply with the fellow's demand. The sight of good English gold coin, coupled with the astonishment of its being accompanied by a stern admonition from *la femme anglaise*— delivered in idiomatic French and with the fractured vowels of a Norman peasant—to drive slowly and carefully so as not to cause distress to her injured daughter, instantly reduced the driver to awed silence. The blanketed girl having been carefully deposited across one of the seats by two obliging crewmen of the *Arrow,* and the astonishing beauty with the silver-gold tresses having taken her place opposite her charge, the fellow cracked his whip, not too loudly, and they set off.

For Purity, though beset with worries about Chastity, it was a journey that was redolent with long-gone memories. Many times, in her girlhood, she had ridden atop a farm cart, from Château Feyelle to Le Havre, along that very road. Some distance on, where the narrow track from Fécamp met the highway, she remembered how she had ridden on Mark Landless's saddle bow, her young body disturbingly pressed against his warm loins, when he had spirited her out of Revolutionary France to become first her guardian and then her husband.

Forget all that, forget Mark. . . .

Chastity had not uttered a word since her first, blessed salutation. She seemed to have succumbed to a lassitude of mind and spirit, lying with her single eye fixed dully upon the middle distance. Nor would she respond to Purity's essays into making conversation; she seemed even not to be listening; and any attempt to trap her into a reply—such as posing a direct inquiry as to whether she was comfortable or not—appeared to cause her so much distress that Purity abandoned the idea. The sole, and curiously heartening, contact between them was that the girl would respond to a smile by smiling, shyly and wanly, in return.

Toward midday, they came within sight of a wide bridge by which the road crossed the Seine, and it was there that, upon an impulse, Purity called out to their driver to halt when they were halfway across. Puzzled, the fellow obeyed, and Purity alighted. She went to the balustrade of the bridge and looked down into the swiftly flowing waters, stained ruddy-brown by the rich soil of Normandy.

With a curious lightening of the heart, she opened her reticule and took out the hated medallion. She had removed it from around her neck before her journey to Norfolk, but some impulse of prudence had prompted her to retain it. The evil green eyes winked up at her, almost as if they lived. With a cry of heartfelt release, she threw the medallion and chain far out into the river and watched it splash there, watched the gold speck wink and shimmer like a turning fish as it sank out of sight. And then she climbed back into the coach, feeling suddenly clean again, as if the river that had nourished the land that had reared her had, by some miraculous means, been capable of washing away her shame.

An hour later the ivy-covered tower of Château Feyelle appeared above the treetops, and they were soon passing between the high stone gateposts and

311

traversing the long driveway to the ancient seat of the De Feyelles.

Home . . .

The evocative word sang in Purity's mind. Before them stood the château, its ivy mantle mercifully concealing the dark scars of the fire that had all but destroyed it in one hideous night of sacking and raping, when the Revolutionary mob from the Paris slums had marched through fair Normandy. Reroofed now, its windows freshly glazed and the great doors rehung, the main building was obviously occupied. She smiled at the homely note of a line of wash hanging out on a pole from one of the top windows—a thing unheard of in the days of the last marquis!

The trim lawns were still well tended, and the ornamental flowerbeds were as primly neat as they had been in the days before the holocaust. And as the diligence passed by the gatehouse, Purity saw *it*. . . .

It was a big chestnut tree, once one of the finest in the province. From its spreading branches, all those years ago, had been hanged the bodies of men, women, and children, so densely packed that the stout limbs of the great tree had bowed low beneath the weight. In later years it had been called—and likely was still called—"The Hanging Tree." On the day that the bodies had been cut down and reverently buried by the survivors of the holocaust, the tree had begun to die, and it came forth with no leaves the following spring. Now it stood stark, bare, and blackened—a terrible *memento mori* to the appalling horrors of civil strife.

The driver halted the diligence close to the splendid portals of the château, where the proud coat of arms of the De Feyelles was etched into the indestructible granite. A middle-aged woman in a lace-trimmed apron and the tall coiffure of a Norman peasant came out of the door and down the steps, a look of inquiry upon her broad, homely countenance.

"Who is it?" she demanded of the driver. "Who have you brought, hey?"

"Visitors—from England," responded the man.

"From England?" The woman peered into the diligence. She saw Purity, her hair hidden beneath a large bonnet. She frowned in puzzlement to see the girl with the ruined face lying across the seat opposite her.

"Don't you know me, Yvette?" murmured Purity. And when the other woman continued to stare at her blankly, she reached up, untied the ribbons of her bonnet, and took it off, shaking out her wonderful hair till it fell in a silver-gold cloud around her shoulders.

"By all the blessed saints!" exclaimed the woman. It is Madame! Madame herself, come back to Feyelle!"

"If you will have us, Yvette," said Purity.

"Oh, Madame, Madame!"

Half-laughing, half-crying, Yvette reached to embrace Purity as she alighted from the diligence. She pressed her to her ample bosom, stroked her hair, squeezed her hands.

"You are looking well, Yvette," said Purity presently. "And how is everything at Feyelle? I see that the château has been completely refurbished and that folks are living in it."

"It was always your plan, Madame," said Yvette, "and we have accomplished it at last. Seven families now live in the building. Mercy me! Monsieur the old Marquis must turn in his grave at the very thought. But why are we standing here? Let us take your baggage indoors and give you and the young lady a glass of good estate Calvados after your long journey."

"Yvette, we have no baggage, save what we stand here in," said Purity simply.

313

"And the young lady"—Yvette glanced into the open door of the diligence—"she is not well?"

"My daughter, Chastity," murmured Purity, "is very badly hurt, in mind as well as body. Can she have a bed, please?"

"At once! Instantly!" declared Yvette. And she shouted, "Claude! Jean-Pierre! Roger! Come here at once!"

In answer to her summons, three strapping young men came out of the château, wiping their lips. They glanced once at the woman with the miraculous hair, then looked a second, and longer, time.

"I see you've been at the applejack again," said Yvette tartly. "Get you hold of the young lady in the diligence. Take her up carefully, mind you, and carry her gently to the empty bedroom at the top of the main staircase. We will follow presently. Look sharp about it, now. My three nephews," she observed to Purity.

"I remember them well," responded the other with a smile. "How they have grown."

The three youths carried Chastity in her blanket up the front steps and into the château. Purity and Yvette followed, stepping into what had once been the great hall of the vast mansion. Now bereft of its carved paneling, with the bare stone walls whitewashed and with clean rushes strewn upon marble floors that had once resounded to the dancing of gilded slippers in the rhythms of the minuet and gavotte. Gone was the elaborate main staircase; in its place was a simple construction of unvarnished timber. Gone, also, was the minstrel gallery with its pipe organ upon which the famous Herr Johann Sebastian Bach had played for the delectation of a previous marquis.

Gone, also—and here Purity raised her eyes with a shudder at the recollection—was the great crystal chandelier from which they had hanged Monsieur le Marquis on that night of horror.

Yvette brought Purity back from her uneasy reverie. "It is here that we take our midday meal, the whole community." She pointed to a bare refectory table that ran the length of the huge chamber. "You will join us today and meet Jacques."

"Who is Jacques?" asked Purity as they climbed the staircase behind the three youths and their burden.

"He is now our acknowledged leader," said Yvette. "And his word is law in the community. You won't know him from the old days, for he's not a Feyelle man; he comes from near Evreux. Our numbers have been greatly increased since your time. There are many faces that will be strange to you."

"Will it be Jacques, then, who will decide if Chastity and I are permitted to stay here?" asked Purity.

"You will stay here for as long as you like, Madame!" said Yvette forcefully. "Let Jacques say what he will. There are still people in this community who know well that the Feyelle land would be a wilderness —and most of us long since dead of starvation—if it had not been for your energy, your inspiration."

"Thank you, Yvette," murmured Purity, feeling close to tears of most profound emotion.

The room immediately at the top of the staircase, where the young men tenderly laid Chastity upon a simple bed, was sparsely furnished with yet another, similar, bed, a chair and table, and a crucifix upon the wall—nothing else. The tall window commanded a view of the moat that encircled the entire building, and beyond that was the stable block and a row of white-painted, thatched cottages that had been the community's only homes in Purity's day.

The three youths smiled shyly and took their leave. Purity and her companion looked down into the ruined face that was now composed in slumber.

"How did such a thing happen?" whispered Yvette.

"It was done by the same beast who did . . . this," replied Purity, gently unfastening Chastity's shirt and baring her right breast.

"Mother of God!" gasped Yvette, crossing herself. "What monster could have . . . "

"I don't know," said Purity. "But one day I shall find out. And if it lies within my power, that . . . creature . . . will pay for what he did to this child. By the way, Yvette . . . " A thought came to her.

"Yes, Madame?"

"Do you recall—I don't know how long ago it was, but it may have been quite recently—an Englishman visiting Feyelle? A big man, with pale eyes, very disconcerting eyes. And it's likely that he was inquiring about me."

"Madame, I remember him well," said Yvette without hesitation. "Last year twelvemonth, it was, just before the time of the harvest. He came here in a fine carriage with a lady companion."

"A lady with a patch over one eye?" demanded Purity.

"The very same!" confirmed Yvette. "Mark you, I did not see her well, for she remained inside the carriage all the time, while the gentleman quizzed us all around. He asked our names and if we had known you well. Me, I didn't take to him at all. He got nothing out of me. But there was Eloise Lamont—you remember what a gossip she is. Eloise told him everything about you; she even took him to see the tomb of your mother in the old chapel."

"He saw . . . that?"

"Yes, Madame." The woman looked at her keenly. "I said I didn't take to him, and it was with good cause, non? That man is no friend of yours, I think."

"He and the woman in the carriage are responsible for this child's condition," said Purity. "It is to escape them that we have fled to France and are throwing ourselves upon this community's charity."

"He—the man who came here—did *that?*" Yvette pointed to the sleeping girl's breast.

"Oh, no, I think not!" said Purity. "He is an evil man, one of the most evil men it has ever been my misfortune to meet. He may well have given the order for my darling to be assaulted, but that he could have . . . no, it's unthinkable. He has the trappings of a gentleman. The creature who did that must be, must look like, *an animal!*"

Yvette reached out and squeezed her hand.

"Have no fear. The community will take you in, Madame," she whispered, "you and the poor, stricken child here. It must be so. It must!"

At two o'clock, the workers came in from the fields, men, women, and children all. With them came other members of the Feyelle community whose skills and crafts served to make the domain of the long-gone De Feyelles almost entirely self-supporting: the thatchers, blacksmiths, wheelwrights, carpenters, and plasterers; those who, like Yvette's three strapping nephews, were still working on the repairing and restoring of the château. They all trooped into the great hall and took their places on each side of the long table. Grace was said. Then in from the kitchens came plump and comely lasses bearing great tureens of onion soup, platters of freshly baked bread, jugs of raw red wine, and the cider of the countryside.

Purity was with Yvette, having left Chastity peacefully sleeping upstairs. They sat together, halfway down the table.

"That's Jacques, right at the head of the table," murmured Yvette. "He's looking at you, wondering who it is I've brought in. I'll introduce you to him when we've finished the soup."

Purity glanced down the table and met the flat stare of a thick-set man of about forty, with a thatch of close-cut hair and a ruddy, outdoor complexion. His shirt was unbuttoned to the waist, displaying a thickly pelted, heavily muscled chest. There was power and domination in the set of his head and the squareness of his chin; and stubbornness showed in the outthrust lower lip.

"He doesn't approve of me," said Purity, "not even at this distance."

"Let him approve or disapprove," said Yvette blithely. "Here you are, and here you stay!"

All around her, up and down the table, people were recognizing the unmistakable silver-gold tresses. Several of them rose and came to her, shaking her by the hand, kissing her cheek, addressing her as "Madame" —the title by which she was known in the old days, in the days of the war, when, with all the menfolk of the De Feyelle estate being away fighting in Napoleon's Grand Army, she had rallied the women and children to feed, clothe, and keep themselves warm by the sweat of their brows.

"It's good to see you again, Madame."

"How is the good colonel?"

"We've never forgotten you, Madame, nor will we ever!"

"This is my little Marie-Claire. She was only a babe at the breast when you left us, Madame."

The interchanges were not lost upon the man at the end of the table, whose brow grew sterner and more sullen by the minute. When the soup bowls had been cleared away, he refilled his glass with a draft of red wine, then noisily thumped the tabletop.

In the silence that followed, he said loudly, "I see we have a visitor from the aristocracy. We are honored." His hostility was quite unmistakable and unconcealed.

"Jacques, this is Madame," responded Yvette stoutly.

"I know well who she is," replied Jacques. "She is Lady Landless, an aristocrat, daughter of an aristocrat. Why has she come amongst us common people again?"

"Jacques, Madame and her child are in need of our help," said Yvette. "She asks to be allowed to remain here."

The statement was greeted by concerted muttering up and down the table, and this was interspersed with comments of delight and approval from all sides. Such sentiments, however, were not shared by Jacques.

"We want no newcomers," he growled. "Every hectare of our land is stretched to its limits to feed us. It's bad enough that you women insist on spawning children like milch cows. Every extra month means a little less food to go around. We don't want the aristocrat and her daughter."

This outburst was greeted by a chorus of dissent. Purity said nothing.

"Madame has as much right here as you have, Jacques," delcared Yvette. "Indeed, she has more, for you were not born on De Feyelle land."

The big man's eyes narrowed with fury. He smote the table again.

"The De Feyelles are all dead!" he cried. "The day of the aristocrat is over! This land is ours, won by the right of toil! And I have won my share with the rest! I say she goes!"

"I say she stays!"

The speaker was a grizzled old fellow with a sweeping moustache that identified him as an old soldier of Napoleon's army, which was further confirmed by the straightness of his back when he stood up. Purity recognized him at once.

"Thank you, Hubert," she murmured. "But I don't want to cause trouble here, and . . . "

"Listen to me, Jacques," said the old soldier. "And all the rest of you listen, too. I am taking you back to the days after the great retreat from Russia, when we lads came back to the De Feyelle estate—a beaten army, broken, demoralized, our emperor taken prisoner, totally without hope.

"For weeks—months—we sat around and played cards and chewed the cud of our misery and our defeat, fit for nothing but to put our wives and sweethearts in the family way. And then what happened? I will tell you. One day this young woman, this delicate young aristocrat, with her soft hands and her puny strength, did harness up a horse and shame us men by plowing the south meadow in full view of us all playing cards under the old oak tree. You may guess what happened next!"

"I know the story well!" It was a voice from the far end of the table. "François Lamont—he who was killed later at Waterloo—took the plowshare from Madame's hands and finished the job. By the end of the week, you were all hard at work!"

"That's true! If it hadn't been for her, you'd all have starved, and I'd have never been born!" one of the young people cried.

"Madame is part of De Feyelle land!"

"She *is* De Feyelle!"

"She stays—or I go, and my family with me!"

Blinded by tears, Purity listened to the testimony of love and devotion that was showered upon her from all sides. She extended her hands to take those that were offered to her and exchanged a fresh flurry of kisses.

"Well, Jacques, what do you say?" demanded the old soldier.

The big man rubbed his stubborn mouth and glowered from under his beetling brows at Purity.

"I've listened to what you have to tell me," he declared at length. "What has she to say in her own favor? Let us hear from the aristocrat herself."

With all eyes upon her, Purity rose to her feet, mindful of the tears that fled unchecked down her cheeks and of her lower lip, which, as always at such times of emotion, was trembling uncontrollably. She took a deep breath, gained a considerable amount of encouragement from a broad and confiding wink that the old soldier Hubert directed at her, and began. "All I have to say in my favor is that I love the De Feyelle land as my own birthplace. I was raised and nurtured here. The De Feyelle earth is part of my bones and mingled with my blood. So much for that. I have nothing else to commend me. I am a weak woman. I have a desperately sick daughter, who will be nothing more than a useless mouth to feed for many moons to come. But this I will promise: if you allow us to stay, if you do not drive us from your door, I will work to keep us here. Let a man labor till sunset, and I will work till the hour beyond. When any take their ease in the shade, they will see me still at my task. That is all I have to say."

She sat down amidst a silence that could have been touched.

From the far end of the table, she heard Jacques noisily clear his throat.

"Well, Jacques?" It was the voice of old Hubert. "What do you say? You are the leader."

"They can stay for . . . three months," declared Jacques. "In that time, the aristocrat must prove her worth afresh—one way or the other."

Purity flashed him a tremulous smile of thanks, which was not returned; the stolid, sullen countenance remained as implacably hostile as ever.

Yvette was a treasure. She was marvelous with Chastity, who, when she awoke, meekly took soup, spoonful by lovingly proffered spoonful, from the strange woman in the curious, tall lace cap. Afterward, Yvette sat with the young invalid while Purity went upon a short pilgrimage of devotion.

The ancient Gothic chapel of the De Feyelle château, built during the reign of the saintly King Louis, in whose arms, so legend went, a De Feyelle Crusader had died within sight of the Holy Sepulcher in Jerusalem in the year 1249 A.D., had been much added to during the years. The night of the holocaust, however, had eradicated—as with so much else, human and inanimate—many of the later refinements: the extravagantly carved Baroque interior, put there by the nineteenth marquis during the reign of Louis XIV; the stained-glass windows that had been the pride of Normandy; the silverware, melted down to make coinage to pay the young General Bonaparte's soldiers who were carrying the message of the Revolution, with fire and sword, in Italy. All that remained, when Purity stepped inside now, were the stark, heavy stone walls of the thirteenth-century architect's design and a simple wooden crucifix set above a plain wooden altar, where once there had been an alabaster reredos carved by the magical hands of Bernini.

To the left of the altar was a wrought-iron gate, and beyond that was a spiral stone staircase that led her down into the burial crypt. The thin light of an autumnal afternoon dimly illuminated the dank cellar through a grating in the roof. By its exiguous beam, Purity picked out tiered rows of lead coffins set in niches around the four walls.

She found the coffin she sought without much difficulty, though it was hard to decipher the name engraved upon the discolored metal. She sank onto her knees in front of it and bowed her head in prayer.

"Oh, mother mine, who bore me in adversity, whose love, whose embrace I never knew, I beg you to intercede for the child, who, like myself, never knew her true mother, and who is in desperate need. . . ."

She stayed for a short time. Then she rose, kissed the cold lead of the coffin, and left that place of death and dissolution to the spiders and to the bats that contrived to edge their way in through the grating and hang, heads downward and leathery wings folded, from the roof beams.

That night, upon bathing and examining Chastity's wounded breast, Purity was horrified to discover that Jack Moonlight's worst fears had come to pass. The two rows of teeth marks that encircled the delicate nipple had taken on, since she last saw them, a distinctly angry hue: a redness, combined with a slight swelling and a feverish warmth to the touch, which betokened the dreaded mortification of the blood. Chastity, who was awake at the time, who had demonstrated a vehement repugnance at having her bosom uncovered, screamed when she saw her mother bring forth the jar of leeches.

Her screams brought the doughty Yvette.

"What's amiss, Madame?" she asked. "What is troubling my lamb, my little angel?"

"Purity took her to one side and briefly explained the danger that had arisen, showing her the leeches. The hideous creatures aroused neither fear nor repugnance in Yvette, whose mother had been *sage-femme* and amateur physician, not to mention layer-out of the dead, to three generations of the local peasantry. Yvette had attended at births and deaths galore as her mother's assistant, and had helped to draw away blood and attach leeches since she was about five. She took the jar and its unpleasant contents, winked reassuringly at Purity, and approached the shrinking girl in the bed.

"Come, now, my flower, my lovely," she murmured.

323

"Let Yvette see what's amiss with you. There's my pet, my angel."

Miraculously, Chastity permitted the woman to remove her hands from her wounded breast. Her dark eyes widened with a fresh horror when Yvette took one of the leeches between her finger and thumb and laid it against her soft, shrinking flesh. But benign Nature, which provided the leech with the means to gorge itself upon morbid blood, also ordained that its tiny bite should be entirely painless. And Chastity, suffering nothing but revulsion, watched with markedly lessening dismay while the woman patiently applied a dozen or so of the little creatures to her breast.

An hour later, or less, the operation was completed. The leeches released their holds, were replaced in the jar, and Yvette declared that the state of the wounds was much improved.

From that day forth, Chastity made a rapid recovery.

As Jack Moonlight had predicted, the contusion around her right eye rapidly subsided, and the discoloration faded also. In a week, she was looking out at the new world around her through a second eye, which, though bloodshot to an alarming degree, saw as well as the other. The broken arm gave no troublesome complications whatsoever. And her tender breast, after the eradication of the danger signal, proceeded to heal itself admirably well.

Not so her mind.

From that moment aboard the *Arrow,* when she had acknowledged Purity by name, Chastity never uttered another word, nor was she to be persuaded to acknowledge, by a nod or by any other commonplace gesture, that she understood what was said to her. Purity might say, "Let us go down to the hall for supper, dear," and the girl would meekly obey, but without a word or gesture.

As soon as Chastity was out of danger—within days of their arrival—Purity presented herself for work in the fields. It being harvest time, the entire community —anyone old enough or able enough to walk—came to help. A simple breakfast of oatcakes and cider was taken at five in the morning. By the first light, the long lines of advancing men were nibbling the edges of the waving corn the way a caterpillar attacks a leaf, moving across its sea of ripeness as scythes and sickles swung in steady unison. After them came the women and children, gathering up armfuls of the sheaves and building them into pile, ten to twelve sheaves to a pile, leaning against each other in two rows, the rows set north and south so that each side received the benefit of the sun.

The sun during that blistering autumn was both a boon and a curse. It rapidly dried out the harvested grain so that the lumbering carts were soon able to come and take it away to the threshing floor; but its searing rays punished the toilers greatly. Though fair-skinned, Purity was not given to rawness and blistering; her skin rapidly took on a most becoming, but unfashionable, tan. Some of the others, the children especially, suffered the agonies of sunburn. The most blessed time of the day—apart from a brief rest at noon, when they ate a frugal meal of bread, sausage, and cucumber, all washed down with the ubiquitous cider—came in the evening, when the sun dipped down below the wooded hills that lay beyond the river. It remained as hot as ever, stiflingly hot in the dusty fields, but one's skin was free from the sun's assault. Then it was a blessed release to strip off one's sweat-sodden outer clothing and labor in just a skirt and shift, moving barefoot. At those times, most of the men —and, indeed, some of the women, the unmarried and unattached—stripped to the waist. Purity prudently was not one of those.

The day's work ended, simply, when there was no longer enough light to see by. Then and only then, the long lines of weary folk wended their way back to the château, the men carrying sleeping children in their arms, the women bearing their husbands' scythes and sickles. The great farm carts were piled high with the good grain, and patient horses pulled the heavy weight.

It was then, at supper in the great hall of the long-gone De Feyelles, that the people of the community enjoyed the best of their reward for the labor that they put into their long days. Supper was always a feast. There would be a whole roast ram, cooked on a spit over the great open fire in the vast fireplace, and it would be served in slices as thick as a man's finger. Upon each table, whole hams, cured in honey and smoked over oak chips in the Norman manner, vied with cold capons stuffed with forcemeat and walnuts, pasties of coney, hare, guinea fowl, pheasant, and partridge. And such cheeses—the delicately blue-veined, the ripe goats' milk, the kingly Camembert. And everywhere there were great flagons of cider, red and white wines, and, for the discriminating palate, tall bottles of Calvados, the applejack brandy of Normandy.

Within two weeks after their arrival, Chastity was able to join the others for supper. During the working day, when Purity was away in the fields, she remained in the care of Yvette, who had charge of the apple orchards, whose fruit provided the community with its cider and Calvados. Apple-picking was regarded as "light work" in the community, and it was delegated to the sick, the very aged, and the simpleminded. It was in the latter category that, much to Purity's dismay, Chastity almost imperceptibly slipped in the eyes of the community. This is not to say that she was looked upon with contempt or distaste. On the contrary, like most primitive, uneducated folk, the Norman peasants treated those who were deranged in their minds with a special respect, almost with awe, as superior beings, almost, who were blessed with strange insights that were denied to common mortals.

Purity and Yvette always sat together at the table, with Chastity between them. Yvette it was who insisted on cutting up the girl's meat and helping her to overcome the disability of her broken arm. They would talk, Purity and she, and Chastity would quietly eat and drink, for all the world as if she were alone.

There was a crippled youth named Etienne: a shy, gentle soul with sad, pansy-brown eyes, who dragged a withered leg. He was, like so many deprived creatures, very good with small children and animals, with which he possessed an almost uncanny communication. His favorite companion was a jackdaw, which he had hand-reared from a fledgling. This quirky black-and-white bird went everywhere on Etienne's shoulder, even to the supper table, where it would remind its master, by giving him a gentle tweak of the ear with its beak, when it wanted a tidbit.

Etienne worked under Yvette's guidance in the orchard, sorting the good fruit from the bad, the large from the small. His lameness permitted him no other form of work. Yvette knew him well, had known him since a babe, long before one of Napoleon's baggage wagons, passing in convoy through Etienne's village on the way to the disastrous field of Waterloo, had driven over the young boy's leg and destroyed its use forever.

Etienne, confided Yvette, had a greater problem than merely being crippled. Abandoned by his unmarried mother as a useless mouth to feed, he was conscious of his inadequacy in the world, and, despite the fact that, as Yvette attested, he was the fastest and most painstaking apple-sorter the community had ever had, he forever remained convinced that he was doing a make-believe job and living on the charity of the others.

Strangely enough, it was this deprived lad who made the first step in restoring Chastity to the world around her. One night at supper he limped over to where Purity, Yvette, and Chastity were seated, and, after exchanging a slight pleasantry with Yvette and a shy smile with Purity, he produced a fine red apple and presented it to Chastity.

The girl stared at him, wide-eyed and slack-mouthed. For one hideous moment, Purity thought that she would scream, burst into tears, perhaps leap to her feet and flee. Etienne continued to hold out the apple, grinning encouragingly and begging Chastity to take it. Finally, slowly, with infinite caution, the terror faded from the girl's countenance and was replaced by the docility that had become her habitual expression. And then—wonders, thought Purity—she reached out her hand and took the apple.

Etienne was overjoyed. His gentle face wreathed in smiles, he went back to his seat, with the jackdaw doing a little hopping dance upon his shoulder.

"They're two of a kind," was Yvette's comment. "Both of an age and both afflicted. I've seen Etienne glancing her way in the orchard from time to time. He's a good boy. No harm in him. I think I'll put Chastity on the sorting. He'll do her good, you see."

Purity nodded agreement, smiling at Chastity, who was taking a tentative bite of the apple and glancing shyly down the table at the crippled lad.

Purity had deliberately been avoiding Jacques, pre-ferring her own unstinted efforts to speak for her, rather than making any attempt to ingratiate herself with the leader of the community. Occasionally, she saw his eyes upon her, reflectively; and it seemed to her that she was being sized up, considered, and, in the final balance, rejected, for whenever their eyes met she saw resentment there.

With the harvest home, the leaves falling fast, and the men out with the plowshares, drawing the long, straight lines over the broad hectares, in preparation for sowing the winter wheat, Purity found an occasion to confront Jacques for a special reason. This she did on a Sunday Afternoon—at the one time in the working week when the entire community was free to do as it pleased.

She found him sitting at the end of the long table in the great hall, a leather-bound book before him. No one else was in the hall. At her approach, he carefully marked his place with a slip of paper and closed the book, afterward removing a pair of spectacles and placing them in a case. A glance at the title of the book told her that he was studying animal husbandry. Jacques never stopped working.

"I want a word with you," she said.

He inclined his head. "Sit down."

She obeyed, noticing as she did so that he had a button missing from his rough corduroy coat, that the cuff of his shirt was threadbare, and the shirt was none too clean. Jacques, as she knew, was unmarried and lived in the bachelor quarters over the stables. She wondered who did his washing.

"It concerns . . . the water meadows."

"What of the water meadows?"

The water meadows comprised the lower part of the De Feyelle estate, beyond the lush pastures and down by the riverbank. In winter, they became a frozen bog; in summer they were mostly flooded, though a few cattle managed to graze there in the very dry weather.

"I think we should drain them," said Purity.

He raised one eyebrow and fixed her with an un-wavering gray-eyed stare.

"For what reason?" he growled.

"So that the land can be tilled. There is nigh on a hundred hectares of De Feyelle land bordering the Seine, and all of it could be brought into use."

He terminated the stare by closing his eyes and not reopening them till he was looking away from her, coldly, into the middle distance.

"That land will never grow an ear of corn," he said flatly. "It is sour, sick ground, and it will remain so till the end of time."

"Rubbish!" cried Purity. "It will only remain so till someone does something about it. And I think we should do it. Now! This winter!"

The gray stare swung back to meet her.

"Impossible!" he said. "By no means on earth could that land be drained."

"It *can* be done!" insisted Purity. "I remember well my stepfather saying it could be done, and I even remember seeing a map of *how* it was to be done."

"Who prepared this map?" demanded Jacques with a sneer.

"It was done by an expert," said Purity, "by a Dutch engineer who was brought in by Monsieur le Marquis." She leaned forward across the table and drew a line across it with her forefinger. "He said that a deep ditch was to be dug straight through the middle of the water meadows. Then lesser ditches were to be dug here, and here, connecting with the river, so that the fall of the land would allow the water to . . . Why are you looking at me like that?" she demanded. "What are you sneering about now?"

"So?" He sat back in his chair, regarding her with his lips curled in a grin of contempt. "It was *Monsieur* le Marquis who gave you the idea of draining the water meadows? And what led that aristocratic gentleman to bother his brain with such trifles, I wonder? Did he tire of deflowering virgin brides on their wedding night? Or of flogging women for stealing the gleanings from his fields? Or of his perpetual roundelay of hunting, gluttony, drunkenness, and fornication?"

She drew in a deep breath, being resolved not to let this insufferable, opinionated man make her lose her temper.

"For whatever whim, I am not aware," she said. "But the marquis *did* summon the Dutch engineer, who said the meadows could be drained, and he showed my stepfather, the estate bailiff, how it could be done."

"And, yet, it was not done," interposed Jacques.

"The small matter of the Revolution intervened," said Purity tartly. "And they hanged the marquis"— she pointed to the center of the vast ceiling—"up there! I saw him with my own eyes, dangling from a chandelier."

The gray eyes wavered. He cleared his throat and rubbed his square jaw, raspingly, with his knuckles.

"We don't have the labor for the job," he said.

"Not in the winter?" asked Purity.

"Even in the winter there's hedging and ditching to be done," he said. "Then there's the lambing, and . . ."

"I have inspected the hedges and ditches," she said, "and they are in an excellent state, requiring only perfunctory attention from a handful of expert craftsmen. Likewise, the lambing can be done by a few specialists. The ditch-digging can be done by anyone—anyone! And that will include *me!*" she added.

He made one final attempt to put up an argument. "There's plenty of indoor work for which we can only spare the time in winter."

"All that can be done after dark!" cried Purity.

"After we come in from digging the drainage ditches!"

"You are a difficult woman, I think," said Jacques.

"And you are a damned stubborn man!" said Purity. "Now, will you give me your answer? Do we drain those water meadows and win another hundred hectares with which to feed ourselves?"

"If you think it can be done," he said. "And if you can persuade the people to dig that quagmire through the winter, you have my permission to try. But don't blame me if you fall flat on your aristocratic face."

"Thank you!" snapped Purity. She rose to go. Then, upon an unbidden impulse, she held out her hand. "You need a button sewn on your coat," she said. "Give it to me and I'll do it now."

He paused for a moment, then took off the garment and tossed it across the table, unsmilingly.

"Please yourself, woman. As you wish."

Insufferable! The wretch was completely insufferable!

Purity bit off the end of cotton, tugged at the button to ensure that it was strongly held, and threw the coat aside. Her victory over the leader of the community—if it could be called victory—had left her with mingled feelings. Foremost was the satisfaction of having bested him in an argument; but what was tempered by the sour thought that she had undoubtedly put her head into a noose of her own devising, a noose with which she could well hang herself. It did not take much imagination to picture what would happen if, following a long winter of cruelly hard labor upon the water meadows, the scheme turned out, after all, to be a fiasco—and the low-lying ground remained what it had always been: dank, damp, sick, and sour.

How the community would revile her. How the insufferable Jacques would sneer.

She glanced out of the window. Coming across the

courtyard from the direction of the diary were Chastity and Etienne. With the apple harvest gathered in, the young couple had been given work in the dairy department: Etienne milking the cows, Chastity learning to make cream cheese, clotted cream, and cheese cake —produce that, sent to the weekly markets at Rouen and Louviers, brought in the revenue with which the community was able to purchase the few things that were not manufactured on the domain.

Chastity had still not uttered a word; but some of the shadow had passed from her eyes and she frequently smiled. She was smiling as Purity looked down at her, presumably at something her companion had said. Etienne limped along beside her—the lame god Vulcan walking with the goddess of spring—chattering away happily. She watched them till they went from her sight.

She supposed she should take Jacques his coat. While sitting at the window, she had seen him walk over to the stable block, his tall, shirtsleeved figure casting a long shadow in the evening sunlight. It was going to be a cold evening, and she knew he possessed only one coat. It was still a couple of hours before Sunday supper, and he might well miss its warmth if she waited till then to return the garment. But the prospect of going over there, knocking upon his door, gave her a small *frisson* of—what?—unease?

Patting her hair into place and arranging her shawl around her shoulders, Purity took up the coat and went out. Crossing the yard, she could hear the rooks cawing in the tall trees across the river, and the sound reminded her of the water meadows. She must start the work almost immediately. Next week. Why not tomorrow? Tomorrow, she would go down and drive in a row of pegs to mark out the line of the main drain—just as the Dutchman had planned it all those years before.

She knew Jacques' quarters, having seen him looking out of the window. The door was immediately in front of her, at the top of the stairs leading from inside the stable.

She knocked. Receiving no answer, she knocked again. There being still no reply, she toyed with the options of either leaving the garment inside or taking it away; she chose the former.

The door was unlocked, and there was a short passageway inside. It was bare of any furniture, not even a chair upon which to lay the coat. It seemed churlish to throw it on the floor. There was a door at the end of the corridor that must lead to his living room. It was slightly ajar. She would put the coat in there.

She heard a movement just as her hand reached out to push open the door: a rustling sound and the creaking of bedsprings. The scene that met her shocked gaze was imprinted on her mind with a startling clearness that remained before her, in incredible detail of pose and nuance of expression, for long after.

There was a girl. Purity knew her well: a flighty little thing of about twenty, unmarried and unattached, and, like so many in post-war France, an orphan. She was one of those who, in the heat of summer's evenings in the fields, was among the first to strip to the waist. Now she was totally nude, and quite uncaring. She merely stared around at Purity with a shameless strumpet's grin.

"Oh! Look who's here!" she exclaimed. "Told you we should have locked the outer door, didn't I, Jacques?"

Jacques was beneath her, and she with her well-fleshed young legs were astride him. Nude, he looked infinitely more impressive than when clothed. Clothed, his thick-set torso seemed disproportionate to his length of leg. When he none too gently shoved the girl aside and got to his feet, Purity was overwhelmed by the perfection of his long and well-shaped legs, and lean flanks, the proud loins.

He gazed at her quite expressionless, his gray eyes searching her for comment.

Purity licked her dry lips.

"I . . . I have brought you your coat," she said. And, after laying the garment upon a chair back, she turned and walked out.

Night and silence.

Only Chastity's regular, quiet breathing in the bed across the room. A patch of moonlight on the uncarpeted floor half-illuminated her skirt lying draped over a chair.

She had made a night shift for herself in the community's sewing room: a thing of coarse calico, whose rough weave curiously excited the surface of her skin as she slipped it over her shoulders, breasts, and hips, then gently kicked it to the bottom of her bed so that she lay nude to her searching fingertips.

Not her own fingertips.

Whose, then?

The broad, coarse fingertips of big Jacques, who took proud-breasted field wenches to his couch? Jacques, of the unexpectedly beautiful, Greek-like nudity that would have inspired Praxiteles to sculpt figures to adorn another, more splendid, Parthenon? Perhaps. Big Jacques it was, certainly, who had inspired her to the warm desire that now overwhelmed her body, so that she was aware of each and every pore upon her skin, and all of them prickling with a restless wanting.

She had drunk deeply at supper that evening. Jacques had not been present (out of shame?—surely not), nor was his pretty little strumpet. Perhaps they had found more diverting pastimes than the Sunday

335

supper at the château. The thought quickened the motions of her questing fingertips.

She had drunk . . . how much Calvados? Two brimming beakerfuls, and her head had swum as she had walked unsteadily up to bed. So drunk, she; but with what vividness she was able to imagine that it was other hands, and not her own, which were pleasuring her body so intimately. And, surely, it could not have been Big Jacques; for only one man in her whole life had been able to call forth the ecstasy in quite the manner she was experiencing now; one lover, only, had ever played upon her like this, as a master musician upon a fine instrument. Had he not taught her, guided her fingertips?

She mounted to the high clouds and broke out into the illimitable blueness. She called his name. . . .

"Mark! Oh, *Mark!*"

Chapter Ten

At dawn, she was down in the water meadows, striding out a thousand paces that comprised the widest length of the waterlogged, semi-swampland bordering the Seine.

Her fingers blue with cold, she hammered in a line of pine stakes, setting them true, one aligned with the other. This was the direction that the main, deep ditch would take, and from it three or four shorter ditches would connect with the riverbank.

Breakfast was over by the time she returned to the château, but the kitchen hands gave her a beaker of hot milk and honey, which revived her and thawed out her fingertips against its warm earthenware. News of her intention had already spread through the community, and anyone with nothing better to do was soon down in the water meadows, sighting along the line of stakes, pointing to the river, speculating on how much oats, barley, wheat, or sugar beets could be grown on a hundred hectares of good soil.

Only . . . this was not good soil. . . .

Old Hubert condemned it before all of them. With

his great soup-strainer of a moustache blowing in the keen wind, he stooped and gathered up a handful of the dank, clay stuff in both his hands. He sniffed at it, pressed his nose into it, tasted it, then spat it out.

" 'Tis sick, rotten muck," declared the old soldier. "Put a seed in this and it would go moldy within a week."

Purity was standing at the edge of the group. Her heart sank to hear the condemnation. She had had high hopes for Hubert's support.

She need not have doubted. . . .

"Well," said the old soldier, stripping off his coat and rolling up his sleeves to show the scars of a dozen battles, "there's no use in crying over this rotten stuff. Best to get it drained. Where's a shovel?"

Shovels were produced as if from nowhere. All eyes were upon Purity, who stood in amazement.

"Who digs the first sod?" asked someone.

"Need you ask?" said another.

"Come, Madame!" Old Hubert held out a shovel for her, his toothless mouth spread in a broad grin. "The honor shall be yours!"

Joyfully, Purity took the keen-edged tool and drove it deeply into the yielding turf, digging out a load of dank soil and throwing it aside. A cheer went up from all around. Others were running down the slope into the meadow, carrying shovels, pick-axes, mattocks, and plaited baskets to carry the soil. She saw Jacques' tall figure watching from afar. He was leaning against a willow at the top of the meadow, his gaze fixed upon the group by the freshly dug patch. When he saw her eyes upon him, he straightened up, tossed away a blade of grass that he had been sucking, and stomped off back to the château. He did not appear down by the water meadows again that day, or for many days after.

Every man, woman, and child who could swing a

pick, heft a shovelful of earth, or carry away even the smallest load put in ten hours' hard labor that first day, afterward returning to their specified indoor tasks in the château or in the farm buildings.

By the end of the week a drainage ditch stretched one-tenth of the way along Purity's first line of stakes. As wide as a grave and as deep as a tall man, it was already filling up with water from the humid earth.

It seemed to Purity that Chastity was greatly improved in spirits. Her arm was out of the splint and had mended perfectly. Her eye had lost the terrible redness, and the angry blemish had faded from her satin cheek. Also, though she was not to be persuaded to bare her breast for inspection, Purity had stolen a glance at it while the girl was undressing, and she saw that she was unscarred.

Light-hearted most of the time, willing and docile all the time, Chastity had nevertheless not recovered her capacity for speech. Moreover, any attempt to draw her out only resulted in, at best, tears, and, at worst, a total withdrawal into herself for several days, during which time she would neither look at, or respond to, anyone—anyone except Etienne.

A smile from Etienne, a look from Etienne, and she would emerge from even her most profound moods of despondency. The crippled lad and his companion jackdaw—which rejoiced in the name of Jacko, and which could enunciate the word quite clearly—had become Chastity's constant companions, a fact that gave Purity a great deal of satisfaction, and just a bit of concern.

One day, while digging the drainage ditch side by side with Yvette, she voiced her slight, nagging doubt. "I hope that Etienne doesn't get himself too—how to put it?—besotted with Chastity. I don't want him to get hurt, or she, either. For, you see, she's not a whole person. And it's possible that she never will be."

Yvette threw another shovelful of dirt out of the ditch and straightened up before replying. "You've got no cause to worry," she said. "As I told you from the start, they're two of a kind—two poor, afflicted creatures who turn to each other for a kind of comfort. Etienne's a good lad. I've known him all his life. I tell you, Madame, nothing but good can come out of the friendship."

"That has always been my belief," said Purity. "But I'm glad to hear you confirm it." She took another stab with her own shovel. "The going's getting easier, don't you think? The soil's much softer at this end of the meadow."

"Time for a rest," said Yvette. "Here comes Eloise with a bucket of good, hot soup."

They took their midday meal in the meadow, huddled behind a rough windbreaker that had been erected against the cruel blasts of winter that were already carrying with them the first flurries of snow, which, as Purity feared, might well blanket the entire province till spring and put an end to all work on the drainage ditch that year.

As they drank their soup and sucked at the fresh bread dipped into the hot, appetizing brew of meat and vegetable stock, they talked, and always of the draining of the meadows, a task that had become a challenge to everyone in the community.

Everyone save Jacques.

"There he is," murmured someone. "Came to see how we're getting along. A good fellow, Jacques, but stubborn as any mule. You'll not see him take a shovel in hand. What's more, he'll not believe the job can be done till it's finished."

"Look at him now," said another. "See, Hubert, he's trying your trick."

Halfway along the line of the deep ditch that by now almost bisected the wide meadow, the bulky figure of the community's leader stooped, took up a handful of earth close to the edge of the ditch, held it close against his nose, and appeared to sniff at it.

"He'll not taste it," chuckled old Hubert. "There's not many who enjoy chewing earth. But 'tis the only way to get the flavor of it and find out its true worth."

"By heaven, he is, though! Look at him!"

A laugh went up. Jacques looked around with a scowl, spitting out a mouthful of earth. The laughter died like a spent candle.

"Back to work, all!" said Hubert. "And I'm next at the deep end of the trench."

Purity put her empty soup bowl with the others, took up her shovel, and plodded through the ooze at Yvette's heels, toward their part of a fresh trench that was being dug to connect the main, deep drainage ditch with the river. It was quite a long walk, and the going was hard. Her *sabots*—the wooden workshoe of the Norman peasant: hard-wearing, serviceable, and filled with straw for warmth—were carrying their own weight of mud.

She and Yvette had reached the lip of the trench when it happened. . . .

"Cave-in!"

"Oh, my God!" cried Purity, whirling around.

"It's the deep trench!" exclaimed Yvette.

"Hubert!"

"Come on!"

They were running. Every man, woman, and child in that wide meadow was running toward a small group of figures at the end of the deep trench, figures that were plying their shovels like mad creatures, but already working with the desperation of those who know in their hearts that they were too late.

Purity and Yvette were the last to arrive on the

scene. The crowd parted respectfully to let Purity through. Three men were still digging at a chest-high mound of newly fallen earth at the end of the deep ditch.

"Is it . . . Hubert?" asked Purity.

"I saw it happen," said a woman. She was weeping, frantic. "Hubert called out that the side was caving in. He shouted to the others to run for their lives. He reached up with his shovel and tried to hold it back as it . . . as it came down on him. He was buried in the instant, still shouting. It was horrible—horrible!"

Now the men had thrown aside their shovels and were scrabbling with their bare hands, plunging their arms deeply into the oooze, probing for their comrade.

"I have him!" shouted one.

Presently, they uncovered a mud-covered head and shoulder. A woman cried out with shocked horror, then another. A child, only half-aware of the tragedy that had occurred within the deep ditch, began to wail plaintively. Everyone edged closer to the lip of the ditch. Purity pressed her hands to her mouth to prevent herself from screaming.

They wiped the moustached old face with their neck cloths as lovingly as any mother would wash her babe. They felt within the mud-caked coat, against the skinny breast, for a sign of a heartbeat.

"He's gone. The old fellow's gone."

"God rest his soul!"

They fell on their knees. Hubert was one of the oldest of the community. He had marched with the Forty-fifth Light Regiment across the face of Europe at the behest of his emperor. Survivor of many battles, he had seen his own son perish by his side at Waterloo. And, now, to die in a ditch in his native Normandy. . . .

Four men bore him away upon their shoulders, wrapped in his coat of honor, like any soldier. Everyone followed, as mourners. All that remained—like so many crosses stuck upright in the mud—were their abandoned shovels.

And Purity Landless . . .

She remained kneeling alone, head bowed, face buried in her hands, her slender shoulders racked with bitter sobbing. Her proud dream was lying in ruins all around her.

She did not look up at the sound of a footfall, nor did she respond to the hand that was laid, none too tenderly, upon her shoulder. Only the voice aroused her—Jacques' voice.

"So . . . a man has died!"

She looked up into his face: the cold gray eyes, cheeks reddened by the biting wind, jutting lower jaw. There was no pity there.

"I killed him," she said simply. "As you predicted, I have metaphorically fallen flat on my aristocratic face."

He rubbed his chin, narrowed his eyes against the wind, and looked out across the Seine, which flowed like a ribbon of cold steel at the end of the water meadows below them. When he spoke, it was as if he was musing aloud to himself.

"Great evils have been done in this land," he said. "Those who ruled in the old days—the aristocrats— matched the atrocities of the Paris mob, deed for deed down through the centuries. My mother, who was born and raised in Evreux, was married in the church there. In the midst of her wedding feast, a simple peasants' merrymaking, the lackeys of the local *seigneur* descended upon the gathering and snatched her away. No one protested—not loudly, not with any violence. It was the law, you see."

"I know of that law," said Purity. "I myself saw it applied here, in our village."

Ignoring her interjection, he went on. "When the

seigneur had deflowered the young bride, he sent her back to her bridegroom with a purse of gold. He—the bridegroom—who had never possessed more than a few *sous* at any one time in his young life, threw the purse into the river and embraced his broken-hearted bride, comforting her as best as he could. A child was born to the couple nine months later."

Purity drew in breath sharply.

He went on. "You find me prejudiced, do you not? You see, it is because I am not sure, nor ever will be, whether I am partly one of that hateful breed or not. Personally, I think—I hope—that I am not. These are not the hands of an aristocrat, you may think; nor this coarse, uncouth face the countenance of a *seigneur's* bastard."

Purity recalled the vision of him nude: the unexpected sight of his elegantly proportioned limbs and torso that had put her so in mind of Greek sculpture. But she held her peace and made no comment.

"However," said Jacques, "to return to the present. Today, the people will mourn the passing of a brave old soldier. Tomorrow, the work will go on, *non?*"

She stared at him in flat disbelief.

"Are you mad?" she cried. "After what happened, do you think that I would try to persuade those people, always supposing that they were fools enough to let themselves be persuaded. . . ?"

She broke off upon seeing him stoop and pick up a handful of the soil. As Hubert had done, as he himself had done a short time ago, he held the dark-colored mass close to his nose, savoring its odor. He bit off a piece, chewed it, rolled it around in his mouth, then spat it out.

"The old marquis was no fool, damn his guts!" said he. "He knew what he was doing when he brought in the Dutchman. The Dutchman knew his trade, right enough. And he earned his fee."

344

"You mean . . . "

"The Dutchman was right. You were right." His face broke into one of his rare smiles. "And I was wrong. The water meadows can be drained . . . are *already* being drained. The ditches you have dug already are taking in the rotten humors of the soil. It is no longer sick and sour. By springtime, if the snow keeps away, the rottenness will be carried away into the Seine, and these meadows will be a sea of corn."

"We owe it to Hubert, for his sacrifice," she said tremulously.

"The rich soil of France is well watered with the blood of her sons," said Jacques, "soldiers and toilers, peasants and aristocrats alike. It is our birthright. We must make it good."

The next day, after old Hubert had been laid in the ground, the work recommenced. And Jacques labored with the rest.

The weather remained cold, making the work a terrible hardship; but the snow held off. When the first wild daffodils showed on the banks, scattered around the nodding willows, the main, deep ditch spanned the meadows, and three lesser ditches were all but joined with the river. The entire system was filled with water, and it was decided that the last few feet would have to be blown up with gunpowder. The date for this, the "official opening" of the hundred hectares of reclaimed land, was set for the first of May.

The mutual respect that had grown between Purity and the leader of the community broadened into a friendship—of the Platonic sort. Jacques, she decided, was a natural bachelor, not greatly interested in women as a sex. He regarded her as an honorary man: more capable, possessing more clarity of mind and masculine authority than the normal run of womankind. His physical needs were easily satisfied upon the bodies of complaisant girls—of whom the proud-breasted little trollop was only one—who gave themselves freely to various men of the community. He never—by word, look, or gesture—made the slightest advance toward Purity.

She was embarrassed—it seemed a markedly special favor, considering her recent arrival in the community—when, by way of a surprise, Jaques presented her with the key to a pretty, four-room cottage behind the stable complex that he, all unbeknownst to her, had been renovating in what little spare time he had. He waved aside her protests and told her not to repine. As former leader of the community and begetter of the drainage scheme, she was entitled to better accommodations than a cramped single room. And, besides, he reminded her, she had Chastity to consider. It was a great burden, he added, to be mother of a poor creature who was not quite right in the head. The extra rooms would make her burden the less onerous. Purity accepted the key.

Chastity progressed not at all, but remained a silent, docile, and amiable creature who was liked by all, who did as she was told, worked hard for her keep (like her friend and companion Etienne, her winter task was to help in the dairy, which was why, blessedly, she had not been present at Hubert's tragic end), and gave Purity no anxieties—save for the hardening conviction that the girl's brutal ravishment had, indeed, altered her mind irrevocably, and she would never emerge again into the real world of people. And perhaps, thought Purity, considering what she had suffered, it was a not unmixed blessing. . . .

On an unusually mild evening in the early spring, Purity walked back through the starlit shadows of the courtyard, from the château (where she had been spending a couple of hours in the dressmaking room, refurbishing her and Chastity's sparse wardrobe) to the cottage. Halfway there, she was shocked out of her contemplations about the possible longevity of her one and only summer bodice by an ear-shattering shriek. This was instantly followed by another. Then came the slamming of a door.

Purity immediately began to run. The sound came from the direction of her cottage. The scream—by its pitch and cadence, by its very sound—she knew to have been Chastity's.

No one else appeared to have heard it; no heads emerged from windows around the stable block. Most of the community was enjoying post-prandial amusements in the great hall: cards, dice, gossip. No one joined her in her frantic, heart-pounding race to see what the screaming was all about.

The ground-floor window of the cottage showed a light; she had left Chastity sitting by the fire with her needlework, so that was to be expected. Flinging the door wide open, she rushed over the threshold, then recoiled to see the wild-eyed figure that backed up against the far wall and defied her: sable hair awry, mouth agape, trembling, frightened, breast heaving— but defiant.

"He deserved it!" cried Chastity. "He . . . he tried to kiss me . . . to paw me! The filthy bastard!"

There was a kitchen knife in her hand. It dripped blood.

Blood also besplattered the whitewashed wall against which Chastity cowered, and there were traces of it on her skirts and bodice. Despite the sudden onslaught of horror, nevertheless, and unmindful of the implications behind the girl's words, Purity's first reaction was that of joy and release.

"My darling!" she cried. "You . . . you can talk again!"

Chastity's lovely face crumpled. The knife dropped

from her grasp. Slowly, she sank to her knees, covering her face with her hands.

"I . . . I didn't mean to hurt him," she sobbed. "But I couldn't bear it, even the thought of it—for a man to . . . to do *that* to me again. . . ."

"Oh, my poor darling!" Purity raced to fall on her knees beside the distraught girl. She wound her arms around the slim shoulders, pressed the anguished face to her bosom. "No one shall hurt you, my precious— no one. I promise you. Rest. Be still. Trust Mama Purity. She won't let anyone harm her darling girl."

They had not moved when, minutes later, Yvette's shocked face appeared at the door. She signaled to Purity, mimed at her to come and join her. Purity, looking over Chastity's shoulder, gave a nod of acknowledgment.

"My darling, I must go and have a word with Yvette," she murmured.

The pretty, tear-streaked face jerked up. The dark eyes widened.

"Mama Purity, don't leave me alone!"

"No, my darling. I promise that I shall be near at hand. I will never leave you again, my Chastity."

"No, Mama Purity, please not. . . ."

Gently, she disentangled herself from the arms that held her. Chastity slumped back against the wall and began to keen in a high-pitched, tremulous wail: the sound that has echoed down the ages; the sound of uncounted and uncountable women raped since time began.

Purity joined Yvette at the door. Heads close together, eyes cocked toward the slight figure collapsed by the far wall, they whispered together.

"Etienne . . . I saw him running toward the chapel. Streaming blood, he was!"

"Oh, no, not Etieene!"

"Madame, I stopped him. She has not hurt him

348

much, I do not think—a slash in the arm. But what has been unleashed—the passions! Madame, I have been so wrong. They were like fire and air, those two. He tried to kiss her...."

"Yes, she told me."

"He screamed at me. She took up the knife and tried to kill him. And now he says that, since she has failed, he will kill himself for what he has done."

"Oh, my God, Yvette! Where is he now?"

"I told you, Madame, he was heading for the old chapel. His jackdaw, that Jacko, was flying above his head and following after him. Madame, he is a good boy. No matter if he tried to kiss our darling, our angel, but I know that he would not have..."

"Of course not!" said Purity. "Listen, Yvette, I will go after him. I think, as Chastity's mother, I may be able to assure him that no real harm has been done; indeed, I can tell him that, providentially, he has renewed her powers of speech. Stay here, Yvette. Comfort darling Chastity."

"Yes, Madame."

Covering her head with her shawl, Purity raced off into the gloom in the direction of the chapel that stood like the upturned hull of a great ship at the end of the château. There was no sound but that of the wind in the high trees, her own footfalls, and the hammering of her heart. But there was no sign of Etienne.

By the chapel porch, she saw that the door was open. There was a small pool of blood there ... and something else.

With a stab of sudden anguish, she saw that it was the jackdaw Jacko. The bird was dead. She stooped to pick it up: a pathetic scrap of feathers and small, delicate bones. The head lolled brokenly, and it was still warm. Someone had wrung its neck.

Not Etienne, surely?

With the thought came the certainty. Etienne loved

the jackdaw, and he would never abandon it to neglect. If he had ended Jacko's life out of mercy, it must follow that he really intended to end his own life, also!

She rushed into the chapel.

"Etienne, are you here? Etienne!"

No reply. By the faint light of the red lamp burning on the simple altar, she saw only shadowed emptiness.

There was a dark archway that led up to the bell tower. It beckoned her. She took the winding stone steps two at a time and arrived, panting and breathless, in the ringing chamber, where by the moonlight that streamed in through the unglazed windows, she could see six bell ropes hanging. Nothing else.

"Etienne! Etienne!"

She heard a sound. It came from outside the window, and it might have been a roosting pigeon, which, disturbed by the sound of her voice, had fluttered and ruffled its feathers. She crossed over and looked out. It was no pigeon.

Etienne was standing three paces from her, his back to the bell tower's ancient wall, his feet half over the edge of the narrow ledge upon which he stood, hands pressed against the stonework at his sides, his eyes—those gentle, pansy-soft eyes—fixed upon hers. Far below, the cobbled courtyard stood out whitely in the moonlight.

"Etienne . . . please . . . " She lifted her skirts, preparatory to lifting a leg over the windowsill.

"Stay where you are! If you try to come out here, I'll jump!" His voice had the wild edge of hysteria to it.

Her mind raced. What to do? Should she fetch help? Surely, Jacques would be better able to deal with the distraught lad than she. But was there time?

She must say something, keep him talking.

"Your arm, Etienne," she faltered. "You must let me bandage it. Show it to me . . . please."

He made a dismissive gesture. "The arm . . . nothing," he said. "What does it matter, anyhow? In a few minutes, when I have thought everything through, I am going to take one step—out there."

"No, Etienne, *no!*"

"Why no?" He seemed genuinely puzzled. "I want to die. I am not needed. I do not even need myself. I am a cripple, a freak. Everyone holds me in contempt, myself included. No girl would look at me twice. Even Chastity, who I thought was my friend, when I tried to show her my feelings, tried to express how her beauty filled me with such strange joy . . . I . . . Madame, I am sorry I frightened her. . . ."

"It doesn't matter, Eteinne," said Purity. "Did you but know it, you have restored her powers of speech. It was the shock, you see."

"The shock!" His voice was harsh with self-loathing. "The shock of being kissed by a freak! A monster!"

"No, Etienne, you're wrong! It wasn't like that at all!"

But he was no longer listening.

"I shall be better dead," he said flatly. "Poor Jacko's gone. I couldn't leave him to grieve for me. And he's the only living creature who would have. It will soon be all over—the agony of knowing that there isn't a girl in the whole wide world who would ever wish to feel my arms around her; envying other men; knowing that in all my life I shall never know the delights that they take for granted. I can't live with it any longer. Chastity—what happened with Chastity was the end of the road for me. But I am truly sorry I frightened her. . . ."

Purity's heart melted with compassion to hear him. How to express to him—quickly and with complete

351

conviction—the truth about himself: that he was no freak, but a kindly, gentle soul who was liked by all who knew him? And, surely, when he learned to overcome his shyness, any girl would look upon him with favor. Why, he was very nice looking. But how to convince a broken-hearted lad with his feet already poised on the edge of eternity?

She must try. . . .

"Etienne, listen. . . ."

"Madame, I wish you would leave me," he said. "Go back to your cottage and shut the door behind you. Forget I am here. Tell no one. It's no use, you see? No one will be able to prevent me. And I want to be alone—quite alone, the way I have been, in my mind, all my life—when I take the step out there."

"You're wrong about yourself. . . ."

"Leave me be!"

He screamed the words at her, pressing his hands against his ears to shut out the sound of her voice. But she persisted.

"Etienne, you are not a monster. Your problem is a problem as old as time. You are a perfectly ordinary shy young man who . . . "

"I am nineteen!" he cried. "Nineteen, and I have never touched a girl's body! Nineteen, and I have never kissed a girl till tonight—and she would have killed me for it!"

"Chastity's not like other girls. You must take that into account. You must!"

"It's always been the same!"

"It will change. There will be women . . . "

"Never!"

"Etienne, I promise you . . . "

"What women?" he blazed. "What woman would let herself be touched by a freak like me?"

"Etienne . . . "

"Would *you?*"

She gave a sharp intake of breath but made no reply. She knew, then, that her course of action had been preordained by fate, and that her compassion, her humanity, her sensibility—her capacity for loving, even—were standing at the bar of her own conscience, and if she let scruples stand in the way of the human obligation she owed to the suffering, bewildered lad on the ledge, she would never be able to live with her conscience again.

Framed in the moonlit window, she unfastened her bodice with fingers that trembled, then let the garment fall around her hips. Her shift followed. The chill, night wind prickled her bare skin as, raising her arms, she unfastened the knot of her chignon and shook out her wondrous, silver-gold hair and let it fall around her shapely shoulders.

"You have my answer, Etienne," she said softly.

He was staring at her, transfixed with wonder.

"I never knew . . . never imagined," he gasped. "I've never seen . . . never guessed for one moment . . . "

"I am just like any other women, Etienne," she said.

"You are . . . *beautiful!*"

"Then why do you tarry? Come. . . ." And she reached out her hand for his, which, being given, she guided it toward her bare breast, placing it upon the peak, with the palm resting upon the taut nipple.

"Oh, my God!" whispered Etienne.

"Come," she said, gently pulling at his arm and stepping back into the chamber, bringing him with her. "We're quite alone here. Just the two of us together. Lie down with me."

Slipping out of her skirts, she spread them out upon the ringing chamber's ancient floorboards—timbers that had survived the holocaust and had been polished by the feet of a hundred generations of bell-ringers—

353

and lay down on the makeshift bed, guiding him to follow her.

"Madame . . . I . . . I don't know what to do." He was trembling.

"Ssh! No cause to worry. I will show you. Only, dear Etienne, you are so big and strong, so be gentle with me, please. There, are you comfortable? Hold me, like so. Does that feel nice?"

Gently, her fingers sought and undid the fastings of his breeches, then eased them over his hips. His shirt followed. He shuddered with passion as her hands slid over his bare chest and encircled him, stroking his well-muscled back.

"You are wonderful—wonderful!" he whispered against her cheek.

"All women are wonderful," she whispered in return. "And I am only your first, Etienne."

For her it had been a journey of curious delight, in which she had been guide and exemplar; and he had been the willing pilgrim, sometimes hesitant to tread strange and unfamiliar pathways, at other times over-eager, hasty to the point of recklessness, breathless to reach his goal.

Released, serene, he now lay in her arms, his cheek pillowed against her bosom, one hand stroking her hip, rediscovering for the hundredth time its suave complexity of shape and texture.

"That was better than dying, I think," she murmured.

"Yes. Oh, yes!" he said. "But . . . you must have found me very stupid and ignorant."

"I found you a very gentle, very satisfying lover in every way," said Purity. "Etienne . . . "

"Yes?"

She touched his hair, smoothing it back from his

brow. "Don't ever boast about having possessed me," she said, "to other men, I mean."

"Oh, no!" He was horrified. "I would never dream . . . "

"You are young, Etienne," she said. "From my experience, the young can sometimes be very cruel. You will have other women—younger, prettier women. And you will look back upon your first time with me as something rather less splendid than you think it to be at this moment. All I ask is that you don't tell anyone. Don't shame me."

He reached up and touched her cheek to discover that she was crying.

"How can you think that of me, Madame?" he said. "After what you have given me. The beauty. My life. Hope for the future. I shall treasure the memory of this night for always."

"Thank you, Etienne," she said, kissing him. "And now, my dear, I think we must go—that is, unless you want me again. . . ."

"I . . . I would love to have you again," he said, "but the way it was—it was such perfection that just to think of it, to remember how we were together, the things you taught me—that is happiness enough."

"You are old for your years, Etienne," she told him. "You have already learned the art of savoring the fragrance of pleasure, which is the opposite of gluttony. Come, now, let us go."

They dressed, then descended the spiral staircase together, she leading. When they came to the porch, he groaned to see the dead jackdaw that she had placed on a ledge by the holy water stoup.

"Poor Jacko," he whispered.

They parted, he to bury his dead friend, and she to see how Chastity was faring.

Yvette heard her approach and greeted her on the

threshold before she had time to unlatch the cottage door.

"Etienne—is he all right, Madame?" she demanded anxiously.

Purity nodded. "I . . . managed to persuade him not to do himself any harm. He was very upset about the incident, but I think that, in many ways, tonight has taught him something."

"The slash on his arm—it's not serious?"

"No. I bound it with a handkerchief. And how is Chastity? How is my poor darling?"

"Better, Madame, much better. I put her to bed and she is resting quietly. But she made me promise to send you to her as soon as you returned. Ah, Madame—to think of it!—our darling girl is speaking again!" The good women dissolved in tears and had to be comforted.

When Yvette had departed, Purity lit a candle and went up the narrow stairs to Chastity's bedroom. The girl lay with her mane of sable hair spread out upon the pillow. Her eyes were bright, her smile a joy to behold. She held out her arms for Purity.

"Mama, dearest!"

"My Chastity, my love!"

They embraced, and it seemed to Purity that a whole world of misfortune vanished at the touch of those soft arms around her, and with the pressure of the sweet lips that rained kisses upon her.

"You can talk again! You are cured!"

"Yes, yes! It was like . . . like waking up from out of a dream. Poor Etienne, he little knew what he had unleashed when he tried to kiss me. How is he, Mama? I behaved so dreadfully, but now that the shock has passed, I am full of remorse. What must he think of me?"

Purity reassured her that Etienne was recovered from the encounter and that the wound was only superficial, marveling as she did so at Chastity's clarity of thought and diction. It was, indeed, as she herself had said, like a return from the limbo of a dream, a somnambulist awakened to the life around her.

Over and over again, the girl expressed her regrets for what had happened.

"To think that I could take a knife to poor Etienne!" she said. "How awful of me! Of course, he wasn't going to rape me, I know that now. But, you see, Mama Purity, in that state between sleeping and waking up, I thought myself to be back . . . back in . . ."

She shuddered. Purity held her more tightly.

"Don't speak of it, my darling. Don't even think of it."

Chastity said, "I will speak of it, Mama Purity. I will tell you everything that happened, as well as I can remember it—but not now, perhaps not for quite a while. It was not what was done to me. That was horrible—horrible! But there was something worse, much worse. And I find that that part of it overshadows all the rest, so that to tell you of what happened to me while I was away, leaving out the really important part [and I can barely think of that, let alone speak of it], would be meaningless to me. Do you understand, dearest?"

"Of course, my darling," said Purity. "And now you must sleep."

"Yes," said Chastity. "Kiss me, Mama Purity."

Purity embraced her again.

Chastity said, "Those men you lay with—the men mentioned on that hateful paper—they meant nothing to you?" There was anxiety in her voice.

"Nothing, my darling," replied Purity.

"And you've never seen any of them again?"

"No, nor ever shall I."

"I'm glad." The girl sighed. "I was so cruel to you

that day, Mama Purity. Things that have happened to me since have taught me to be more charitable. We all make mistakes. We all sin. And do you know something?"

"What, my darling?"

"I have already forgiven you."

Already she was forgiven for playing the whore! If only the man she loved could find the charity in his heart to do likewise. . . .

"Thank you, my darling," said Purity brokenly.

The day following the "official opening" of the reclaimed land, when Purity lit the powder fuse that exploded the charge and blew up the last few feet of ditch amidst general rejoicing, Etienne announced that he was leaving the community, and he came to say good-bye to Purity and Chastity.

"I have confidence that I can learn a good trade and make something of myself," he said, and the inner meaning was all for Purity. "First, I think I will travel, see something of the world, for I have never been farther than Evreux in my life."

Since their single, rapturous encounter in the bell chamber, he had neither by word nor gesture importuned a repeat of her favors, nor presumed upon the slightest familiarity, but had continued to treat her as he always had: addressing her as "Madame," according her the utmost respect as a member of the gentle sex, a person older and wiser than himself, and an aristocrat to boot.

Purity wished him well in his enterprise, gave him her hand, and kissed his cheek. And she was mightily glad when, after the briefest moment of hesitation, Chastity did the same. Together, they watched Etienne limp across the yard, out into the world beyond the confines of the De Feyelle domain—and out of their lives.

The month of May sped past. No rain fell, and the drainage ditches in the water meadows dried out, amply demonstrating that the soil had rid itself of the sick, dank humors that had made it useless since time immemorial. Jacques visited the meadows daily, testing the earth with eye, nose, and mouth. On the first of June, a calendar month after the "official opening," he declared the reclaimed land to be ready for the plow.

That night the community feasted—a gala feast—in the great hall.

Purity and Chastity had been anticipating the event for weeks. They had spent long hours with their needles and had made feast gowns for them both. They were not gowns of silk, satin, or velvet, trimmed with fine lace and hung about with jewelry, the like of which they had known in other, different, circumstances; they were simple creations of snowy-white muslin that admirably set off their excellent and contrasting figures; the older woman fair as a Viking goddess, the younger as darkly radiant as a gypsy princess.

Purity sat in the place of honor at the head of the long table, with Jacques on her left and Chastity on her right. The bill of fare was both lengthy and complex, including as it did the classic dishes of the province, together with the finest wines and ciders that the domain produced, and the inevitable Calvados.

Most of the men, and not a few of the women, got themselves mightily drunk. Though he had imbibed as much as anyone, Jacques hauled himself to his feet at the clearing away of the final, fifteenth course and delivered a totally coherent address, in the process of which he praised his former rival and present friend Purity in the warmest of terms. She replied in a brief speech, which—seeing the earnest and passionate glances that Jacques' bold-breasted little bedmate was throwing in his direction, and the sidelong glances that he was giving her in return—she made all the briefer. It was past one o'clock when the community rose from the table and proceeded for the most part unsteadily to their respective—in some cases each other's—beds.

"Mama Purity, darling, what a wonderful evening!" Chastity embraced Purity when they had entered the cottage and lit the candles. "You looked so beautiful, darling, so radiant and regal. Oh, you are my despair! How can I ever hope to emulate your beauty and presence?"

Purity squeezed the girl's waist fondly. "I do not notice many glances aimed in my direction when you are at hand, my dearest," she declared. "As I predicted once"—she paused, as, with a sudden pang of deprivation, she remembered it was in Brighton, on the never-to-be forgotten night of Chastity's kidnapping, that she had made the prediction—"as I said once, the time has come when no one will spare me a glance when you are around."

Chastity hugged her anew.

"You flatter me, darling Mama, but there is a very special pleasure in being flattered by one of the great, acknowledged beauties of our age. How generously the gods of Parnassus endowed you, and how . . . Mama Purity, what *is* it? What ails you?"

Purity's torso had suddenly stiffened within Chastity's grasp. Her harsh intake of breath, followed by a cry of alarm, appraised the girl that something had gone terribly amiss.

She glanced up into the face of the older woman. She was shocked at what she saw recorded there. She followed the direction of Purity's wide and staring eyes—to the window.

Chastity's scream echoed deafeningly in the narrow confines of the cottage living room. She swooned in

Purity's arms. Purity held her fast, then remained holding her, murmuring over and over to herself as she did so.

"There's no escape! No escape! How did I think I should ever escape. . . ?"

The face at the window had at first been a fleeting vision: now appearing, now withdrawn. After Chastity's outcry, it remained steady.

The benign waters of the Seine River had not, after all, washed away the image of the goat's head; it remained with her, it was staring at her, in near and terrible reality, through the glass pane, eyes blazing with a terrible triumph.

She could not have dragged her gaze from it for her soul's sake. She was still staring, still holding onto the limp form of the girl, when the door burst open.

There were three of them: big fellows, roughly dressed, and they spoke English—Cockney English. She fought them when they tore Chastity from her arms. But they laughingly restrained her, warded off her raking fingernails, lasciviously pawed at her body in doing so, ripping the shoulder of her white muslin feast gown.

"Leave her be, you dogs! That one is *mine!*"

The specter in the goat's mask stood in the doorway. The big louts obeyed instantly. They gathered up the girl between them and carried her to the door. Purity made a move to follow after, but she was immediately intercepted by goat-head, who stepped swiftly forward and seized her by the wrist in a steely grasp that brought a cry of pain to her lips.

Her cry, or the rough motion of being borne off, aroused Chastity from her swoon. The last thing outside of Purity's own personal horror, before the goat-headed creature enveloped her, was the girl's despairing plea: "Don't let them take me! Don't let them ravish me again, Mama Purity—*please . . . !*"

The door slammed.

She was alone with the masked figure.

The voice, muffled as on the previous occasion by the enveloping mask, was insinuating itself upon her ears, and the powerful hands were imprisoning her wrists.

"You will remember your solemn oath, the exchange of the four unholy kisses that we made together, each to each. You recall that? *Answer!*"

The strong fingers pinched deeply into her tender flesh.

"Yes . . . *yes!*" She screamed the reply.

"You have broken that oath, woman, and you no longer wear my representation around your neck upon a chain as you were ordered to. For that, your eternal soul is forfeited. But, before then, your living body must be chastised!"

"No . . ."

She shrank away from him, backing up against the wall as he released one of her wrists. She screamed as his free hand, taking the neck of her feast gown, rent the white muslin to the waist. She screamed again as he slapped her across the breasts.

It was but the beginning.

Deliberately, insanely, after the manner of those perverted creatures who followed the precepts of Donatien Alphonse François, Comte de Sade, he punished the fair body of Purity Landless, with deliberate attention given to those parts of her that might have been thought to inspire the most tender of passions in the heart of a man. He brutally chastised her rounded buttocks, ill-used her peerless bosom, and marked her face—that countenance which had been the toast of society.

And when he had slaked his darker passions upon

her, the monster in the goat mask bore her to a couch, where, divesting himself of his nether garments, he threw himself upon her quivering, pain-racked body, and with unfeeling brutality proceeded to despoil her, again and again. Goat-like in his attributes, he did not flag in his assaults. And Purity was still lying in his grasp, and enduring the most soul-racking excursions into abodes of pain and horror, when the first light of dawn dimly illuminated the scene of his frenzy. Then, and only then (for evil shrinks from its works upon being subjected to the clear and dispassionate scrutiny of the sun), did he dismount from his swooning victim, and, with one last brutal blow across the tear-streaked face, leave her to live or die—depending upon the caprices of Fate, Nature, and the capacity of her mind and body to absorb the protracted torments to which they had been so persistently subjected.

Chapter Eleven

"The king is dying. . . ."

The news passed by word of mouth throughout the capital. The bloated wreck of a man who was titular head of the most powerful nation on earth lay dying in Windsor Castle. More correctly, he sat a-dying, for he was forced—by reason of his overtaxed heart, which made lying down an agony—to sleep in an easy chair with his head in his hands and resting upon a table.

The tidings did not cause any undue concern amongst his subjects, satiated as they were with years of the monarch's carryings-on; some speculations about how his debtors must be hammering on the castle gates for settlement before his demise; scurrilous suggestions concerning Lady Conyngham. (It was rumored that she had already seized all the portable valuables she could lay her hands on and had dispatched two cartloads of plate and jewelry from Windsor to her family home; there was even a cartoon about it in all the print-shop windows, entitled: "A Moving Scene.")

That June Sunday, as a church clock chimed six in the afternoon, the Duke of Wellington took out from his fob an enormous half-hunter watch, checked it carefully, then replaced the timepiece. He then turned from the window that looked out over Hyde Park Corner and readdressed his attentions to his companion: a short, stocky, and quirky-looking man of about forty-five, with a shock of prematurely gray hair. The latter was dressed in civilian clothes of subdued color and material but of excellent cut. He was seated facing the duke's ornate desk, with its elaborate appointments of inkstands commemorating past victories, a pair of ornate reading lamps held aloft by gold and onyx statuettes representing the spirits of Valour and Patriotism, and a writing case that had once belonged to Wellington's arch-opponent Napoleon.

"What you are suggesting, Strickland," said the duke, "fills me with considerable concern. If true, then we have little time in which to act."

"The king's passing is imminent, sir?" asked the other.

"I expect the news any moment," said the duke. "It is only the tatters of a formally excellent constitution that keep him hanging onto life. I was at Windsor yesterday. The dropsy is now so advanced that his legs are swollen to enormous size and hard as stone. They pierce the soles of his feet to tap the fluid, and that gives him some small relief. Would you believe it? He rallied slightly yesterday and spoke of visiting Brighton! As if Lady Conyngham would permit it, even if 'twere possible! That woman will run off with the crown jewels if I don't prevent her. Oh, yes. Brother William will be King of England by this time next week; you may depend on it."

"Or . . . some other personage," said Strickland quietly.

Wellington frowned, stroked the side of his prominent nose, and eyed his companion fixedly. Strickland was reminded that here was the man who had held the fortunes of all Europe in his hands on the day of Waterloo.

The duke said, "I am conceding that William, Duke of Clarence, is not *my* ideal of a prospective monarch, but he will serve his purpose, which is to occupy the throne till his niece, Princess Victoria, achieves her majority. And he *was* a good friend of Nelson's, which counts in his favor with the vulgar populace. I should need a very great deal of convincing that there is really a serious conspiracy afoot to upset that eminently convenient arrangement."

Strickland leaned forward in his chair, taut as a compressed spring.

"I have evidence—patchy evidence from here, there, and everywhere—which, taken together, might well convince you, sir."

The duke spread his hands. "Tell me of it, Major Strickland," he said. "It was to bring such matters to my attention that I caused you to be appointed to your present secret office."

"Firstly, sir, I have to tell you that certain disaffected officers—officers who have neither the financial means to purchase promotion, nor the talents to merit the same—have been bribed."

"Bribed by whom, and for what purpose?" demanded Wellington.

"By whom, I have not been able to ascertain," said Strickland. "As to why, there seems to me to be only one reason for suborning an officer, and that is to secure his services for some reason."

"But for what reason you have also not been able to ascertain, I presume?" said Wellington dryly.

The major's heavy countenance flushed darkly. "A reason may emerge when I have related more of my evidence, sir," he said.

"Pray, proceed," bade the duke.

"In addition to officers, there is slight, but persistent, rumor that whole bodies of troops have been suborned," said Strickland, "though I am glad to report that I have found no evidence to support the rumor."

"I am mightily relieved to hear that!" exclaimed the duke. "The prospect of a Sovereign's Escort of the Household Cavalry attacking the royal coach on the way to Westminster Abbey is not to be contemplated lightly. But I interrupt again. Please continue."

Strickland said quietly, "There is at present a bill before the House of Commons that contains a proposal to abolish the Royal Marriage Act prohibiting members of the royal family under twenty-five from marrying without the king's consent."

"Yes, yes," said the duke dismissively, "sponsored by that pushy jackanapes Hardcourt. But I can promise you, Strickland, that it is a piece of legislation that has as much chance of becoming law as I have of being made queen of the May."

"But the bill has been drafted, sir," persisted Strickland. "It is in the process of being put before the House. Given certain conditions, it could speedily be passed and made law."

"Given what conditions?" demanded Wellington in a bleak voice.

"An insurrection," replied Strickland, "a popular rising, in favor of another candidate for the succession. A popular and *successful* rising. And another thing . . . "

"What's that?"

"The bill contains a clause making the abolition retroactive."

"The devil it does!"

"Which means that any marriage that the present

sovereign made before his alliance with Queen Caroline could be legalized."

"The devil it could!"

"The marriage to Mrs. Fitzherbert, for instance."

"My God, you're right, Strickland! And that damned brat of hers—devil take it, I can't even remember his name—the fellow whom that fool Charlie Strickland would have for our king in place of Princess Victoria . . . he could be . . . "

"I think not, sir," said Strickland. "It is my belief that the conspiracy—if there is a conspiracy—concerns itself with another possible candidate for the succession, a pretender of whom no one save a very few have ever heard."

"His name, sir?" demanded Wellington.

"The personage is a female, sir," replied Strickland. "And I believe her name to be Elizabeth."

The duke's incredulity was apparent. He tapped his fingers upon the desktop and eyed his aide with the air of a man who has been greatly put upon, and who has had his time wasted, by a fool. When there came a discreet knock upon the door, he called for the one outside to enter. It proved to be his private secretary.

"Your Grace, Lady Landless has returned. Shall I tell her that you cannot see her today, after all?"

"Devil take it, I can't send the poor, wretched woman away yet again," said the duke. "I was closeted with the Home Secretary when she called earlier, and I promised to talk to her for a few minutes after six. Will you bear with me for a few minutes, Strickland? No, don't bother to leave. I think you will find the encounter of interest. Pray, ask her ladyship to attend me, Ponsford."

The secretary bowed and withdrew, closing the door.

"Lady Landless?" mused Strickland. "Not *the* Lady Landless, sir? The one who . . . "

369

The duke nodded significantly. "The very same. Mark you, I think the scandal was greatly exaggerated. Personally, I have always greatly esteemed Lady Landless. She is a lady of excellent parts, and greatly put upon. Her husband, you know, has deserted her, along with the boy. *Cave!* She is here."

He rose to his feet, and Strickland did likewise, as the secretary ushered in through the doorway a figure dressed all in black from head to foot. Even that somber covering could not conceal the glorious body that lay beneath: hints of a superb bosom, an unbelievably slender waist curving out into generous hips, long and shapely legs. Her face was almost entirely hidden by a heavy black veil. And Strickland noticed, when she crossed the room with her hand extended to Wellington, that she walked with the aid of a parasol that was of such a robust construction as to resemble an invalid's stick.

"You Grace! So kind of you to see me."

"My dear Lady Landless, ma'am, an honor, I assure you. Allow me to present Major Strickland of my staff. Pray, let me assist you to a seat. You will find this most comfortable, I think. Will you take some refreshment? No? Then how can I be of service to you, ma'am?"

Purity inclined her head in Strickland's direction.

"You informed my secretary, ma'am, that the matter was one of some delicacy concerning your daughter," said the duke, divining the reason for her glance. "I may tell you that Major Strickland's occupation is concerned with delicate matters. If you can bring yourself to speak before him, it is possible that his counsel may be of some benefit to you."

"I gladly seize upon any counsel, sir," replied Purity. "For I have to tell you that the unrepeatable has been repeated, the horror piled upon the horror. My daughter Chastity has again been taken from me—and by the same creatures who kidnapped her on the previous occasion."

Wellington rubbed his jaw, looked puzzled, and said, "Ma'am, I confess myself to be a little confused. Had I not heard—had you not communicated it generally?—that your daughter had returned to you of her own free will one day last year, and that, again of her own free will, she immediately departed again with those with whom she had been staying?"

Purity made a frantic gesture. The heavy veil prevented them from seeing her expression, but it was obvious that she was greatly distressed.

"That is true, sir," she said tremulously. "But those with whom she freely left caused her to be treated with such brutality, such hideous cruelty, that when she was returned to me it was many, many months before she was whole again in both mind and body."

"What manner of brutality, Lady Landless?" interposed Major Strickland.

"She was . . . raped and beaten," said Purity.

"Raped, was it—or seduced?" asked Strickland. "You will forgive my asking, ma'am, but the distinction is rather relevant, in view of the fact that, as you admit, your daughter had gone away with these people of her own free will on at least one occasion."

"She was raped!" It was almost screamed.

"And now you say she has gone away again."

"She was *taken!*" cried Purity. "They dragged her from the refuge to which I had taken her in France."

"They—who were they, who took her?"

"I . . . I don't know. I didn't see any of their faces."

"By force, they took her?

"Yes, by force! They dragged her off, with her struggling and screaming to me to save her from ravishment. And I know well that that was their intent, for when they had taken her, I was . . . was . . . " Her voice trailed away.

371

"Yes, Lady Landless?" demanded Strickland. "You were saying that when they had taken your daughter you were—what?"

The slender shoulders sagged in defeat.

"Nothing," sighed the voice from behind the heavy veil. "It . . . it doesn't matter."

The duke glanced at his watch, cleared his throat, and said, "Ahem! If I may interject a question, ma'am. I am a little puzzled over one point. You said at one point that the girl had been returned to you—and in some state of distress. By what agency did she return on that occasion?"

"She was returned to me through the good graces of a common servant girl," said Purity, "a scullery wench at the house where her kidnappers reside."

The duke tapped his chin, cocked a glance at his aide, and then looked back to Purity.

"Now, that is very odd, is it not?" he said. "That these people, who, on your evidence, have kidnapped the girl on no less than two occasions, should not only permit her to come and visit you at your house on Half Moon Street, but also to let her slip through their fingers through the—as you say—good graces of a common servant girl? Now, ma'am, I find that all very inconsistent—not all of a piece, if you follow me."

"That was the way it happened," said Purity desperately. "I can't explain all the whys and wherefores. I only know that they took her, and she is now likely to be at Jermyn Abbey."

"Jermyn Abbey!" The interjection was from Strickland. "The D'Eath place in Mill Hill?"

"That is so," said Purity. "Captain D'Eath and a woman named Madeleine were with her when she came to me at Half Moon Street. They are behind all this business. They have my daughter."

"Well, that explains a very great deal," said Wellington. D'Eath is a blackguard. I warned you about him once, ma'am. You should have heeded me and not allowed that giddy young daughter of yours to get herself mixed up with that fellow. He's a bad lot with women, from all I've heard."

"Sir, you don't understand!" cried Purity, rising. "This is not just a matter of a giddy girl who has gotten herself infatuated with an adventurer! They have stolen her from me twice! They have abused her body and assaulted her mind! They have . . . "

"Ma'am, time is passing and I have much to do," said Wellington firmly. "For sake of the high esteem in which I hold both you and your husband, my former comrade-in-arms, I would do much to assist you. But I am not quite clear about what it is you require of me, save advice."

"Sir, I beg you—I entreat you—to send an armed body of men to Jermyn Abbey to search the place and find my daughter and return her to me," said Purity.

"Out of the question!" said the duke.

"But . . . "

Wellington rose and nodded to Strickland, who quietly crossed over and pulled a bell rope to summon the secretary.

The victor of Waterloo gazed at Purity, not unkindly, and said, "From what I gather, ma'am, this is not a police, but a family, matter. Your daughter has fallen amongst bad company. Well, she's not the first pretty young filly to fall into the hands of a blackguard, and she'll not be the last. My advice to you is to swallow your pride and discuss the whole matter with that husband of yours. Let him settle with D'Eath. But, if you want another piece of advice, you'll prevent Landless from challenging the fellow to a duel!"

"My husband is not in England, sir," said Purity

dully. "I don't know where he is, but I promise you that, if I did, my pride would not prevent me from crawling on my hands and knees to the ends of the earth to go to him—and not only on account of my poor, darling daughter. Good day to you, Your Grace. I thank you for your counsel, and I am sorry to have taken up so much of your valuable time. Good day, Major Strickland."

The secretary was hovering at the open door. The duke and his aide watched as Purity turned and went out, walking heavily upon the stout shaft of her parasol. When she had gone, they resumed their seats.

"A lovely woman," said Wellington. "A tragic woman. Did you observe her limp? And strange that she should not have unveiled. Do you suppose she is suffering from some terrible affliction? 'Twould be a tragedy if such a splendid creature were sticken down in the full flower of her beauty. Now, to revert to the business at hand. I have to say that I was both intrigued and disturbed by your evidence. As to the conclusion you draw, I can only say that you stretch credulity to its uttermost. There is a royal pretender named Elizabeth, hey? Well, Elizabeth—that's a royal name to juggle with, and no mistake. What price Queen Elizabeth the Second, hey? Come now, Strickland. I can see by your expression that you have a tale to tell. Out with it, man."

"Sir," said the aide, "do you recall the story of he who was known as 'Pretender George'?"

"Pretender George . . . Pretender George?" Wellington leaned back in his chair and stared up at the ceiling, as if to gather inspiration and enlightenment from the elaborate plasterwork there. "Was he not a low actor fellow who claimed to have royal blood in his veins? And did he not have a somewhat lurid end?"

"His claims—in private, at least—were more detailed and specific than that, sir," said Strickland. "As to his end . . . yes, I would say that it was as lurid as any cheap tragedian could have devised."

"Tell me all," said Wellington, "from the beginning. I'll not interrupt you."

Nor did he . . . much.

"Pretender George," began Strickland, "made some small clatter in the summer of 1805, when he was taken up by the cheap broadsheets regarding his claim to royal descent. George Whalley, to give him his baptismal name, was the leading actor of a group of traveling players who, after the manner of their kind, fell upon evil times in London when their manager absconded with the purse—and the leading lady. The company was at that time engaged in presenting *Hamlet* and *King Lear* upon alternate evenings, with matinees on Wednesdays and Saturdays, at the Mercury Theater in Stratford-atte-Bow, with not a penny to bless themselves, with a theater proprietor demanding a settlement for beer and amenities provided against future profits by the end of the week, and with not a single advance booking, nor any real prospect of a break in the inclemently hot weather, which might have induced a few of the inhabitants of Stratford-atte-Bow to venture inside the airless confines of the Mercury Theater.

"It was at this critical juncture that Whalley made contact with various local, small newspapers of the sensation-seeking and ephemeral kind, offering each and every one what he described as the full account of his life as a true member of the Royal House of Hanover, and by descent through the House of Stuart to William the Conqueror. As I have said, sir, it was an oppressively hot summer, the summer of that year, and the sale of newsprint, like all else, having suffered in consequence of the people's disinclination to do anything but lie in the shade, the gentlemen of the Fourth Estate rallied to Whalley's offer with more enthusiasm than they otherwise might have.

"The account that George Whalley gave of his parentage was instantly dismissed by all the journalists concerned, as so verging on the treasonable, not to say the high treasonable, as to expose its publishers to the grave dangers there inherent. Nevertheless, the general tenor of Whalley's account was so convincing, and the appearance, manner, and demeanor of the claimant so impressive [George Whalley was unquestionably one of those actors who rendered a better performance on, rather than off, the boards] that most of them printed a watered-down version of his story, suggesting, merely, that the leading actor of the traveling company presently playing at the Mercury Theater, the young and personable Thespian who bore such a staggering likeness to what one remembered of the then Prince of Wales when he was young, was indeed connected with the royal family—like so many others in this land—by ties of bastardy."

"And was it bastardy?" Wellington made his first interruption.

"That, sir, would depend upon the law, both as it stood then, as it stands now, and how it might conceivably stand sometime in the near future," replied Strickland.

"You possess better evidence than was published in 1805?" asked the duke.

"Sir, if I might possibly continue my account in chronological sequence?" said Strickland stiffly.

"Please do, please do," replied Wellington. "I will interrupt no more."

"I thank Your Grace," said Strickland. "Now, contingent upon the publication of those sensational accounts of a supposed royal bastard playing the leading roles in both *Hamlet* and *King Lear* [and you may wonder at the pretensions of a Thespian for attempting two such disparate roles on successive nights, not to mention the matinees on Wednesdays and Saturdays], the people of Stratford-atte-Bow, and others in great numbers from wider afield, flocked to attend the performances. Not only did the traveling company survive the critical week, but they played throughout the summer of that year to packed houses, mainly, one may suppose, because the newspapers continued to flirt lightly with high treason by coyly hinting at new and sensational revelations shortly to be published about he who, by late October of that year, rejoiced in the nickname of 'Pretender George, the Man Who Might Be Next on the Throne of England'!

"In short, Pretender George's brief hour of fame lasted the entire summer in that year of 1805—till an unprecedented event wiped the story of the high-flying actor from the journals of this land, together with other such ephemera that the gentry of the Fourth Estate had concocted."

The duke pointed a finger in the air.

"Trafalgar!" he exclaimed.

"Precisely, sir," said Strickland. 'News of the victory and of Lord Nelson's death put an end to Pretender George as a public figure. There were attempts on the part of the more sensational journals to revive him the following winter, but they came to naught."

"I met him, you know," mused the duke thoughtfully.

"George Whalley, sir!" exclaimed Strickland in surprise.

"Nelson, you .fool," growled the duke. "We met only once, and quite by chance. It was in a waiting room. Only for a very few minutes. A curiously inconclusive encounter. Please, continue."

"As I have said, sir," resumed Strickland, "the

journals had printed only a watered-down version of Whalley's alleged life story, eschewing what in newspaper circles is known as 'the hard stuff.' However, one of the gentry of the Fourth Estate, acting in the role of common informer, gave a full account of Whalley's allegations to my predecessor."

"The devil, he did!" said the duke.

"My predecessor took no action upon what was, in effect, a treasonable claim to royal parentage," said Strickland. "But the document in question remained in the records. And it is here." He took from his pocket a sheaf of papers.

"Give me the gist of it," said Wellington.

"Briefly, sir, Whalley claimed that his mother, a Miss Lucinda Chambers, an actress, of Bury St. Edmunds, in the county of Suffok, went through a form of marriage with a gentleman in the year 1782." He paused, as if for effect. "And that gentleman was our present monarch, then George, Prince of Wales."

"Good God!" cried the duke. "You mean, before he got himself illegally wed to Mrs. Fitzherbert?"

"Three years prior to that unfortunate match, sir," confirmed Stickland. "The prince would have been twenty-one at that time. Miss Lucinda Chambers was thirty. She bore a son the following year."

"George!"

"Precisely, sir."

"But, why the surname Whalley?"

"Whalley, as I understand it, sir, was Miss Chamber's mother's maiden name."

"Is this . . . this Chambers woman still alive?"

"She died in childbirth, sir, not, I hasten to add, in bearing George. There was another fruit of the match—a stillborn."

"Thank God for that," said the duke feelingly. "We already stand neck-high in royal bastards."

"In George's case, sir, the bastardy might, as we

have already speculated, became questionable," said Strickland quietly.

The cold eyes of the victor of Waterloo stared at Strickland down the long length of the imperious nose.

"Are you about to tell me, Major Strickland, that you are in possession of a valid marriage certificate relating to the joining of Lucinda Chambers, actress, with the man who is dying up there at Windsor?"

"Such a certificate is—or was—in existence, sir," said Strickland. "I have here the informer's testimony of having witnessed it in George Whalley's possession, together with Whalley's own marriage lines and other documentary evidence."

"Continue," said the duke in a tone of resignation.

"It was in 1816," said Strickland, "and the personable young actor who, thanks to his brief notoriety, had enjoyed a brief season of success at the Mercury Theater, Stratford-atte-Bow, and was by then far gone with drink and gluttony, and penniless to boot, attempted to sell these documents to the informer's journal. The offer was turned down. But, as I have said, the facts were given to my predecessor."

"Yes, yes, go on."

"In 1814, George Whalley married a young woman by the name of Alice Wright, a doctor's daughter from Islington. She died a year later of the consumption—but not before she had produced a daughter."

Again the pointing finger.

"Elizabeth!"

"Precisely, sir."

"Good God! Why did I ever leave the army?"

Wellington rose to his feet, walked over to the window, and looked out over the wide, rutted carriage road.

"This child—do we know what became of her, Strickland?"

"Just prior to his death, Whalley placed the child

in an orphanage, sir," replied his aide. "It is possible that my predecessor would have apprehended Whalley and questioned him further on the matter—discovered the whereabouts of the child—but Whalley died before this could be done."

"Killed on a stage, was he not, during a theatrical performance?"

"While playing the role of Polonius in *Hamlet*," said his aide. "It was at that juncture where Hamlet, becoming aware that someone is hidden behind the arras, makes a pass with his sword and kills the eavesdropping Lord Chamberlain—that is to say, Polonius."

"I am familiar with the work, Strickland," said the duke dryly.

"Quite so, Your Grace. It appears that Whalley was given a chalked mark, on the floor behind the arras, on which it was safe to stand, permitting Hamlet to make a thoroughgoing, realistic thrust. But he was too drunk to see the mark. They say that before he died he was giving one of the best performances of his career. By irony, it was at the Mercury, Stratford-atte-Bow, that the tragedy occurred."

"Leaving us—leaving England—with a child who, given certain circumstances, might be thought to have a better—a far better—claim to succession than the Duke of Monmouth ever had," said the duke. Then he added grimly, "And look what *his* attempt at seizing the throne brought the country to."

"Insurrection. Nigh on civil war, and a bloody battle at Sedgemoor," said Strickland.

"Or Lady Jane Grey," said Wellington. "A better claim than that unfortunate young woman had, some might think."

There was a brief silence, and both men exchanged glances.

Strickland said, "Lady Jane Grey was only a cat's-paw, but that did not save her from being beheaded on Tower Green. She was seventeen at the time of her execution. The child we are discussing—if she lives—must be around the same age."

"Indeed, she must," said the duke.

"If my speculations about a conspiracy are correct, if an attempt is made to secure the succession for this girl Elizabeth, and assuming that the attempt failed —as fail it surely would—what would be her fate?"

The duke readdressed his gaze out the window.

"The law would likely as not follow the precedents established in the cases of Monmouth and Lady Jane," he replied. "At least, women are not hanged, drawn, and quartered, since that is deemed to be an unedifying spectacle for the common people to witness."

"She would be executed for high treason?"

"As likely as not, yes."

"I will pursue my inquiries with renewed haste and vigor, sir," said Strickland quietly.

Still looking out the window, Wellington said, "They are not popular in the country, the House of Hanover. Descendant of Prinny or no, this child would be regarded, by the common people, as being the bright promise of a new dynasty. We could have another civil war staring us right in the face." He spun around, eyes imperious. "Yes, see to it, Strickland. Find that girl. Find who's supporting her, if anyone is indeed supporting her. Nip it in the bud—now, before the king dies."

"Yes, Your Grace."

"As for that bill before the Commons, the bill to abolish the Royal Marriage Act, I'll have that quashed first thing tomorrow morning. It will never even be debated. And that fellow who's sponsoring it—what's his name?"

"Hardcourt, sir—the member from Stoke-by-Zouch."

"Take him into custody—on any pretext you choose. I will accept full responsibility. Hold him till after the king's death, and for as long after that as I deem suitable."

"I will attend to it at once, sir."

Major Strickland, in the event, did not have the opportunity to leave before a messenger riding posthaste from Windsor brought news that George IV had died, and with him a whole era.

Quintin was ministering to Madeleine's needs; she face down upon the sofa, he bending over her, his skillful fingers probing the deep muscles of her bare back and her buttocks.

She gave a sigh of pleasure, then turned over and presented the front of her superb body to his eyes and hands.

"So it is to be tonight," she murmured. "The last act of the charade."

"The final ceremony that will bind those twelve men to us forever," said Quintin. "I will presently go out and secure some pretty little slut to spill her blood for the cause."

"You must find someone particularly toothsome for the final event," she said.

He wrinkled his nose in distaste. "The creatures are invariably unwashed and lousy," he said. "Before they go to the altar, I have had to persuade them to bathe and submit to having their fingernails and toenails cut."

"Poor Quintin," she mocked gently. "The things you have endured for the sake of the cause. Will the king die tonight, do you think?"

"He cannot possibly survive till dawn," said Quintin. "There are things that should have been done to him this morning—extreme palliatives which, if repeated at intervals, would have protracted his agonies for a few more hours—that have not been done."

"And our friend the physician, who should have carried out those palliatives?"

"By now he should be on the overnight packet that leaves Tilbury for the Hook of Holland, where his small act of professional neglect will be rewarded with a sum of money that will keep him in considerable style for the rest of his life. And how is our dear Elizabeth?"

"I have had to drug her heavily, but she is docile. Quintin, I am worried about . . . you know . . . "

"That he will get at her again? It is nearly the full moon, certainly, and he becomes particularly dangerous and lustful at such a time. But I have locked him in his room, and there he will remain till the time comes for him to perform the virgin sacrifice."

"He was locked in his room the last time," said Madeleine, "but he got out and ravished her, all but ruining the entire conspiracy. He could have killed her. Thank God it occurred to me to arrange for her to be released to her mother. And how thoughtful of dear Lady Landless to take her daughter to France and keep her safe from him till the time came for us to retrieve her." She gave a brittle, heartless laugh.

Quintin frowned. He drew his fingertips firmly down the woman's torso; breasts, belly, thighs. "It was a damnable thing to happen," he said. "We had her eating out of our hands till he raped her."

"But the position can be retrieved," said Madeliene "Using your methods, we can again suborn her mind to our will."

"It will take time," said Quintin. "Much ground has been lost. The principal barrier to the breaking of her will—the thing she clung to through all the privations to which she was subjected, and the tender ministrations that followed, and by that I mean the devotion that she bore for her adoptive mother—was only shattered by our denouncing her mother to her as a whore and a hypocrite. She has to a very great extent forgiven the woman. That will have to be reversed before we can begin to get anywhere with her again."

"Meanwhile, we rely upon drugs to keep her docile."

"Drugs . . . and dear Cornelia."

"She appears to have cooled somewhat to dear Cornelia," said Madeleine.

"Then why do you not feed her with the extract of the Spanish fly that we discovered to have such a beneficial effect upon dear Cornelia?" said Quintin suavely.

Purity knew that in all London there was only one man to whom she could turn, and that man was Jack Moonlight.

He, and he alone, would respond to her plea and help her to rescue Chastity from D'Eath and Madeleine. The sincere love he bore for her, proved in many nights and days of idyllic passion upon the islet in "The Devil's Hundred," would ensure his unquestioning support. There might—indeed, there almost certainly was—a danger in the enterprise. It would not deter the physician-turned-thief.

Only she did not know her way through to the islet. Though she had traversed the secret path with Jack, the tortuous, unmarked route through the treacherous swampland was of the very complexity that provided the highwayman's hiding place with its security, and she could recall none of it. To her knowledge, only three persons knew the route: Jack himself, Barney Bates, and Barney's brother, Wilfred.

One solution alone presented itself: she must seek

Jack, or the Bates brothers, in the St. Giles "Holy Land," at the Hare and Hounds tavern. The prospect of again entering that foul alehouse where she had been flogged on the bare buttocks and nearly raped for the delectation of the ragged clientele was daunting to the extreme, but she was not daunted now.

From the locked drawer of the library at Half Moon Street, she took the pistol with which Mark had provided her, then loaded it as he had instructed her: first a capful of powder, then a wad, then one of the lead balls, then another wad, and a pinch of powder in the frizzen. One shot—to kill any man who made an attempt upon her.

She dressed sensibly against the night and what it might bring: a riding skirt, a frogged tunic. Eschewing a bonnet, she bound her silver-gold hair in a long plait around her head, afterward concealing its luster beneath a Cashmere shawl.

She looked at her reflection in a mirror. A scar ran down her left cheek; this was where she had struck herself against the wainscotting during her struggle with the beast in the goat mask. The hideous bruising that had ensued as a result of his blows had all but faded away. Her right leg, severely sprained during his insane frenzy to mount and violate her, still hurt intolerably. There was a stout walking stick in the hall stand. She took it with her, both to aid locomotion and as an additional weapon.

Except for the butler and two footmen, all the servants had left the establishment. No one saw her let herself out and walk swiftly away into the night. Half an hour later, she was entering the dark alley that led into the heart of the rookery, and she did not encounter a soul till she came to the sign of the Hare and Hounds, opened the door, and gazed around her with trepidation.

All eyes were immediately directed to her—all, that is, save his. . . .

He was seated in the place by the cock-put where she had first seen him. Caped coat hung around his shoulders, hat tipped jauntily over one eye, hands in pockets, his booted feet propped up on the low table that formed the cock-pit. He appeared to be either asleep or drunk.

They recognized her at once, the clientele. No woman of such quality as she had been laid bare and flogged in the Hare and Hounds before or since; she was already a legend, to be savored and mulled over with licentious attention to detail. And now she had returned. Was it too much to hope, thought many, that Sam the landlord would put the belt to her again?

There was no cock-fighting taking place this night. Purity walked through a sea of speculative silence to the figure seated before the table. She had scarcely reached him, was stretching out a hand to touch him on the shoulder, when some ingrained sense of proximity made his eyelids snap open, and she saw, from the glorious light that suddenly suffused his eyes, that her coming had brought an unfathomable joy into his life.

He rose, embraced her without a word, held her close to him, stroked her head—and all with the clientele of the tavern looking on and wondering.

And then he said, "What has happened, my Purity? Only ill tidings would bring you to this hole of evil. And your face . . . my God, who has done this to you?" He traced a finger, delicately, along the line of the scar.

"They . . . they have taken Chastity again," she said.

She told him all. When she had finished, Jack sent one of the serving men to fetch Barney Bates from his lodgings. The little Cockney arrived soon after and flashed a gap-toothed grin at Purity.

"Barney, get horses for yourself and the lady," said Jack, pressing guiness into the lad's hand. "The best you can hire. We've a long ride ahead of us tonight, and we will leave immediately upon you return."

"Right you are, gov'nor," said Barney. "Where are we a-ridin', if it ain't a rude question?"

"Mill Hill."

"Mill Hill—ah!" The boot-button eyes slid swiftly to Purity.

"Off with you, then, Barney," said Jack.

"One thing, gov'nor . . . "

"Out with it, lad. No shilly-shally."

"There's rum goin's-on in the rookery this night?" The youth took off his tall hat, scratched his ginger stubble, and also contrived to cast a swift look around the taproom. He resumed speaking in an undertone. "The private army what's been formed—the rough-and-tumble bully-boys I spoke o' once—they're under orders to march."

"We are not concern with them this night, Barney," said Jack. "Bully-boys or no, we're off to Mill Hill on an errand of rescue. So, mind you, bring your pistol."

"Right you are, guv'nor," said the diminutive Cockney. And he was gone in a trice.

The highwayman's pleasantly ugly countenance broke into a heartwarming smile as his gaze fell upon Purity once more.

"Well, my dearest Purity," he said, "there's time for us to drink a bumper measure of brandy in celebration of our reunion before we depart. Ho, there, wench! Two large measures of brandy. None of your swipes. The best French brandy that was ever smuggled ashore at dead o' night under the very noses of the excise men!"

They rode under a nearly full moon through a drizzling, fine rain that quickly turned the highway to a fine mud that soon had their mounts plastered to the shoulders, and themselves splattered from head to foot with muddy droplets. It was hot, an airless sort of night, and the mounts were giving off fine plumes of steam from their sweating hides.

Jack had called for a brisk canter, then slowed down every so often to a short walk, and dismounted, the riders leading, cavalier fashion. During the walks, they talked. . . .

"What news of your husband?"

"None."

"Where is he?"

"Out of England. No one knows where—or won't tell me."

"And if you knew where he was?"

"Earlier this evening, I answered that question of the duke. Do I have to give *you* the answer?"

"You do not. You would walk through fire to get to his side, for you love him still—God help me! Mount up, you both! On to Mill Hill on this next gallop!"

He was off. So wild and breakneck was his pace that they had difficulty keeping up with him.

Upon arrival at the lowering, dark vales and heights of Mill Hill, each promontory topped by a windmill and ever mill-sail stilled in the airless night, Barney assumed guidance of the party, for he alone knew the way to Jermyn Abbey.

Following him in line, and progressing by cart tracks through a sleeping hamlet, past a silent blacksmith's forge, past a steepled church with an eternally sleeping graveyard, with the fine rain still sluicing down, they finally came to a high stone wall that stretched to left and right as far as could be seen.

" 'Tis the outer wall o' the abbey grounds," said Barney, dismounting. "The gatehouse be guarded an' the gates shut, day an' night. When I did meet my little sweetheart for to pry a bit o' news from 'er, not to mention a bit o' the handy-dandy, she did earnestly recommend me to climb the wall at this spot, for, as she did say, it gives a good approach to the abbey buildin's, with plenty o' cover, from rhododendrons, box hedges, the wall o' the kitchen garden, an' so forth." He grinned at both of them. "We always did meet behind the stew ponds for this an' that."

"I am greatly obliged for the information," snapped Jack Moonlight, slipping out of the saddle. "Sometime, when we are not engaged upon such pressing business, you must provide me with further and better details relating to what must surely have been a romance to rival that of Antony and Cleopatra, Dante and Beatrice, Heloïse and Abélard, Tristan and . . . damnation, I have dropped my pistols, both of them, in this confounded wet bracken! What hope for the priming to have remained dry?"

"You should stay calm, gov'nor," said Barney without rancor. "You really should. It ain't like you, it really ain't, to get so heated at such times."

"Shut your damned mouth!" snapped Moonlight. "Help the lady down from the saddle. "Thank God, yes, here are the pistols. But there's no way of telling, in all this wetness and darkness, if they are going to serve me."

Purity was handed to the ground by the little Cockney. The three horses were tethered to a nearby tree.

Jack Moonlight pointed to the wall. "Over with you first, Barney," he ordered. "I will assist the lady over and follow after."

The Cockney youth scrambled up and over like a

spider. Jack turned to Purity and put his hands at her waist, preparatory to picking her up. Their eyes met.

"I'm sorry, my dear," she said. "I wasn't able to lie to you. Does it show very badly?"

"That you still love that husband of yours? Yes, it does. You once told me that you were no longer a whole woman, that you have given your love away and that nothing remained. I think you were right about how you were then. But you have changed. I saw it in your eyes tonight and hoped that it might be because of me. But it is not."

"Oh, Jack!" She touched his cheek.

"One kiss, lass," he said lightly, "one kiss to last forever, for I have immortal longings in me this night."

Their lips met in a kiss that was at once chaste and passionate.

He said, "You are sure you won't stay here and leave it to Barney and me? It will be dangerous."

"You know I have to come with you."

"Of course."

He lifted her up, and her hands, scrabbling at the top of the wall, secured a hold and enabled her to draw herself to a kneeling position on the rough stonework. She saw Barney in the shadows below her, and as she lowered herself down, the lad made a foot stirrup with his hands. Moments later, Jack Moonlight joined them.

"Lead the way, Barney," whispered the highwayman. "We'll make a quick entry, find the girl, free her, then shoot our way out if need be. Speed and surprise —that's the ticket. Let's go!"

They proceeded through wet, knee-high grass, under dripping trees, and out onto a driveway that curved up a steep incline at the far side of a large ornamental lake. Set upon the crest of a low hill beyond the silvery water was the dark, ragged shape of a great medieval house, with tall and twisted chimneys in the Elizabethan manner, and a myriad of diamond-paned windows that reflected moonlight in a million pinpoints of light. Set close to one end of the mansion was a steepled chapel. This was Jermyn Abbey, abode of the mysterious Captain Guy D'Eath.

With Barney leading, they skirted the lake, avoiding an obvious crossing provided by a many-arched bridge, till they came to a thicket of laurel bushes that appeared to give cover as far as the rear of the house and the kitchen quarters.

Purity followed Jack, her eyes fixed upon his broad back, her hand slippery with sweat on the butt of the pistol she carried, her heart thudding so fiercely that she could hear it.

Suddenly, there was a noise ahead, the sound of something plunging through a hedge.

"We've been rumbled, guv'nor! Run for it!" It was Barney's urgent shout.

In the confusion that followed, Purity was hideously aware that dark forms were looming up all around her. She was close to Jack Moonlight when he raised his arm, pointed his pistol, then gave a curse when the hammer fell with no effect.

"Fall down flat, Purity!" he shouted. "And you, Barney! Don't stand looking, man! He's going to fire!"

There came the deafening discharge of a pistol, accompanied by a blossoming of orange flame. Jack Moonlight, who had been in the act of shoving Barney to the ground, clutched at his breast, gave a choked cry, and sank to his knees.

"They've got the guv'nor! The bastards have got the guv'nor!"

Purity saw the man who had fired: a dark shape topped by a tall hat, standing beyond a line of laurels. She cocked her pistol, took wild aim, and pulled the trigger. The tiny weapon discharged with a deafening crack. The figure slipped from view. Suddenly everything was very quiet.

Barney was on his knees beside the stricken highwayman, pillowing Jack's head in his arms, sobbing heartbrokenly.

"Guv'nor, guv'nor," he wailed. "You shouldn't 'ave done it. You shouldn't 'ave taken the bullet for me!"

As Purity knelt also, the highwayman opened his eyes.

"You are a sentimental fool, Barney, lad," he said. "I've warned you time and again to leave me be and go find honest work. . . . Is that you, Purity?" His voice was very weak.

"Yes, Jack," she whispered, tears blinding her eyes.

"Sorry I . . . failed you, my dear," he said.

"Jack, you've done everything a friend could do," she assured him.

"Get you gone, both of you," he said. "Split up. Make your separate ways to the horses. Those fellows are lying low, but they'll be back as soon as they've gotten over their scare about being shot at. . . . Purity, are you still there?"

"Yes, Jack, yes! How could I leave you?" She took his hand.

He smiled, then coughed. A thin trickle of blood issued from the corner of his mouth.

"That gypsy woman . . . she told me I'd never hang," he whispered.

His hand tightened for an instant in hers, then went limp. His head lolled sideways.

"He's gorn!" cried Barney Bates.

A shout from beyond the nearby thicket roused Purity to the import of the highwayman's dying instructions. Jack had given his life for her cause; she could not let the little Cockney lad perish also.

"Run, Barney, run!" she ordered him, giving him a shove. "That way!"

"I . . . I can't leave the guv-nor!" he said, anguished.

"He needs you no longer, and no one can harm the dead," replied Purity harshly. "Get you gone! Run!"

Barney's diminutive figure scrambled away into the darkness. Purity waited a moment, listening. An owl hooted in the distance. No other sound. Stooping, she planted a kiss on the head highwayman's brow.

"Good-bye, Jack," she whispered. And she rose to go.

Then they were surrounding her: dark figures leaping out from all sides; calling out in triumph to each other; expressing astonishment when they discovered that their captive so easily overpowered—was only a weak woman. And, when they had brought a torch more closely to examine their catch, they rejoiced to find her a woman of most delectable and rare beauty.

They took her to the mansion, mauling and pawing at her all the way, exchanging brutal obscenities one with the other. Then they bundled her into the presence of Madeleine.

Madeleine was seated in a vast, glass-walled fernery, with exotic fronds reaching high to the ceiling, and a water fountain was splashing into a medieval basin in the middle of the stone-flagged floor. She was dressed all in black, her hair drawn back into a severe chignon, her single eye fixed unwaveringly upon the newcomers.

"Purity! So you were the cause of the shooting!"

"There were three of 'em, ma'am," said one of Purity's captors, an unshaven lout from one of the rookeries, from his looks. "One of 'em's now graveyard meat. The other took to 'is 'eels, but the lads'll catch 'im. Then there's this little charmer." He grinned at his prisoner. Her unbound hair and the particular state of her clothing bore testimony to the sort of licentious manhandling she had received.

393

"Is my daughter here?" demanded Purity. "Have you got Chastity in this very house?"

"That I have, Purity," responded Madeleine. "And you may not see her. Next question."

"Why . . . *why?*" pleaded Purity.

"All in good time," purred Madeleine. "All will be explained to you." She transferred her gaze to someone who had entered the fernery. "Ah, Quintin, dear. Have you obtained a girl to play the leading part in tonight's final charade?"

"No, I have not, my dear," replied Quintin. "Indeed, I am just about to depart upon that errand." He paused as he drew abreast of the woman held in the grasp of the grinning ruffians. His dark eyes flickered over her. "Lady Landless," he murmured.

"And very providentially arrived, do you not think, Quintin?" said Madeleine. "You are saved the errand, and here is a lady who will not need to be bathed and have her fingernails and toenails trimmed for the ceremony.

"What more perfect subject to play the leading part? And on this night of all nights!"

Chapter Twelve

They came, as always, separately, each in his own conveyance, the younger and more agile on horseback. As ever, they were received by liveried lackeys who conveyed them to the candlelit chapel, where drinks of all kinds were set out for them.

Familiar, after so many meetings, with the proceedings of the society, the twelve greeted each other affably and broke up into three distinct bodies: three groups of members drinking and conversing together.

One group of four centered on the member of Parliament from Stoke-by-Zouch. They plied him with questions.

" 'Tis certain, then, Hardcourt, that he's gone?"

"A general announcement has not been made," said Hardcourt. "But, yes, I had the news from our informant at Windsor. The Bishop of Chichester was with him at the end. Lady Conyngham has already decamped with every piece of portable gewgaw she could lay her hands on. I shall have the bill rushed through the Commons tomorrow. You and I, gentlemen, will be Cabinet Ministers and Privy Councillors by the end of next week."

"And you Prime Minister, eh, Hardcourt?"

Hardcourt looked as modest and self-deprecating as he could. Then he cocked an eye toward the other groups, the nearest of which was the Marquess of Strachan with a couple of his cronies.

The glance was not lost upon Hardcourt's companions.

"What are we going to do about the others, eh, Hardcourt?" asked one. "What of Charlie Strachan and his wild talk about Mrs. Fitzherbert's brat?"

"Strachan will do as he is told—or hang," replied Hardcourt. "And his friends, likewise."

"And the others—Browninge, Davenport, and the rest?"

Hardcourt smirked. "They are footing the bill for this enterprise, for which each will be rewarded according to his needs. It is really quite simple, gentlemen."

"Devilishly clever. Devised by . . . *him,* of course."

"Who else?"

"We still haven't received our orders for tomorrow."

"I understand we are to do so tonight," said Hardcourt. "Ah, here comes that fellow Quintin. I may say that I have never taken to befriend Quintin."

"Slimy individual."

The epicine Quintin had entered the chapel, clad in black, as usual, with a deferential smile upon his countenance as he bowed to the assemblage.

"My lords, gentlemen, once more I bid you welcome on behalf of my master. Please sign the visitors' book in the customary manner and then robe yourselves. As some of you will be aware, tonight is to be the climax of our proceedings. Immediately following the sacrifice, a proclamation will be announced."

"Proclamation? What the hell do you mean—proclamation?" The brandy-colored, belligerent voice of Charlie Strachan spoke out.

"That I am not at liberty to divulge, my lord marquess," responded Quintin smoothly. "But the proclamation, when it is read to you, will be entirely self-explanatory."

"Humph!"

The lackeys entered, bearing the ceremonial robes of the society, which the members, having appended their signatures to the leather-bound tome upon the lectern, proceeded to put on, afterward taking their respective places in the pews. When this was done, Quintin bowed low to them and departed.

There was silence in the ancient chapel, broken only by the wheezing breath of the Marquess of Strachan.

Twelve waiting men, each with his own separate thoughts, yet every mind was directed to the experience that lay immediately ahead: the supreme erotic indulgence that had, by then, eaten into all their souls and destroyed them for all else but its pursuance.

It was useless to tell themselves—as some of them did—that it was madness or self-destruction to continue attending the unholy monthly rites at the dark chapel; as the fateful eve drew nearer, each passing month, the blood ran hotter, the loins ached more urgently, and the ancient bloodlust that had been overlaid by a thousand years of civilization spilled over.

There stood young Gervase Browninge, as handsome as a Greek god, with all that wealth and beauty could have provided—everything except what had by now become a craving. Well might his tender conscience haunt his dreams, making him cry out in his sleep. He had witnessed ritual butchery upon his own raped victim. And he craved more.

Others among them had no qualms at all; no dream-haunted nights.

The pipe organ took up the *dies irae*. And the congregation shifted with impatience, all heads turning to look down the aisle to the direction from which the sacrificial victim would be brought in.

They came, the two nude men, padding barefoot on the flagstones, holding aloft in their upraised hands the body of a lightly draped woman whose wealth of silver-gold hair trailed like a stream of light around the men's heavily muscled shoulders.

"By heaven!" gasped the Marquess of Strachan hoarsely. "Do you see who it is?"

"Zounds!" Angus, Lord Houghton, one-armed now, after his duel with Mark Landless, recognized her at once, and he was consumed with anticipation of supreme lust.

Young Gervase Browninge all but cried out. He had an impulse to denounce the proceedings as monstrous. But he held his peace and felt his passions stir.

She was known to all of them, by fame and by notoriety. And half of that company had already possessed her according to their differing tastes.

They laid her upon the altar. Unlike the other women who had been placed there, her wrists had been bound behind her back, likewise her ankles.

For, unlike the others whose life's blood had been shed upon the cold marble, Purity Landless had been told of her true fate.

She lay very still when the bearers left her, willing herself to remain staring up at the hammer-beamed ceiling far above in the shadows beyond the wavering candlelight. Her mind was racing, fighting to encompass the truth or falsehood of what she had heard.

Chastity was safe and well, and she would remain so—that much Madeleine had assured her. Proceeding from that, the woman had, quite suprisingly, kept her promise to explain the reason for Chastity's abductions. Indeed, she had explained . . . everything.

It was madness, surely. . . .

Madeleine had revealed the truth of Chastity's birth and origins, had shown her documents and letters, incontrovertible evidence to support her wild assertion that Chastity was . . . who she was.

That in itself, whether true or false, would have been fantasy enough. But what had followed—the woman's carefully detailed exposition about what advantage she and her associated intended to take of Chastity's secret—that was madness.

She had pleaded with Madeleine; begged upon her knees to be allowed to take the girl away; offered to keep silence before the world, never to set foot in England again. The woman had laughed at her.

She was never to see Chastity again. Madeleine had brutally explained the reason why they had made her into a whore: it had been to turn Chastity against her. And they were even now in the process of seducing the girl's mind again, the more easily to bend her to their insane plan. The sight of "Mama Purity," whom Chastity had learned to forgive, might put the girl's mind beyond reach of their evil intent, and set at naught their attempts to vilify her adoptive mother.

She was going to die. Now. This very night. Madeleine had told her that, quite unconcernedly, relishing the telling of it. She had ordered her brutish minions to strip their captive and dress her in a shameless scrap of transparent silk. Then the men themselves had stripped naked, before the lusting eye of their mistress. It was they, nude and hideously masked, who had ceremoniously borne her on high into the place where she now was. They had carried her past the regarding, suddenly astounded gaze of robed men, some of whom she had fleetingly recognized as members of the hateful society, and as partners with her in acts that had shamed her to the very soul. She had seen young Gervase Browninge; the frenzied utterance he had made in his sleep, that afternoon aboard his yacht, now took on the hard edge of comprehension. . . .

It was cold. She shivered and saw her lightly draped breasts quiver. All she could see when she lowered her eyes was her own body and the shaft of one of the two tall candlesticks that flanked the altar. The men in the pews were lost in shadow beyond the loom of candlelight.

The organ music ceased. She heard a rustle, as when a congregation rises at the appearance of an officiating priest. Indeed, a line of impersonal faces, pale in the gloom, bobbed into her view.

A footfall beside her . . .

She screamed and writhed in her bonds . . . *as the beast with the goat mask loomed over her!*

She still screamed to shut out the sound of his voice as he declaimed the Black Mass. She was still screaming when, having filled the silver chalice with the hellish brew and having partaken of it himself, he passed it among his congregation, so that the last vestiges of reason and humanity were plucked from their minds and they became like ravening wolves.

She screamed till her strength would bear no more. Then she lay still, panting and helpless and waiting for her fate. There was more profane mumbo-jumbo from goat-head, followed by frenzied responses from his followers. And then, shrinking with apprehension, she was looking up into the glittering eyes behind the goat mask as, reaching out, he took the vestigial shift in which they had clad her and ripped it, in one swift movement, from neck to hem, rendering her nude.

There was a clamoring in her ears. They were crowding all around her, faces familiar and unfamiliar: Strachan's face; the handsome Gervase Browninge, the brute who had claimed her for his in Berkeley Square; all wild-eyed and baying like hounds at the chase, pawing at her breasts and her thighs.

And the last thing she remembered, before merciful Nature drew the veil of unconsciousness over her horror-stricken mind, was the sight of the beast in the goat's mask, who, having severed the bonds that secured her ankles, had mounted the altar and was straddling her with vile intent. . . .

She was back at the château, and it was springtime. There were cowbells tinkling down in the water meadows, and fields of lush grass, blue-green in the brilliant sunshine. She was alone. No one in sight.

She walked through the archway that led into the courtyard in front of the château facade, with the flight of deeply indented steps that led up to the great porch and its iron-bound doors. The hum of bees in the blossomed trees was curiously soothing.

He—the beloved—would be waiting for her in the great hall of the château. She quickened her step as the notion sprang, unbidden, to her mind. She ran lightly up the ancient steps, pushed open the creaking door, and stepped into the solemn splendor of the vast chamber, with its richly carved paneling, with the lines of gilded frames that enclosed the portraits of long-gone De Feyelles, and with the minstrel gallery, with its lofty pipe organ upon which the miraculous fingers of Herr Johann Sebastian Bach had once sketched out his incomparable variations. And she looked around for her beloved, calling for him by name.

"Mark . . . Mark . . . Mark . . ."

Someone answered her from above. Looking up, she saw Monsieur le Marquis De Feyelle, hanging by his neck from the great central chandelier, turning, turning. And the next time he turned to face her, she saw that his eyes were open and fixed upon her, red-rimmed and protruding, and that his purpled face and livid lips were alive and straining to produce sounds.

She screamed, frantic to shut out the message that might come from those dead lips. Still screaming, she emerged from unconsciousness and saw the last of her tormentors—it was young Gervase Browninge, his too-perfect countenance drained by the release of his passions, and suddenly sweet and vulnerable. He withdrew, and the oppressive weight having been taken away, she was aware only of the pain that the protracted violations had wrought upon her.

And now the twelve members of the congregation, having satiated themselves upon the peerless body of Purity Landless, had returned to their seats, tremulously to await the bloody climax of the ritual slaughter of the sacrificial victim. And, as always, the greater to whet the passions of the participants, it was not done without protracted ceremonial pomp. The goat-headed celebrant must intone the second half of the Black Mass in its entirety, and he standing before the defiled altar in his naked pride, with the similarly naked congregation screaming the unholy responses, and their eyes never leaving the beautiful creature laid out to receive the kiss of the sacrificial knife.

The final profanation having been declaimed, the last frenzied response made, the congregation craned forward, slack-lipped and wild-eyed, as the celebrant unsheathed the knife and turned to face the altar. He looked down at the shocked countenance of Purity Landless and gazed upon the lovely body laid open and uncovered to his thrust.

She closed her eyes—and knew a sudden peace. Before her, like the groundswell in a mighty ocean, there swept a majestic vision of love, and she saw all the past sweetnesses of her life: the friendships and the loyalties with which she had been enriched; the feel of her babe suckling at her breast; Chastity's trusting small hand in hers; and then, in a swirl of wonder and light, there appeared the smiling countenance of Mark saying that nothing had changed, that he loved her, and that there was nothing to repine, nothing to forgive.

There came a rushing in her ears. A moment of confusion, when the vision shattered and dispersed.

A shout echoed hollowly in the lofty edifice: *"Monster—see what you have done!"*

Purity's eyes opened. She was a witness, with all the rest, to the sight of Madeleine framed in a halo of light from the candelabrum held in the hand of her companion. Quintin stood at her elbow, his head bowed.

Madeleine's glory of bronze-colored hair was wild and unbound. Unbound, also, and sweeping low to the stone-flagged floor, was the hair of the girl who lay in her arms. She was white-faced, eyes staring, her head hanging slackly upon a broken neck.

"You have killed her, beast! You have raped and killed your own daughter—and she a child of your rape upon my own body!" The awful denunciation rose to the high rafters and died away in silence.

In silence, Madeleine laid the body of her daughter upon the altar steps and advanced toward the nude figure in the goat's-head mask that still stood, knife in hand, by Purity Landless's side. The glittering green eyes burned unwaveringly upon the woman with the bronze-colored hair as she came nearer, her arms extended.

"Why do you tarry?" Madeleine demanded. "You have taken the life of my child, why not mine? You have the means in your hand. Thrust now! Destroy my life as you once destroyed my beauty!"

For answer, the creature in the mask threw back

his head and laughed: deep-throated, insane laughter that was a defilement to the ear. He raised the knife, pointing its keen edge toward the advancing woman's proffered breast.

"Madeleine . . . *no!*"

The epicine Quintin, it was, who, hastening forward to draw Madeleine away from the sweeping knife thrust, took the point under his extended arm. He cried out in pain and reeled back into the arms of the woman.

"Quintin, Quintin—you fool!" she screamed. "Why couldn't you let him kill me and have it over with? Oh, my dear, are you greatly hurt?"

Goat-head made no move to stop her as she half-dragged, half-carried, the wounded Quintin down the altar steps and into the shadows. He remained where he was, bloodied knife in hand, head erect, eyes blazing from the twin cavities of the hideous mask.

There then came another disturbance: a hammering upon the outer door of the chapel, running footfalls, lights bobbing past the stained-glass windows. The congregation rose, suddenly shocked to sanity and sobriety, as the outer door burst open and a file of tall-hatted and becloaked men strode swiftly up the aisle.

"Let nobody move!" came the harsh command. "Remain where you are, or be shot where you stand!"

Purity had been staring at the bare back of the masked beast. She was still staring when he turned around and, taking a swift stride toward her, raised the knife aloft to strike her dead where she lay.

There was a thunderous discharge, followed by an instant stink of powder smoke. Goat-head let fall the knife, which clattered to the altar step, and stared down in seeming disbelief at a scarlet furrow that had appeared on his bare forearm.

Purity felt the weight of a warm cloak enveloping her nudity, and she looked up into the shrewd, quirky eyes

404

of the man she had been introduced to by Wellington at Apsley House.

"You are freed, Lady Landless, ma'am," murmured Major Strickland with a truly commendable imperturbability. "Pray, permit me to assist you to arise."

There must have been ten or a dozen newcomers: hard-faced individuals, all armed with pistols, carbines, or cudgels. They were shepherding the horrified members of the unholy society out of their crested pews, treating them with scant courtesy, even those who, like the Marquess of Strachan, had already recovered enough of their high-born arrogance as to be blustering their names and titles and demanding to be treated with the proper respect accorded to their rank. Strickland's men would have none of it. Charlie Strachan was roughly bidden to cover his nudity and stand over by yonder wall with his hands above his head like the rest.

Two men had pinioned goat-head by the arms. He had offered no resistance, but stood meekly in their grasp.

Strickland knelt by the body of the girl with the bronze-colored hair that lay on the altar step. He touched the head and noted how it lolled brokenly on the riven neck, like the head of a broken doll thrown by a child in a temper tantrum.

"Whose work is this?" he asked gruffly.

Purity pointed.

"Him?"

She nodded. "Yes."

"He is the ringleader of this . . . obscenity?"

"I . . . think so," said Purity.

Strickland eyed the man in the goat's-head mask for some moments before he reached out, and, taking hold of one of the great, sweeping horns, ripped the hideous covering aside and threw it to the floor. Two green glass eyes shattered to pieces at his feet.

Purity recoiled with a cry of horrified recognition, to which was also added a feeling of disbelief at what had been wrought upon the countenance before her, the unbelievable change from the coldly self-possessed personage who had once caused her such strange and disturbing promptings.

Strickland was callously dismissive.

"This fellow is no ringleader," he said. "Couldn't lead a parched horse to water. Why, he's as mad as a March hare!"

It was true. Gone were the assured, ice-blue stare, the full and sensuous-lipped smile that had stirred dark urges in the heart of Purity Landless. The man whom she had known as Guy D'Eath was now presented to full view as a raving maniac, with eyes that protruded from their sockets, and teeth bared in a rictus grin, with a trail of spittle coursing from a corner of the slack, idiot's mouth.

"No, ma'am," said Strickland. "We'll have to look elsewhere for the mind that has been directing this . . . Now, by all that's holy, what's this?"

She followed the direction of his astonished glance. "Chastity!"

Chastity came out of the dark alcove that lay behind the altar. She walked like a person who has risen, still sleeping, from her bed: the eyes open, but lusterless; the step unsteady, wavering with every slow pace.

"Good God!" gasped Strickland. "We've found . . . *it's she!*"

She was garbed in a sweeping gown of white samite interwoven with gold, as was worn by medieval queens. Over that was a robe of purple velvet trimmed and lined with ermine, with a train that swept grandly over the cold stone and seemed too heavy by far for the slender shoulders that bore it. In one slim hand she carried a queenly scepter, in the other a golden orb that winked diamonds and rubies. And on

406

her sable-dark tresses she wore a diamond-studded crown of crosses and *fleurs-de-lis*.

Pausing by one of the tall candlesticks that flanked the altar, she gazed around her irresolutely for a moment, seemingly unaware of the eyes that were directed toward her from all around. Then, like some small child who has with difficulty learned a lesson by rote, she piped up in a clear, pure voice: "My lords! I am Elizabeth, the Second of that name. By the Grace of God, Queen Regnant of England, Scotland, and Ireland, Defender of the Faith . . . "

"Chastity, my darling!" Purity's rounder, deeper voice joined in counterpoint with the other's, silencing it. "No! *No!*"

The somnambulistic eyes clouded with dismay. They flickered unsteadily toward the sound of the interruption. Lighting upon Purity, they sparked recognition.

"Mama . . . Mama Purity. Don't . . . don't be angry with me. That . . . that's what they told me to say. . . ."

Orb and scepter clattered to the floor, and the splendidly robed figure slowly followed, the billowing cloud of velvet and ermine enveloping her in her fall.

Purity was the first to reach her; but it was Strickland who, bringing his nostrils close to the partly open, coral-tinted lips, gave a scowl of distaste.

"Drugged to damned stupefaction!" he growled.

Oddly, in all that had passed, no one had commented on the disappearance of Madeleine and the stricken Quintin.

They had made their retreat, painfully, she supporting him with his arm around her shoulder, urging him on with anguished whispers, till they came to an alcove in the bridge that spanned the lake, and there he collapsed and could go no farther.

She had seen the arrival of Strickland and his men and made a guess as to their intent. Peering over the balustrade of the bridge, she could see their horses tethered among the dark trees by the chapel. The lighted windows of that building were waveringly reflected in the dark surface of the lake. The full moon had gone down.

"Madeleine, I am done for," he whispered.

"We are both done for, my dear," she replied. "And the game was so nearly won. Two barefoot children from the St. Giles rookery, who so nearly were queen-makers. And I dearly wanted to be a duchess. Does it hurt badly, dearest? Let me see."

He would not let her touch his wound, but kept a hand pressed hard against his side. With a lurch of the heart, she saw that a dark pool was already beginning to form in the stonework beneath him, crawling in the cracks, spreading wider by the instant.

"Don't leave me, Madeleine," he gasped. "Talk to me."

"I'll never leave you now," she replied. "We were so close to success, dear Quintin, were we not? Tomorrow morning the mob from the rookeries would have marched upon St. James's. She would have been proclaimed queen before all. Instead of that . . . oh, my darling Cornelia, how she must have suffered! Why did we need to use that monster, Quintin, why?"

"There was no one else who would suit our plan," said Quintin. "You know that as well as I. Most of the time he was the urbane gentleman of society. Only you and I were aware of what he was capable of doing when the moon was full. We needed him, my dear. Could *I* have slaughtered those wretched women!"

"We should never have used him!" cried Madeleine.

"We knew there were inherent perils . . . "

"Inherent perils! Ye gods! Can you imagine what

that fiend must have done with my darling Cornelia before he broke her neck? We should have foreseen it. He took every woman by rape and violence—even Purity Landless, whom he could have had at any time, merely by showing her a medallion. Even with her, lusting for her as he did, he had to wait till the moon was full so that he could take her in madness. How long, I wonder, had he lusted for my darling Cornelia? And she—his own child!"

"I think you loved him once," murmured Quintin.

"I would have walked naked through hell for him once," she replied. "My body and my soul were his for the taking. He took me—the way he took all the others. Even after that—even after he had destroyed my face—there were happy times, as when we traveled to Normandy together to look into Purity Landless's background and determine if she was, indeed, an aristocrat and a suitable adoptive mother for a future Queen Regnant."

"Madeleine," he whispered, "the pain . . . is more than I can bear. . . ."

"Oh, my dearest!" She laid her cheek upon his sweat-streaked brow. " 'Tis just like it was when we were children. At the end of the day, when all your bright schemes had come to naught, you had need of Madeleine, always Madeleine." As she whispered to him, her hand was stealing to the pocket in her voluminous black skirt and was drawing something out. "Just as, when everything was awry with me, you were able to minister to my needs and comfort me. In some ways, we have been so good for each other; in others, we have destroyed us both—utterly."

"Madeleine . . . the pain!"

"Peace, my dearest, my darling brother," she whispered. "It will soon be over. See, I will kiss you now. I will still be kissing you when you are at peace, and all pain is gone."

He gave no more than a harsh intake of breath when she drove forward her hand, thrusting a needle-pointed bodkin between his ribs, straight to the heart. And her lips remained on his till his breath—his last expiring breath—had joined with hers. Then she sat back on her heels, threw back her splendid head, and stared, dry-eyed, up at the stars.

She covered his face with his coat. This done, she took from his breast pocket a sheaf of papers, which, having given them a cursory glance, she proceeded to tear up, sheet by sheet, into very small pieces, finally throwing them into the dark waters below the bridge.

"Good-bye, Elizabeth," she sighed. "There goes your birthright."

Lifting her skirts, she stepped up onto the low balustrade and stood there for some little time, poised above the surface of the lake like some tutelary goddess of the deep. And then she let herself fall.

"You have done well, Strickland," said the duke. "Brandy?"

"I thank you, Your Grace," said his aide.

They toasted each other in silence.

The military clock on the mantelpiece struck the hour of noon. Wellington grunted with satisfaction.

"The earl marshal and his heralds will be assembled on the balcony of St. James's Palace," he said. "By the time we have finished our brandy, Strickland, they will have proclaimed the new king."

"To His Majesty, King William the Fourth, sir," said the aide. "And long may he reign."

"The king!" responded Wellington. "As to length, I would say that if poor Willie were to shuffle off this mortal coil in, say, ten years' time, ready for Princess Victoria's coming of age, he will not entirely have wasted his life."

They drank deeply.

"What of the prisoners, Strickland?" demanded Wellington. "They have all been arraigned, eh?"

"For murder, sir," said Strickland. "All have confessed, or have accused each other, of complicity in the brutal and senseless slaying of at least fifteen young woman. Only D'Eath was unfit to plead. He is mad, quite mad."

"Nevertheless, he will hang with the rest," said Wellington. "I always said that fellow was a blackguard, but it seems I didn't know the half of it."

"His . . . peculiar vices were vital to the conspiracy, sir," said Strickland. "With his aid, Quintin and his sister were able to bind to them with ties of blood the twelve men in all England who could either best assist them, or most effectively oppose them, or provide them with the monies to pay for the insurrection."

"And what happened to the insurrection?"

"I am informed, sir, that the mob was assembled in the rookery awaiting the order to march before dawn. The order was never sent. However, having received half of their promised payment, the ragged army dispersed to the alehouses, where I confide they are all now safely dead drunk. The suborned officers who were to have led this rabble have been arrested and placed in the Tower."

"They will also hang," said the duke. "The fellow Quintin is dead, you say?"

"And his sister also, sir," said Strickland. "My fellows found her body floating in the lake at dawn."

"A rum pair, Strickland," said the duke.

"Indeed, they were, sir, to have come within an inch of making the biggest constitutional upheaval we have had in a century and a half. And they were stopped only becuase I was on my way to arrest Hardcourt—and ran him to the ground at Jermyn Abbey."

"And what of the gel, hey, Strickland?" asked the

411

duke, stroking the side of his nose. "What of the Landless gel?"

"She is in my custody, sir, awaiting your instructions," replied Strickland. "Will it be high treason, or not?"

The victor of Waterloo took a large handkerchief from his coattail pocket and blew his nose loudly in reply.

Strickland said, "Lady Landless is waiting outside —has been there since early morning."

"I will see her at once, Strickland," said the other. "My God, I had rather face a charge of Napoleon Bonaparte's Old Guard than confront that unhappy lady, for I know what she will want of me."

"Shall I remain, Your Grace?"

Wellington shook his head. "I thank you, no, Strickland. Best for all concerned if I do what has to be done in some privacy—if only out of regard for the poor creature's feelings."

"There is no hope, sir?"

Wellington stared at him, affronted.

"Of allowing the gel to go free, you mean? Come, man, you know better than that. I have no jurisdiction in these matters. The law is the law, and it must take its course."

"Yes, Your Grace." Strickland bowed stiffly and withdrew.

Wellington was standing by the window, hands clasped behind his very straight back, when Purity entered. He turned and greeted her effusively, speaking loudly and at a fast pace. "Good day to you, ma'am. Pray, be seated. Would you care for some refreshment? A glass of Sherry, perhaps? Tea? Coffee? Well, I think we are in for a thunderstorm, don't you? Are you quite comfortable there, or would you prefer a chair with its back to the windows, so your eyes aren't strained with the light?"

"Sir, you know why I am here," said Purity quietly.

"Ah, I can hazard a guess, ma'am," admitted Wellington.

She was all in dark gray, with a high-necked coatee and a bonnet that was lightly veiled, so that only a hint of her perfect profile was visible to him. She had entered the room with something of the limp that he had observed on the previous occasion; but of the ordeal she had suffered the previous night, there was no evidence.

"My daughter is innocent of any crime, sir," said Purity.

"That will be for the courts to decide, ma'am," said Wellington. "That judgment, I am happy to say, does not lie with me."

He was standing. His richly appointed desk was between them. Purity rose to her feet and approached him. Leaning with her hands upon the desktop, she shouted into his face, "Spare me your cowardly evasions, my lord duke! Is it, or is it not, your opinion that my child was implicated with those creatures? Answer me straight!"

For a man quite unaccustomed to having the epithet of "coward" thrown into his face, Wellington received her outburst with a stoical calm. He merely raised his proud head a little higher and made his reply.

"I cannot give you your answer, ma'am, and for two reasons: first, I have not made up my mind as to your daughter's guilt or innocence; second, my opinion matters little one way or the other to the issue. But . . . " He paused.

"But?"

"The issue, when it is brought to court, will present, in my opinion, at least one very grave obstacle to the securing of a verdict of innocence. I refer to the matter of your daughter's brief return to your house on

413

Half Moon Street and her almost immediate departure, of her own free will, with two principals of the conspiracy. That, in my opinion, is a point, a damning point, which simply cannot be talked away."

Purity smote the desktop with her two small, bunched fists.

"But I have explained that to you already!" she cried. "Her mind was assaulted in some way, so that she was totally confused, so that she scarcely knew right from wrong. Oh . . . !" She broke off, pressing her knuckles to her mouth, hideously aware of the trap she had sprung for herself.

The duke spread his hands. "There you have it, ma'am," he said. "Out of your own mouth, you have condemned her. 'She scarcely knew right from wrong.' That, as I understand the present state of our law, is a perfect definition of the criminal mind. It is entirely possible that in some future and more . . . uh . . . enlightened age, a gentler interpretation might be placed upon such a definition. But it will not do here—now. We have our law, and we must live with it—or die by it!"

"If she is found guilty, sir, will she be condemned to die?" asked Purity quietly.

"It is . . . possible, ma'am," said the duke, avoiding her eye and addressing his gaze to the gold-and-onyx statuette of Patriotism that adorned one side of his desk.

"Likely, perhaps?"

"More than likely, ma'am." He met her gaze again, unflinchingly.

"And you will stand by and allow it to happen, my lord duke?" she blazed. "You, who were comrade-in-arms to my husband—my husband, who followed you through the hell of Spain and Portugal. Who stood with you at Waterloo!"

"Madam, do you not realize that my own obligation

to your husband torments me constantly in this matter?" he blazed, and with a fury equal to her own.

"Ah, I have drawn blood!" cried Purity with grim satisfaction. "The great, the imperturbable, Wellington is rocked on his heels. Will he not now unbend and utter the one word that can spare the life of a poor, deluded child who had the misfortune to be born of a prince's caprice and to fall the victim of scoundrels?"

The duke's aquiline, high-nosed countenance was darkly flushed. He waited the space of three deeply drawn breaths before replying, and when he did, it was with a simplicity, an unaffected dignity, that brought a stab of remorse to Purity's heart.

"Ma'am, Wellington concedes that he is in complete disarray," he said. "But, trounced though he be, he cannot surrender principle to sentiment. And that's an end to it." He bowed his fine head.

Desperation for Chastity's plight, remorse for her cruel assault upon a man who had shown her and hers nothing but kindness and favor—both emotions fought for supremacy in Purity's mind as her need dictated her will, and her will dictated her hand. . . .

"And if Wellington will not surrender to sentiment, will he then surrender to the gentle blandishments of . . . l'amour?" she said, reverting, in that moment of supreme testing time, to the language of her childhood.

Wellington glanced up. His eyes widened to see that Purity's slender fingers were slowly unbuttoning the high-necked gray coatee, under which she was wearing nothing but a flimsy shift that did nothing to hide the delicate structure of her superb bosom.

"Ma'am, I beg of you!" In three strides, he was around her side of the desk, reaching for her hand.

"Sir, I had not thought that you would be so eager," she said, with a vain attempt at coquetry that died on the instant, then gave way to tears.

"Dear lady, do yourself up, I beg you. My God, how you must have been tried, to resort to such desperate measures. Sit you down, I beg you. I will pour you a glass of brandy. There, there, don't carry on so. No harm has been done."

With his own large, somewhat clumsy hands, the victor of Waterloo himself rebuttoned the bodice for the distraught and weeping woman. He placed in her trembling fingers a tidy-sized glass of spirits and urged her to drink it up. By the time Purity had done so, and had somewhat composed herself, Wellington had made several swift traverses of the large room, hands clasped behind his back, deeply sunk in thought.

"Sir, I am so sorry for . . . " she began.

He silenced her with a gesture—a gentle gesture.

"I'll hear no repining, Purity," he declared. "Your man did stand with me at Torres Vedras, and again at Waterloo. For that, if for nothing else"—and he crossed over to her, took both her hands in his, and looked earnestly into her eyes—"if only for the inestimable honor that you have lately offered to bestow upon your obedient servant . . . "

"Sir, I . . . "

"No more! Here is what you will do. You will return to your house on Half Moon Street, and there you will pack such necessities as would be required for two ladies to make a long journey under somewhat straited circumstances—as, for instance, if they were fleeing the country a short head in front of their creditors. Do you follow me?"

"My lord!" She shook her head, bemused, suddenly alight with hope, halfway between laughter and tears.

"That's the ticket. You will manage very well—a soldier's wife—with such simple instructions. Mark well that you be ready by"—he consulted his pocket watch—"let us say ten-thirty, when it will be dark. A carriage will pull up to your door. Stand not upon ceremony, but run out and join those whom you will find awaiting you there. Now, I beg you to be gone, ma'am. You have much to do. For a lady to select an unlimited wardrobe for the purpose of traveling is a matter of minutes, merely; such a vestigial selection as you must take in this enterprise must be a day's work a-choosing."

She touched his hands, her eyes brimming.

"Sir, I shall never be able to thank you enough," she whispered. And, reaching up, she planted a kiss upon that austere cheek. "You have given me back all life, all happiness."

He watched her go out of the room. Then, crossing over to his favorite spot by the window, he looked out toward the distant towers of Westminster.

"If I were to tell anyone, they would never believe me," he mused aloud. "To have said 'no' to one of the finest lookin' woman who ever walked the earth! Unbelievable!"

At fifteen minutes past the hour of ten, Purity was ready and waiting. Dressed in a dark costume, bonnet, and shawl, with a slender wardrobe of suitable attire for herself and Chastity strapped inside a small valise, she stood by the window of her sitting room, heart thudding, dry-mouthed, waiting.

Supposing, she told herself, that the plan backfired? Supposing Wellington, reconsidering his position and the risk of professional obloquy that the unofficial release of Chastity might pour down upon his head, had changed his mind, after all? Somehow she did not think it possible of such a man. But other factors might intervene. Supposing, during the day, the matter had been taken out of the duke's hands—and that officers of the court had already taken the girl into custody. Supposing—dreadful thought—she was already incarcerated in the Tower of London, that grim

417

fortress where so many traitors, religious misfits, and royal adulteresses had eked out their final days?

Supposing . . . ?

What was that?

A carriage lumbered down the rutted road from Piccadilly, lamps winking in the gloom. Approaching her house, its pace was checked and it headed toward her door. Purity was halfway down the stairs, hefting the heavy valise, by the time the knocker sounded out, hollowly, in the dark hallway.

No servant came in answer to the summons, for those remaining were doing so only with sufferance, and paid not the slightest heed to their duties, but spent the time playing cards and drinking their mistress's cellar dry down in the kitchen quarters.

Two men with unsmiling, neutral faces stood on the steps.

"Lady Landless?" said one.

"Yes," replied Purity. "Are you from . . . "

"Quite correct, ma'am. This way, please." The speaker took her valise, handed it in through the open door of the carriage, then gave her his hand to help her inside. The door closed, leaving the two men outside her house.

"Good evening, ma'am," came a voice from out of the shadows opposite: a voice she recognized.

"Major Strickland . . . good evening." She looked around her in sudden dismay. "But where is . . . "

"We have a rendezvous south of the river to join the lady in question, ma'am," he said. "At my house in Wandsworth. In view of last night's events, and the slight possibility that the mob from the rookeries might take it into their minds to earn their pay by running amok in the city tonight, I ordered the bridges to be guarded and all conveyances crossing them to be searched. In view of this, I deemed it . . . impruden‍ . . . to bring the lady here with me." He laughe‍

418

shortly. "It would be folly, indeed, would it not, to be caught in one's own trap? Drive on, coachman."

The vehicle lurched to a swift start. Looking out, Purity was surprised to see that the two men, far from taking their departure, were again knocking upon the door of her house.

"Why . . . " she began.

But Strickland must have seen her glance and divined her puzzlement. "They have gone to arrest your butler," he said flatly. "The fellow was in the service of the conspiritors, reporting all your comings and goings and those of your husband, too."

"My God, they were thorough!" cried Purity.

"That they were, ma'am. That they were."

They traveled in silence, down Piccadilly, past the lighted windows of Apsley House, down the long wall of Buckingham Palace's gardens.

It was Strickland who broke the silence. Reaching out, he placed an envelope in Purity's hand.

"That is a letter of introduction to a gentleman acquaintance of the duke's," he said. "The gentleman in question, a Mr. Clement Browne—spelled with an 'e'—owes the duke a certain obligation, in addition to which he is a most agreeable person, likewise his family. The letter of introduction requests Mr. Browne to accept both of you as his guests and to afford you every means of help and protection till you have, so to speak, found your feet in America."

"America! Did you say . . . *America*, Major Strickland?"

"That is so, ma'am," responded the other blandly. "We deemed it to be safest. Mr. Browne's residence lies some fifteen or twenty miles from the city of Washington, in the state of Virginia, on the banks of the Potomac River. I think you will find the district very agreeable, ma'am. One is informed that the climate is mild, and the rainfall is not excessive. The state has also, from your point of view, the tremendous advantage of having been colonized by the English. So pleasant to be among one's own kind, don't you think?"

Purity did not reply, her whole attention being devoted to the notion of being whisked away, at half a day's notice, with scarcely more than she stood up in, to the far side of the ocean. To America!

Strickland did not permit her the opportunity to dwell upon the implications of his bombshell.

"We have deemed it prudent for you—for the time being, at least, till you have put ashore from the English packet that will be taking you across the Atlantic —to assume the name of Mrs. Fazackerley, and for the young lady to call herself Miss Fazackerley. Upon your arrival in America, the matter of reverting to your own name and title will be entirely up to your own judgment, of course. The Americans, so I have been informed, are not over-fond of titles," he concluded.

America! As the carriage slowed down at a bridge, and she saw the Thames reflecting the lights of the Surrey shore, and heard the homely accents of a Cockney voice demanding who they were and whither bound, she was filled with an aching sense of loss. To be so far from home meant to be that much farther from Mark and Robbie. While ever she had been near London, and, in consequence, not far from Brighton, or even Clumber, she had felt the reassurance of proximity should Mark and Robbie ever return from abroad. But America! A place she had always regarded as the end of the earth!

They had satisfied the guards on the bridge of their *bona fides,* and they were on their way again.

Strickland was talking to her: "I have been at Mill Hill all the day," he said, "in search of certain documents that establish Miss Chastity's parentage, documents that it seems certain Quintin and his sister purchased from the young lady's father in order to serve their own ends. They have quite disappeared. Not, I should think, that it will be any cause for regret to yourself, ma'am." He paused, then went on, conversationally: "A most curious incident occurred. In the mid-afternoon, a pair of common young fellows, brothers by the look of them, arrived in a donkey cart, claiming for burial the body of a comrade whom, so they averred, had been killed the previous night while trying to enter Jermyn Abbey and rescue Miss Chastity. Did I hear you exclaim, ma'am?"

"It . . . it was nothing," whispered Purity.

"They led us right to the spot where the body still lay," said Strickland. "And one of my men, a former member of the Bow Street Runners, was able to identify the corpse as that of a notorious highwayman who rejoiced in the alias of Jack Moonlight. Did you . . . ever hear of such a person, Lady Landless?"

"I . . . think I may have," murmured Purity.

"Howbeit, we had no need for the body, and the young fellows—their name was Bates—said that they intended to give their friend what they were pleased to call 'a slap-up send-off.' So we let them take the body away. Now, was that not a very curious thing, ma'am? One asks oneself: Why should a common highwayman and his assistants interest themselves in the rescue of your daughter? It is a rhetorical question, of course, don't you agree?"

"Yes," said Purity, eyes prickling in the concealing darkness inside the carriage.

They clattered through rural Clapham, with the dark humps of sleeping cows scattered around the common, and the sound of voices raised in raucous song in an alehouse. Everything looked very peaceful.

"And to think, ma'am," said Strickland, "that, but for the providence that sent me trailing after Hardcourt at Mill Hill, in order to arrest him, and except for divers other imponderable factors, we might now be living in a country ruled by a pretender. And all London would be given over to sack and pillage at the hands of the mob."

They will give him a good burial, thought Purity, perhaps somewhere in "The Devil's Hundred" that was so much his own; to lie with the sedge and rushes all around him, and with the call of the wildfowl filling the lonely air.

Chastity was borne on a litter to the carriage, having, as Strickland explained, been given a soporific by his physician, the better to combat the effects of shock and the noxious drug that she had imbibed. She recovered consciousness in the early hours of the next morning, when, with Winchester towers behind them, they were bowling down the ancient Roman road, straight as a die, through the clear dawn. Chastity reached out a small hand and took Purity's, then smiled with a sweetness that touched the heart, and closed her eyes again in peaceful sleep.

Strickland's agent had ridden on ahead the previous afternoon and had secured for "Mrs. and Miss Fazackerley" a decent, two-berth cabin and sitting room on the packet *Esmeralda,* bound for Norfolk, Virginia. *Esmeralda,* a superannuated East Indiaman, made up in comfort for what she lacked in seaworthiness, having been originally fitted out for the transportation of East India Company nabobs and their families. The dining salon was decorated in the then current Oriental style, with Chinese wallpaper depicting exotic birds perched among bamboo trelliswork; it put Purity suddenly and nostalgically in mind of the Royal Pavilion at Brighton.

Chastity, who had said little upon her awakening that morning, declared herself fit to rise and partake of dinner. They dressed together in silence. Through the bottle-glass window of their cabin could be seen the sweep of Southampton water and the masts of the ships alongside the piers and jetties of Hythe. They were on their way.

"Dearest, would you fasten the buttons at the back of my dress, please?" murmured Purity.

She turned. The fingers behind her deftly completed their task, paused, then slipped around her waist. With a low moan of something between relief and contentment, the girl laid her head upon the older woman's shoulder.

"Oh, darling Mama Purity—to be free of all that horror at last!" she cried.

Purity faced her, joined her embrace, kissed her upon the cheek, the lips, stroked her mane of luxuriant hair, gloried at the feel of the wondrous soft flesh and the delicate bones beneath; she felt the primeval surge of motherhood's passion.

"My dearest—that you've been returned to me!"

The girl drew away and looked at her, eye to eye.

"Mama, you will remember, back at the De Feyelle château, when I was able to speak again, I promised you I would tell you everything that had happened to me while I was away from you, but that there was something—something terrible—that was like a locked door, shutting everything in. Well, that door has been flung open now, and I can speak out."

"If you want to, my darling," said Purity. "There is no hurry. Tell me, piece by piece, as you choose, as you feel the desire for release."

Chastity took her hands from around Purity's waist and walked over to the window and squatted there upon a comfortable, low seat. She looked down at her long, slender fingers.

"They told me that Cornelia is dead," she said. "I asked about her, you see. I was in love with her— once."

"Oh, my dearest!"

"She was Madeleine's daughter, you know. We lay together and made love—often, sometimes many times a day. Do you think that was very awful, Mama Purity?" The luminous, dark eyes fixed Purity with the light of candor.

"If you were both in love, there is no cause for you to repine," said Purity quietly.

"I think—I know now—that she was not in love with me," said Chastity sadly, "but that it was all a pretense to entrap me. You see . . . when I was . . . when he . . . " Her voice wavered.

Purity ran to her side.

"Dearest, don't continue if it distresses you," she murmured.

The candid eyes, moist with bitter tears, met hers.

"The night that he—the man they called D'Eath—came into my room and raped me," she said, "Cornelia entered also. She carried a candle, so I could see her face clearly. I called to her to help me, to fetch Quintin and Madeleine. She would do no such thing. Instead . . . oh, Mama Purity, hold me tightly!"

"My angel!" Purity pressed the young face to her bosom.

"Instead of fetching help, she closed the door," said Chastity in a voice of sudden calm. "Then she brought the candle over to the bed and held it aloft, the better to see the things he was . . . doing to me. She watched it all!"

"Shh!" Purity would have given the world to have staunched the agonized outburst, while knowing all the time that it was like a putrified wound upon the child, which, having been lanced by clean steel, must be allowed to pour out its poison.

"She laughed to see what he was doing, Mama Purity! She encouraged him! Called me a whey-faced bitch who deserved all she got!"

Chastity gave a shudder and fell silent. The wound had shed its poison.

After a while, she added, "Now she is dead—and I am free."

The voyage passed exceedingly pleasantly, with the cumbersome *Esmeralda* making good westering with calm seas and a steady breeze. The inactivity of shipboard life provided Purity with ample opportunity for thought, in which she was not greatly interrupted by Chastity, who early formed an attachment to a family of Americans returning to their home in Baltimore. They comprised father, mother—both of Purity's age or thereabout—two daughters younger than Chastity, and a son of twenty. It was the latter, a straight-eyed and good-looking lad, to whom, in Purity's guess, Chastity was most attracted. The young couple was often to be seen taking a stroll around the deck, throwing scraps of food to the dolphins that constantly plunged and dived under and around the ship's stem. And it gave Purity a warm feeling in her heart to see that, after all her hideous and unnatural experiences, Chastity had not forgotten how to be at ease with a young man of her own age, nor—let it be admitted—to flirt with him.

To her own wry and secret amusement, Purity herself was not devoid of admiration. There was an Englishman, a planter traveling back to his sugar plantation in Barbados, who attached himself to her after dinner on the first night out. He had served in the Peninsular War, knew Wellington by sight, and—as Purity had been able to elicit by diplomatic questioning—had met the young Mark Landless several times, knew him by reputation, and admired him greatly. For that reason, and that alone, Purity encouraged their acquaintance, where otherwise she might not have. She always sat with this gentleman at mealtimes, and she walked with him often on the sunlit deck. For his part, the planter behaved from first to last with the utmost correctness and circumspection, never presuming to address his shipboard friend as other than "Mrs. Fazackerley, ma'am," nor so much as to touch her hand when they were promenading around the deck. He constantly regaled her with tales of his life in the West Indies and of his former days in the Peninsula—more often the latter. And it must have been a constant source of puzzlement to him that, while speaking of his army days, the conversation invariably turned to the subject of "the gallant Captain Landless, of whom you spoke the other day. . . ."

On the bustling quayside of Norfolk, Virginia, piled high with hogsheads of tobacco, where black children splashed and shrieked in the shallows, and narrow-eyed men in Panama hats sucked at thin cigars and thought of money, the planter from Barbados—without losing an iota of circumspection—proposed marriage to Purity at, literally, their moment of parting. She—who, simply by not denying an assumption he had made that she, an unaccompanied lady with a grown daughter, was a widow—was only flattered by his proposition, and she told him so. The half-relief in his transparently honest eyes when he, a self-confessed bachelor, was released from the consequences of his impulsive act, was a joy to see. They parted company the best of friends.

Purity had secured a public conveyance to the city of Washington, together with the information—imparted by an extremely agreeable young man in the ticket office on the levee who could scarcely keep his gaze from wandering from the woman with the silver-gold hair to the younger woman with the hair of sable-black who stood behind her, then back again to the forner—that she would find plenty of cabs in Washington, and riverboats, also, to take her up the Potomac to her final destination.

The conveyance deposited them at a decent inn on the outskirts of the city, where they were able to obtain a room with a double bed for the night. Purity spent sleepless hours with her arms clasped around the sleeping girl, her mind racing about the implications of the morrow.

The day they had spent—their first day ashore in a new land—had been the beginning of a new life for them both. She and Chastity had arrived as anonymous immigrants from Europe's teeming shores: unknown, untitled, not even having the right to the names they bore. She had with her a purse full of gold guineas, enough, she reckoned, to keep them in decent style for a year. In her reticule, also, she had the letter of introduction from the high and mighty Duke of Wellington, requesting and requiring Mr. Clement Browne (spelled with an "e") to afford every means of help and protection to Lady Landless, alias Mrs. Fazackerley, till she had established herself and her daughter in the New World.

Established herself and her daughter as what? Doing what?

The duke's intention was clear. His demand upon Mr. Clement Browne was no more than this: in return for the obligation that Mr. Browne owed to the prime minister of England—who, incidentally, was also arguably one of the most famous men in the world, and certainly one of the most influential—Mr. Browne would take in Lady Landless and her daughter (or Mrs. Fazackerley and her daughter, depending on how the lady desired to style herself in the latter-day cradle of democratic philosophy) as permanent pensioners upon the charge of his no-doubt limitless purse.

"To hell with it!" exclaimed Purity aloud.

And when Chastity stirred in her arms, she added, more softly, but still aloud, "What in heaven's name would Jacques and the folks back at Feyelle think of the both of us if we spent the rest of our lives as pensioners living on the charity of a rich man?"

Nevertheless, the next day they went to see Mr. Browne's lovely home on a bluff overlooking the Potomac, traveling there in a hired carriage. The main building was in the Colonial style of the previous century: with a row of noble columns spanning the well-proportioned facade, and a cupola surmounting the center block. In front of it, the brilliant green parkland descended to the shore of the wide river, all set with cedars of Lebanon and sentinel cypresses, elms and sweet chestnuts.

They saw it from afar, across the wide river. Even from that distance it was a place of enchantment. As they watched from their halted carriage, a figure on a white horse emerged from the stable block at the side of the mansion, cantering through sunlight and shade, with a black dog bounding along at the mount's heels. A little later, a personage with a black face laid out some startlingly white sheets to air on the veranda. And the clock over the stable struck the hour of noon.

With a sigh, Purity gave the driver instructions to return to Washington. Mr. Browne's home was lovely beyong imagining; but her overnight resolve that she and Chastity would stand, from first to last, on their own two feet in their new, adoptive land remained unshaken.

"Good-bye, Mr. Browne. We never met you. It would have been delightful to have lived in your beautiful house overlooking the wide river. But we are Thursday's children; we have come a long way and we have still a long way to go."

They remained at the inn that night and the night after, while Purity busied herself in finding work: applying at various emporiums around the city with the view to becoming a counter assistant; also reading through the small advertisements in the local journals, in one of which, the *Alexandria Gazette,* she found a most promising offer of a position as cook-housekeeper for a doctor's family, with a decent wage and accommodations for two or more in quarters above the coach house.

Dr. Delaney and his large and rambunctious family of six girls under eighteen lived in Alexandria, a small, sleepy town about six miles from the capital. The good doctor, who turned out to be a stout, bright-eyed gentleman and a devoted rider to the hounds, was a widower, his spouse having died in bearing their last child. He took to Purity instantly, and she to him. The bargain was struck and sealed with a handshake. In employing Purity, and her daughter with her, without the provision of proper references, Dr. Delaney showed his excellent judgment of character, just as Purity demonstrated her obvious probity. Concerning herself, she was perfectly straightforward with her new employer, frankly admitting that she was estranged from her husband. She offered no information about Chastity, save to present her as the daughter of that marriage. And she had long ago decided to remain "Mrs. Fazackerley."

The Delaney household was easygoing to the point of laxity, for the previous housekeeper had left the children to fend for themselves in matters culinary; consequently, the once well-appointed kitchen was now in a dreadful state, as was the remainder of the rambling, Colonial-style house. Dr. Delaney had no eye for his surroundings; he did not distinguish between tidiness and chaos, but was only concerned with his hunting and his considerable medical practice. He left the running of the household entirely in Purity's hands, with complete *carte blanche* to manage as she chose. Purity shooed the rambunctious girls out of her kitchen, persuaded them to put their individual rooms in apple-pie order, and had the house clean and tidy within a week.

Dr. Delaney, in addition to keeping his own hunter and a pair of carriage horses, which were looked after by a black groom and coachman, possessed a couple of hacks for the girls. Chastity, who doted on all things equestrian, took it upon herself to care for and exercise the latter. She also helped Purity in the general running of the household.

So began a vastly different period in the lives of the former Lady Landless—society beauty and chatelaine of a country mansion in Wiltshire, a town house in London, and a seaside house in Brighton—and her daughter, who had been expensively reared to take her place in the same lofty social milieu. It spoke volumes for Purity's stern, Norman peasant upbringing—as well as for the excellent precepts that she had passed on to Chastity—that neither of them was in any way dismayed by the change in fortune as such. They simply applied themselves well in the large and happy Delaney household, with mutual advantage to all.

It was about a month after their arrival in Alexandria, when they had comfortably settled in, that Purity decided that she must write to Wellington, thanking him for his kindnesses, and explaining why she had decided, after all, not to avail themselves of the letter of introduction to Mr. Browne. It was not an easy letter to write, but write it she did, then mailed it off to England.

The days passed easily, with plenty to be done and with ample rewards coming from the quite delightful and appreciative Delaney girls, with their father beaming vague approval in the background.

It was the nights that weighed heavily upon Purity's heart and mind. She ached for the giving and receiving of love, the lack of which made a desert of her emotions. And, since she was a passionate and sensual woman, her body was similarly lacking.

One night, in her lonely room over the coach house, she stripped herself nude and made a frank assessment of what remained of the beauty of face and form that she had, unself-consciously and without the slightest conceit, known to have been hers since girlhood; she determined how many years of such beauty might remain to be enjoyed.

Her face, she observed in the looking glass, showed not the slightest suspicion of a wrinkle, nor was there a hint of telltale wrinkling at the neck or around the eyes. Her hair, her crowning glory, might be showing a touch more silver than gold; but it was still luxuriant, gleaming, stunning to behold.

Of her body, she was more critical. Though her waist remained as slender as ever, she detected a silent increase of the fullness at bosom and hips, though her breasts, always unsupported by tight-laced stays—which she could never abide—were as firm and upstanding as they had been in her girlhood. Her good friend, the late Madame Dupuis, the dressmaker of Bond Street and sister of the vinegary Mademoiselle Hubert, had been a great authority on, and a tremendous advocate of the preservation and care of, the *poitrine*. She had declared Purity to have been, in that department, the most magnificently endowed of any woman in London society. Madame's test was to place a pencil under the bosom. Should a woman be able to hold a pencil under her bosom, Madame had averred, then her figure was finished. That night, in the little bedroom over the coach house in Alexandria,

431

Purity submitted both halves of her *poitrine* to the pencil test. And she came through it with flying colors.

The nights were so long. Restless and deprived in mind and body, she was only able to woo sleep by resorting to fantasies that relaxed her. The fantasies were all concerned with being loved, and they were not always of the sort that strict moralists would have regarded as being particularly edifying; for the human mind, the mind of a beautiful woman who has known much fulfillment, and is then reduced to a lonely bed and the prospect of a loveless, celibate future, is not much concerned, in its wayward fantasies, with the niceties of morality. Purity's waking dreams, as she lay, nude and panting, within her lonely, narrow bed, rose to forbidden heights of erotic fancy.

But always, in the climax of her journeys into the blinding light beyond reality, one name and one name alone rose to her tremulous lips. . . .

"Mark!"

The fall of the dying year turned the shady, tree-lined streets of Alexandria to avenues of russet and gold, and the air was perfumed with the heady scent of burning leaves.

On such a day—a Thursday in late October—Purity was alone in the house preparing luncheon for the girls, whom she expected home from school, or from their various activities in the town. Chastity was riding out on one of the hacks, and Dr. Delaney had gone to a medical conference in Washington and was not due to return till the weekend.

She put an apple pie into the oven, assured herself that the saucepan of good French-style onion soup was simmering nicely, then went upstairs to the linen room to make sure that the laundress had not neglected both to iron and to examine the week's wash for those items in need of repair or replacement. The linen room was on the second floor. Busily absorbed in her routine task, she heard with half an ear the return of one of the older Delaney girls; it was the second daughter, Alice, who had taken the carriage into town to buy some dressmaking material. The clatter of the carriage in the coach yard was followed by the sound of Ben the coachman unharnessing the horses and leading them into the stable. She heard Alice cross the parquet floor of the hallway below and enter the drawing room, humming to herself.

Purity paid little attention when, soon after, another conveyance drew up on the road outside the house; nor did she look up from her task when there came a rat-tat on the street door knocker, for it was immediately followed by the sound of Alice going to answer it.

The ensuing conversation came clearly to her up the stairwell and through the open door of the linen room, with the voices slightly muffled and distorted by the acoustics of the large, empty hallway. She listened, first with only half her attention, then with rapidly mounting interest. . . .

"Good day, ma'am." A man's voice.

"Good day. Can I help you, sir?" That was Alice.

"Is this the residence of Dr. Delaney?"

"It is."

"Ah. And does a Mrs. Fazackerley reside here also, ma'am?"

"She does, sir."

Purity raised her head. Quite distinctly, she felt her skin prickle, and the hairs at the back of her neck stirred and stood on end.

"I have a letter here for Mrs. Fazackerley."

"I will see that she gets it, sir," came Alice's answer.

"That is kind of you, ma'am, but my instructions— from the gentleman in England who sent the letter—

433

are that I must hand the letter to Mrs. Fazackerley in person. . . ."

Purity was now on her feet, though, upon rising, she found that her legs seemed to have been deprived of their power to sustain the weight of her body; moreover, she was trembling from head to foot. Nevertheless, she contrived to reach the linen room door and, by means of supporting herself against the wall, gain the landing and stairwell beyond.

Two steps brought her to the balustrade, which ran completely around the stairwell. Below her were the sweep of stairs, the wide parquet floor of the hallway, with a band of sunlight from the open front door, and the shadows of two figures therein.

"You had better come in, sir, and I will fetch Mrs. Fazackerley."

"You are most kind, ma'am."

The door closed. Footsteps moved across the hall. In an instant they would come into sight below her. Her fingers tensed upon the rail. Her heart turned over.

"Are you from England, sir?" asked Alice.

"Originally, ma'am," was the reply. "I now live at a place farther upriver. Incidentally, I am most remiss in having neglected to introduce myself. My name is . . ."

"Mark!"

Purity uttered the name in the instant that the two figures appeared below her. He was hatless and wearing a caped coat. There were new streaks of gray in his dark hair, and he walked with a pronounced limp; but his face, and the expression upon it, as, at the sound of her voice coming from above, he jerked up his head and met her gaze, was unchanged and familiar to her as her own: known and adored in a thousand nights and days of love.

"Purity! Oh! Oh, my dearest!"

Then came the headlong race down to him, and he rushing to be with her, while the astonished Alice was a witness to it all. They met partway up the stairs and joined, each to each, in an embrace that spanned a lifetime of love and misunderstanding, of sins forgiven and forgotten—and of the promise of a future that would have no end.

That afternoon Mark took them both home. Home was Mr. Browne's lovely house overlooking the Potomac. They drove in his carriage through the autumnal gloaming, hand in hand, all three, with Mark in the middle, and his wife and daughter at either side.

Mr. Browne, as he explained, was a *nom de guerre* that he had employed while doing various enterprises of a confidential nature for Wellington after the war. The duke, having discovered his whereabouts in America, had sent Purity to him unannounced, and, upon receipt of her letter, had made yet another attempt to bring the two of them together again. His message, sent via Mark to the elusive "Mrs. Fazackerley," was typically brief and to the point, consisting as it did of only two words:

Good luck!

They came to the nobly proportioned house on the bluff above the river, the white walls pinkly glowing in the dying sunlight of that perfect day.

As their carriage rattled up the steep driveway, a figure on a white horse detached itself from the bank of trees screening the rear of the house and came galloping to meet them, a black dog bounding behind.

It was her son—Robbie.

Epilogue

In any event, King William IV—"poor Willie," as Wellington had designated that undistinguished but well-meaning monarch—did not survive the ten years that the duke had considered to be the optimum span of life remaining to him, taking into account the extreme youthfulness of the heiress presumptive, Princess Victoria. Poor Willie lasted only for seven years.

At five o'clock on a mid-summer's dawn, the Archbishop of Canterbury, together with Lord Chamberlain and the king's physician, arrived at Kensington Palace, where the eighteen-year-old princess—already, did she but know it, a queen—was asleep in the bedchamber that she shared with her domineering mama.

Her mother, the widowed Duchess of Kent, refused to awaken Princess Victoria. It was only when Lord Chamberlain demanded to see "the Queen" that little Victoria, in dressing gown and slippers, descended the stairs and, with the fortitude that was to characterize her throughout her long reign, offered her tiny hand for the messengers to kiss. The Victorian Age had begun.

Early in the following year, there arrived a communication at the Landless mansion above the Potomac. It was from the Duke of Wellington. No longer prime minister, he was, nevertheless, able to inform his former aide that his adopted daughter Chastity had been declared to be free of any suspicion of complicity in the conspiracy to set her upon the throne, and that she was consequently at liberty to enter England without fear of arrest. And that, wrote Wellington, was of some immediate import, since Colonel Sir Mark and Lady Landless and family were to be invited to attend the coronation of the new sovereign in Westminster Abbey next June 28.

Purity, Mark and Chastity rose before dawn and walked through the windy streets in order to be at Westminster Abbey when the doors were opened at seven. It would have been out of the question to have taken a carriage through the packed thoroughfares, even if the military had not closed off the environs of the abbey to all traffic since the night before.

Mark was in full-dress uniform, with the medals of his campaigns glittering upon his breast. Purity and Chastity, both in cloth-of-gold, could have passed as sisters, save that one was as fair as a Viking goddess, the other splendidly dark in her maturing young womanhood. Many were the admiring glances from the packed crowds massed around the entrance to the ancient seat of coronation as the trio entered and were ushered to their places, along with distinguished veterans and their families, in the towering nave of the great edifice.

The service of coronation, which lasted five hours, and was enlivened by a ninety-year-old peer catching his foot in his robes while ascending the steps of the throne to pay homage to the young queen and rolling to the bottom, reached its finale with the processional march, when the freshly crowned monarch, amidst shrill fanfares of trumpets, passed down the long aisle and out into the sunlight of her new reign. It was a specially proud moment for the Landlesses—mother, father, and daughter—for following behind as escort, bright and smiling and looking, to Purity, like the very image of his father as she had first known him, was young Robbie, a newly commissioned officer in his father's old regiment the Life Guards.

The Duke of Wellington sought them out after the ceremony. The victor of Waterloo was gray-haired now, like his former aide, but ramrod-straight of back and bright of eye. Mark, who was conversing with a former comrade from the Peninsular campaign, and Chastity, who was watching with awe the passing procession of peeresses in their ermine-trimmed robes and silver-gilt coronets, were not witness to the ensuing exchange between Purity and the duke.

"Well, ma'am," said Wellington, "it is over. We have a lady queen, and you may mark my words that she will do well. There is not much of her, but she will make a clatter, of that I assure you." His gaze turned to Chastity. "What of our little pretender, eh, ma'am? I must say she has grown exceedingly handsome."

"She has indeed, sir," agreed Purity. "Remembering Prinny as he was in his declining years, it is difficult to imagine that they were kin—and so closely related."

"Ma'am," said Wellington, "I direct your memory back to a certain portrait of a golden Prince Charming to which I once drew your attention at the Brighton Pavilion. All that bright promise we thought we had lost. That young lady, ma'am—our little pretender, as I insist on calling her—is that bright promise brought to fruition. Alive. And with us."

"Yes," whispered Purity. "Yes, my lord, you are right."

With the last fanfares dying away in the great, vaulted nave, and a new era begun, Purity was suddenly seized by a sense of completeness, as when, after the protracted agony of a difficult delivery, one lies in blissful repletion, with a new life cradled in one's arms. She glanced over to Mark—young no longer, but as vigorous as ever and everything she had ever wanted in a man—as he conversed animatedly with his old comrade.

She had scarcely needed to confide the secret of her shame on that long-gone October day seven years previously; the mutual and all-embracing joy of their sudden and totally unexpected reunion had driven out all need for explanation and forgiveness for anything but the bliss of being two persons when for so long they had each been only one.

She had told him why she had taken on the mantle of a whore, and Mark had raved with fury at those who had despoiled her. It was the first time in all her knowledge of Mark Landless that she had ever seen him weep.

By a mutual and unspoken agreement, they had never told Chastity the reason for her adoptive mother's sacrifice, reasoning that the burden of guilt and remorse would have been too much for Chastity to bear.

Mark looked around, met her eyes, and smiled. The years rolled away. She was back in a cabbage field in Normandy, where they had first met: she a scrawny young girl who was disturbingly conscious that, the lacing of her shift having come untied, the tall man on the tall horse must certainly have seen her bare bosom beneath.

She returned his smile.

Purity Landless, formerly Purity Jarsy, of Château De Feyelle, in fair Normandy. Delivered, through passion, through ecstasy, through shame, to the peace that comes with serene contentment.